W9-BUJ-973

Rocket Man

Also by William Elliott Hazelgrove

Ripples
Tobacco Sticks
Mica Highways

Rocket Man

William Elliott Hazelgrove

PANTONNE PRESS INC.
27 W. WACKER DRIVE
CHICAGO, IL 60606

Copyright © 2008, by William Elliott Hazelgrove

Rocket Man

A Pantonne Press Book

Pantonne Press Inc.

27 W Wacker Drive Suite 828

Chicago, IL 60606

This book is a work of fiction. Names, characters, places, and incidents either are products of the author's imagination or are used fictitiously. Any resemblance to actual events or locales or persons, living or dead, is entirely coincidental.

All rights reserved, including the right to reproduce this book or portions thereof in any form whatsoever. For more information contact. Pantonne@gmail.com

Fax 775-540-8700

SAN 297-5815 www.pantonnepress.com

Library of Congress Control Number: 2008929300

ISBN 978-0-615-21307-1

Printed in the United States of America.

For Clay, Callie, Careen, and Kitty
My Stars.

Acknowledgements

Many thanks to the Ernest Hemingway Foundation of Oak Park for giving me a key to a very old house. It's not everyday one gets to write in the birthplace of Ernest Hemingway. The view has been amazing.

W.E.H
July 2008

"I am not to be denied…"
　　　　　　　　　　–Walt Whitman

Preflight

My father is a traveling salesman, that peculiar brand of Willy Loman that actually loves the natural flight of American selling. When I was a boy, I thought of him as a man who appeared on Fridays when we had a steak and ice cream for dessert. After dinner, my father would watch whatever football game was on television and fall asleep with his mouth open, tie loosened, hand over his brow as if he had just finished one hell of a race. I usually waited until he woke to tell him of my latest achievement and show him my banana bike and collection of baseball cards. But I had a brother who demanded his small time with him also, so when my time came, it was usually just before he ran for his car, briefcase in hand, and waved away another week.

But there was one time I remember where I had him all to myself. For Christmas, my parents had given me an Estes Rocket Set. It was an amazing toy with a launcher, rocket engines, and the giant Saturn Five Rocket that had conquered the moon a decade before. I stayed up late gluing the white fuselage together, packing the parachute, and inserting the four D engines. The day after Christmas, my father and I walked to a field to launch my rocket. We walked through the tall weeds painted orange by the low sun. He kept his hands in his pockets while I carried the rocket and the launcher packed with batteries to fire the rocket. We crunched through frozen mud until we reached the middle of the field. Twilight simmered beyond the big pines and thin blue snow dusted the ground. I put the launcher down and stretched the wires to the control pad. My Saturn Five rocket was a beast. It took four D engines with two parachutes and four wadded sheets to keep the ejection charge from burning the chute up.

"Looks like we are launching Apollo 11," my father murmured while I threaded the Saturn Five onto the launch wire.

I connected the igniter wires to the four D engines. All four engines had to ignite or my Saturn Five would go off at a crazy angle and heave into the ground. I checked the igniters and made sure they were shoved far up into the engines. My father stamped his feet and kept his hands in his pockets.

"You think this thing will go, boy?"

I looked at the man smoking a Pall Mall, his long Brooks Brothers coat waving.

"Think so."

"So this is what you do all week while I'm gone, boy?"

"Yup."

My father smoked without his hands.

"Well, hurry up, boy. It's going to be dark soon."

I turned and walked back to the launch control and inserted the key. The light glowed ready.

"You might move back, Dad."

He looked over and snuffed the cigarette out, crunching through the frozen mud. He was already looking at the distant cars on the highway, thinking about his next appointment, gassing up, pointing that company car back to the highway. He turned back and nodded to me.

"Well, blast it off, boy."

I stared at my Saturn Five, a colossus of white and black with USA going up the side in red letters. I began to count down.

"Five, four, three, two, one ... "

I pressed the button on my launcher as the ready light flickered out. There was the slight hiss of the sulfur igniters, and for a moment the rocket didn't move. Then the four D engines caught fire, and whoosh! The fire bent out and burned the weeds below the launcher and suddenly the Saturn Five was gone. A fiery tail burned high up in the cold sky as the rocket leaned over slightly and left a white vapor trail across the early stars.

"Jesus Christ!"

My father continued staring up while I stamped out the weed fire. The ejection charge fired and the chutes blossomed, but I could see the Saturn Five had gone too high for the wind and the time of day. It was getting dark, and that rocket was sailing fast into the west, a white satellite against a darkening blue palate.

"I'll be goddamned," he muttered, shaking his head. "Boy, that sonofabitch really flew."

I put my hand up and saw the Saturn Five drifting away; a gold colossus hanging by four parachutes.

"Aren't you going after it, boy?"

I shook my head solemnly.

"No, it's gone," I murmured, watching the rocket drift past the field. "There's too much wind."

"You sure about that?"

"Yes."

My father kept his neck craned to the sky, then put his hands on my shoulders. That's what I remember. I think it was the only time we were really together, watching that rocket disappear into the coal sky.

1

T-6

...and counting

Sunday

HAIR of the dog.

The vodka is fighting the tomato juice, but it does the trick, and I mitigate the vagaries of selling popcorn at the Kane County Fair with ten screaming Cub Scouts, Bloody Mary firmly in hand, shades firmly affixed. The margaritas from the night before are a headache I'd rather be doing without, but osmosis and a little old-fashioned self medicating has gotten me to the point where I can drive Cub Scouts and be the charming father of two, husband of one. But I have to make a decision.

We are constantly presented with rules that we can either choose to follow or break. Does one go through the unmanned toll? Does one pay for the case of water in the bottom of the shopping cart that no one sees? They are small, middle class rules, but rules all the same. My choice is simple. Do I take the time to hang a big looping U-turn and return to the highway for the Dairy Queen I missed ... or do I cut into the McDonald's parking lot and plow across an excavated field of old pipes and earth movers, past the surveyor posts flapping like markers of the road not taken?

These are the choices of our lives now. The big choices are mostly behind us by middle age, and we are reduced to schoolboys trying to whisper when the teacher's back is turned.

What the hell.

"Dale ...Dale, *what are you doing*," Brad Jones of Pack 155 Boy Scouts of America (BSA) demands while hanging on to the handrail of my white Yukon urban assault vehicle.

I look over at Brad in his camouflage green BSA hat, aviation sunglasses from 1975, and scout leader shirt tattooed with badges and ribbons like something General McArthur had worn. His cell phone and pager are clipped firmly to more drab olive green, his outfit finished out with knee-high socks also in the color of combat regalia. He is the scout leader alarmed, his Chicago accent giving way to a more high-pitched tenor, speaking as the leader of the pack, but also as a man who realizes he has suddenly lost control. His day up to now has the tenor of all scout functions—monotony on par with a kid's show, sprinkled with flares of patriarchal conformity. This is the way Brad likes it. He *likes* control and conformity, and he *loves* uniforms. Give the man a gymnasium and a microphone and captive parents and he becomes *Aerosmith*—the neo-Nazi of the last sanctioned paramilitary organization in America—the Boy Scouts.

A finger jousts the air between us.

"Dale, you can't do this!"

I have turned my warlord Yukon XL into the vacant field between McDonald's and Dairy Queen, veering around a drainage culvert, avoiding a berm, crushing a few neon orange surveyor posts. From the recesses of this wagon on the rampage comes the dulcet tone of my wife. She is occupying the third seat along with a rafter of Cub Scouts, Tiger Scouts, and a desultory Boy Scout who has suddenly perked up at the prospect of a little off-road four-wheeling. That would be Brad Jones Jr, who is headed for an Eagle Scout badge, and in unguarded moments, I can see he thinks his father is as big a geek as I do.

"Dale … *what are you doing?*"

This is the question of the day really. I glance into the dim recesses of my cavernous SUV and can see lovely blond hair in a sea of blue Cub Scout hats. *What am I doing?* I have made a choice outside the purview of the modern father. "Dad" would not do such a thing, although I can imagine my own father plowing his dusty Buick across a field in Mississippi. But those were different times. Conformity was still just a word to men who had only four channels, and those were grainy at best—mass culture was yet to do its collective tap dance on our consciousness. But a modern man with a Blackberry and an iPod and a thousand-dollar bicycle would not *knowingly* break the law unless he was a criminal. I know I am alone in my choice to bash through barriers and take the shortest distance between two points.

The noise level in our caravan has reached something resembling an airplane going into a nosedive. The scouts are being jostled and have just realized something really cool and different is going on outside the purview of the grab-ass melodrama that is their everyday existence in the far west suburb of Charleston, Illinois. Kids are still open to a good time; it is the adults who have become a drag. Our move to the land of the moral majority has put me many times in sympathy with the Lilliputians who skirt the radar screen of overgrown men and women. I am in sympathy with these ten-year-olds who just want to have fun, because *I* just want to have fun, and it is my brethren that seem intent on stopping anyone from having a good time

"Dale! *What are you doing?*"

I look into the mirror of our command vehicle.

"Just taking a shortcut, honey," I shout above the squeals of scouts in motion, enjoying the massive amount of sheer power a man processes when imprisoning people in a large truck.

"Dale, this is *illegal,* and you are setting a bad example for the boys," Brad Jones warns while I skirt a large drainage culvert and several nasty-looking steel pipes sticking out of the ground.

I glance at Brad and gesture to the moonscape we are bouncing over like two men in a pogo contest.

"Calm down, Brad, calm thyself," I tell the leader of Pack 155. "You are always talking about how we have to teach the boys to be prepared and how we have to learn to think creatively in the wilderness and deal with the unexpected. Well," I continue, motioning to the excavated plain, "here is the unexpected."

Brad Jones turns to me, his olive skin turning darker. This is not something that a man who clips a cell phone, a radio pager, and a large keychain to his belt every day envisions as a possibility. I imagine Brad standing in front of his bathroom mirror with the coffee-induced circles less prominent under the brim of his BSA hat. His Chicago accent falls away as he readies himself for the pack meeting in the gymnasium, enjoying Andy Warhol's fifteen minutes of fame with an hour and a half of droning announcements to a captive audience of parents. I know Brad loves wearing the Scout uniform the way a senior citizen likes wearing a crossing belt. A sense of purpose descends over one Brad Jones when the olive drab covers his body and the 155 tattoos his shoulder—something being the manager of Best Buy does not provide.

"*Dale!* Driving across private property does not teach *leadership skills,*" Brad hisses, holding on as the front left tire finds a hidden chuckhole, eliciting howls of delight from our young protégées.

"Well now, Brad, this may not be the same as blazing a trail through the boundary waters, but we are men who are confronted with modern problems, and our boys could well find themselves faced with this very same choice one day," I point out, swerving around a sewer grate.

Brad stares at me as if I had just asked him to go into a gay bar. He is from Chicago and has equated escaping the city with material success and carries none of my suburban angst. He is never happier than in heelless slippers, grilling burgers on his deck, looking out at fifty other homes just like his. Brad Jones has made it in the immigrant sense and has left the squalor of dark brown stones and strange accents and landed in the cradle of the suburban middle class. I know we are different men, but still I try and enlighten Brad just the same.

"What choice," he sputters, turning bright red.

"Whether or not to take the road less traveled," I point out. "I could have turned around in the parking lot and reentered the highway, but instead I opted to take the road less traveled—to blaze my *own* trail, as we all must do."

Brad stares at me as if I have just told him the world is flat. My philosophy of the writer-adventurer finds no port in the Jones sea, and I see now we are back in the Westside neighborhood, and Brad and his dad, in their sleeveless T-shirts, are shaking their heads on the stoop, saying, "That guy is a fricking whack job."

Assistant Scout Master Jones then frowns, shaking his head.

"I don't think four-wheeling is one of the merit badges our scouts should be working toward," he says with more sarcasm than I thought he was capable of.

"You got me there, Brad," I nod, holding my drink aloft, which Brad is now scrutinizing like a cop. "But I am *problem solving* aren't I? I mean, I could have gone back into traffic and taken all that time waiting to turn into the Dairy Queen. Instead I took the shortest distance between two points," I point out again, watching parents and kids abandoning picnic tables on the edge of the field.

I imagine to them I look fairly menacing, this large white

whale of a truck plowing across this dusty sea of prairie grass and excavator glory, lunging toward the middle class families enjoying a little ice cream on one of the last warm days in October. Brad Jones now has the look of a librarian who just caught some boys jacking off in the bathroom. His eyes have narrowed and the clipboards and scouting manuals in his lap give him moral support as he levels his charge.

"I know that's not *tomato juice*, Dale," he informs me, leaning across the space in our cockpit as I wheel past two men in orange surveyor jackets, looking up at Moby Dick's passage. "I can smell the *alcohol,*" he hisses like a woman, all the outrage of a hijacked Assistant Scout Master in transit making his voice unsteady.

It is true. I did lace the V8 with some Smirnoff at the last minute. The party around our marble bar on the patio was dried up salsa and obelisks of salted rims that had dashed many a margarita the night before. The thunder that is tequila felt like cracked ice in my frontal lobe, and so I employed the homegrown remedy of lessening the departing alcohol with just a splash of vodka. The cure had worked, and my headache had mostly left, leaving only the short temper of a hangover to be mitigated. Little did I know I would share a ride with the temperance league. It was just a splash, after all.

"Brad ... come on," I say, feeling the bite of my hangover in the form of this pestering neo-Nazi. "Just a little hair of the dog, buddy."

I am sure Brad Jones would have made a great Brown Shirt in Hitler's legions, informing others how their shirts weren't tucked in, their swastikas sewn on in the wrong spots. His fellow Nazis then would groan as Brad took the podium and proclaimed in fine German, "Now, just a few procedural announcements before the Fuhrer comes on." Then Brad would drone on for a good thirty minutes about the Nazi campout, the Nazi popcorn drive, the Nazi Merit Badge awards that would go for another thirty minutes. Soon, the entire SA would suspect that Brad actually *liked* all the mind-numbing procedural protocol, and they would begin to plot to shoot him in the back when they reached the Russian front.

But Brad's observations on my habits, my choices, my very being are all for naught. I have just bumped over the curb barriers and left the desert of our conquering. Dairy Queen families have clustered around one lone picnic table, outraged fathers in shorts with fat calves and black socks, shaking their heads at the audacity of someone crossing the Mohave desert. They said it couldn't be done, but I say, "*Acaba!*" I feel the elation of Lawrence of Arabia when he cleared the desert and snuck up on the Turks. It is not so much that I crossed the field to Dairy Queen with my two-ton vehicle, but that I have *broken* a rule in the land of rules. So I raise my drink.

"To your health, buddy. We did it."

I wheel across the parking lot in a victory arc and pull into an open spot. The high of selling popcorn at the Kane County Fair has now been lost on Brad Jones, along with his gratitude for giving him and his popcorn salesmen a ride. He fumes silently, scribbling on a clipboard. I feel like I am a boy again and a teacher is writing me up for talking in class, spitting out the window, or four-wheeling to the Dairy Queen.

"I'm going to have report this to the council, Dale."

I raise my eyebrows.

"Does this mean I'm off the hook on Rocket Day?"

There is now silence in my Scout bus, and I know the ears of one Wendy Francis Hammer has zeroed in on the conversation.

"I think we will have to review the *entire* situation," Brad says ominously, writing something on his clipboard that I'm sure says something like, *Said subject did in fact knowing and with forethought drive across an open field to the Dairy Queen with scouts in vehicle under the influence of alcohol. Faithfully submitted, Brad Jones, Assistant Scout*

Master 155, BSA.

I shrug. I have always lost with men like Brad. Sooner or later they know there is a spy in the organization.

"Do what you have to do Brad."

"I will," Assistant Scoutmaster Jones responds, clicking his BSA pen.

2

"What the hell was that?"
–Astronaut on Apollo 12

D. T. Hammer lobs one from the free throw line, and the ball rims the basket, then sails off as the crowd groans. Basketball is a game of physics, and some in the crowd doubt a forty-six-year-old man still has the ability to conquer those physics. Now the young upstart thunders down the driveway, neatly sidesteps the old man, then turns and jumps from the side court, swishing another. The crowd goes wild for the rookie. I take the ball, chagrined that my almost-ten-year-old son is kicking my ass. Since when did he have a half-court shot that makes him look like one of the NBA stars he has plastered on the underside of his bunk bed?

"You got PI, dad."

"I know, I know," I mutter, wheeling and blowing a simple hook shot.

The game of PIG came about when Wendy disappeared into the house and I saw Dale junior shooting baskets. Basketball being infinitely preferable to a discussion with Wendy Hammer about four-wheeling and related matters—I jumped at the opportunity for some one-on-one. The hangover had settled into a dull headache and I wanted some time to strategize about the latest developments in the life of D. T. Hammer.

Dale junior misses a simple lay up. I take the ball, bounce twice, and then shoot from the side. I'm about to lose the game when the basketball defies physics and sails around the rim twice before plopping into the ratty net.

"Not out of it yet," I shout.

Dale junior gives me a look, and I have one of those odd moments all fathers experience where they see themselves in their sons. The eyes are Wendy's, but the face, the large teeth in front and the skinny legs with too-big tennis shoes and the easygoing persona are mine. I was always messing around, shooting baskets, hanging around the garage with the tools and the mowers and that gassy oil smell so much friendlier than the institutional scent of a school. The truth is I like hanging out with my kids and doing nothing. I do all the required activities—scouting, little league assistant coach, spectator of numerous musical reviews. But I really like just messing around with Dale and Angela, doing nothing together.

With Dale junior there is another element lately. He is nine, soon to be ten, and I notice already he distances himself from me at school when I drop him off. I notice the calls to his friend over a game of catch with his dad. I have done the math, and in a scant eight and half years, he is off to college. Soon he will be asking me for the keys to the car.

I take the ball again and plunk one in from the side.

"So how's school?"

"It's all right," he shrugs, dribbling, passing the ball between his legs.

I nod, patiently hammering away at the wall of nine-year-old indifference.

"You liking Mr. Boner any better?"

"No."

Mr. Boner—a twenty-something, gelled-hair bodybuilder who teaches elementary kids the finer points of dodgeball—had been riding Dale since he arrived last year. Extra laps and extra pushups had been dished out for not listening to the tactics employed in flag football. I had done what any self-respecting parent would do and vilified the square-headed Mr. Boner. I put him into the general area reserved for cinder-blocked, suburban elementary schools with pointy-headed principals who wear suits ten years out of style. I feel genuinely bad about Dale junior landing in the narrow confines of Prairie Farms Elementary. To say it was different from his old school would be an understatement—progressive, integrated, maybe even cutting edge, Whitley Elementary had successfully walked the line between black kids from the ghetto and the white upper middle class. Now Dale junior was under the tutelage of men and women who rarely even see an African American.

"Well, I'm sure it will get better," I assure him, swishing one from the center.

My son takes the ball and shakes his head doubtfully.

"I don't think so, Dad."

I line up again, disturbed at the futility in my son's voice.

"So how's the bus?"

I dunk the ball and know this is unfair, but hey, I've got PI. Dale junior takes the basketball and I can see I've hit paydirt. The eyes are down, and his face has lost all the sunshine.

"Not so good," he mutters.

He shoots, more like *slams* the ball, and misses the backboard entirely. I recover the basketball from the garage, considering how to proceed. Another difference from our former life is that my son now has to take a bus to school. In the city I enjoyed the relaxing moment of walking my son to his school every morning. I usually had a cup of coffee, and the walk was our time to chat, to bond. On snowy mornings, a snowball fight sometimes developed, and on crisp autumn days, we meandered along, kicking leaves, spotting new pumpkins on our block. Usually we saw neighbors walking their children and this turned into a time to complain, empathize, discuss the issues of the day—to chat. I now live in a neighborhood of stick men in the distance, waving across wide two-acre lots.

"So, what's not so good about it?"

Dale junior is staring at the ground.

"Nothing … it's all right," he says and shrugs.

I nod slowly, blowing a free-throw shot.

"Well, *something* must not be right about it."

Shrug. Shrug. The basketball clears the backboard and rolls off the roof. Clearly there is misplaced aggression now in our game of PIG. I give him back the ball and this time he just holds it, staring down at the orange sphere.

"It's just …" My son breathes heavily. "It's just I have to sit next to Derek on the bus."

"Derek Slug?"

He nods stonily.

I now see a framework for his despair. Son of a man of many big screen televisions, a traveling salesman with every conceivable technology stuffed into his basement—Xboxes, Playstations 3, 4, and 5, the Wii, computers galore, a home theater, more mp3 files than any other *Homo sapiens* in the Western Hemisphere—Derek Slug was brought up to be the techno child. Into this techno maelstrom of fast action thumbs and glowing blue screens comes the son of a man who writes and reads. Our sons were destined to brook no stream together. The only thing that could make it worse is that Derek Slug is a boy who has a proclivity to hit.

"So …" I dribble the ball. "You have to sit next to Derek on the bus?"

"Right."

"And …"

Dale junior shrugs again. Clearly he is distressed. *I'm distressed.*

"And ..." He shrugs again, mumbling, "... he hits me."

I take the basketball. Our game is no longer. PIG has lost all relevance. I turn, bearing down on the five-foot replica of myself.

"What do you mean he *hits* you?"

He shrugs again, eyes down. The parent has been fully activated. Not good. He gives up several more shrugs.

"He punches me in the side," he says down to the black tar of our driveway.

"For no reason?"

Dale junior continues staring down at the driveway and I see he regrets telling me this. I have to get a grip. *Rational.* My son shrugs again.

"He thinks it's funny."

I'm in full fight or flight mode now. All my suspicions of the Derek Slug clan have found purchase on the totem pole of upper middle class white culture. I am sure Derek Slug views his persecution of my son like a video game where points are scored by picking on the sensitive city boy. Extra points are scored by punches in the stomach while riding on the bus. A win is achieved by throwing the city boy off the bus while in transit.

"Dale ... look at me." My son looks up with real pain in his eyes. "Are you saying that Derek hits you every morning for *no reason?*"

Dad is not that swift. He needs repetition of the crime for it to sink in. My son nods silently like a convict. I squeeze my nose, feeling the return of the margarita headache.

"Why don't you just move?"

"Assigned seats, Dad," he says and shrugs again. "It was on the day Mom gave me a ride. No one else wanted to sit next to him ... so I ended up sitting next to him."

Now I feel like shit. It is my fault, *our fault,* that our son has to sit next to a bully for a ride to school. It's our fault we gave in to white flight and the desire for a bigger house and ran to the far western suburbs. It was my fault for not knowing my son and daughter would be the real victims of middle-class conformity. I count up my transgressions for the millionth time since moving and come to the same conclusion—it was a terrible, terrible mistake to move.

I throw the basketball against the backboard and it bounces clear of the warrior ship.

"Wow, Dad."

"Listen, you don't ride the bus anymore! I'll give you a ride every day."

"Really …"

"It's not a problem," I say, doing quick math, reorienting my day that usually didn't really begin until ten or eleven anyway.

"Okay." He looks up. "Are we going to finish our game?"

I shake my head. The boy may be ready to move on, but the parent wants restitution. The parent needs action to salve his bitter wound.

"Listen, champ … I better go talk to your mother … we'll finish it later."

"All right, Dad," he says, hooking one from the far left.

Of course, it's a beautiful swisher.

Wendy is in the library, scanning my bookcase of novels, literary criticism, and author biographies. Only the real shit makes it into my bookcase, and that's why I am amazed to find my wife perusing these dusty old books seldom moved. She usually prefers nonfiction with a thriller plot of the *Da Vinci Code/Devil in the White City* variety. My books are thumbed, creased, and yellowed, from Dostoevsky to Joyce back to Hemingway and Fitzgerald. My small library is a study in the secret guilt all writers carry—here are the books you *should* read and not necessarily the books you *want* to read. Wendy carries no literary guilt and indulges in only the books she wants to read and quickly throws those over if they don't hold her attention.

I fall onto the couch.

"What are you looking for?"

"Stephanie wants to get John a collection of Hemingway short stories for Christmas and I told her I would get the name of a good one because I know you have—"

"John Winston reads?"

Wendy turns around and gives me her best "don't start" look.

"No really." I hold up my hand. "I didn't know BP corporate executives with boatloads of stock options who have second families of kids he never sees ever considered the irony of an Ernest Hemingway short story as something valuable to have as mental pabulum."

Wendy once again gives me the flat blue eyes of a beautiful blond.

"It's for his son in college," she informs the buffoon.

"Oh," I nod. "For his son in college. Then I suggest *The Snows of Kilimanjaro.*"

"All right," she says, sitting down in the Queen Anne opposite me. "I'll tell her."

Our little library is a study in modern efficiency. I have seen the blueprints of the house, and the man who built this cedar-sided country squire abode really did have this ten by fifteen room marked as a library. It is a token library with a fireplace and three floor-to-ceiling windows. The two French doors ensure the world at large can be sealed off, but the other entrance is wide open. I had studied the blueprints closely and saw that originally there was a plan for a sliding door to block off this entrance, but at the last minute this door had been eliminated. A modern man cannot *really* block himself off from the television, the Internet, the talking heads of our lives. A library in this day and age is really nothing but a quaint footnote to a quieter day.

I lock my hands, thinking how best to proceed. Wendy turns another page of Hemingway.

"What?" she murmurs.

"Do you know what is happening to our son on the bus every day?"

This gets her out of the land of one true sentence, her blue eyes looking for the mirth, the hint of disingenuousness that will let her off the hook. I see the neighbor kid, Derek Slug, out in the cul-de-sac. He is pulling branches off a lone tree.

"Do you know what's going on with our son and that little Nazi Derek Slug?"

Wendy's eyes dull. She has become used to my assignations of fascistic intent to the prowling youths of the hood. I plunge on, building up righteous steam.

"Do you know what is happening *every day* on that bus?"

The lawyer who once cowered felons in jail cells now confronts the hostile witness. The witness is known for diatribes laced with invectives pitting the world at large against the lone artist. He is fond of the epigram, "You will never go broke underestimating the intelligence of the American public." Another favorite is, "Patriotism is the last refuge of scoundrels," followed by the famous Napoleon quote, "You don't govern men who don't have religion, you shoot them." The lawyer has heard all this before and braces herself to guide the witness slowly back to earth.

"No, I don't, Dale," she replies dully.

I stand up in our small library, spying the collective works of D. T. Hammer on the mantle. I pace, four steps one way, then back. The man really should have built a larger library. I wheel.

"That little shit is hitting our son every day on the bus!"

"Keep your voice down," Wendy says, glancing into the next

room where Angela is watching *Blues Clues* for the thousandth time. "What little shit?"

This is a favorite tactic of the lawyer, if not the wife. She gloms on to some inessential piece of my diatribe, thereby draining off the thrust of my charge. I have seen Wendy's mother do it to her father with the cunning of a double agent for years. But I am focused now. The assault on my son has kicked off all sorts of guiltinomics, and I have found a convenient outlet in the five-foot-one, crew-cut automaton from across the way.

"*Derek Slug!* The kid is punching Dale every day on the bus!"

Wendy rolls her eyes and becomes calmer. I know she has heard confessions of murder, rape, incest, and burglary. I know those machine-gunner blue eyes have coolly met men with murder in their heart. Still, I want a reaction.

"Dale has to get along with all sorts of boys. He has told me about Derek on the bus, and I told him to just tell Derek not to hit him anymore."

I stare at my wife in her pink jumpsuit. "You don't *tell* a boy like Derek Slug not to *hit you* anymore," I explain to her, realizing the *Romper Room* tactics Wendy employs have now been given to our hapless son to combat the *predator Slug*. "You either flatten the kid, or you avoid him all together. Mental midgets like Derek don't give a shit about a request."

The lawyer surveys the pacing, sweating man in front of her.

"You are overreacting, Dale. Your son does not have any friends in the neighborhood. He is not interacting with the other kids."

"That's because they are all cretins, Wendy. We screwed him by moving out here."

"You were the one who wanted to move, Dale," she points out calmly.

I stare at the lawyer.

"I think you wanted to move also."

"No, Dale. You were the one who called the realtor. You were the one who declared crime in Oakland had reached intolerable levels—"

"After a woman got mugged on a Saturday night on our street—"

"You were the one who suggested we move to the country."

The lawyer had made her point, and besides, we go over this terrain daily. Like some sort of jogger who ignores rain, sleet, and hail, we circle back around to this one theme—who *really* was responsible for the move out into the middle of nowhere. I look for cracks in the Maginot line of her defense, but I am always left with the single invective—*you* are responsible, Dale.

"Well, that may be, but I'm not going to have my son getting molested by some fascist on a school bus every morning—"

The blue eyes register amusement.

"Molested, Dale?"

I stare at the lawyer lying back in the Queen Anne and throw myself on the mercy of the court.

"You know what I'm saying, Wen," I mutter, flopping down on the couch, losing steam suddenly. "I really think we should move."

"Fine," she says and shrugs. "Put the house up for sale."

"I think we should go back to Oakland."

"We are not going back to Oakland, Dale."

I stare at this woman so calmly countering my every thrust.

"Why not? It's where we belong. It's where our kind of people are!"

The eyebrows dance high.

"Is that why you hated everyone on our block, Dale? Is that you and Frank Goldstein hated each other so much I couldn't talk to Joanne anymore? Is that why you were so paranoid you ringed in our entire yard with an eight-foot fence and put motion lights all over the house and spent hundred of dollars on an ADT system?”

“You wanted the fence, too,” I point out weakly.

Wendy shakes her head.

“We are not going back to Oakland. If you want to move, then fine. But we are not moving back.”

The stalemate of our daily conversation about moving has been reached. The two joggers have completed their circuit for the day and it’s time to hit the shower. Maybe tomorrow we might go a little farther.

“Anyway, I told Dale I would give him a ride to school from now on.”

The eyebrows climb for the ceiling again.

“So you can start work even later?”

I let this one pass, as we both know this is a slippery slope down into our financial abyss. Wendy looks up suddenly.

“Did you call Jim Mesh back?”

I shake my head, feeling the distant thunder of new artillery.

“What about Dean Heinrich?”

“No,” I mutter.

Wendy frowns, examining the enigma that is the man she married. Contradictory is the way she summed me up once and I suspect she is right. Even I know that I am a walking antithesis, if an adverb can be a noun. I can’t even follow my own logic most of the time.

“Are you going to just *not do* Rocket Day?”

“Brad says I might be out of it anyway for four-wheeling,” I say, shrugging.

The machine-gunner eyes are back.

“That was asinine, Dale.”

“Oh come on … so I drove across an empty lot. Big deal.”

“With a drink in your hand,” the lawyer finishes.

I frown.

“Did I miss something? Or is prohibition back?”

"It's against the law, Dale, to drink and drive," the litigator informs the obtuse witness.

"Oh come on, we're talking about a splash of vodka."

Wendy shakes her head and stands up. I am treated to a full view of ten-thousand-dollar breasts. It is not incongruous that an intelligent woman with a law degree and a healthy understanding of the trappings of bourgeois life should want to have breast implants. I myself have been a Rogaine habitué for years for extra hair along the frontal lobe region. Young is what we are and young is what we will always be. At least before we turn fifty.

"You know, Wendy," I begin, employing a different tactic, "we always said that after three years we would evaluate the move and decide if we had made a mistake or not."

"And?"

"It's been almost three years, and we have never had that conversation."

Wendy rolls her eyes, gripping the mantle where the literary outpourings of D. T. Hammer are a scant two inches away. I hope this will give me some weight. Surely, a man who wrote *three novels* must have something on the ball. Wendy turns and I see the cool objectivity has given way to a withering despair.

"Dale, we have that conversation *every day*. You are obsessed with it and I can't stand much more of you talking about the same thing over and over. It's so … *blah!*" Wendy says, using her favorite expression when it comes to me. Normal language is no longer sufficient to sum up the habits of her husband.

"What … talking about what?"

"Moving! You talk about it all the time, but you never do anything!"

I nod slowly, conceding the point.

"Well, my income's been a little off …."

"That's an understatement," comes the deadpan reply.

"Anytime you want to go back to work, let me know," I say

lightly.

"You say that every day too, Dale."

I hold up my hand.

"I don't want you to work, but when you attack my earning capabilities …"

The lawyer is now bored.

"I wasn't *attacking you,* Dale."

It is true. There is not a day that goes by where I don't think having the mother of my children at home is a great thing. But a single household income is a balancing act few can afford to play, and we are certainly one of the few. A new topic looms on the horizon. Wendy sits back down in the Queen Anne interrogation chair.

"Why did you cut down the sign, Dale?" she asks quietly.

I return to the visit from Charleston' finest. The two strapping young men who sat in this very room had asked me the same question. I met them with the same blank stare. *Where did such a canard get started?* Who would perpetuate the fiction that I would rise in the dead of night and go cut down an ugly subdivision sign? True, it was the type of sign that engendered the misgivings I have about our new surroundings—unimaginative, sterile—an electric eighties blue banner with ducks and children playing under the moniker Belleview—a real republican sign.

"I didn't cut down the sign, Wendy," I say tiredly. "But I might as well have, because everyone has convicted me already."

"That's because you have been *very* vocal about what you felt about the sign, Dale."

"I was just messing around," I say indignantly. "It was an ugly sign, but that doesn't mean I would go cut the thing down!"

Wendy fixes with me with her best lawyer stare.

"Anyway, it's gone, so it doesn't matter now," I say, pushing us along.

"No, it doesn't."

Topic number three now looms.

"I'm having my parents over for dinner this week."

I look up, all bells and whistles going off on the good ship lollipop.

"We just saw them last week."

"Yes, but they are leaving on a month-long cruise, and I want to see them before they go."

I feel the strange tightness in my chest. The shuddering of adult independence begins with financial dependence, and then the host of other goodies moves in—loss of individuality, loss of political views, loss of self. Not that Wendy's parents were offering us money, but the moniker of a stable Midwestern family was planted years ago and my own decentralized family is but a feather against the death star of home and hearth.

"I really don't think we need to see them again," I say.

The lawyer shrugs.

"You don't have to be there."

I don't want to be a bad husband, all opinions to the contrary, but lately I feel my identity slipping like a ship taking much water, and Wendy's parents seem to carry a billboard—*become stable and well meaning, and all your problems will vanish.* This terrifies me more than anything else. The dullard has always been my nemesis, and I feel he is now riding shotgun, waiting to take the wheel.

"What were you talking to George Campbell about?"

I look up and shrug again, thinking about the neighbor whom I had accosted on the drive back from four-wheeling. George lives directly across the street and for two years we had stared at each other from our respective two acres. He had become our ambassador to the land of zero turn mowers when we first saw him cutting his grass like a man riding a recliner. After four-wheeling, I felt I wanted to traverse another forbidden field and actually speak to my neighbor.

"Nothing ... I just asked him why we never talk."

For the first time, Wendy looks alarmed.

"You didn't."

I hold my hands wide.

"Why not? I thought we had a pretty good conversation for two men who have lived across the street from each other and never spoken."

My wife frowns at the bully.

"He's shy, Dale."

"You are shy when you are fifteen. At forty-seven it's just fucking weird."

"Well, George is shy."

"Then I helped him out," I say and nod. "How do you know he's shy?"

Wendy looks at me dead on.

"Because I don't attack people, Dale. I *wait* for them. George is a very nice man—"

"Whoa—since when did you ever talk to Campbell?"

My wife looks at me like I'm a child.

"I don't know. I'll just be outside, and he will come over and talk to me."

"*Campbell does?*"

"Yes."

"He has the hots for you."

"Don't be ridiculous."

"No." I nod. "He does … I can tell."

Wendy sits back and smiles in spite of herself. The absurdity that is me still can break through and give her a laugh. She breathes heavily and leans back in the chair.

"So what did George say when you accosted him?"

I squint, thinking how all conversations eventually circle around to a central theme. I look at my wife and shrug.

"He asked me why I moved out here."

3

"Five ... four ... three ... two ... one, and engine start!"
–Mission Control

Straight through Charleston turning to the north, we are the furthermost outpost of civilized suburban life before farms take over, consisting of dilapidated barns, neurasthenic cows, displaced sheep, and a cacophony of farm equipment complete with a rusting Hudson on its side. These farms are a paean to the diminishing life of rural America. The excavator will have its day; already the fields are dotted with orange flags marking our avaricious appetite for more shopping malls, more tract houses, more parking lots to park our newer and bigger cars. But for now, we still have the cornfields, and they are just a turn to the left after the jagged peaks of the desecrated Belleview billboard.

This rural oasis is the place I go for refuge, pedaling out under the wide sky that cares not for million-dollar houses—just honest men doing labor under God's light. Anyway, there are some great biking trails out there. So I am suiting up, snuggling my way into black Gore-Tex and padded biking shorts, when my cell phone rings.

"This is Dale."

"Dale?"

"Yes."

"Dale, this is Barb Smithy."

I should not have picked up this call. It is the Scoutmaster's wife—a woman with a hairstyle twenty years out of date and horn-rimmed glasses that have come back in style. She is imposing in her BSA uniform and brooks no shit from the committeemen, of which I am one. I have already dodged several meetings at the Smithy home concerning Rocket Day. Barb has accosted me at pack meetings, left numerous messages on my phone, and bombed me with emails. Many of her invectives close with an accusing, "You are Rocket Man, and you have responsibilities!" I consider the capriciousness of cellular phones as an excuse—a quick, apologetic closing of the phone— "I don't know what happened, Barb." But guilt keeps the phone riveted to my ear.

"Hello, Barb," I say, half dressed in my biking garb of skintight pants and a neon-green biking shirt that is to keep one D. T. Hammer from becoming road kill.

"Dale ..." There is the teacher's pause. "Dale, have you called Dean Heinrich about Rocket Day?"

Dean Heinrich—Rocket Man extraordinaire—a man who would impart the secrets of Rocket Day if I would only call him. Why is it that the simple tasks seem so daunting?

"I tried, Barb, " I continue, one foot in a jockstrap and one foot out—if only Barb could see me now, surely she would not care about Rocket Day. "But I didn't get an answer."

"Did you leave a message?"

"Did I leave a message?" I repeat, rummaging for just the right sweatshirt to wear under my green jersey. "I think I did ... I'm *sure* I did."

"I just talked to Dean and he says *no one* has contacted him, Dale. *Ever.* "

Amazing how one word can change the context of a

sentence—*ever.*

"Well, I called him, Barb. I would be happy to call Dean Heinrich again, but *I did* call him," I say with as much sincerity any lie can generate. *"Believe me."*

The pregnant pause is brilliantly executed, dripping with guilt and unfulfilled expectations—Barb is truly a master.

"Dale. It is too late to cancel Rocket Day, and I'll bet you have done nothing about *ordering* rockets, have you?"

"Ordering rockets," I stammer, selecting a very soiled biking glove at the bottom of the dirty clothes mountain. "I was just going to get on that, Barb ..."

I'm treated to several long breaths of exasperation. They are the breath of the disappointed mother, the breath of all womankind disappointed in what colossal fuck-ups certain types of males seem to be.

"Dale ... when you volunteered to be Rocket Man, you took on the responsibility of that job. Now, you have put us all in a predicament. We have eighty-three boys who have signed up for Rocket Day, and I see no preparations *at all.* We are headed for a disaster. What if you can't get the rockets? Have you even *thought* of that?"

Barb is truly a specialist at targeted guilt, and I appreciate the deft quality of her charge. I had been to the Smithy household only once and sat in their pine-walled den with German beer mugs bordering the fireplace mantle and flowers in the fireplace. Mike and Barb were probably quite the couple in 1975—the poster couple for *Whatever Happened to The Carpenters.*

"I've thought about that, Barb, and here is what I propose," I say, picking up my biking shoes. "I think we should consider balloon rockets as a backup. We will just give every kid a balloon, and he can blow it up and let it fly. It may not be the same as the rockets Dean Heinrich blasted off, but there is a war on, and I think we should all do our part and economize, and maybe

Rocket Day will have to change during the war years."

There is a long, humming silence. I have not folded under the guilt Zeppelin Barb floated and this has surprised her. Barb speaks in a quiet, cryptic voice.

"What war?"

"Why, the war against terror, of course."

I can hear clothes drying in the background. Barb had been doing laundry when she decided to vivisect the errant *Rocket Man*. I imagine bras and underwear, Mike's socks, Mike's comfort fit jeans, all spinning just below Barb in her efficient laundry room, taking down another male as she folds her husband's jock strap into a neat square to be snuggled next to his balled socks.

"You're kidding, right?"

"No, not at all, Barb. I think we all have to do our part and conserve. Those rocket engines might be better used to fight the *evildoers*. I mean, do we really need propellant-powered rockets when we can teach our scouts the finer points of rocket propulsion with nothing more complicated than an ordinary balloon?"

I hear explosions of breath, then a very curt, "I'm going to have Mike deal with you." The line mercifully goes dead as the dryer sings out its buzzer, letting Barb know it is time to fold. I close the phone and open the door from our walk-in closet when the phone rings again.

"This is Dale."

"Dale ... Mike Smithy."

It is the signature of the modern patriarch. The name is stated, and this is the modern equivalent of the calling card, the sword drawn, the gauntlet thrown down. *Mike Smithy.* It is a fierce declaration. He is the Scoutmaster after all.

"Mike, how's it going?"

"Dale, what's this I hear about *balloons* for Rocket Day?"

"I was just telling Barb, Mike, that as a backup, we might employ regular balloons and have the scouts blast those off ...

besides, there is a war on."

Pause.

"What war?"

"Why, the war against terror, of course."

The Scoutmaster's silence is much stronger than his wife's. There are no short exclamations of breath, but a somber no-bullshit question.

"You got to be kidding me."

"Yeah, I am, Mike. I was just trying to get Barb to lighten up a little."

There is a short, gruff chortle on the line.

"She takes her job very seriously Dale and thank God she does … it makes my job a *whole lot* easier."

"Oh, I can see that."

"Now … .Dale, I'm going to give you Dean Heinrich's phone number one more time. I want you to contact him and try and get over there tonight if you can. Then I want you to order the rockets for the scouts and whatever else you need."

I nod in the darkness, anything to get off the phone now.

"Yeah, all right. Can you call back and leave it on my voicemail, Mike? I have the kids right now, and I'm giving my daughter a bath."

"Will do, Dale. But just remember, you're the *Rocket Man*. The scouts … the boys, are *depending* on you, and one thing I will not abide, Dale, is someone letting down *my boys.*"

"I agree, Mike," I say, head against the wall.

"Now," his tone is helpful, even friendly, "I'm going to leave you the number on your phone …"

"Perfect, Mike."

"Oh, one more thing … I got a crazy call from Brad Jones, saying you went four-wheeling with some scouts from the Kane County Fair popcorn sale …"

I open my eyes and lift my head from the wall.

"I just cut through the lot between McDonald's and Dairy Queen, Mike."

"Hmmm … he also claimed you had an alcoholic drink."

"… tomato juice, Mike."

Long pause.

"All right … well, let's straighten up and fly right from here on, Dale. I'll leave you the voicemail now."

"Great."

I hang up the phone, walking out of my closet like the chastised boy I am.

The garage smells like freedom. The scent of internal combustion engines in an enclosed space along with decaying grass from the mower hearkens back to my own childhood. I clack past the white whale of our lives and thread my way past the new John Deere tractor. The tractor is green, has a hydrostatic transmission, drives like a car, and cost a cool six thousand dollars. I know the world is truly on its head when my mower costs more than my 1997 Explorer. I really should be driving the mower and cutting the grass with the Ford.

I take my mountain bike down from the wall and thread my way back between twin SUVs—*gas crisis? What gas crisis?* Reaching the driveway, I pull a bottle of water from the old refrigerator and slip it into the cradle. Sunglasses on, bike helmet pulled low, I am ready to leave this world for the next.

I hear crying.

I dismount and walk outside to the driveway and around to the patio. It is my five-year-old, Angela. She is sitting astride her bike with one training wheel on and one angled back to the point it is no longer rolling. Angela looks like Annie Oakley— long, curly blond hair and blue saucers for eyes. She could stop a Hessian at full march when she turns on the water. Some children make adults act like fools, and Angela has that ability. She has an artist's temperament, the innocence of an angel. She is five. This is the age where the world is still wonderment, Dad still is a hero and there is nothing old about the human condition. She is trying on new words, learning to add, wants desperately to move beyond crafts in kindergarten, and sings Christmas carols all year round.

"*Daaaaadddddy …*"

Her bangs hang flat and her long, curly blond hair spreads on her shoulders. Lately, I see my mother in my daughter. Angela will be washing her hands at the sink in the fastidious way my mother used to wash her hands. Her smile, even the way she prances when she walks, reminds me of the little girl I have seen in old photos. My mother's art covers our walls, but it is my daughter who brings into relief the knowledge of her passing six years before.

"My … bike won't work … *waaaaaaaaah.*"

Another cliff of tears, and I'm on the job. I examine the Barbie two-wheeler. It is my own doing. When I assembled the bike, I put the training wheels on, but they never remained tight. I know I did something wrong, but mechanics is not my strong suit. I move the stabilizing bracket forward and reposition the wheel.

"No problem. Daddy will fix it." I wipe away her tears and stand up. "I have to get a wrench and it will be good as new … all right?"

"All right, Daddy," she says and nods, sniffing.

I head back into the garage and confront my workbench. I have been given tool sets for Christmas by my father-in-law, who has an abiding hope that one day I will turn into a normal man. The tools, along with paint cans, dried brushes, paint trays, extension cords, paint canvasses, insect repellent, cans, and jars of foreign substances, have ended up on the plywood-topped work bench. I had great plans of becoming the organized man and attacking this mess, but all I do is add to the carnage by throwing more tools into the pile.

I find an adjustable wrench in a big plastic ice bucket and head back out of the garage. Angela has now become distracted with the dandelions that have defied drought, seasons, weed killer, and my own maniacal attacks with a weed whacker that left great brown patches on my lawn. That is the beauty of children, to pass swiftly from crisis to the placidity of blowing petals from dandelions. I quickly tighten the errant wing nut on the bracket and make sure the training wheel will not collapse back into its folded state.

"There," I say, holding her pink Barbie cruiser out for her. She lets fly the last white gossamers of the dandelions.

"Yaaaaaa!"

Angela jumps on and starts cruising back toward our patio.

"Thanks, Daddy," she sings, tooling around the brick patio, veering around the fire pit, marble bar, and sitting walls. Whenever I look at the patio, only one word comes to mind, one word, and I am Dustin Hoffman again, graduating into a world I know not—*plastics.*

Time to go for a ride.

"All right, sweetheart. Daddy is going for a ride now."

"Can I come with you?"

"Honey, Daddy is going to take a long ride by himself."

The tour of the patio comes to a stop.

"Why can't I go with you, Daddy?"

"Well, because sometimes Daddy needs to ride far."

Angela's eyes widen, a fresh army of tears at the ready.

"Daddy, I want to go with you."

"How about when I come back, Angela? Then we can *both* go for a ride!"

She looks down, lip extended.

"All right, we'll go for a ride when you come back," she says, dismounting suddenly for another dandelion in the yard.

"I'll see you in a little bit."

"All right, Daddy," she calls out, blowing gossamers into the air, sending more nascent dandelions to the far corners of my beleaguered lawn.

Riding like the wind, I clear the last house of Belleview and turn left into the setting sun. I put faith in my glowing green jersey and the mercy of truck drivers and stressed-out mothers not to clip me into the cornfields. The sprawl of suburbia is left behind and I am running past the high-tasseled corn of October. I pass a farm on the right and smell the cool air of raw earth, then fertilizer, pumping my legs faster to get momentum for the hill. I can hear my breathing and with each deep breath, alcohol and stress is given away to the cooling evening. Riding has become my religion. It is the one thing in my new life that is real.

The road levels and I pedal for Coron Road, an even more desolate farm road. But there is trouble on the horizon here as well. Surveyor posts picket the landscape like ancient graves. Orange tape trails in the wind, and I can already see the excavator tracks going into the middle of what used to be a farm field. I see the houses and the kids and the SUVs fighting for space on the narrow two lane. It is disturbing, this rampant sprawl. The strip malls down the road from us are a study in bad taste. Target, Walgreen's, McDonald's, T.J. Maxx, Bank of America, Sportmart, Petsmart, Club 19—a coliseum of economic titans spread out over acres and acres that used to be farmland. The rumbling tide of development is headed west, and I know forces are already in motion that will eventually eliminate my country sojourn.

I pedal past McMansions in the distance, six-thousand-square-foot monsters that snuggle up against each other like city lots. I can see the white squares advertising incentives in the million-dollar and up price range. These ugly monsters are a testament to the real estate crash a year ago. The brightly colored banners have been sheared by wind and pools of muddy water collect in unlandscaped yards. Port-a-potties have not been hauled out. The entire neighborhood is a set piece to years of waste and excess—if only the middle class could have held out a little longer, dragged themselves a little more in debt. Now it is a totem to all that has been wrong for the last twenty years.

I pedal on, passing farther into the country, but now the first wave of bad food and latent alcohol has burned off and I am in a freefall. My legs are slowing and my breathing is becoming that of an exhausted locomotive. The toxins are doing their job. There is no denying that the trick of drinking and biking does not work anymore. I am reduced to a man looking down at the road while breathing like an asthmatic. I always could count on my energy before, but there has been a sea change as of late, and the fatigue is so daunting that it gets me off the bike.

I am in front of a white farmhouse. I lean against a rickety old fence and hold on, trying to catch my breath. The ride should have been a swift ten miles to the country store in Wasco where I turn around and bike for home. Now I am the old man who has run out of gas, looking for support from a post driven into the earth during the last century. Years of bad food has caught up with me, and the next trip to the doctor will be a trip to bypass central, where I will emerge like a former president, washed out, pale, old.

I look up at the farmhouse surrounded by towering oaks. Aunt Em surely came out of the back porch and down the short cement stairs, heading toward the barn with eggs in her apron or biscuits for the field hands. Wendy and I were supposed to end up on a farm. There was a small ad in the paper announcing a farm in Geneva for sale and that's what got us looking. We walked around the "farmette." There was a barn where I was to write and a working silo that I could walk into and stare up at the open sky when I wasn't writing. The house was beautiful on the outside and a nightmare inside—bare and utilitarian, with an in-law apartment tacked on the back straight out of Menards. So we ended up in that curious blend of rural and urban where no one is happy.

My heart has slowed to the point where I don't think I'll be found laying face down in the grass. The light is in the top of the trees and the evening becomes inviting. I stare across the fence, seeing a man walking toward me. He is in farmer's jeans and has a hat pulled low. I consider biking away, then tell myself I have done nothing more than lean on his fence.

"Hallo," he calls, walking with the long-legged stride of a man used to crossing rows upon rows of crops.

"How ya doing?" I say, sounding more Chicago than I wanted.

"Beautiful evening," he says, hooking a boot up on the bottom rail of the fence.

I hook a biking shoe on the fence.

"It sure is. I bike past your farm every day, and I always stop to admire it."

He pulls his hat off and I am treated to a dome brown as worn leather.

"Do you now? Earl Sheboygan," he says, extending a hand that could easily crush mine.

"Dale Hammer."

"Well, nice to meet you, Dale."

He spits off to the side and I follow suit. His spit goes much farther.

"I take it you own this farm."

"You take it right," he says, smiling, a row of teeth pushed out along the bottom, laced with tobacco stain. "Been here eighty years."

"Wow. You must have seen a lot of changes in your time,

Earl."

"Oh yeah…lots of changes. Wasn't any of this here before? They ruined the land is all they done."

I nod slowly.

"I've only been out here a few years."

He frowns. "You in them new houses up the way?"

"Yes. That's where I am … we wanted something like this, but we ended up in a subdivision."

He glances at my glowing green jersey. I must look like a spaceman or a fool. I must confess something. It wasn't the house that really killed the farm for us. It was living out among the empty fields and *really* going out to the country. I knew we had stopped just short of agrarian reality because we couldn't leave the heroin of too many people in too small spaces. Even though our yard is an acre and a half, the presence of our neighbors and their opinions, politics, and prejudices seeps into our daily lives. Even the mantra of "doing it for the kids" pales as I realize we simply didn't have the guts to become this man with a boot hooked on his fence.

"Do you ever think of selling, Earl?"

He glances at me, shaking his head.

"Nope. I got eighty acres left, and I intend to keep them."

I nod slowly.

"Don't care about the money then?"

Earl Sheboygan looks me dead in the eye and sends the spaceman back to his planet.

"Who gives a damn about money, when it's your home?"

The return trip is much better, and I am able to keep a steady pace all the way back to the Belleview entrance. The slanting sun clearly shows a madman has attacked the two Belleview signs. Someone had attempted to piece the signs together and propped them on the two concrete posts that anchored the plywood.

There is a jagged cut between the *Belle* and the *view* on each sign, and the attempt to meet these two halves caused the *Belle* to lean toward the ground and the *view* to tilt toward the sky. Not content to deface, the perpetrator then attacked the two ends of the sign, not cutting close to the brick supports, but jaggedly cutting a third of the way out.

I coast down the hill farther and feel better as I pass a cluster of trees that escaped the bulldozer. The man who built my new house clearly had an ego; he positioned his house on the second crest of a hill that looks out over a valley of wetlands and farms in the distance. But the real reason he built on the hill is the cul-de-sac of stone forts directly below. He wanted to make sure he dwarfed all his neighbors, and it didn't really matter if his neighbors' homes were bigger than his—he was *higher* than they were.

There is something impudent in the wraparound porch and the galloping horse wind vane over the garage, the three chimneys, the cedar siding defying the neighborhood of brick and mortar. Stately is a word that comes to mind, followed by excessive, grandiose, pretentious, overblown, and elitist. These are my adjectives; for another man the word might be bucolic. I do admire the house, I really do, but I can't help but wonder—who would live in such a house?

4

"We're docked, no noticeable oscillations, very smooth."
–Astronaut Neil Armstrong

I see an unmarked blue car parked in front of the garage. It's one of those police cars that every one knows is a police car because of the *M* on the license plate and the small stubby antenna by the trunk. I consider turning around and riding off into the evening. People would always wonder what happened to D. T. Hammer. He just rode off one night and never returned—one of those John Updike characters that just leaves suburban life and takes the road less traveled. I go through the ritual of hanging my bike on the wall and leaving my hat and sunglasses on the handlebars.

I emerge from the garage and face a Lilliputian.

"Daddy, are we going riding now?"

My son appears.

"Hey, Dad, we going to throw the football like you said?"

I look at Dale junior and Angela, deciding which crisis to address—promises broken or the police.

"You told me yesterday that we would play football today," Dale junior complains.

The memory of elephants these children have.

"Listen, guys, I have to go in and talk to this man—"

"You mean the cop?"

"Right, the cop," I nod. "But after that I'll go riding with you, Angela, and throw the football, Dale."

The round tears descend from my daughter.

"You said we'd do it now ..."

"Angela, quit crying."

I glare at Dale junior

"Let me handle this, son."

The lip quivers, the eyes flood over.

"You said we'd go riding ... *waaaaaaaah!*"

The light of the kitchen breaks into the garage.

"Angela, Dale ... Grandma's on the phone." My wife then looks at me. "You can cook the burgers when you are finished with your ... visitor."

A conversation with Grandma breaks the spell of a ride with Dad and I am suddenly alone in the garage. Wendy peers at me from the lit doorway.

"He's in the library."

"Yeah, I know," I say, trying to sound as casual as a man can when the police are waiting for him.

I am now annoyed. If this was real crime, then the cop would not be waiting for me. He would be in the kitchen with a warrant, running into the garage when the perpetrator rode in. I circle the house and enter through the front door. It's better to show ownership than sneaking in through the garage. I make a great show of coming in the front door and shout toward the kitchen, *"Honey, I'm home."* Just to show what a *Leave it to Beaver* family we are. I then turn toward the library, where a man in jeans and tennis shoes is sitting in one of the Queen Anne chairs. He carefully puts my second novel into the wedged containment of the mantle.

"So you're a novelist," he says, shaking my hand. "Brian Clancy."

"Dale Hammer" I murmur, falling to the couch.

Brian Clancy shakes his head slowly, and I see a man about my age in the official uniform of Charleston leisure attire—a checked shirt and comfort fit jeans with new white tennis shoes. But he has the cop squint with cold blue eyes that are already taking in the man in green Gore-Tex.

"I've never met a novelist before." Brian Clancy shakes his head. "I used to think about writing a book."

"You should then," I say and nod.

He smiles, rubbing the bristles of his peppered crew.

"No time between the job and kids … maybe someday."

I pop off my riding shoes, rubbing my feet.

"Are you here to back up One Adam Twelve—Reed and McCoy?"

The cop smiles again, but I see a small vein appear next to his right eye, a throb below the temple. He crosses his leg and rests one hand on the rubber sole of his Puma running shoe. I am referring to the duo that visited my house at nine AM to inquire about the destruction of the Belleview sign.

"That was Reed and *Malloy* in One Adam Twelve, Mr. Hammer."

I frown. Popular culture is one thing I pride myself on knowing, especially old popular culture from my childhood.

"No, I think it was Reed and McCoy."

Brian Clancy shakes his head.

"No sir, Reed and Malloy, but yes, I'm here to back them up. I'm actually a good friend of Dr. Petty; I live just across the wetland."

"Ahhh, a friend of Dr. Petty," I say and nod, thinking of the good doctor who has sold me down the river.

"Actually, my wife and Tammy Petty work at the same hospital

… this is really an unofficial visit."

"Good, I was worried it might be official and I would have to call my lawyer."

Clancy laughs, shaking his head.

"No need for that. Like I said, I'm just a personal friend of Dr. Petty here to … well, see if I can clean up the situation."

The situation? The blanks filled in, I'm ready to dispense of Sergeant McGruff in tennis shoes.

"Just one big happy family," I murmur.

The eyes turn into a cop as he leans forward.

"Listen, Mr. Hammer—"

"Dale, call me Dale."

He nods, not listening anymore, interrogating.

"Dale … Dr. Petty filled me in and wants this to be taken care of quietly." Brian Clancy hooks a thumb on his running shoe. "Dr. Petty doesn't want to create a rift in the neighborhood, and I think he wants to avoid legal action if at all possible. So, again I've come over here in an *unofficial* capacity to act as intermediary."

I lean back into the couch, nodding slowly.

"Oh…unofficial capacity. You should have brought a station wagon then and left the squad at home."

He lets this pass, his eyes growing duller by the second.

"My point is I think Dr. Petty would be fine if you would just pay for the sign and have it restored to its previous condition. I then can get the police report, and no one will be the wiser."

The friendly blue eyes are now like two small bullets.

"So what you're saying, Officer …"

"Detective. *Detective* Clancy."

The eyes are now downright hostile. I am clearly the criminal.

"What you're saying, Detective Clancy, is that if I confess to a crime I didn't commit and pay for a sign I didn't destroy, then there will be no charges filed?"

"What I'm saying, Mr. Hammer, is there is no reason to make this a *bigger* thing than it is. I think you agree that we should handle this quietly."

I lean back on my couch, conscious that I am wearing a fluorescent green biking shirt and skintight shorts—not the kind of attire a man wants to have on when dueling with the law.

"That would be fine, Detective, if I in fact I *did* cut down the sign."

Detective Clancy studies the perpetrator.

"Mr. Hammer...why do you want stir up all this shit? I know a little bit about you. I know you don't exactly fit in. I know you moved from Oakland, and I probably know why. You got a lot of yuppies who want to live by the big bad city until their kids get mugged and then they run out here with their liberal bias and they don't call it white flight; they call it buying a bigger house."

"Oh, so what ... you investigated me?"

Detective Clancy raises a finger from the armchair and looks bored. Clearly, there is a football game on tonight that would be much more interesting than playing dueling banjos with a writer.

"Look, you moved out here, Mr. Hammer. And you have got to fit in now. This is where conservative people live who want to raise their families." Detective Clancy shakes his head sadly. "Ain't no rebel without a cause out here because there ain't no causes. You want causes, go back to Oakland. I know you cut that sign down. *You know* you cut it down. So why don't you get out the yellow pages and get some sign guys out here to replace it?"

I'm up now. *I'm really up.* Detective Clancy watches me as I pace in my small library. I wish I was wearing something other than Gore-Tex, but we can never really pick our moments.

"Is that all, Detective?"

It's a puny response, but I can't really think of anything else to say. He shrugs and looks up sleepily. Time to go watch some football and leave this whack job in the zoot suit.

"I guess so, Mr. Hammer."

I make a great show of opening the front door. Detective Clancy has a faint grin on his lips as he pauses in front of me.

"You know we're going to have to prosecute you," he says in the tawny light of the front porch.

"Let me ask you something, Detective Clancy ... don't you have any *real* crime to solve? Don't you have anything else to do but drive out here and accuse someone of cutting down *a sign?*"

He frowns, then shrugs.

"No. So now I can spend all my time riding your ass. Have a nice night, Mr. Hammer."

I slam the door and walk back into the library. I sit down in the Queen Anne and stare at the collected works of D. T. Hammer on the mantle.

"Reed and Malloy," I mutter, realizing he was right.

5

"That looked like a slice to me, Al."

—Mission Control to Alan Sheppard, first astronaut to golf on the moon.

After Detective Clancy left, I returned to the driveway to find a black Jaguar parked in the middle. A man with a silver goatee in loafers and a pullover sweater from Brook Brothers is shooting baskets. I stop and watch the man with little hair, charming blue eyes that can stunt a bull, a surprisingly light step, make a free throw that rims the basket. He runs after Dale junior who is laughing in a way I haven't heard for a while.

"Granddad ... don't ..."

Even though the man wears a Brooks pinpoint shirt and Wejun loafers, he moves like a center for the Chicago Bulls, all animation, circling my son, taking the ball, hooking a shot that goes in dead center. My father screams, holding up his hands in victory.

"*Yeaaaaaah!*"

"Granddad!" Dale junior yells, running after him.

D. T. senior wheels and knocks the ball from his hands, dribbles away, letting loose his version of the Rebel Yell. "Ahhhhhhhhh!" He executes an impressive lay up and only then does he slow down and take a breather. Not bad for a seventy-three-year-old man.

One shouldn't be surprised if a parent pays a surprise visit to his son. Wendy's parents drop in randomly to see their grandchildren, fix a toilet, or drop off an outfit for Angela. They are the grandparents in the classic mode. My side of the family is more modern, dysfunctional, scattered, divorced, and decimated by death and rancor—your run-of-the-mill modern American family. It is easier to pull teeth than to get my side of the family together, and my father *never* just drops in.

D. T. senior is breathing hard and shakes my hand weakly. I'm hoping he hasn't pushed himself too hard, but I know this is an errant thought—D. T. senior has *always* pushed himself too hard.

"How are you, boy?" he shouts.

"This is a surprise." I nod as he recovers his breath, cell phone ringing, slipping it up from his waist with the speed of a gunslinger. "Dale Hammer."

I take the ball from Dale junior.

"Jack … that's a bunch of shit, and I'll tell him that to his face!"

D. T. senior is now cluing my neighbors and my son into his profession. I know what is coming next, and I want to put my hands over Dale junior's ears.

"That's *whoreshit,* Jack, and I don't care what he says, they aren't going to do me like that! That really pisses me off!"

Horseshit pronounced "*whoreshit*" is the lead-off word, usually followed by *pisses me off … asshole* should be coming. All fine Mississippi patois.

"Jack, the man is a complete and total *asshole,*" D. T. senior bellows toward Georgia Barnes's house down the road.

I imagine Georgia sitting down to dinner with her two sons, the window open to the breeze. Along comes an errant southern voice on the autumn tide, *"Jack, the man is a complete and total asshole."* These invectives are the classic rock of my family history. Many a cereal bowl was inhaled with *asshole* and *whoreshit* swirling above. A salesman's son, I became used to the animated man in voice and body. The hard sell, the pitch, the attack mode was my father's own brand of selling in the rough and tumble world of industrial sales. I swore early on to become a writer and not the purveyor of coarse assassinations over the breakfast table.

"Listen, Kingfisher … I don't give *a fuck* what he says …"

"Why don't you go see if Mom needs some help with dinner," I say to Dale junior, figuring I have given him the short version of four letter words.

He frowns, brow descending.

"Aw, can't I stay and talk to Granddad?"

"Jack. The man is a bonafide prick!"

I know my son wants to see this elusive man who usually only appears at Christmas. D. T. senior has a perfect record when it comes to my kids' birthdays—consistently forgetting every one and never appearing at the birthday parties where Wendy's entire family is in attendance. I dutifully invite him every year, and he dutifully murmurs, "I'll let you know, boy," and we both let it pass in mutual conspiracy to the utter dysfunctionality that is the hallmark of my family since my parents divorced. The remaining glue in the bonds of our family certainly dissolved with the death of my mother six years ago. I face my son, trying to reassure him my father will not just jump back in his car and vanish—something I am not all that confident about.

"Granddad is on the phone right now…discussing…business. We'll be in a minute," I say, watching D. T. senior pace as animated as any rapper. The only thing missing are the baggy pants, low-riding underwear, and backward baseball cap, because D. T. senior could go toe-to-toe for down and dirty lyrics.

"The man is a total and complete *fuckhead,"* floats across the lawn as Dale junior goes into the garage.

"Complete and total fuckhead," brings back fond childhood memories. The lexicon D. T. senior uses is really an exercise in recycling, and as a writer I find it amazing the same phrases can be employed in such a variety of ways. I expect a summation from my father soon, a sort of incantation of invectives that employs the repetition Gertrude Stein experimented with so many years before.

"That's whoreshit ... whoreshit ... whoreshit ... that's just whoreshit!"

D. T. senior is showing his age. *Whoreshit* is not of the current vernacular when it comes to swearing. This comes down from D. T. senior's birthplace of Mississippi. As a child, I grew up with *whoreshit* floating at me from all parts of the house. D. T. senior still has the heavy molasses of a Mississippi accent, speaking like he has a watermelon (pronounced *watahmelon*) in his mouth. D. T. senior's accent is so heavy that many times people think he is black. During the CB craze of the seventies, my father bought a CB radio and took us for a ride to demonstrate his prowess in this new form of communication.

"Breakah breakah, this is the Mississippi kid," he said, employing his handle.

"Are you black, boy?" Came back from the truckers on the highways of West Mississippi.

Another time I stayed over at a girl's apartment only to have the phone ring at six AM. I had just graduated college and was staying with my parents. The twenty-three year young lady picked up the phone, and then stared at me with large eyes.

"It's a negro," she exclaimed, betraying her Georgia roots. "And he's asking for you."

"That's my dad," I nodded.

Now I see DT Senior is going for a summation. He is leaning back on his heels, arm tucked into his side, one hand on that smooth dome of a head. I have seen this over the years too. I know the line; I *feel* the line coming in every bone of my body. It is the state of the Union address for D. T. senior. I could tell this man on the line what his proctologist is about to instruct him to do.

"Oh really, Jack," D. T. senior says dropping his arm, holding his cell phone with one hand to get maximum projection. I hope Georgia Barnes has closed her window and is holding her hands over her daughter's ears.

"Well listen here, Kingfisher ... YOU CAN JUST SHOVE THIS WHORESHIT JOB RIGHT UP YOUR ASS, YOU DIRTY COCKSUCKAH!"

Again, *cocksucker* is pronounced in the Mississippi patois of "cocksuckah." The phone closes; another business call for one D. T. senior has ended. I take the basketball and loft a swisher.

"Another happy client, Dad?"

'The bastards fired me," he grumbles, taking the basketball and hooking it so hard it pounds the backboard like a rifle. "The dirty cocksuckahs!"

I recover the basketball and pause.

"I'm sorry to hear that," I murmur, blowing a free throw.

I don't feel any real shock. It's not that I am cold hearted, it's just I grew up with a man who changed jobs the way other people change shoes. As long as the job was in the food industry, had a hefty expense account, and allowed one D. T. senior to travel until the cows came home, he would take it. The truth is, I don't know enough about my father's life to gauge this latest blow to his employment. I assume he already has something lined up. That was the D. T. senior style going back as far as I can remember—landing on his feet the very next day with a new job, a new car, and sometimes a new house in a new city.

D. T. senior leans back for a free-throw, the dress of the University of Mississippi, Class of 57 clinging to him even now—

loafers, no socks, open collar shirt. No women, of course. Ole Miss was just for men. The athlete D. T. senior used to be still clings to him as he dribbles around me and takes another shot.

"I'm going to sue the bastards ... it's goddamn age discrimination, (pronounced discrimiNAtion)."

"Do you think you have a case, Dad?"

D. T. senior stops suddenly, and I can see he is gone. I follow his line of vision and see the auburn haired and very languid Georgia Barnes walking down her drive. She is wearing a white jumpsuit with her long red hair trailing behind her. From our vantage point, she looks like a much younger woman. I assume she is coming down to find out what miscreant is filling the calm country air with Howard Stern invectives. I stare at my father and remember again who I am dealing with.

"My, my, goodnight, Mrs. Agnus, she is not bad."

I heave the basketball and miss, bouncing off the backboard and hitting the front of his Jaguar. D. T. senior picks up the ball and stops, a hint of tragedy in his blue eyes. I feel a second bomb rolling under my feet.

"Doris threw me out."

Now I stop. Doris is a little older than myself and the latest wife to take the Dale Hammer Senior Course in Loneliness and Debt. All of D. T. senior's wives, except for my mother, started out as career women whom he promised a life of leisure. They then quit their jobs and stayed at home while D. T. senior disappeared Monday through Friday on the routes of the traveling salesman. His wives then slowly began to lose their minds in the small town D. T. senior picked—usually close to a golf course that he could get a quick nine holes in before he left again. Wife number two turned to the bottle before having a nervous breakdown and returning to the home of her parents in Kansas. Wife number three, "Doris" is a tough Jewish woman from New Jersey who had seemed to weather the D. T. senior regimen, but now there was this.

"What happened?"

D. T. senior shrugs away the vagaries of conjugal relations.

"She said she had to find out who she is and that I am keeping her from doing that by isolating her in Langford."

I nod slowly, not sure what do with this.

"Anyway," he continues, dribbling again. "She says we should separate for a month so she can find herself."

I can't say I blame Doris for this. D. T. senior's constant, frenetic, passive aggressive, if not outright aggressive, persona, could eventually drive a sane man or woman crazy. He is the permanent man in motion right up to where he falls asleep in front of a movie. My father has two speeds—full throttle and passed out. He is a movie freak and will watch anything the video store will rent him. Pornography, action adventure, comedy, drama, it doesn't matter—as long as D. T. senior can turn it on, have a bowl of ice-cream, slump back on his couch, tilt his head toward the ceiling, let the credits roll, and then snore open mouthed through the movie.

I stare at him, not quite grasping the full implications, but feeling a rumble in the unsettling terrain that is my life. *Doris* has tossed him out, and he has lost his job, and now he is here. This is not the normal D. T. senior ritual of controlled chaos. Time will bring most freaks of nature to bay, and I think the sands of my father's egregious lifestyle have called their marker due. It is then I see the hanging shirts in the back of D. T. senior's car, the overnight bag, his briefcase, and what looks like an assortment of shoes on the floor of the front seat.

I stand up from the D. T. senior chariot and turn.

"What are you going to do now?"

The master salesman swishes one in from the half court. The blue eyes crinkle, closing the mark.

"Move in with you, Kingfisher."

I know I am a testament to the man; it's when I am cantankerous, shooting off passive-aggressive missiles like the Russians at the height of the Cold War, leaving the house in a huff of silence, pushing away the vagaries of intimacy with the clean air of action. D. T. senior is all about action. It is the action taken that matters. Get on the plane, drive like hell, make the call, get the deal—take the action even if it's the *wrong* action. The bull in the china shop cares not for the pastels of human relations—that was my mother's stong suit. When they finally split up, after twenty years of therapy, I think they were both relieved. My mother could admit my father was incapable of change, and D. T. senior could get back to the business of being a balls-to-the-wall salesman.

When I think back on my childhood, I remember a man coming home through the twilight, his suit smelling like pencils, dashing in with burgers from the grill or a rare steak pooling in blood, a rolling dervish in the backyard, faking, running, absurdly fast for a forty-five-year-old man, disappearing suddenly to play tennis or golf, his new car gone before the dawn on Monday, not to appear again until Friday, the consummate salesman, the man with the twinkle in his eye and the confidence of a history major from the University of Mississippi, inheriting only a good old Southern name and the feel-good mantra of the seventies combined with a work ethic that bordered on being a narcotic—good luck defining the most elusive man on the planet.

D. T. senior played halfback in football at the University of Mississippi. I bring this up because to understand the man, you have to understand the genesis of his twisting, dodging, faking way of life. When we would play football, my father would run straight at me, then shift his hips one way before faking again, going two ways at once before shooting off to the opposite way. Twinkle toes best describes the way he runs—leaning forward, up on the front of his feet, dancing along, and then just when you think you know where he is going, *wham*, he shoots off the other way and scores the goal. The important thing for D. T. senior is to keep moving, keep faking and dodging. Once, I asked him why he never stops and he replied—"Boy, if I stop moving, then I'll die."

Saying all that, I didn't take my father seriously. D. T. senior has said on many occasions he was going to come stay with us for a weekend only to call in a breathless voice that he suddenly was called out of town. My father visits in short power visits, much the way he sees customers. A lot is crammed into a very short amount of time. Suddenly we are going to lunch after seeing a movie, then going bowling or miniature golfing, picking up a new pen from a vintage store, with a final stop at his favorite ice-cream shop, and then he is in his car already driving hell to leather for home, and you realize the man had been with you all of four hours.

So when my father said he was going to be staying with me, I expected a last-minute phone call from *Doris* with D. T. senior swinging back into his silver Jaguar, saying, "Sorry, boy, she took me back," and that would be that. But his cell phone only rang with his cadre of cronies supporting him in his new battle against a billion-dollar corporation. D. T. senior is the king of victims and never more energized than in a fight. "Those Yankee, mother-lovin' sonsofbitches will rue the day once I launch my class-action age discrimination suit."

I helped him unpack his car, carrying in the ten pairs of Florsheims and twenty boxed shirts from Brooks. I had just put down his last pair of shoes when Wendy came in the kitchen.

"How is the best looking woman north of the Mason-Dixon line?"

D. T. senior hugs a few seconds longer than is in-law prerogative.

"Fine, fine, Dale," Wendy murmurs, the tone of a teacher with a problem student. "This is a surprise …"

It is the lawyer, faintly amused, slightly suspicious, and *extremely* apprehensive. I can't say I blame her when I consider the client is now running from a five-year-old like another five-year-old. Angela shrieks as my father rounds the couch with his hands up like Frankenstein, walking stiff legged.

"He got canned, and Doris threw him out," I explain quickly in a low voice. "I think he is just going to stay with us a few days. I can put him up in my office."

Wendy's eyes narrow, watching the stiff-legged monster chasing our daughter.

"Ooohh, I'm going to get you!"

"Your father ..." Wendy stops, staring at the seventy-three-year-old man with the Burl Ives goatee running backward in her family room. "Here," she says retreating into logistics. "You and your father can go grill the burgers ... there should be enough."

I hold the plate of raw meat, navigating Angela who just dove at my feet, and Dale junior, who brought the basketball inside and is dribbling on the hardwood floor.

D. T. senior chimes in with his best Uncle Tom. "Don't worry about a thing, Miz Scarlet."

Wendy frowns.

"Dale ... you know I hate that sort of thing."

My father looks at her wide-eyed, holding an innocent hand to his chest.

"What? Did I say something offensive?"

"That ... that ... racial pantomime."

D. T. senior looks hurt, and then suddenly falls to a knee.

"Mammy ... mammy ... sweetheart ... where are you ..."

Angela is now crying for no discernable reason. The basketball has just slipped from Dale junior's hand and bounced once on the kitchen table before bowling down a vase of wilting two-week-old roses. There is silence as everyone pays respect for the sound of breaking glass and sloshing water.

"*Dale junior,*" Wendy shouts, pointing to the garage. "Get that basketball out of here!"

"Yeah," I say ineffectually. "I told you about balls in the house."

My son, a carbon copy of myself, stares at me dead on.

"No, you didn't."

We have already graduated to the age of contradiction where my son specializes in showing me up in front of other people.

"Seems like somebody going to the woodshed," Dale Senior rolls out in deep molasses, winking at Dale junior.

"Dale," I say, grasping for the patriarchal tone, "*Do as you are told.*"

"And that goes for you too," Wendy says, while I stand with the plate of ground beef patties like some serf of the bovine. "Take your father out there and cook those burgers so we can get this dinner over with!"

Dale Senior turns on the charm, never better than in shifting gears.

"C'mon, son," he says, holding the door. "Let's do our part."

Suddenly I'm twelve again and D. T. senior is telling me to take out the trash or rake the leaves. I stare at him and wonder how he so deftly changed from MC of a minstrel show to supportive father-in-law.

"Don't worry darlin', I'll have them for you in fifteen minutes," he drawls, closing the door behind us. *He walks* toward the grill, taking in the patio he's never seen. "Well now, look it here, *Tara* done got a patio." I know what is coming; I feel it in every bone of my body. "My, my, some folks got all the monies." He rolls his eyes. "You in high cotton now, boy."

"More like high debt, dad," I murmur.

"Sitting walls, a fire pit, and a marble bar," D. T. senior looks around, nodding slowly.

I know this has sent him churning because it underlies a basic fact neither of us have recognized—my house is bigger than the small Cape Cod he and Doris inhabit. It is not that I am doing any better financially, but we somehow managed to sell in an area that led the real estate bubble. The upshot was a home larger than either of us had imagined in an area where we sit in the back of the income bus. Still, to my father, if you lived in a big house, then you had made it.

"This patio must have cost some buckos, boy," he continues, running his hand over the marble remnant we had glued to an L-shaped stack of bricks.

I light the gas grill and begin trying to scrape off mutilated remains of chicken.

"Wendy's cousin did it and gave us a deal."

D. T. senior sits down and looks up at the house.

"Boy, when you sell out, you *really* sell out."

I frown at him.

"What's that supposed to mean?"

He shrugs, crossing his Wejuns, leaning back.

"Oh nothing, boy. Just that I never thought I'd see you in a *big* house like this, out here in the suburbs with all these *Yankee tight asses.*"

I put the burgers on the grill, knowing what he is up too. The best salesmen in shoe leather can smoke out people faster than anyone else on the planet. He is a genius of the well-placed insult.

"Dad. I told you it is only because we were able to sell our house in Oakland for top dollar that we could get into this house." I put the top of the grill down. "My mortgage is actually less than before."

D. T. senior digests this, which means he has not heard a word. The mark of any great salesman is the ability to ignore all objections.

"I mean, Mr. Benny," he says in the old radio show voice of

Rochester. *"You must really be doing lots of mortgages to support all this."*

I turn around from the grill. He is referring to the job I took as a mortgage broker three years ago when it became apparent no publisher was interested in a D. T. senior fourth novel.

"Don't you read the newspapers, Dad? Haven't you heard about the sub-prime crisis, debt implosion, and skyrocketing interest rates?"

"Uh huh, what's all that mean?"

"It means I'm in a slump, if you really want to know."

The salesman takes this in and nods sagely. He closes one eye. Now we are in his territory.

"Don't keep enough in your pipeline, do you, boy? That's what happens. You get a few big months, take on this *nigger rich* lifestyle, and then there's nothing to back you up. That's what all this sub-prime crap is, people who bought too much house and now they can't afford it."

Willy Lowman meets Al Jolson.

"*Nigger rich* lifestyle, Dad?"

"That's what they call it where I come from," he says and shrugs.

"Well, you're in the North now, Dad. We call it living beyond our means, something I think you know about as well."

D. T. senior nods and I know he has not heard a word. Counter views are to be ignored, lest they make sense. He nods to my grill.

"Your burgers are burning, boy."

I turn to the raw beef that has turned into a cauldron of fire.

"Didn't I give you that grill?"

"Yes," I shout, inhaling smoke, seeing the grill has caught fire on the inside.

D. T. senior turns down the gas.

"You have the heat too high, boy! You'll burn those patties to black turds."

I stare at the man enveloped in white smoke.

"Dad!

"Just tryin' to give you the benefit of my wisdom, boy," he says, slipping into a Foghorn Leghorn vernacular. He returns to his sitting wall and looks around. "So, you're still writing?"

I turn back to the grill and finish arranging the burgers. When I was publishing novels every two years, I was the best-selling novelist who would support him in old age. When I first began writing, D. T. senior saw it as nothing more than a diversion from real work, a ploy to put off the inevitable nine-to-five job. Now that almost a decade has passed since my last book, I have returned to the status of the twenty-five-year-old who is writing to put off the real work of a job.

"I'm working on several things," I murmur.

D. T. senior shakes his head.

"Well, I'm going to tell you your problem, boy."

"I can hardly wait," I mutter, dropping the grill lid.

My father gestures to the setting sun.

"The problem is, boy, you are writing books that are *too good*. What you need to do is write a *shitty book* so you can make some money."

I consider not dignifying this pearl of wisdom, but I can't help myself.

"A lot of people write shitty books, Dad, and they don't make money."

D. T. senior holds his arms wide.

"Yes, but you know how to write *good books*, so if you wrote a *shitty book* it would probably be the best shitty book out there. You see what I'm sayin'?"

I stare at Edmund Wilson and realize our literary discussion has ended. I lift the grill again, satisfied that the grill fire is mostly out and the burgers will not become black turds.

"Good Golly Miz Molly. There she is again."

I turn and see Georgia Barnes pulling up her trashcan from the curb. She waves and D. T. senior sends back semaphore with a series of hand motions. I am apprehensive. Georgia became wealthy after her husband left her for his secretary and paid for it with DHL stocks options. We have talked several times over coffee when she picked my brain for a career in real estate. I know she is lonely and that is Morse code to an Indian like D. T. senior, hanging around the telegraph line, waiting for the next damsel in distress.

"Nice body," D. T. senior nods, pronouncing body like "bahdy."

"I think you have enough on your plate, Dad."

My father has his arms crossed, tracking Georgia Barnes's ascent up the road. Her house is two houses down from mine on the access road, a stately home complete with columns and a porch that would make any Southerner envious.

"She's a fine-lookin' woman … lives in that big house down there does she?"

I turn around with the plate. The master salesman is already sizing up the prospect, the hop to the next turning log where he will not get his feet wet. I begin to throw out obstacles.

"That's right. They divorced last year." I turn and frown. *"Why?"*

D. T. senior turns and looks at me, and I cringe. The gleam in the eye is there, the vision of himself firmly ensconced in a new life. He shrugs innocently.

"Just making conversation, boy … I assume she is all alone, then?"

I wipe the tears from my smoked eyes.

"No, she has two sons, so she's not waiting for a salesman from Mississippi to sweep her off her feet."

He turns back to surveying the Georgian colonial.

"Lot of house for just one person."

"Her sons are with her too. I heard Georgia is going to be engaged to some man from Texas, and he has lots of kids, and I think her parents are living with her also."

I could tell D. T. senior the whole Notre Dame football team was living there, but I know he hears none of it. The instinctive nose of the salesman smells the deal, and it would be easier to pull a bloodhound off a convict than to deflect my father from a customer. The door opens then and Wendy comes out looking more composed.

"Are the burgers almost finished?"

"Two minutes, darling," Dale Senior informs her, only lacking the white Panama to sweep off. "I promise. "

His charms are not lost on a woman with children who just clear her waist. She turns and goes back in. D. T. senior tracks her every step.

"So when is your wife going back to work?"

I stare at my father and feel the blithe slap across the face.

"She's not…we have kids at home."

"Well I think *she better*, you obviously need the income, boy."

"Dad! It's not your right to comment on whether or not you think my wife should work… I mean what the fuck!"

D. T. senior smiles sagely. He has successfully sounded out the target after much evasive action, skillfully dropping his charges at different depths until I surfaced. Now he heads back to base.

"Son, I'm sorry. You are so right. I have no right to comment on your wife's lifestyle. If she wants to stay at home and fuck off while you go down the shitter, that's her business."

"Dad!"

D. T. senior holds up his hands.

"That came out wrong, boy. I am sorry if I offended you, son. Lord *knows*, I don't want to offend my hosts."

My father is almost believable when he turns on the Southern charm. I turn back to the grill of black turds and scoop off the remaining burgers

"You just let me stay in one of the sharecropper shacks, and I's behave myself," he intones while I shut off the gas. "Really, son, I am sorry."

I shake my head and know I have lost on every front.

"Yeah okay, fine. Let's just fucking eat," I mutter.

D. T. senior pauses.

"Now, does this Georgia woman work?"

"Dad!"

6

"Apollo 8 you're looking good ... ten seconds to loss of signal."
–Mission Control

Wendy has put out the china for D. T. senior, and I'm touched she would take this extra measure for a man she could clearly do without. The dining room has a converted gas chandelier on a dimmer, and she has lit the candelabra, and I toss a log into the gas fireplace. We are from the South, and I would like to think I inherited that fine oral tradition of spinning a good yarn that must have come from long, hot evenings with little else to do. My memory is one of laughing around the dinner table while my father trotted out the latest adventure of the traveling salesman complete with denouement and surprise ending. I pride myself on the fact that the stories I tell are more intricate, fully imagined, and less obvious, but there are moments I suspect I am nothing more than the typical Southern blowhard, looking for the cheap laugh.

D. T. senior has regaled the dinner table with several stories and is fast approaching the climax of his third one when I see Wendy grimace. She has laughed grudgingly, giving my father more than enough rope to offend, insult, and hang himself, but now I see he has used up that reserve of patience with this latest yarn of fiber pills taken while traveling on the highway.

"… so I did what I had to do after taking those fiber pills, I ran into the field and relieved myself, except it got all over my pants, and so there I was on the side of I74 without pants, and I had to get back to my vehicle."

"Ohhhhh, Granddad went potty in a field," Angela grimaces.

"Eat your food," Wendy says, frowning.

"That's funny, Granddad."

"So, I had you know what all over my pants, and I start back toward my vehicle and this trucker slows down and says, 'Boy, where are your pants?'"

"Dad," I say, leaning over. "Maybe a different story while we are eating."

D. T. senior leans back, and then holds up his hands in supplication.

"My apologies to all concerned."

"I want to know how Granddad gets back to his car without any pants," Dale junior complains.

"Later," I say.

"I will tell you later, and then it will be our secret," D. T. senior whispers. He raises his wine glass suddenly.

"Now I have a question for you fine rich folks. Who attacked your sign at the entrance with a chain saw?"

"We don't know. It happened last night," I answer, taking the reins.

D. T. senior is now smothering his blackened brick with ketchup. He raises his eyebrows tragically.

"Well in my humble opinion, I can't say it is any loss. That was one butt-ugly sign … if you pardon the expression, ma'am."

Wendy smiles for the condemned.

"Speaking of signs, John Petty called." Her eyes pin me to

the wall. "There is an emergency association meeting tomorrow night at eight."

Wendy turns to my father.

"Dale is on the committee of the neighborhood association."

D. T. senior sits back, and I want to qualify her assertion. I was never *elected,* no one else would do it, and I made the mistake of saying I would be on the committee to replace the sign if they would replace the sign.

"Well, madam, I must say I always said the boy would go far and that the apple does fall from the tree," D. T. senior nods slowly. "So how are you liking it out here now, Miz Wendy?"

She drinks from her Chablis, raising her eyebrows.

"We're getting used to it."

My father sets down his silverware and becomes somber, looking out the window at the lone streetlight in our cul-de-sac.

"I really don't understand why you people left such a cultured, progressive town to move out to this *cultureless* vacuum." D. T. senior stares out the window as if he expects to see the cultureless hordes in the street. "I just never would have thought you two would move out to this wasteland. But," he says, raising his eyebrow, "everybody has a selling point, and I guess it's just a matter of price."

I lean in.

"Crime, Dad. Remember? There was a lot of crime in Oakland." I look at the man with ketchup on his cheek, a napkin stuffed into the neck of his shirt. "You're the one who said it was too dangerous for kids."

D. T. senior's eyes grow big, holding up his silverware.

"Oh *I know,* boy. Your mother [pronounced *mothah]* and I used the same rationale when we moved out to that God-awful Hanesville. Well, it's all how you paint it, right? We knew it was better for you kids, and that's why we did it, but that Oakland, what a great community. Progressive, artsy, beautiful old homes, a *great town*. And for a writer, I would think it was fantastic ..." DT senior looks out the window tragically. "The problem out here is you just have too many white people in one place."

Wendy sets down her Chablis and speaks in the logical tone of the litigator.

"Dale, we could not afford a bigger house in Oakland. So, it wasn't a matter of choosing one community over another. We simply did not have the option to stay in Oakland."

"Oh I know, *I know*," he says and nods broadly. "Like I say, Miz Wendy, we *all* do things for our chillun'. Do you think I ever wanted to live among all those tight-asses in Hanesville. No, your mother and I did it for yawl," he continues, nodding to me. "So I do understand why you ended up in this sterile, Godforsaken suburb."

"Dad, we don't think it is sterile out here—"

"So, Dale, I heard you've lost another job."

Wendy has had enough. Her eyes are smiting. D. T. senior sits back in his chair with the smile of the practiced commander.

"That is true, Miz Wendy," he nods slowly, his eyes darkening. "They let me go, but they are hiding under production (pronounced PROduction) numbers when it's age-related, and these bastards are going to rue the day."

"You think you have a case?" the lawyer coolly asks.

D. T. senior tilts his head.

"I have always produced well beyond expectations."

Wendy touches a fork to her glass, rolling her tongue inside her mouth.

"But is there history here, Dale? Haven't you bounced around from one job to another because you have been disruptive, acting counter to management's objectives?" The lawyer settles down on her elbows, raising her wine glass. "Couldn't this company point to these reasons rather than age, which is very hard to prove in court?"

D. T. senior frowns, staring down at his plate. "I know it is unpopular to say it, but this is one reason I voted for the current president! He is trying to limit frivolous lawsuits and get rid of these *parasitic lawyers* ruining the fabric of our country." My father leans back and spreads his arms. "I mean, here you are, Miz Wendy, bearing down on a poor ol' man with your *lawyerly tactics* when your energy could be better spent somewhere else."

"Dale," Wendy says gently. "You are the one bringing the frivolous lawsuit on an age discrimination case that probably doesn't exist."

"Well, you know what Henry the Fifth said," D. T. senior faintly sings. "The first thing we do is kill all the lawyers."

"All right, you kids almost done," I say, looking at my two children eating under the barrage flying overhead.

"That was Henry *the Seventh*, Dale," Wendy sniffs. "Don't quote someone unless you are sure of the source."

D. T. senior rolls his eyes and drops his mouth open.

"Well, Miz Scarlett, I knows one of them kings done said it sure enough."

"And that idiot in the White House knows nothing about the legal problems of this country. He is a monkey who says what his advisors tell him to say."

"Whoo, whoo, whoo," D. T. senior intones. "Better than that party of gays and talking heads [pronounced *haids*] giving away all our money to them welfare queens, I say."

Wendy sits back from the table.

"Dale, your money goes to a toilet in a B1 bomber. The amount of money spent on true social programs in this country is laughable."

"Daddy, I want some more mac and cheese," Angela sings out.

D. T. senior shrugs and sits back from the table.

"All I know is that I'm seventy-three and will have to work

until the day I die." He touches the napkin below his chin and looks at my wife. "But I don't go looking for any government handout to bail me out. No sir!"

Wendy smiles faintly.

"Dale," she says gently, "the reason you will have to work until the day you die has nothing to do with social programs. You have placed yourself in your situation. You are the product of two divorces. I really don't think someone earning *six figures* is on the same level of a woman with children barely existing at poverty level."

D. T. senior spreads his bands in benediction.

"Well, I don't think anyone here has a pension, so we will all be working well into the twilight years."

DT senior finally dabs the ketchup from his cheek, his tunic blotted red.

"But, for my money, I would say Elliott is the only really smart one from our family. He works half the year, has the summahs off, gets sabbaticals, has tenure, and will retire with a big, fat pension." My father looks around the table. "And he's doing something he *believes in*—more than I can say for anyone sitting around this table."

I breathe heavily and stare at the table. When in doubt, *insult grandly*. I had seen this tactic for years when D. T. senior would launch into polemics that offended my mother, gross generalizations designed to incite riots. My father has brought out his weapon of choice—insult by lauding a sibling. D. T. senior waves the finger of denigration.

"Now, *he's* a man of integrity!"

"Oh, and we're all just a bunch of whores, Dad," I say dully.

My father holds up his hands in surrender.

"Just saying, boy, your brother is a man of *high ideals*."

I close my eyes, absorbing the blows rooted in pitting my brother and me against each other. Different from birth, we were not allowed to forget we occupy opposite ends of the ideological spectrum lest we develop a rapport. D. T. senior is the true policeman of filial discord and has kept us apart with his basic mantra—you and Elliott are just different.

"Just speak for yourself, Dad," I say warily.

My father holds his arms wide like Cassius.

"All right then, son. I will speak for myself. Here lies a man who sold food additives! That's what my tombstone will read. Here lies a man who writes mortgages will be on yours—"

"Dad, I've written three novels," I point out, my voice edging up.

"Fine son, *fine*, we all have our dreams, and you were able to touch yours, but that's not what you're doing now, son. But your brother is influencing young minds, see, making the world a better place, and he will retire while the rest of us go with this whoreshit grind." He shakes his head regretfully. "I tell you, boy, there are days I could just sell everything. I told Doris the other day, why don't we just go live in the woods and live on half what we live on now."

"Is that before or after she threw you out, Dale?"

The blow from my wife is ineffectual because D. T. senior is already hitting his central themes. A Thoreau existence coincides nicely with sibling success as a poster board for what we all should have done. It is no coincidence our middle name, father and son, is that of the sage who went to live by a lake. Forget the Southern madness of everyone naming each other by the patriarch—we are all saddled with this philosopher/writer's legacy, one, two, three of the misanthrope in waiting. Only my brother the professor, man of many wives and no children, escapes this latent yearning to escape and has of late become the flag D. T. senior waves over my head in times of need. Here is the answer—*the life of the academic*. If only we could have been so smart.

"Well, Miz Wendy," D. T. senior continues. "It was before

we agreed to a trail separation while Doris finds herself. Confidentially, she is going through the change' and I have seen this sort of thing before—"

Wendy frowns.

"The change? The change, Dale? I'm afraid to ask, but what is *the change?*"

"Why, the menopause," D. T. senior says and shrugs. "It makes women bitchier than a cat in a washing machine. And Doris's has been having some bad troubles with her hormones that I think it is responsible for her erratic behavior," he says and nods slowly. "But, I think with some good therapy she will find herself."

Wendy is staring at D. T. senior as if she has just discovered some unknown sea creature on the beach.

"*What?*"

"What?"

"What are Doris and the therapist working on?"

"What I said, Miz Wendy," D. T. senior nods sagely. "She is trying to find out who she is."

Wendy stares at the man with the napkin in his neck. If she had a gun, D. T. senior would be no more.

"And you are paying for this, Dale?"

D. T. senior nods again, playing the role he was destined for all his life—the sugar daddy, *the patriarch*, the man without a pot to piss in who will not allow his wives to work.

"I personally don't care if Doris ever works. I like the thought of her being home when I get there. I couldn't travel knowing Doris was not covering my backside. So hell yes, I'll pay for her therapy! I always will support Doris in whatever midlife changes she has."

Burt Bacharach had just come in the door in skimpy tennis shorts. The switch to the seventies do your own thing mantra is too much for Wendy. The catacomb of issues concerning my father is her undoing. She is used to taking on one legal issue at a time. D. T. senior is a walking fifty-count indictment. He literally overwhelms the judicial mind, and it is really better to move on to the next case.

"I'm out of here," Wendy murmurs, rising with her plate.

DT senior has returned to his turd burger and dabs his mouth once again. He has clearly won, having swept the field of players.

"My my, it's good to have some good old home cookin'!"

"Granddad's funny," Angela says and giggles.

Al Jolson returns.

"Zippity do dah, zippity day, my oh my, what a wonderful day!"

D. T. senior is unpacking his clothes in my office while I wrestle with the new math of my nine-year-old. My cell phone sounds the alarm.

"This is Dale."

"Dale … Jim Mesh."

"Hey, Jim, how's it going?"

"Not so good, Dale," he says, sounding not unlike Detective Clancy. "Let me ask you a point-blank question."

"Sure."

"Are you or are you not the Rocket Man?"

Jim Mesh is very point blank with his point-blank questions. I smile at Wendy, throwing daggers down the dining room table where she is now working on basic geometry with Dale junior She is not up for cellular communication during homework.

"I just got off the phone with Barb Smithy, and I assured her I have everything under control."

This does nothing. Jim Mesh has a large salt-and-pepper mustache, and I have seen him at pack meetings in business casual with a Blackberry clipped to his belt and a Hartman briefcase under his arm. He drives a pickup with "*Jim Mesh Party Catering*" on the side. I know a man who erects inflatable Moonwalkers—navigating stressed out mothers and psychopathic children at birthday parties—will probably not buy any of my bullshit.

"Have you ordered the rockets, Dale?"

"I was just going to do that."

"Dale, I don't want you to take this wrong way ... but don't bullshit a bullshitter."

"Ha," I say to Jim.

"Listen to me, Dale, and listen good. I'm busy, *you're* busy, so we're going to stop fucking around here and get this thing taken care of."

"Ha."

"Here's what I'm going to do for you, Dale. I'm going to *order* the rockets, and you're going to call Dean Heinrich and go see him tonight. Then I want you to come by my house so I can get you up to speed on the rockets."

"You know, Jim, I'd love too, but it's getting late—"

"You don't understand, Dale ... I'm not asking you. *I'm telling you.* If you don't do this, then I am going to tell Mike and Barb Smithy that you are *not* Rocket Man and I will withdraw my offer of help and support."

I stare at Dale junior hovering above his calculator. I have been MIA on a lot of father-son activities and missed the last two campouts. Wendy has been taking him to soccer, and I missed curriculum night last week. Volunteering for Rocket Man is directly related to my shortcomings as a father. Dale junior has already mentioned the various benefits to my being Rocket Man. He will get to stand inside the yellow tape that separates Rocket Man from the kids and parents. He will be able to assist in the launching of up to a hundred rockets. Now, Jim Mesh is about to torpedo my engineered coup d'etat against the government of guilt and recrimination.

"I'll be there," I mutter, glancing at my watch.

"Good," Jim "the Closer" Mesh says. I know he is the man to call for a Moonwalker.

"I'm going to call Dean Heinrich and let him know you're on the way. Now I'll give you both addresses."

"Can you call my voicemail, Jim ... I don't have a pen on me right now."

"I can do that."

"Thanks. Tell Dean I'll be there in a half an hour," I say, giving him back a little of his own.

The silence is palpable. Dale junior is erasing like a madman. I hear my father laugh loudly out on the front porch. A man who inflates a large balloon for children has just chastised the provider. Wendy sends Arctic air down the table.

"You're leaving."

It is not a question.

"Yeah, I have to get the rocket stuff from Dean Heinrich and then I have to go see Jim Mesh about ordering rockets." I shake my head. "Boy, that Mesh is really pushy ... you think the guy would have something better to do with his time."

"If you returned his calls, then he wouldn't have to be so pushy."

That I am on the knight's mission of Boy Scout business cuts no weight with Wendy. She is a den mother and once a week trots off to the controlled mayhem of den meetings. Her husband has been visited by the police twice in one day and is now shooting out the door. Not good.

"When will you be back?"

"Soon. Maybe an hour."

"Where are you going, Dad?"

The earnest eyes of my wife stare at me from Dale junior. I smile and ruffle his hair that is long by suburban standards. The standard crew has not come into the Hammer household.

"To get the equipment for Rocket Day."

"Can I go?"

"No. You have homework," my wife tells the son. "Your father is going to get this … *stuff* … then come straight back."

"Yeah, better I go, Dale," I say and nod seriously. "We'll go over all the stuff when I get back."

"Can I go, Daddy?"

"No," Dale junior answers for me.

Angela's eyes well up, and the lip quivers.

"*Waaaaaah … I … want … to … go!*"

I stare at Dale junior and shake my head.

"She has two parents, Dale, she doesn't need another."

"You always take her side," he mutters, his cheeks becoming red.

"No I don't," I say over the wall of sound coming out of a five-year-old. "But I don't need you answering for me."

Dale junior crosses his arms, mumbling darkly.

"You always take her side."

"You know, Dale, I'm doing this for you—"

"Shut up."

I stare at my first-born. The command came out in a short machine gun burst; a flip, no nonsense eruption from the mysterious sanctum of nine-year-old hubris. No doubt about it, he had just told me *to shut up.*

"*What?*"

Dale stares at me in mortification as if his mouth had betrayed him. He turns red, and I feel myself turning red.

"Go to your room, young man!"

Dale's eyes spill over as he runs from the room. I stare at Wendy and shake my head.

"Can you believe what he said, when I'm doing all this for him!"

"Don't even go down that road."

"What do you mean?"

"I mean, don't even go there," Wendy, says again, her blue eyes hardening.

I sit back.

"So it's all my fault. Is that it?"

"No one said that, Dale," Wendy says in a bored tone. "But you have hardly been around lately."

I sputter, blink, and open my mouth. I am the twenty-first century homebody. My office is over the garage, and there are weeks where I literally don't leave the two streets of Belleview.

"What are you talking about? *I'm always around.*"

"No, you're always in your office, doing God knows what."

"Working is what I'm doing."

Angela is still crying. Wendy shakes her head.

"Just go, Dale."

"I'm going," I say, heading for the back door.

"Make sure your father has sheets for his bed," she murmurs, picking up my son's books.

"I already made it."

"Then water the trees."

I stop at the door and stare at the black skeletons breaking the horizon. "Water the trees," had become our equivalent of "Fuck you." The trees are a ten-thousand-dollar disaster. We moved into a house surrounded by a field. After a month of roasting July days, we pulled the now-famous equity line on the house and had the mother of all patios constructed, complete with marble bar and seven thirty-foot trees complete with support cables. We thought we could combat the sterility of open fields by bringing flora and fauna into the land of burned grass and miniature pines.

"Now, you got to water these trees or you are going to be singing the blues," Charlie O'Brien of Charlie's Trees said with my ten-thousand-dollar check in his pocket.

Then came the drought; the worst drought in fifty years. The drought destroyed the soybean and corn corps, turned lawns into nuclear-blasted landscapes, and torched our newly planted trees into black, leafless, thirty- foot skeletons. Our well could not pump enough water for the seven giants rudely taken from the primal forest and left in a hot, featureless field. They began to die one by one.

Charlie returned and shook his head and explained the one-year guarantee was only good if it wasn't *anybody's fault.* "But these trees died from lack of watering," he said with an accusing gray stare that matched my wife's. So now, *water the trees* had become an exercise in futility, a nascent hope the trees would somehow return with hundreds of gallons of water.

I stomp out the door and stumble around in the darkness of our acre and a half. I finally locate the hose, dragging it to the nearest denuded edifice of my own shortcomings as a yardman. I stare up at the seven skeletons, clinging branches curled to the heartless sky. I am convinced it will never rain again. We have gone five months without rain of any sort, and I can't even remember what rain sounds like anymore. Every day is clear and blue with the sun beating down on the plains of Illinois.

I walk to the house and turn on the water and feed my dead brethren.

7

"… something is wrong in the computer. I've got a bunch of computer alarms. Abort the landing … Abort!"
–Flight Simulation, Mission Control

Dean Heinrich is the Von Braun of Rocket Day. His house is in the older area of Charleston. A small ranch in a cul-de-sac, his house predates the wave of super houses. I see Dean in his garage with his son. He has the same glasses, short blond hair, and knee-high socks. Nothing is out of place in this garage. The minivan is immaculate. The lawnmower is a modest John Deere with no trace of grass clippings. Dean reeks of a man who does not carry debt, a contented man. The torch was being passed from Gibraltar to Gallipoli, and I am not the Turks.

We shake hands and mutter our names.

"This is my son, Dean Heinrich Jr."

"I have a son, Dale Hammer Jr."

Dean Heinrich and son look at me oddly. I have struck no responsive chord. I look around the garage and notice the walls are covered with tools. I walk closer and see a piece of yellow masking tape with a number below every tool. I look at Dean Heinrich.

"What's with the numbers?"

Dean walks closer, adjusting his glasses.

"Every tool is numbered to match a schematic I have of the garage. I know exactly where they are."

"You're kidding."

Dean frowns.

"No. I don't believe in wasting time."

"Dad has five hundred tools," young Dean Heinrich offers.

"Five hundred and ten," older Dean counters. He looks at me over his glasses. "Pack 160 is coming by also. They wanted to be briefed on the equipment."

"Oh ... are they using the stuff too?"

"No." Dean Heinrich shakes his head gravely. "They just know I've been Rocket Man for the last five years and requested I go through the equipment so they understand the procedure for Rocket Day."

"Dad is the best Rocket Man there ever was," young Dean assures me.

Dean Heinrich turns to his son.

"Will you go down to refrigerator number two and get me a 7 Up?"

"Yes sir," young Dean replies, disappearing into the house.

Another minivan pulls into the drive, and two men with brown hair and long shorts mutter introductions. We stand around, listening to the beginning rain outside the garage. "All right, I can begin." Dean leads us across the immaculate garage with the air of a man about to give up the secret of the atomic bomb. "These are the totes," he informs us, pointing to two rubberized green totes.

"Ah the totes," corporate man number one murmurs, looking

at corporate haircut number two. "I really wish I had brought my digital camera or video equipment."

I look at him.

"So you know what a tote looks like?"

His eyes are scary—brown, dull, devoid of questions. He wears heelless sandals and long shorts, and I can see where a razor scoured his neckline. Not one hair is out of place and not one pimple blanches his skin.

"No, so I can go over what Mr. Heinrich is about to impart in the privacy of my home."

"A good porno sounds better," I joke.

The two men and Dean scour me for signs of an Al Qaeda link. There is something un-American in a man who would ridicule a tote. Dean motions to two long, yellow two-by-fours.

"These are the barricades. It is very important you erect these no less than fifteen yards from the site of the launch. At no point can the scouts go beyond these yellow barriers."

The second man with dull eyes poses a question.

"Now let me get this straight. What you are saying is that the scouts must at all times stay behind these barricades."

"That's right."

"You know, I should have brought my Blackberry. Then I could take notes and transcribe them later for the pack."

"Why don't you call yourself and leave yourself a message on your voicemail?" I say, gesturing to his phone.

"I have all this in handouts I will give you at the end of our meeting," Dean informs us.

My cell phone rings, and I see by the number I shouldn't pick up, but I do anyway. I walk into the outer darkness.

"Yes, Jed."

"Dale … Dale is that you?"

"Yes, Jed, it's me," I answer dully.

"Dale, what *the fuck* is going on with our loan?"

I can hear the mighty sixteen-wheeler screaming along in the background along with country western's finest twanging away. My lone client is upset, hands on the big steering wheel, drinking truck-stop coffee, navigating the dark highways of overland commerce.

"Yeah, what the fuck is going on with our loan?" squeals another voice from the interior of the cab with the compressed, nasally pitch of the backwaters of Mississippi.

"Dale, that's Ellie Mae, and she says that you are ripping us off … so I'm going to put her on."

I cringe. When I began brokering mortgages three years ago to supplement my writing income, it didn't seem like a bad gig. I could work from home, never see clients, and the money was good. The biggest thing was that I was invisible, a voice from the mysterious void of the Internet answering questions about interest rates and closing costs. Jed came to me from a referral from his sister, busting into his house where I waited to take his application, screaming: *"Who's the nigger that blocked the drive?"* I stood and identified myself as the man who had blocked his jacked-up, Confederate flag-waving four wheeler from the garage.

Now a month later, he and Ellie Mae, a woman he met on the Internet from Alabama who looks and acts like Ellie Mae of the *Beverly Hillbillies,* have become my only prospect to get a check for the month, to say nothing of keeping my job. The man who hired me, a Filipino who attends a mega-church and declared me a good family man, had let me know that unless I brought Jed and Ellie Mae to the closing table, then I could find employment elsewhere.

"Dale!"

Ellie Mae's voice is so high, so perfectly modulated to drive dogs and potential rapists away, that I close my eyes.

"Yes, Ellie Mae," I answer dully.

"Dale … you are fucking ripping us off again!"

I breathe deeply. I have learned to endure tirades, being sworn at, and even the threat of bodily harm in my role as a purveyor of mortgages. I view myself as one step away from the tin men of another century, men whose income depended on the inclination of Americans to always believe there was a better deal out there. But it doesn't mean that I don't grind with desire to tell the miscreants of my fiduciary responsibility to go to hell and never ever call me again. But of course, I need the money and so I breathe deeply, look to the stars, and smile.

"Now, Ellie Mae, we have been over this. You and Jed have low credit scores, and Jed has a child-support judgment for eighteen thousand dollars, a tax lien, and a spotty employment record, and so that is why—"

"Dale, I watched that fucking black Oprah in the truck this morning, and she had on that Suzy Orman, and she said that the reason everybody is losing their homes is because of *mortgage brokers,* and she said that yawl are paid by giving high interest rates, and I told Jed then that you were ripping us off and we could go on the Internet and get a better rate!"

Ellie Mae is the antichrist of reason. She routinely scours the Internet for fantasy rates that she shoves in front of the unwitting Jed, the bearded, tobacco-chewing driver of tractor trailers through the Netherlands of the Deep South, hauling the electronic goods of Best Buy and Wal-Mart to ports distant. I know that Jed just wants to close on his bungalow in the valley, that he wants to watch NASCAR and drink *Bud* and have Ellie Mae prancing around in the skin-tight shorts she paints on, screeching into the phone with her cousins from the backwoods of Tennessee. But Jed is to gain no peace until his Internet bride is satisfied by men the telegenic gods purport are the cause of all her problems. So we dance on.

"Ellie Mae … we have gone over this," I say gently. "Those

rates on the Internet are not real rates, they are for people with A credit and—"

"How much are you fucking making? Suzy Orman says that you can reduce the rate of our mortgage if you want to … I told Jed that I'm going to go to a bank and get us a better loan unless you fucking do something for us."

"Ellie Mae …" I point out patiently. "You are closing this Friday. We have worked very hard to get your loan approved with the child support judgment and the tax lien and the bad credit—"

"We don't have bad fucking credit. The man at the car dealer told me we had *A Plus* credit, and he wouldn't of sold me my *Trans Am* if I had bad credit. All my life I been ripped off by you yuppie assholes, and I told Jed we ain't going to close on this house if the numbers don't look right and—"

"Ellie Mae, Jed has an eighteen-thousand-dollar support judgment—"

"And he's been fucking paying it!"

I breathe, taking in the logic of a woman who views five dollars a month on eighteen thousand as constituting a *good faith* payment. The bank doing Jed and Ellie Mae's loan is the last remaining sub-prime bank, and I am hoping they stay open long enough to finish it.

The phone takes air and Hank Williams moves in with a refrain.

"I can't quit you until the morning, darling …"

"Dale, this is Jed."

"Yes, Jed."

"Now I told you I can't go above sixteen hundred on my payment."

"Ask him how much he is making," squeals Ellie Mae against the hum of no less than eighteen wheels.

"Now how about that … how much are you making, Dale?"

"Jed … I don't even know anymore—"

"Well, I don't give a shit how much you are making, but I'm not going to pay more than sixteen hundred, and if its one penny more, then I'm walking out of the closing room and—"

"He's ripping us off, Jed!"

"Will you shut the fuck up, I'm trying to talk and drive here …"

"Don't tell me to shut the fuck up when he's ripping us off."

"Jesus, *quiet the fuck down* … Dale, listen, I'm driving down a fucking two-lane in the backwoods of Arkansas with a full fucking load, and I don't need to worry about this loan shit and Ellie Mae is—"

"Ask him how much he's making!"

"Will you shut the fuck up?"

"Jed … can I make a suggestion?"

Hank Williams moves in and I can tell Ellie Mae is slowly wearing away the resolve of one truck driver to purchase a home. I have to move quickly or the last fan of *Dukes of Hazard* will torpedo my only hope of gainful employment.

"All right … go ahead, Dale."

"Let's meet on Thursday before the closing and go over the numbers. If the numbers don't look good to you, then we won't close. It's that simple."

"I'll be back from a run that morning…sleep a few hours. How about three o'clock then?"

"I'll see you there, Jed."

"Ask him how much he's making—"

"Will you shut the fuck up, woman?"

I close my phone to leave the land of NASCAR and Dollywood when the lights blaze to life again. It is my boss who I haven't seen for the last month.

"Hey, Jerry."

"Dale, is that you?"

Jerry speaks in the short sentences of the immigrant. He donates Bs to very and cherry and has no idea what makes Americans laugh, forever cracking bad jokes with the timing of a savant. He has a Land Rover, a Jaguar, and a Jeep Cherokee, and his house is stuffed with furniture and neoclassical clocks. Jerry has bought every trapping he can get his hands on, from a thousand-dollar treadmill jammed up against a pool table jammed up against a shiny Nautilus workout system. He is a pudgy bald man who doesn't work out but sucks on an inhaler and views the world through thick lenses he is forever cleaning. Materially, Jerry has made it.

"Dale, where you been, man?"

"Getting loans, Jerry."

"Oh man. I know you been out there sleeping, going on vacation, living the good life on my dime."

He says all these American idioms in the clipped voice of the Filipino. His attempt to be hip and sling the shit American style makes it even worse, but I play along; he is my boss, after all.

"You got it, Jerry. With all the money you pay me, I'm laughing to the bank"

"That's what I figured, man. I said to my wife the other day, damn, I haven't seen Dale for some time now. I wonder if he has quit on me."

I laugh lightly.

"No, no … I've been out there looking for loans."

"No really, Dale. What have you been up to? You haven't closed a loan in two months, man."

The "man" is now tacked on, street patois giving way for corporate speak, which is the preferred mode of Jerry Manara conversation.

"I know. I've got a big closing coming up this Friday…a purchase."

"Oh … a purchase, that is good, good. You need to close

a loan, Dale, or you know, I'm going to have to let you go … man."

He says this in the same kind of singsong voice, giving none of the American pauses or the drop in tone to the dark dirge of canning somebody. This more than anything else lets me know that after twenty years, Jerry still doesn't have a clue what makes Americans tick.

"So, you need to close this loan, Dale."

"I know, I know, this one is going to close."

"Well, that's fine, Dale, but like I said, I hired you because you were a go getter, but now all the go is gone."

This is not an attempt at humor. Jerry dissects the English language like a scientist and the fact "go getter" is a euphemism does not cross the Asian brain. The *go* left the *getter,* and that is enough to can someone.

"Jerry, the whole industry is collapsing."

"Oh, I know. Many companies [pronounced cumpuies] are failing, but I must protect my company, and I need go getters or I'll be gone." He laughs. "Seriously, though, Dale, I like you, you a good family man, but business is business, and if you don't close this loan this Friday, then I have to let you go. No hard feelings."

"No … no hard feelings."

"Okay … well, go get 'em, *tiger.*"

"Sure, Jerry … talk to you later."

I close the phone and take a deep breath, trying to refocus. I have just been told I will be fired on Friday if Ellie Mae and Jed don't close. I walk back into Dean Heinrich's garage, where he is now opening a tote, bringing out wires perfectly coiled, attached to a large switch. There are copper clips attached to the coiled wire and a long, snaking orange cord leading to what looks like a remote control with a silver button.

"This is something I designed."

"What is it?" the two men from pack 160 want to know.

Dean Heinrich raises his glasses mysteriously. The light rain outside is now pattering just inside the garage.

"It is a kill switch. There can be no launching until the button is pressed," Dean Heinrich says with much gravity. "But it also has a dual function. In the first position, rockets can be launched individually. This is what I strongly recommend. It allows the Scouts to pursue their rockets and is much safer."

Dean pauses, eyes hardening.

"But if you press it all the way down, then all the rockets are live. You could, if you wanted, theoretically, launch up to one hundred rockets at once, but I *would never* do anything like that. It is actually a flaw in the design … I tried to get rid of it, but well, just *never* launch more than one rocket at a time. "

"Of course not," dull eyes intones. "You know I have to say, I'm a corporate trainer, and you are conducting your seminar in a very interesting manner."

"I just want everyone to be safe," Dean says grimly.

"Of course, being safe is what we are all about."

"That's right; there is a war on, after all."

Dull eyes frowns at me.

"What war?"

"Why, the war against terror of course," the corporate trainer answers.

Dean and I load the back of my old Explorer with the rockets, barricades, green totes, and twenty stakes for stringing yellow police line tape. Fric and Frac have left already and so it is just Dean, the stars, a low moon, and myself in the driveway. We shake hands, then he pauses.

"You know being Rocket Man is a big responsibility."

I nod gravely.

"I understand, Dean, and I will do my best to live up to your legacy as Rocket Man par none."

His glasses are catching the moonlight and I feel like I am talking to Lunar Man.

"No, I don't think you do," he says, shaking his head. "The kids look forward to this all year. It's one of the few Scout activities that are not geeky and boring. They spend real time building their rockets, and then they hand it over to you, *the Rocket Man*, to blast them off and bring them back again."

I have stopped moving the totes around the back. Any time I hear real emotion expressed in the suburbs brings a stunned tribute from me. Dean's eyes have actually become wet.

"I loved being Rocket Man," Dean confesses. "It's really about space, the final frontier ..."

"Star Trek?"

"*Star Trek* was the best show on television in the last fifty years," Dean says with no humor. "Do you know each of us has star dust in our bodies?"

"I didn't know that, Dean."

"Oh yes." Twin moons bob up and down in the curvature of Dean's glasses. "We have traces of iron that has come from distant stars, meteorites that have blasted into our atmosphere. I mean, we are really *all stars* when you think of it that way, and watching a rocket blast toward the heavens brings us that much closer to who we are."

I am waiting. I am waiting for the joke. Here we are moving through the soft butter of suburban life and I'm facing a man who is telling me I'm full of stardust.

Dean Heinrich shakes his head dismally.

"But my son isn't in the pack anymore and I know that is over. A lot of things are ending in my life now. Our family cat just died. He's been in the family for eighteen years, and he lived in the garage." Dean pauses and breathes out heavily. "I spend a lot of time in the garage and it's pretty lonely out here now. It's not that I did that much with the cat; it's just I knew he was always there."

Dean shakes his head slowly.

"Now my son is going into seventh grade, my wife doesn't know I'm alive half the time, and I'm an electrical engineer."

"Dean ... I don't know what to say—"

"I know you're doing this because someone roped you into it." He stares at me. "But I gotta tell you, it was one of the few real things in my life. I fuck around in my garage most of the time and talk to my neighbors, but they aren't really my friends. I guess I really don't have any friends anymore, just acquaintances. But when I launch those rockets ..." He shakes his head. "I feel them lifting off from the earth, I feel them jutting way up there, and for a moment I feel like a boy again, I feel ... free."

Dean is now facing the moon in sacrificial awe.

"It's like I'm leaving with the rocket and then they just arc over and the chute comes out ... and they float back to the earth like, like ... like blossoms of childhood."

There is silence while Dean contemplates space.

"Dean ... I really—"

"No, that's all right." He shakes his head. "I don't expect you to feel the same way I do." He puts his glasses back on and sniffs. "But I want you to promise me, that as Rocket Man, you will give the rockets a good launch, do a countdown for the boys, let them press the button, let them blast off their rocket, because I'm here to tell you it gets harder and harder to leave this earth and for a lot of them, it might be their only chance."

I stare at this man with twin moons in his glasses.

"Well ... I better get going, Dean. Jim Mesh is expecting me."

I'm not sure weather to shake Dean's hand or call for the boys in the white suits. He puts his hand out and we shake. He clasps my hand with both of his, eyes wet.

"Well good luck! I'm sure you'll be a good Rocket Man."

"I won't let you down, Dean," I assure him.

He smiles suddenly.

"How about those other two guys?"

I open the car door and get in.

"Yeah ... they were different."

Dean Heinrich stands in front of his garage and shakes his head.

"Were they *anal* or what?"

Charleston is in every respect a river town. The prized Hotel Brewer is on the river, and there is a dam that saves the town from being washed away in floods. The town hasn't undergone the makeover of the other suburbs, but still has the old ma and pa stores advertising "VCRs Fixed and Prescriptions Filled." Three bridges divide Charleston with old smoke stacks from closed mills picketing the riverfront. People no long travel from Chicago to get their fill of river aquatics. The cottages on the east side of the river now have Trans Ams, dune buggies, and an occasional washer in the front yard. The residents are bus drivers, construction workers, factory workers, carpenters—a Mecca of men and women who work with their hands. This is where Jed and Ellie Mae are purchasing a home, and this is where I found Jim Mesh's house.

Jim's house turned out to be a small ranch with an SUV in the drive and a yard bereft of the newspapers and the occasional soggy American flag adorning his neighbors. I can see in the open garage the habits of another organized man as I walk up the drive and see children in the picture window and Jim watching television. I ring the doorbell as an avalanche of kids and dogs crowd into the small foyer.

"Daddy, someone's here," a girl's voice sings out.

The dog decides the someone is an intruder, and I'm treated

to the bared teeth of a Cocker Spaniel. Jim moves into the door and expertly moves the dog with his foot.

"Tessy, get back!"

All ferocity leaves with the name of Tessy.

"Hello, Dale … found the place all right?"

"No problem," I say and nod, counting two girls around seven or eight with blond hair and Jim's large, sad blue eyes.

An anemic boy has already returned to his model car, some sort of combo drag racer and *Star Wars* Cruiser. He looks like Jim without the mustache and peppered hair. The furnishings of the house are spare—a television just below big screen, a couch, couple of chairs, no dining room furniture. Dinner hovers in the air—French fries or fish sticks. There is no doily under the Sears lamp on the side table. The remotes for the television are lined up in precise order on the coffee table. Four prints of Thomas Kincaid's take on agrarian life square the room. The couch is utilitarian and brown; a lazy boy takes center stage. It is all Jim right down to the dust buster mounted on the kitchen wall and a coffee mug with "JIM" on the side.

"It's my day with the kids," he explains, ushering me through the girls, who have returned to another television in the kitchen.

"We just got another hit, Dad," his son calls out.

"Keep me posted, we're heading down to my office."

"All right, Dad."

I follow Jim down into a cellar smelling of natural gas and some sort of sulferous radon mixing with the perfumed heat of a dryer. Dual fluorescent tubes light a smooth, bald-headed mallard on a workbench with a perforated backboard. Enamel paints and brushes are lined up in the same order as the tools hung on the backboard. Even the boiler is bereft of the normal dust and strange coatings of oil and dampness that seem to cling to steam-generated heat.

Jim crosses to a desk where a computer hums along.

"Have a seat."

The sight of technology in a nineteenth-century basement goes along with Jim living in a part of town composed of men with tattoos and pickup trucks. The computer is the latest of the small but very powerful desktops along with a top-of-the-line scanner and laser printer. The old metal desk is clean. I lean back in the swivel-back chair while Jim frowns at the screen.

"I ordered you two hundred and fifty rockets ... fifty for each den," he murmurs, clicking away, stroking his mustache. "I'll break them out for you," he continues as the printer ejects paper and he hands me two flyers. "Just make copies and insert one in each rocket pack ... it gives instructions on how to construct the rocket and also directions to the site of Rocket Day."

"Will do."

"The rockets should come in on Tuesday. I'll give you a call and you can pick them up from me or if you want, I'll drop them off."

The dryer buzzes and the rolling thunder ceases. Jim looks up from his monitor.

"Any problems with the equipment?"

I shake my head.

"Dean showed me the ropes."

Jim leans back in his chair and smiles.

"He's a little weird about his rockets."

"Yeah, I can see that."

"But he's been the best Rocket Man we've ever had. Hell, he's been the *only* Rocket Man we've ever had," he says, grinning.

"I'll do my best to follow in the Dean Heinrich shadow."

Jim stares at me and shrugs.

"Yeah, well, you do a lot of shit for your kids. I never thought I'd be sitting in the corner of a basement watching the washing machine ... but life gives you some strange curves."

"Where were you before?"

"Lakewood … had the big house."

Lakewood has even bigger houses than Belleview. Seven hundred thousand is the starting range with a covenant so anal people have to get their Christmas lights approved.

"Yep," Jim says and nods slowly. "That was to be our dream home. I designed it, was GC on the job. We bought the lot first and it had a lot of trees, couple of acres." Jim leans back in his chair, his blue eyes finding me among the boxes and discarded toys. "Everything seemed fine. My wife got a boob job, I got a promotion, and then one day … a woman in the neighborhood tells me I should come home from work early and see what's *really* going on."

Jim shakes his head.

"I had just started this business on the side, and I had to sell the house, pay off the wife, and move into a house a quarter of the size." He glances around the basement. "But I never thought I'd end up here."

"The east side?"

"Yeah, the guys are okay though. They helped me swap out a water pump on my truck. I don't think that would have happened in Lakewood."

"No, I don't think so," I murmur.

"Dad, the Sox just scored again," comes from the stairs.

Jim tilts his head up.

"What's the score?"

"Three to two, Sox."

"Keep me posted." Jim grins. "So anyway…that's how I ended up in a basement." He leans back in his chair. "You live in Belleview?"

"We moved out here three years ago from Oakland."

Jim puckers his lips.

"Wow." He whistles low. "That's a great town and is a long way from here ... how'd you end up out here?"

It is the question, one that I ask myself every day. Depending on my mood, I have produced several reasons: crime, bigger house, a desire for country air, and then the one for which I have no clear answer—a vague yearning to become someone I always detested—a successful man with a large house.

"Daddy!"

We are back upstairs in the middle of two little girls tugging on a Barbie doll.

"Girls ... girls ..." Jim says, trying to stop the flailing hands.

"She hit me!"

"Now girls ..."

"Dad! The Sox got another hit!"

I turn and see the bedrooms just off the kitchen. The hastily constructed beds have new pink dressers and matching quilts. I see Jim going to Sears and buying complete bedrooms straight off the floor. He has no time to construct a new home for his 50 percent family. He has no time for his son's room with the new wallpaper of baseballs and bats and the pennants tacked to the wall. The kitchen has the magnets on the fridge with pictures of the kids in order. I see the whole re-creation of a family life and I know Jim probably had it all set up in a week.

The chaos has slowed down to a mild riot. We move toward the door.

"I'll give you a call when the rockets come in."

"Great."

"Thanks for coming by, Dale," he says, shaking my hand, one eye on the game, his son, his daughters, and the dog. "Bye," the kids scream.

I wave and walk to my car, passing a faded plastic Jesus someone had stuck on old Jim's mailbox a long time ago.

8

"Christ, Wally, all you gotta do is flip a switch."
–Mission Control

The light is on in my office when I return. My office came about after much negotiation. I gave Wendy trees and a patio and she signed off on finishing the space over the garage. I saw my office as the oasis where I would compose great work separated from the general chaos of a family of four. The only egress would be a tortuous route around our monster vehicles, threading past the tractor, tool bench, rakes, pooling oil and water on a dirty concrete floor to reach a stairwell of unfinished pine that opened to a sanctuary of hardwood floors, can lights, and two dormered windows.

I climb the stairs, rapping lightly on the door.

"Come in, boy."

My father is sitting at my desk, reading.

"So did you get the deal?"

"It was just scouting shit."

D. T. senior drops the *Reader's Digest* to my desk and shrugs.

"Never know where you can pick up a deal, boy. Did you give everybody a card?"

I plop down on the futon, shaking my head.

"Nope."

"See, now that's why you are in the situation you are in. You have to *always* be selling, boy. Never lose an opportunity."

"Yeah, okay," I nod, noticing the sepia light from the lamp playing across my father's Hartman briefcase. After working in a pine-slicked bowling alley, I had purchased a futon for reading and editing and sleeping when the need arose.

"You want to make your bed?"

"Sure, boy."

We spread the sheets, then D. T. senior tests the Chinese water torture bed, lying back and staring up at the dormered ceiling.

"This will do," he nods, pulling up his suitcase. My father travels amazingly light—a scuffed brown suitcase, a briefcase, and a leather workout bag. Of course the ten pairs of shoes and boxes of shirts were still in my front hallway.

"You can put your toiletries and whatever else on this table, Dad ... use it for work if you want."

My writing table had been rescued from the Belleview garbage. The chairs had all lost their seats, but the table had fit into one of the dormers quite nicely.

"This is great office, boy." D. T. senior is out of his sweater and gray slacks, sitting on the futon in his T-shirt and BVDs. The light from my desk casts a hard shadow and without the bravado, my father seems suddenly old and frail. I want to assure myself he will be back tomorrow, sassy, full of vigor, and immortal.

"Dad, the bathroom is just inside the kitchen door. I'll leave the light on in the garage. If you want anything to eat, just help yourself."

"I'm fine, son."

He pulls a red nightshirt from his suitcase, then stands up, yawns, and looks around at the long room.

"These are top notch accommodations, boy."

I feel bad about the trek D. T. senior must take in the dead of night to relieve himself.

"If you want to sleep on the couch in the living room, then you would be closer to the bathroom."

"No, no," he says, climbing into the water torture bed. "This will do just dandy."

D. T. senior is willing to risk bodily injury to ensure he has privacy from the family in motion. Many times he would come through our fair town on business and elect to stay in a motel. This drives Wendy crazy, because the implication is that he is a man who doesn't value seeing his grandchildren. But my father is a man of single focus, and that focus has always been work.

I pause in the doorway, hearing the low clatter of frogs in the wetlands. The wind moves the trees, and it's not unpleasant in this hidden space. D. T. senior pulls the covers up to his chin.

"All right ... let me know if you need anything."

"Will do ... there is one thing, boy."

He is laying on the futon with his eyes closed. I'm not sure he is awake, prescient, or if it is just the D. T. senior clock winding down with a final send-off question. He rises to one elbow like a man from the dead.

"There is another reason I came out here."

A faint warning light on the control panel of my life glows. I slowly sit down on the desk chair of my writing table. He frowns in the gloom and looks up at me.

"Do you know that that sonofabitch has the plot next to your mother?"

I stare at the man in the futon.

"You're talking about, Al?"

D. T. senior nods somberly, anger flashing across his eyes.

"That's right, boy. He's got the plot next to your mother!"

I lean back slowly. I had been to my mother's grave in Mississippi several times. I had stood in front of the large stone, realizing it had been six years since my mother succumbed to cancer. In my mind it was always just a few years back—a confusing time of an aggressive disease that carried her off in less than a year.

"I mean, the sonofabitch didn't even *wait a year* before marrying another woman," my father cries out in moral indignation.

Never the man to play the role of the prig, I am faintly amused. Al had shocked everyone when he married a woman half his age less than a year after my mother died. He had been the doting husband all the way through my mother's illness, then a small four-by-six card arrived inviting us to a wedding. Al confirmed he had fallen in love and hoped we would understand. We did—everyone except the last of the Latin lovers.

"That's a family cemetery! The man is a Midwesterner, for God's sake!"

"You mean you have to be Southern to be buried in Alton Cemetery, Dad?"

"You *should be* boy! Half your relatives are buried there, along with thirteen thousand Confederate dead, and some of them are your relatives too, boy!"

I squint at this man slapping his sheet, upset over a Yankee being buried in the hallowed cemetery of the old South.

"I'm missing something here. I mean ..." I lean closer. "What do you care?"'

D. T. senior stares at me as if I'm the dumbest man on the planet.

"Boy, *I* should be the one buried next to your mother! He's not going to take the plot—he's going to be buried with that woman he married."

"Oh." I sit back slowly in my chair. "I see."

D. T. senior shakes his head doubtfully.

"Look, boy, I don't have much time left."

"You are sick?"

"Nooo ... I'm just saying, in the grand scheme of things, there will come a day, and I think it is right that I be buried with the love of my life."

I stare at my father and begin to laugh.

"It's not funny, boy."

"I'm sorry."

"What?"

"Your marriage didn't exactly work out with Mom."

D. T. senior stares at me, his blue eyes suddenly naked.

"Just because we couldn't work things out,doesn't mean I don't *love her* any less, boy."

I lean forward, rubbing my forehead.

"Does Doris know about this?"

"Lord no! I would never tell her this … hurt her feelings."

"You sure about that, Dad?"

D. T. senior looks down the run of my office, clearly done with the obtuse man in the chair.

"Look, boy, I know I did things that I am not proud of with your mother."

I lean back in my chair.

"How do you think Mom would feel about this?"

"I would say she wants me to move in."

"You know this?"

D. T. senior sits up, clearly animated now. I know now that something has grabbed the traveling salesman in the dead of night at a Motel Six and caused him to lose his equilibrium.

"Yes, I do, boy! We raised you kids together, and we knew each other since the days when we were kids." D. T. senior looks down. "I know it's what she'd want … and it's what I want now that my time is limited."

I come forward, leaning on my knees.

"You still didn't tell me, Dad, what you want from me."

D. T. senior holds his arms wide and looks at me like I'm too dumb to breathe.

"I want you to ask that sonofabitch to give up the plot!"

I stare at this man of my flesh.

"You're kidding."

"Hell no, I'm not kidding, boy! You are the oldest male with my name, and it is your duty to see that I have my wishes on my final resting place, and I wish to lay next to your mother."

I don't move, thinking only an alien abduction could make the day stranger.

"You want me to go to Al and ask him to give up his plot so the ex-husband of his wife can move in?"

"Tha's right."

"Why don't you ask him, Dad?"

"I don't even know the man."

I get up from the chair, shaking my head. Clearly this belongs in the category of a strange dream that one shakes off in the morning.

"Dad, you've lost your mind."

"What do you mean?"

I stop at the door.

"No way."

D. T. senior stares up as if I had just betrayed him.

"Well, why not, boy? It's the most natural thing in the world!"

"Dad, there's nothing natural about you. Besides … Al was there at the end for her."

D. T. senior waves away "'til death do us part" like an errant wind.

"That doesn't have anything to do with it, boy."

"Why not?"

"Because blood and birth are thicker than water, and *you* are Southern, and your *mother's* Southern, and *I'm* Southern. This is your duty, boy. She only married that carpetbagger because he had a lot of money."

"Al didn't have a lot of money, Dad," I say dully.

"Had more than I did."

"What's that say?"

D. T. senior guns his finger.

"You know what I'm asking here, boy."

I breathe in defeat and shake my head. The thought had occurred to me that Al would be buried with his current wife and not my mother. Still, the reality of asking for the plot seemed ridiculous.

"I'll think on it."

"That's all I ask, boy," he says turning over, ready to retire now that the pitch is over.

"You and your wife all right, boy?"

"Yeah … we're fine, Dad."

"Just checking," he says, eyes closed, his mouth moving like a dead man. "… it can all turn on a dime, you know, boy. You can't tell where the fork in the road is … then suddenly you're sleeping over a garage."

I stand in the open door and pause.

"Maybe Doris will call, dad."

I look up, but he is already snoring.

Our house is dark save for a lone light over the kitchen table where Wendy sits with her reading glasses slicking light. A wooden Moet wine case is open, and anyone else might think she might be sampling the vineyard's best before turning in, but I know what this nocturnal ritual bodes. The Moet box has been batted around like a bad shoe, each person taking a stab, trying to establish the Maginot line against debt and dissolution, only to give the box back in desperation. The box has a history. We had it in the city when times were good, and we uncorked our grapes from small pine boxes. In those days, the box was not odious. Words like foreclosure and bankruptcy carry much more mileage than credit card debt. The pinched forehead, the hair cliffing one side, even the overhead light all presage a moment of reckoning.

"That bad," I say gingerly, sliding into a chair.

"That bad."

She has several piles of bills in front of her and a check book.

"We can't pay our bills," she declares, crossing her arms.

It is a simple fact, and one we have both taken turns in uttering. No matter how cavalier one is, how much *carpe diem* one professes, the inability to pay one's bills harkens back to a frustration felt in childhood.

"Forget the bills, we have to pay the taxes," I mutter.

Wendy looks up as if I have just punched her. Her face drains of color.

"When are they due?"

"This month.'

"How much?"

"Five grand.“

This is the torpedo beneath the water line. Wendy sits back slowly in the chair, pulling off her reading glasses. We sit and stare at each other in wonder, each secretly wondering how the other person put us in this predicament.

"What are we going to do, Dale?"

We face each other from opposite ends of the table, the titular king and queen of middle class debt ruling over a kingdom of two children, a goldfish, one guinea pig, and a crayfish hacking it out in polluted waters.

"I have a closing this Friday … I should make close to that."

Even as I say this, I hear Ellie Mae's nasally twang, "Ask him how much he's going to make." I wasn't reaching into Jed's pocket and asking how much he was going to make for hauling Best Buy's plasmas to market.

"Is it going to happen?"

"I think so."

Wendy bites her lip, whispering.

"How did we get so fucked up?"

Two people who refuse to take money seriously might be one answer. An inability to be organized might be another. But I suspect it comes more down to this—we find fiscal responsibility boring. A hundred-dollar dinner, a night in city, or a quick, irresponsible vacation seems to carry the nectar of life. Of course, now we are choking on the dregs.

"Don't worry … we'll find a way," I say, standing up and walking behind my wife.

She knows what I am up to and makes no move to stop me. The massage begins at her neck and moves down to her shoulders.

"You know … this isn't gong to help," she moans lightly.

But it does. The one deal with the owner of the Moet box is that the other person must administer stress relief in whatever form they choose. She stands up and looks at me in the darkness, her body cutting the light like a goddess.

"Sex is not going to help anything," she says lightly, walking toward the bedroom.

I know her words are true, but I am a writer of fiction, after all.

9

T-5

… and counting

Monday

On Monday I give Dale junior a ride to school. I like this time together. It is one of the few times my son and I are together alone. I still remember sitting at the bus stop with D. T. senior in the winter darkness, listening to a distant radio station. These small moments make up childhood, and I know I will remember them the rest of my life. An early frost glistens as we wheel out of the drive with the sun rimming the trees. Smoky mummies wrapped in scarves and skullcaps people the corner bus stop with a few parents waiting in SUVs and Hummers. I pick out one lanky boy in an orange skullcap who is pushing a smaller boy.

"Is that Derek Slug?"

Dale junior presses his face against the window and nods slowly.

"Yup."

We clear Belleview and settle onto the two-lane. I glance in the mirror.

"So Monday … what happens on Monday?"

My son shrugs and settles back in his winter parka.

"Not much … Dad, can I go to another school?"

I look in the mirror.

"Another school?"

"Yeah, the water tastes horrible in the water fountains in this school. In Oakland, the water tasted great."

I squint down the road, thinking chlorinated water should not precipitate such a big decision. But then I realize my son's range of options is limited and one of the options is to turn the handle on a porcelain fountain. Our old town of Oakland was fed by Lake Michigan water, while Charleston pulls off underground aquifers. One would think the water out here would be a little cleaner, more pure somehow, but I'm not drinking out of instructional fountains either.

"Well … how about I give you some bottled water for school?"

"Sure, okay."

Problem solved. No change of school today, at least not before nine AM.

"So, what classes do you have today?"

"Science, math … gym."

"Well, gym is good."

"No, it's not," my son says darkly. "Mr. Boner hates me."

I glance in the mirror. The indomitable Mr. Boner has once again entered our world and I consider a boy not liking gym class. Gym was always my favorite; a chance to run, a chance to break out of the dull routines of the classroom.

"I'm sure he doesn't hate you, Dale—"

"Yes, he does. He made me do extra pushups and run extra laps again."

I look in the mirror.

"He did?"

"Yes!"

I feel a small dart of alarm and press down on the accelerator.

"Why does he make you do pushups and run laps?"

115

"Because I forget to wear my gym shirt sometimes," he shrugs. "Or I forget to wear my stupid socks."

I look in the mirror again.

"You don't wear a shirt?"

"No," Dale junior shrugs again. "You're supposed to wear a red shirt on some days and a gray shirt on others, and I forget sometimes. It's stupid."

I am now speeding. The rage that is directed toward Mr. Boner is translating into miles per hour. I am like this. The more agitated I become, the faster I drive. It is something I inherited from my father, who gave us all a stiff neck from pulsing acceleration, something that drove my mother crazy.

"That doesn't seem fair," I say darkly. "You shouldn't be doing pushups or extra laps just because you wore the wrong *shirt*." I look in the mirror again at my young charge. "How about I talk to him?"

"He won't like that, Dad. He's pretty mean."

I laugh and raise one hand off the wheel.

"I can handle him," I say, zooming past two black-and-yellow sawhorses that say, "School Crossing" and "15 MPH."

Several things then happen at once. I see a woman with a bright red stop sign in her hand. Dale junior screams. The woman screams. I slam on the brakes as two tons of metal comes to a screeching halt just outside the second yellow sawhorse. The dash lights up like a small airplane as the engine dies.

"Jesus, Dad!"

We are all victims of our past transgressions and mine is right beside the car. I had on several occasions blown through the fifteen mile an hour zone at a steady twenty and been treated to the bullhorn voice of the matriarch screaming, "*Slow down!*" Now I have lost the fine art of escape. I turn slowly to a heavy woman outside the passenger window. Her mouth is moving under the silver bowl of her hair, but the sealed glass window is robbing her of sound. I am like a duck hit on the head and for a moment I do nothing.

"You better put the window down, Dad," Dale junior mutters, the veteran at calculating authority rage.

I hit the button. A hail of words crosses the still morning air.

"You stupid jerk! What's wrong with you? You nearly killed someone!"

I see a fleshy woman. Molars. Coffee breath. Washed out blue eyes. Her mouth moves nonstop and I no longer hear her voice. Like the writer I am, observant to freak phenomenon, it occurs to me that this verbal alliteration is amazing. How could anyone spew forth with such rapidity so early in the morning? Then, like a radio being turned up, she comes back into my hearing.

"... and I'm sick and tired of jerks like you endangering our children. You think you can do whatever you want because you drive a big truck. Well let me tell you, you can't!"

The woman is now leaning into my car, blasting me with rancid coffee and maybe an earlier cheese croissant—this is clearly the breath of the sweaty middle class.

"I'm going to report you! What's your name?"

I stare at this short woman with silver hair and wind-burned cheeks. She wears a bright neon green smock and sun-darkened glasses. The stop sign is behind her head like a billboard for the defrocked safety guard. I begin to backpedal.

"I'm sorry, I didn't realize how fast—"

"Names! I want names!"

She is shouting. Cars are lined up behind me. People are honking. I am stopping the morning pogrom of taking children to school.

"I am sorry—"

"I want names, and I want them *now!*"

Her breath has changed again; it is now a strange mixture of coffee and garlic. Dale junior looks like he is trying to press himself into the backseat. She spies my ward and attacks, going for the easiest target—the children.

"Young man, what is *your* name?"

"Dale Hammer," the prisoner gives up.

She turns to me, a gleam of triumph in her eye.

"You will be hearing from the principal."

Then she stomps away with incredible buttocks and begins redirecting the traffic bottlenecked behind. I move off at a conspicuously slow fifteen miles an hour.

"Oh man, are we in trouble now," Dale junior groans, shaking his head.

I clear my throat trying to retrieve the ten-year-old in myself. I know what Dale junior is feeling like, because I feel the same way. We are all bad little boys for most of our lives.

"She overreacted," I say, trying to give some perspective to my son. "I'll call the principal and explain what happened."

My son jumps forward.

"Don't do that, Dad!"

I turn into the school driveway and glance in the mirror.

"Why?"

"Just don't. You've done enough," he mutters.

I feel chastised, another failure of the modern patriarch. We round the circle drive where mothers are dropping off their children. I see a man with a blond crew cut in Target blue sweat pants, a Bears sweatshirt, and top-of-the-line Nikes. Something about the square jaw and the absurdly white teeth tells me I am staring at the indomitable Mr. Boner.

"It's Mr. Boner," Dale junior groans, falling down on the seat.

I feel his lack of faith acutely. It's time to make something right in the world. Mr. Boner is acting as a greeter, opening the doors for parents dropping off their kids. I see my opportunity to buttonhole this storm trooper of physical education.

"I'm just going to have a word."

"Oh no," my son groans. "I'm doomed."

I throw our troop ship in park and figure I have thirty seconds to set this pituitary case straight. Dale junior has already alighted from the car into the throng of students. He is running from the showdown between Mr. Boner and his old man. The gym teacher is already looking at the next car when I reach him.

"Pardon me ... ah, Mr. Boner?"

Dull blue eyes turn on me. The waffle crew cut is marine, the jaw chiseled like a brick, the brain utilitarian. I can handle this guy.

"My name is Dale Hammer," I say extending my hand.

He dismisses my overture and gestures to my Yukon.

"Sir, you have to move your vehicle."

"I will, but I wanted to talk with you. My son is Dale Hammer Jr ... he is in your PE class."

The blue eyes flicker, a faint curl in the right lip. I notice then how close his eyes are together, the protruding frontal lobe—definitely the primal hunter-gatherer.

"Oh right," he says. "The kid that can never remember what shirt to wear."

I feel the right hook. It is deft, straight, and fast. The gloves are off. I laugh shortly.

"Well, I think *the kid* can remember—"

"And you think I'm picking on your kid," Mr. Boner continues, looking down from his six-foot-three height.

I smile, giving him the benefit of the doubt.

"Well, I think laps and pushups are a little harsh for forgetting to wear a shirt," I say gingerly.

Mr. Boner's line of cars are now all screwed up because of my white whale in the drive. He turns the force of his square jaw on me, complete with chest-thumping finger. It would seem there would be some edict in the teacher handbook about thumping a parent in the chest.

"You know, I'm really sick of *you parents* telling me how to do *my job*. I'm not picking on your son! It is a basic responsibility for him to know what *shirt* to wear, and if he can't remember it, then he might think again after some laps and a few pushups! But I am not going to put up with any more *bleeding heart parents* who think their precious kid is being treated unfairly. You got a problem with me, then take it up with the principal. Now, kindly move your vehicle before I have it towed. Got it? *Good!*"

Mr. Boner moves off to the traffic jam behind me. I feel the burn on my cheeks and the finger thumps on my chest. I consider several replies or hitting him in the back of the head with a tire iron. But the moment has passed and I slowly get back in my command ship and drive off, a fifteen-mile-an-hour dog with his tail between his legs.

Oakland is the anomaly of Illinois. Liberal, Democratic, integrated, ridiculously progressive, offering up legends from Hemingway to Frank Lloyd Wright, honeycombed with charming nineteenth-century homes, wide lawns, trendy restaurants, bookstores, organic grocery stores, yoga salons, art leagues, writer groups, book clubs, a real old movie theater that gets current movies and manages to thrive despite the mega theaters, independent bookstores that survive despite Borders and Barnes and Noble— the rock in the heel of a conservative state, a Studs Terkel city, and a myopic country that promotes diversity with the lackluster effort of a nun in a brothel.

I love this village.

I drive under the canopy of Elms and Oaks clustering the streets and shoot down through the middle of town, heading for my first port of call, The Bread Shop. This coffee house produces bread, killer pecan rolls, and a latte to die for. Some would think it strange I drive a full hour east to have a cup of coffee and work on a stalled short story, but here among the disenfranchised, the down and out, the yuppies and the artists, the professors and the professionals, I can find myself again. I enter The Bread Shop and throw my knapsack on the bar running the length of the floor to ceiling windows. Here one can watch the old freight trains, the sleek commuter trains, the long cars of coal heading for Chicago and the yellow Pacific and Atlantic diesels that pass six at a time, all while sipping coffee and eating hot bread. The Bread Shop is a writer's paradise. Plenty of newspapers to read and a big old clock over the Oakland station to watch time be slowly swindled. A man with a heavy beard and curly black hair is behind the counter. He smiles, reaching over the glass barrier of rolls and pastries.

"Hey, long time no see, author."

It is George Demopolis, the owner, a man who rises at four thirty to make sure the bread is ready. He looks absurdly like John Belushi and is a great fan of the written word. I had actually met George in one of the many writing seminars I headed up for the local community college. When he told me he owned The Bread Shop, a beautiful friendship was born. He wanted to learn to be a writer and I needed a place to call my own.

"How ya doing, George?"

He shrugs, scratches his beard, frowns.

"Can't complain. Business is good. How's the writing?"

"Great. Just great," I say, feeling for a moment that it is great.

"Working on a new book?"

I look at George and see hope flickering in his eyes. He actually is waiting for me to write another novel, and this makes me feel like buckling down and producing that elusive fourth book. George has read all my books and made a point of citing favorite scenes in each one. For a writer there is nothing more satisfying. I determine then and there to begin a new novel. It's not that I haven't written any novels in the last seven years; it's just I haven't written any *good* novels.

"Always," I answer, eyeing the pecan rolls beneath the glass, changing the subject lest he ask what this new epic is about.

George hovers close, spying the novel in my leather coat.

"What are you reading?"

I pull out the book of essays I've been carrying around for six months. I have to pull it out because I forgot the title.

"Jonathan Franz's *Essays.*"

"I read those," he says and nods quickly, and I know he has. A short, swarthy bald man with curly brown hair ringing a baseball cap—he is an unlikely literary man but inhales the printed word and thinks writers are something next to God. This is not a bad setup for a man on a limited budget.

"I really enjoyed his essay on the death of the American novel," he continues, interrupting my examination of the rolls. "I mean, I agree with Franz, I'm not sure the novel *is* capable anymore of depicting the American landscape; the culture is too ephemeral, vatic, polarized, changing with nanosecond speed. How can a novelist today take that on? Even Hemingway couldn't have done it!"

Hemingway is next to God for George. He can readily quote passages from *A Farewell to Arms* and has memorized "Up in Michigan," which he claims is the most perfect short story ever written.

"Maybe the blog is the new novel of today—up to the minute, updated daily, a mutable form that cannot be made obsolescent."

I was thrown way back with the word *vatic.* George is in love with polysyllabic words no one uses and speaks of *masticating* when chewing and *fecundation* when fucking. I mumble something about the American novel and then swing into the real business at hand, picking the most luscious pecan roll with the maximum amount of caramel. But George has been energized.

"I agree with Tom Wolfe's assertion that no one is writing the great social novel anymore; all the novelists are either regional or derivative of old classics, but no one is *really* taking on the cultural landscape of this country. Hell, Gore Vidal said the American novel was dead back in the sixties and that film was the new novel and now charged with interpreting American life. I agree with Franz's assertion that the digital revolution is the next step and that the Internet generation will come up with a whole new art form unknown to us and *that* will be the new novel of the twenty-first century."

I look up from the rolls. George is sweating, a vein throbbing at his temple. I remember this type of person now. He is a man who really *cares* about things, who is able to work into a lather over an editorial in a newspaper. The people I come in contact with seem as if they are all on low-level valiums.

"Did he really say all that?"

George nods earnestly.

"Oh yeah. He said that when he gave up his television, he basically lost touch with reality and that is a futile gesture, because *everyone does* watch television, and how can you reference the correct cultural landmarks if you are ignoring them?"

I nod, thinking I really should read the book of essays I've been carrying around in my jacket.

"How about that one all the way in back," I say, pointing to a particularly caramel-smothered blob.

George seems deflated that I am not going to enter into a literary discussion on the death of the American novel. It is a topic I have given much thought to over time, and I don't like my own suspicions that the bulk of the American populace would rather watch *American Idol* than be tied to the rack of a good book.

"Oh sure ... and a latte, right?'

"You got it, George."

He sets the mother of all rolls on the counter and goes off to steam milk. I carry my roll to the long bar along the window. A freight train of bloated chemical cars is silently going by the window and I feel a great peace coming on. A day of reading and writing looms ahead. I have turned off my phone and I have the old excitement when a new idea is quivering on the horizon. I pause as something drops from under the bar to the floor directly in front of me. I stare at the long, reddish-brown creature on his back, antenna waving, legs pedaling air.

"Oh fuck!" I scream involuntarily. *"Holy shit!"*

The few mothers with children look my way; commuters pause with their coffee. I have directed the attention of the entire coffee house on this *mega*-roach. He is panicked, his many legs angling wildly. I imagine he has feasted on warm, yeasty bread for years, traversing the underside of the bar when he fell. There are no roaches in Charleston. There are spiders the size of your fist, there are beetles and flying bugs no man could safely identify, wasps that hover like small aliens, but there are no roaches. I had forgotten about these urban creatures I had once taken for granted.

My scream has activated the ever-vigilant George. He rounds the counter and approaches the giant bug still trying to right himself while all the patrons of The Bread Shop watch. George takes one step in his black combat boots and smashes the roach with a crackly splat that ricochets off the back wall and sends a collective *ugh* up from his patrons. George, never a man for delicate moment, a man who puts on a T-shirt, jeans, combat boots, and a flour-covered apron every day, then smears what is left of Mr. Roach all over the floor like someone trying to get mud off his shoe. The patrons of The Bread Shop have had enough. The door bell jingles continuously as commuters and would-be scribblers depart. George watches his paying customers leave with flour still on his cheeks and a fine sheen on his brow. The bell quits ringing, and all is silent. There are only the remains of Mr. Roach, myself, and George.

He glances around his now-empty establishment. His eyes travel across the empty chairs and tables, then slowly come to a halt. The look of reverence has been replaced with the black eyes of disdain.

"Thanks a fucking lot, Dale," he grumbles.

I feel horrible. My reaction was visceral, automatic, maybe primal. I don't know why I screamed, really, but I see George blames me for nothing less than possibly torching The Bread Shop. It doesn't take a rocket scientist to figure out that news of giant roaches prowling a certain coffee establishment could mean death for a coffee house.

"I'm sorry, George … it's just … it freaked me out!"

George looks down at the long brown smear.

"I thought writers were supposed to be subtle," he mutters, leaving to get a mop or a fire hose to deal with the remains. I look around and realize The Bread Shop is no longer my haven. I gather up my knapsack as George returns with a mop. I wonder if there is a graceful way to leave. I have no appetite, no desire to sit at the bar where other mega-roaches could be prowling.

"You don't have to go," he mutters.

"Ah … I'm late … I've got a class," I say suddenly.

George glances at me and starts mopping.

"Don't forget your roll."

"Right."

I pick up the roll I will pitch the minute I leave.

"Ah … take it easy, George."

He walks to a yellow bucket and wrings his mop.

"You know, I heard a weird rumor about you. I heard you had moved to the suburbs. Someone said you had bought some big fucking house way in the middle of nowhere."

He pauses, resting his hands on his mop. "But you know what I said, I said, '*Nah.* He'd never fucking do that. Turn tail and run, I mean. He's not that kind of guy.'"

I look down and can think of no reply. This village on the edge of the city is a place I did abandon three years ago. I told few people we were moving and enjoyed the assumption I was still in my 1892 frame house on the east side of town. But I see now the cat has been out of the bag for some time. I know now that like my youth, one cannot return to that golden time.

George shakes his head and begins mopping again.

"Maybe Franz was right."

He wrings his mop, fixing me with a final accusing glance.

"The American novel *is* dead."

The Belleview Association Meeting is at seven thirty. I had gotten back from Oakland around five thirty and had time for some quick dinner, scooping up D. T. senior and a notebook from my office. The moon is low over the wetlands and pallors the white stucco forts and brick castles. D. T. senior and I cross the wide lawns of my neighbors, my father's loafers swishing through the early dew. He is quiet, walking with his hands in his pockets, glancing across the acre-and-a-half lawns at the various displays of early century architecture—Georgians, Colonials, Tudors, Victorian country. It is balmy and the breeze carries the hint of distant oceans, seasons past, youth. I can't help but feel we are the field hands on someone else's plantation. In my family we never had any real money, so now, confronted with obvious wealth, D. T. senior and I are the two lounging youths gawking once again at the mansion on the hill.

"They do have the buckos," he murmurs, staring at the looming castle of one Dr. Petty.

One of the few times I hear real respect come out the mouth of the progenitor is in the recognition of wealth. Money is the only thing in this life that will draw reverence from D. T. senior. All my life I heard the summation of the world in terms of economics … "There is so and so. He has a lot of fucking money." The tone in my father's voice told more than the actual words—wonderment, awe, a puzzling ache for what he could never have.

"They have mortgages, Dad," I say, nodding to the castles illuminated by landscape spotlights.

D. T. senior shrugs, catching my eye.

"Maybe so, but they have money too, boy."

I sigh, wanting somehow to nudge my father into my side of the boat. In truth, he speaks of the same issues I have wrestled with for the last three years—money and my relation to it. I live among the wealthy, yet I do not possess this money and have landed only in their kind vicinity because of a real estate bubble that refused to burst. I am the poor boy looking in the keyhole, wondering when I will be discovered.

"Perception is reality, Dad. You were the one who always said that," I point out.

He nods, glancing at me in the half darkness.

"My perception is that these folks have a lot of fucking money."

I have no reply as we reach the Petty castle. I see the illuminated blue eye of a pool. A soft whirring of pumps and chlorinators hum as background music. D. T. senior takes in the skyscraper diving board and the soft whoosh of water circling over the wavering eye of illumination. There is a whirlpool and a steam room and an outdoor gym complete with Nautilus work out equipment. The Pettys have managed to put on an unusual display of conspicuous consumption in the land of conspicuous consumption.

"Jesus," D. T. senior swears softly. "goddamn, these cocksuckahs have some money here."

In this moment I feel sorry for the bull of Mississippi. The

Pettys will lounge by their pool and sip margaritas while my father drives to some plant in North Carolina to have lunch with a man who can barely scrawl his name. The bottom line is D. T. senior will have to work until the day he dies. I know this because I will share a similar fate, while the Pettys are already looking at retirement homes. I could become depressed over the unfair allotment of destiny, but then I know D. T. senior has brought his own suitcase of misery, and I suppose I have too.

We circle around and reach the front porch. The street is in quiet dusk and the houses are subdued, their garish facades secluded by night and for a moment, my neighborhood looks almost bucolic. I imagine the houses as belonging to people who are middle class with the same dreams and frustrations I possess, struggling to pay the bills and looking for the weekend. But I know this is my fantasy and belongs to the last neighborhood I lived in.

"Dad ... listen. This meeting could be a little heated. It concerns ... the sign. *Promise* me you won't say anything."

D. T. senior holds his hands up in divine retribution. He had expressed interest in the association meeting, and I knew this came from boredom, but also a yearning to be back in a business environment of meetings and people wrangling, any type of organized activity that involves procedures and negotiation.

"Son, you have my *word*. I will be a quietly supportive."

"Really, Dad ..." I say, ringing the bell. "No matter what you hear, don't say anything."

"Mum is the word," he says solemnly as the door swings back.

A tall woman with dark, Laura Petrie hair, silicone breasts, and absurdly white teeth, is munching on a piece of celery. Her expression reserved for mad dogs and black men lets me know she already thinks I desecrated the sign.

"Why hello, Dale," she rushes out in the strange falsetto of the disingenuous.

"Tammy...my father, Dale Hammer senior...Dad, Tammy Petty."

D. T. senior bows and takes her hand.

"The pleasure is all mine, madam," he drawls.

The celery stalk suddenly disappears as Tammy Petty lights up.

"Oh, do I detect an accent?"

I remember then that Tammy hails from some backwater town in Tennessee, remembering the cracker roots behind the framed five-by-ten monster over the fireplace of the good doctor, Tammy, and their two adopted sons, in photographic nirvana.

D. T. senior bows farther, holding onto her hand. She is mere putty now.

"You do indeed, madam. Mississippi is my mother, and my people go all the way back to the Mayflower."

Tammy Petty cannot hold out against the man in the pullover sweater and shined loafers. The distinguished gray goatee and the accent conjure up the man she did not marry. Dr. Petty is a manicured Jewish man who says, *Life is fine, life is fine,* when queried, but here is the secret Southern aristocrat of her heart—a man who wouldn't let her in the front door as a child.

"Oh, I'm from Chattanooga, Tennessee," Tammy drawls like a Southern belle.

"Ah," D. T. senior nods. "A fine state, Tennessee, and their woman are some of the *prettiest belles* in the Union."

I now see we are in *Gone with the Wind* and the darkies have just been let in the front door. D. T. senior has taken the pulse of the madam of the house and the rest of the night is now a foregone conclusion—the master salesman is on the premises.

"You didn't tell me you had such *a charmer* for a father," Tammy chides me.

"I didn't know," I mutter.

Tammy stares at me. Clearly, the son does not measure up to the father. She takes us past the picture of framed family life. D. T. senior stops below the three people clustered among Grecian columns with Dr. Petty looking like a buffoon, Tammy against him like a seductress, and their two adopted Japanese sons in round spectacles, smiling toothily behind the imperialist dogs. Three trained halogen spots light the entire photo. This is the Belleview coat of arms that I have seen in several other homes—a paean to Western European roots canonized in the plasticity of American upper middle-class suburban culture. The first time I saw these mounted horrors, I wanted to run and hide.

D. T. senior turns to Tammy and the smile belies him. The picture certifies everything he has always known about Yankees—a crass, boorish people who can only advertise the basest of American virtues—money.

"A fine, fine photograph of a very attractive family."

"Thank you," Tammy gushes, and suddenly becomes shy, lowering her voice. "We thought it might be a little, well, *self serving*, putting the picture over the fireplace."

"Nonsense," D. T. senior declares, framing the colored phantasmagoria like a movie director. "Madam, I think you put the picture of the family where it was *always* meant to go."

Tammy beams while D. T. senior winks at me, his expression like a man watching a fish squirm on a hook. She touches my father's arm, bending down to D. T. senior who is a good five inches shorter. I have found that Belleview women are just taller in general. Maybe it's the hard water or the milk.

"Can I get you anything to drink, water, tea ... a mint julep?"

"You are too kind, Miz Tammy. But I am fine."

"Well, everyone is in the basement," she says, still looking at the picture, assuring herself that she really is that seductress.

D. T. senior bows again.

"Lead the way, madam, and we will follow."

I give my father a warning look, but he merely smiles as the two conmen descend into hell.

We emerge into Brazilian Cherry and more plasma screens with a marble bar and a pool table that has never been used, along with the leather couches never blanched—this, then, is the Dr. Petty lair. There are signed Bears jerseys in glass cases mounted on the walls along with a baseball bat laying in a long glass case like a corpse. A home theater complete with a row of red velvet theater chairs dominates the far side of the basement. The lore is that Dr. Petty procured the theatre seating on eBay and had them reupholstered. I see the good doctor and Tammy cuddling up in the theatre seating, the movie playing out in unearthly Dolby sound to the exclusive audience of two.

D. T. senior and I take a position toward the back and close to the stairs. I think this is prudent if a quick retreat is necessary. Dr. Petty's Brazilian basement is filled. The last meeting evinced less than half the residents in attendance, but I see a full quorum. The good doctor is standing in front of his gas fireplace with a sweater, mustache, and soft-soled shoes. He is the paragon of all that is good and decent and rich in Belleview. All he needs is a pipe.

"Okay, that brings us to new business," the doctor announces after the droning minutes of the last meeting are dispensed. "And I think we all know the reason this meeting was called."

Dr. Petty pauses dramatically. He is a well-built man who wears a Southern Plantation Owner costume every year for Halloween. I suspect he sees himself as a landed man in the late eighteenth-century mode, more enlightened than Scrooge, but approving of the debtors' prisons all the same. He looks at the number-one debtor and plows on.

"Two nights ago," he begins somberly, reading from a paper. "Someone deliberately attacked said sign and with forethought and malice, effectively destroyed the said sign at the entrance to Belleview."

Said sign I mouth, but on one else seems amused. Dr. Petty pauses again, stroking his waxed mustache. I remember then another plank of the Petty legend. The lore is that the doctor was an Olympic swimmer, or that he competed to be an Olympic swimmer, or maybe he just *looked like* an older Olympic swimmer. One thing I have learned about Belleview is that no one has a normal job or a normal history—everyone is either a heavy hitter, CEO, retired movie star, Olympic swimmer, or just mysteriously and gloriously rich.

The doctor drones on in a pseudo-*Dragnet* voice.

"I have contacted the police, and a report has been filed. And I will say there have been *several interviews* conducted with the possible suspect."

I wonder who else has been interviewed as a possible suspect. I consider that maybe there was some good cop/bad cop design going on. Maybe several residents of Belleview have come under the suspicion of the long arm of the law.

"Frankly, I think this changes the whole landscape in regard to the proposed replacement of the sign. I think now the first order of business is to find out *who* is responsible for this ... this ... *carnage.* " The good doctor's face has turned red, fine, shining beads of perspiration appearing on the frontal lobe. "And then take appropriate actions."

There is a chorus of general murmuring, then once voice rises above the rest.

"Do we have any leads?"

This comes from a man sitting in the center of the room. I can only see the back of his head and don't recognize him, but this isn't surprising, as I don't know most of my Belleview brethren.

"Yes," Dr. Petty nods gravely. "We do have some leads, and

frankly, I have to say it involves someone on the board ... someone who has been *very vocal* in their criticism of the sign."

An audible murmur passes over my suburban brothers and sisters. Seventy-five miles west of Chicago, this is big news—someone, *one of us*, a *white man no less*, has turned traitor and sawed the ugliest sign in the Western world in half. Men are nodding knowingly, wives are checking cell phones. If the man would cut down a perfectly good sign, God knows what he is capable of next. A good thing the children aren't here. *Hacker! Blasphemer! Democrat!*

"Well, I think we still have a motion on the table that has to be acted upon."

This comes from Anna Corning, who sits on the landscape committee responsible for the grounds and the sign. It is her committee that has been considering proposals to replace the sign. I had entered the fray proposing to make the sign happen last year. I had hoped to have some impact on my surroundings, taking on the issue of the sign as my lightning rod for everything I detested about my new surroundings. Then I hit the obfuscation, backbiting, and equivocation that is the Belleview Homeowners Association. I quickly realized that while five years was a long time to consider the proposal of a new sign, it would probably take another five years before anything would happen and I quietly withdrew, but not before a farewell speech that has since come to haunt me.

John Petty frowned, losing the momentum of his lynch mob.

"That's true. We do have a motion, and it concerns replacement of the said sign now defunct. I suppose we really have to discuss this motion, because in effect our hand has been forced now. A motion to discuss?"

"I make a motion," the same man in the center of the room calls out.

Anna Corning raises her hand again, long hair trellising

down her back.

"Well, I don't see how we can do anything at all now. We still don't have the funds because of our landscaping requirements."

It is the pedantic I first noticed in Anna when she asked me during a barbecue if I wanted one pickle or two on my hamburger. I was touched she should care about my pickle desire, but then I realized she was that exacting about everything, from pickles to the amount of sex allotted for a normal housewife in the year 2008.

"But we have to do *something*," another man with his back to me complains.

Dr. Petty nods meditatively, holding the gavel under his arm.

"The problem is we now have two issues confronting us. Do we try and fix the damaged sign? Or do we replace it?" the doctor asks.

Anna shakes her head. She could be the thorn in the Petty kangaroo court.

"We can't do either," she states firmly. " We do not have the *funds*."

"Why don't we have the funds?" the man in the middle wonders.

"Because we never *allocated* money for a sign," Anna replies.

"Well, the dues cannot go up to cover a sign," another woman from the leather couch says.

Anna turns and faces her audience.

"Dues haven't gone up for years … it's time we increased them," she states crisply.

"I want to know who *destroyed* our sign," another man sitting on the couch calls out.

"And if you know who it is, then tell us and we can prosecute him!"

Several other men call out in agreement. If this were the old west, they would be looking for a tree.

"We still have a motion on the table," Anna Corning reminds everyone.

"I don't even know what *the motion* is," another woman declares.

"It's parliamentary procedure," the doctor informs.

"I know what *a motion* is I just don't know what *the motion* is," the woman complains.

The good doctor smiles deferentially, raising his hands.

"I think we are all getting beyond the real issue here. And that is bringing to justice the person or persons responsible for destroying the sign and then we can make them or *him* pay for it!"

"But John, we don't know *who* that person is," Anna points out logically.

The doctor nods slowly, ominously, one eyebrow tantalizing. He then looks directly at me, and D. T. senior turns. I feel heat in my face.

"I have a good idea. A *very good* idea."

"Do you want to share that with us, then?" Georgia Barnes demands, sitting by the fireplace.

I had seen her when we walked in and so had D. T. senior. She is appointed with a turquoise eagle and a buckskin coat—a sort of seventies Annie Oakley with long, red hair. Dr. Petty turns and looks at me again.

"I think it is the person who was *most vocal* on their criticism of the sign and who at one point threatened to destroy the said sign."

I begin to stand up slowly, feeling my heart.

"You people are worse than a bunch of scalded cats in a whore [pronounced *hoah*] house!"

The voice comes from beside me. The room turns as one to the man in the yellow sweater. D. T. senior has broken his pledge and is now standing, facing the collective residents of Belleview. I feel a great avalanche descending toward me as my father levels a finger at the Belleview quorum.

"A bunch of goddamn *whoreshit* is what it is! You just have too many goddamn white people living out here!" he declares, waving his arms. "What's all this shit about a sign? If someone tore up your old sign, then *replace the goddamn thing!* It is a disgrace because ya'll are too cheap to ante up and get a respectable sign. But I'd like to thank the man who had the courage to do his duty and destroy that butt-ugly sign."

"*Dad,*" I hiss, thinking any chance I had was slipping away with *whoreshit* and *butt ugly sign.*

"Sir, you are out of order," Dr. Petty censoriously informs the rebel.

I see D. T. senior's jaw drop, and I feel what is coming. The bad boy who has stomped on the toes of authority all his life has been told to shut up by *a Yankee.* I consider a quick exit, but D. T. senior grabs my arm, steadying me for the blowback of his assault.

"Out of order my ass, Kingfisher," he drawls on. "*You aren't talking to some Negro boy!*"

The good people of Belleview are reeling from the words "*Negro boy.*" D. T. senior jabs his finger at Dr. Petty like a gun.

"Who the hell are you, cocksuckah, to tell me I'm out of order! What a bunch of whoreshit … you may have one big-ass house, but you're just a fat -ass Yankee boy with a fancy pool in my book!"

Women are blushing, and men are reaching for their dicks. D. T. senior has stunned his audience and is now maneuvering.

"Now, you want to sit in here and piss and moan about your sign and try and figure out who sawed that piece of shit in half, then you can, but I'd say that's a bunch of whoreshit, because you aren't addressing your basic problem!"

D. T. senior looks slowly around the room. Upper middle-class white people from the North are truly outgunned against a man who will say anything. My father is now leading a sales meeting, telling his salesmen how to solve the problem—*know your decision maker, and identify the problem that needs to be solved*. He begins to pace, hands in his pleated slacks, gesticulating to the red-faced Dr. Petty.

"I have sat through more fucking meetings than all of you combined, and I'm here to tell you most of them are a bunch of whoreshit! You have one problem and *one problem* only, and that is you don't have a sign anymore." The motivator stops his pacing and wheels for his summation. "So, what I suggest is this: quit worrying about who hacked apart that sorry plywood excuse of a sign, and get to work *replacing it.* "

The room is quiet. The fine people of Belleview have been treated to more invectives in three minutes than they have heard in a year. Dr. Petty is burning up. His wife looks like someone who just let a cat in who pissed all over the place. D. T. senior looks around the room of budding salesmen and sees none of the natural ability so necessary for the successful purveyor of goods and services. It is the guile of the burglar combined with the stealth of the cat and the sleight of hand of a magician. I can see he is clearly disappointed no one has thanked him for his message of redemption. *Move on. No prospects here.*

Dr. Petty holds his gavel, trying to decide what to say to a man who has just called him a *cocksuckah.* His wife is staring at him. All of Belleview is staring at him as the doctor considers the options left open to him. *Should he ask the man to step outside? Should he crush him with rhetorical wit? Should he banish him from his domicile?* In truth, the doctor is not equipped for the man who shows no respect. It has been years since he has had his authority questioned and he has forgotten how to punch.

Finally, Dr. Petty decides on a course. He should be beating D. T. senior to death with his gavel, but he weakly motions to my father and does the only thing he can—identify the interloper.

"And you are?"

D. T. senior glares at the good doctor, warning off Dr. Petty with the crazy violence that is my father.

"Dale Hammer the first," he answers defiantly, pointing to me suddenly. "And this here's my boy, you arrogant cocksuckah! "

10

T-4

... and Counting

Tuesday

It is 1968, and the ride is called the Rocket. I hadn't seen a ride like that before. The cars spin around on a spidery spoke that levitates up and down like a giant tarantula. The street fair is winding down. Evening breezes pass down the old main street. Autumn is still sniffing around but has not managed to push out the dog days of September.

My father smokes a Pall Mall and shrugs when I ask him if I could ride the Rocket. I know the ride is mine. I had passed up shooting out a target with a pneumatic BB gun and throwing ping-pong balls into goldfish bowls. With D. T. senior, you had to strike a deal. You either got ice cream or candy, but not both.

"All right, boy," he says and nods, patting the breast pocket of his Brooks suit, feeling for his cigarettes and the bronze money clip. "But after that we are heading home. Your mother is not feeling so good." He nods to where my mother is behind the stroller in her wing-tipped sunglasses.

The man takes the two bucks D. T. senior offers. He is a man who never removes the cigarette from his mouth with greased hair and blue tattoos and no teeth. He looks like one of the men I sometimes saw picking up trash on the side of the highways in the blue jump suits.

"All right, sonny," the man says, opening one of the cars that looks like small, round pods.

I sit down with the bar in my stomach the man has lowered. I had never shrunk from any ride. Roller coasters did nothing to me. A ride called the Predator that dropped straight down from an enormous hill barely got my blood moving. I was always looking for the next thrill. I figured the Rocket would prove nothing more than a distraction at a local fair that had filled me with cotton candy, pop, and peanuts.

The man walks away from my car and goes into a small shack. I see D. T. senior standing just outside the gate, smoking another Pall Mall. I wave as the ride shudders to life. The Rocket begins with a lift. The tarantula of pod cars uses pneumatic pistons to levitate up and down. I am bored. This was the Rocket? Come on. The giant spider then begins to move in a concentric circle. I feel myself push back against my pod. The bar in my stomach keeps me immobile. Things are getting better. I am really beginning to move. I feel the Gs push me harder against the seat. The great spider is rotating and moving up and down. At least I am getting my money's worth. I wave to D. T. senior and then my mother. Then without warning, the Rocket changes.

My pod begins to rotate on its own axle. The force of the Gs built from the tarantula moving in big circles has now transferred to my car. The Gs double. My car zings into crazy circles. I begin to move at unbelievable speed. The force pins me against the back of the car. I can't lift my hand. Then I hear the motor roar. The man with no teeth and tattoos and greasy hair has blasted off the Rocket.

I feel my stomach pin back. My jaw slaps side to side. My neck rivets against the hard plastic and all the blood in my body goes to my back. Then my lunch comes up. I feel it hit my forehead. I try to raise my hand, but the world is a blur. I can't see. I want off, but I can't move. A great darkness moves in and the world is down a long tunnel. The Rocket presses the blood away from my brain. I can no longer breathe. I shut my eyes and see no more. I hear a word come from my mouth, a faint cry for help, a final missive from the abyss.

"... *Dad.*"

I open my eyes to the voices of children.

"I get to look at the box!"

"No, I get to look at the box!"

"Don't throw it ... don't ... Angela!"

"*Wahhhh!*"

"He ... hit ... me!"

"No, I didn't. She's lying."

"Dale ... Angela!"

"That's my box!"

"Angela, I need to pour my cereal!"

"*That's my box! Waaaaaaaah!*"

I lay in bed and pull up the watch of my burdens. *Seven AM.* Things could be worse. My kids could be fighting, and the dream of my father returning could be reality. I smile at such foolish thoughts, then hear the voice of a man. I throw on last night's jeans and a new T shirt and tackle the first real crisis of the day— who gets to look at the back of the Sugar Smacks while eating.

Wendy is making coffee. D. T. senior is sitting at the kitchen table in a dark blue suit with a red power tie and vest. I am twelve again and my father is making notes for his day, lining up appointments, clearing the rest of the world with a five AM internal clock and frenetic energy while I am still looking for a coffee cup. I find a Literary Festival mug featuring a host of writers printed down the side. I notice the "DT" of D. T. Hammer has faded, so I am left with "Hammer."

I stare at the man still working quietly at the table with the intense concentration that is the hallmark of any great salesman. The red power tie is a flag in my kitchen of tawny browns and Formica. I sip the bitter brew and consider I have been long shut of the corporate world and a swing back to the fashions of the eighties could have occurred. D. T. senior continues scribbling away in his leather day timer. Wendy is watching her two children and D. T. senior warily—individuals who are keeping her from having her morning cup of coffee. She turns back to the slow gurgle of Mr. Coffee.

"Hey, Dad ... sleep well?"

"Like a top, my boy, like a top," he nearly shouts, writing furiously, making notes, swirls, and squiggles, all in the University of Mississippi epistolary style. DT Senior has a vast collection of pens and always carries a *Waterman* secreted on his person somewhere. The gold *Cross-pen* he is now using has a black tip and is long and sleek. I write like a caveman and have always admired the beautiful cursive of my father's elegant hand. His signature is a study in graceful swirls and arcs while mine is wholly illegible. I know it is generational—a gentleman of the South writes like a gentleman.

My son breaks the peace.

"ANGELA!"

Sugar Smacks explode across the table as Dale Jr rips the box from the grasp of my five year old. DT Seniors legal pad, cell phone, HP calculator, leather day timer, *Hartman* valet, are all littered with honey coated puffed wheat. I hold down my Literary Festival mug, staring at the repository of my hopes and dreams and a trainload of expectations. Angela is screaming and like any parent I reach for the closest fire extinguisher, caring little for reason or culpability.

"*Dale!* What did you do that for?"

"What?" He looks up with the wide eyes of the wrongly accused. "It's her fault, *she held the box!*"

I really don't need this at seven AM. All my muscles, synapses, endorphins, don't begin to function properly until noon. A modicum of solitude is desired and conflagrations are to be avoided. Dale Jr. is really dealing with a stacked deck. The Angela wail pierces the morning air, complete with large blue saucers leaking down her cheeks.

"WAAAAAAH!

"...DONT...HAVE...THE...BOX...OF...CEREAL...WAAAAAH!"

My nerves crack and I buckle under the load.

"Look what you did to your sister!"

DT Senior has the expression of a man who has been without children for well over twenty years—something along the lines of—*my, my, what the fuck?* Wendy is standing behind me while I purge, knowing I am in the wrong.

"Couldn't you have just let her have the cereal...is it worth this, Dale?"

"Dad..." My son's yes fill. "I just wanted—"

"Couldn't you think ahead? You have a good brain, *use it!* I don't need this shit first thing in the morning!"

He is crying, but I can't stop myself.

"But—"

"Next time, you two sit far apart and eat different cereal," I shout, holding Angela while glaring at my son.

Dale junior turns red and his eyes fill. He runs from the table and goes upstairs. By the time his door slams, I know I did it again. I feel unreasonably irritated with my son. Just tying his shoes can send me over the edge. I already carry the unfair expectations of a father for his son.

"Son, I don't really think it was his fault."

The man in the Brooks Brothers suit weighs in. I glare at D. T. senior and I know the irritation of my wife at that moment—*why did my father pick the kitchen table for his new office?* My son had just caught a mouthful of stress over the man in the gray-flannel suit.

"Dad ... don't worry about it, all right?"

Wendy says nothing, turning back to her coffee pot. D. T. senior has the expression I know from experience. It is the fighter who has just woken, the impish smile of the bad boy. He sits back in his vest, looking like an accountant. Angela has turned off the siren and is munching happily on the captive Sugar Smacks. I have been played and consider going back to bed and starting over.

"Son, I think you better get up there and make peace with that boy."

"Don't worry about it, Dad."

He puts down his pen and picks up several Sugar Smacks.

"Go ahead. I will watch Angela while Wendy makes us all some coffee."

I turn and look at Wendy, who is keeping her back to me. D. T. senior hooks his thumbs in his vest and looks absurdly like Atticus Finch. I consider having a kitchen installed over the garage.

"Come here to your Papa, little darling."

I am amazed as Angela jumps into his lap.

"Papa!" She squeals.

My father looks up at me in quiet victory.

"We have it all under control here. Go on, son. Tell your boy you're sorry."

I take a deep breath, ready to tell the fine old gentleman from the South to get back in his car and just keep driving.

"Dad—"

"He's right, Dale. Go up and talk to him."

I turn and stare at Wendy, who is still quietly facing Mr. Coffee. I have never heard my wife say my father was right about *anything*. Encircled, I give up the ghost and put down my defunct mug.

"Fine."

"Papa, Sing a funny song again!"

"Well, how about 'Swing Low Sweet Chariot'?" D. T. senior drops down to a deep bass. *"Coming to carry me home ... "*

I head up the stairs as the old Negro spiritual sounds through the floors.

I face the six-paneled white door of my son's garret. Dale junior's door is locked, of course. This is something that coincided with my son turning nine and the beginning of the barrier between father and son. The locking of the door to his room presages all sorts of events: descending to a basement with friends to get stoned, descending to the basement with a girl, locking the door to his heart, locking out his parents and all the other obtuse bastards trying to make him comply with unreasonable demands. I try the knob once more. All moral indignation has passed and I am left with the guilt of the drunk now sorry for his rampage.

I rap the door lightly.

"Dale … Dale, open the door."

"No!"

I can hear the breathy sobs of a little boy. Those years when it was just Dale junior and I are fast behind us. I remember once when we went to a hardware store on a spring day and sat outside eating potato chips and drinking pop. An older man paused in front of us and smiled. "You want to cherish these moments," he said as he nodded to me. "They go by you in a flash." I feel I have already lost those moments. It is right that he has locked the door—*make the sonofabitch suffer!*

I knock again, trying for a parental tone.

"Dale … please unlock the door."

There is a long pause, then the sound of his footsteps crossing the carpet. I give him a moment before pushing open the door to my son's room. There are the bunk beds built with red wood— some sort of pine stained red with a built-in desk and various hutches. The whole motif was to be a Northwood's cabin with pictures of wolves and a bear rug mounted to the wall. Then the motif became overwhelmed with baseball. There are three shelves of baseball trophies and no less than ten major-league pennants tacked to his wall with baseball cards of famous players framed in rows above his dresser. Dirty clothes are on the floor, along with all the strange little odds and ends that make a boy's room. Everything is in place except for the intruder; he is the odd toy, the man who doesn't belong.

Dale junior sits on the lower bunk with red eyes, wiping his nose, staring straight ahead. I see then he has several books on the shelf by his bed. I spy an old Tom Swift novel I had given him and realize how little I know of my son now. What does he like to read? Is he thinking about girls yet?

I pause, looking for my footing.

"You like that Tom Swift?'

He glances at the book and shrugs.

"It's all right," he mumbles.

I sit down next to him on the bed and stare at my hands, the hands of a forty-six-year-old man riddled with carpal tunnel from twenty years of typing. I wonder why these hands are such insensitive bastards, why they scar and hit and destroy things with the abandon of an adult ego run amok. I can justify just about anything really, crime, embezzlement, knocking down old ladies, but I just can't find the neat rationalization for hurting my children. Every great liar meets his match eventually, and I cannot save myself on this score.

"Look, Dale," I begin, turning to accusing eyes. "I'm sorry. I should have listened to you … I have no excuse for yelling at you. I am sorry."

"You always take her side," he sobs, fresh tears coming to his eyes. *"All you do is yell at me and take her side! "*

I clasp my hands. What he says is not untrue. I have taken to yelling at my son whenever an unreasonable expectation surfaces. Why I would yell at my son when I would gladly die for him? I have no idea. But there is this duality. As adults, we want the easy, smart child who reacts like an automaton to our every wish and desire. We want the child who can perform and then gracefully melt into the television until adult prerogative beckons again. But the child who is sensitive, who thinks before acting, who we perceive as slow, lax, lazy, who doesn't move to our overcharged schedule—he is then suspect, and we blow down on his small ego with adult fury. I am guilty as charged.

"You're right. I do take her side," I murmur, nodding. "And it's unfair. It's unfair because I try and head off her crying, and that's not right. I apologize for doing that, Dale, and I'll try and listen more before jumping to conclusions. I promise you I will do better. I love you, son, and I don't want to be ... the type of father who doesn't listen to his son."

Dale junior wipes his eyes, staring down at his nimble hands, so sensitive to all the things I have lost.

"You always say that, and then you do the same thing," he mutters.

Guilty as charged again.

"You're right, Dale. But give me one more chance. I don't want to be a jerk of a father ... you going to give your old man one more chance?"

Dale junior hesitates, then nods and allows me to hug him. I feel his ribs and smell the scent of boy sweat in his hair. So uncaring, so happily oblivious these children of ours are that we should think we have some sort of answer. The sniffing is slowing down, the nose wipes less frequent. I look around his room and see a White Sox poster.

"Hey ... what do you say you and I go to game this year."

Dale looks at me, his eyes wide.

"You mean the Sox?"

"Absolutely."

He looks down at his hands, suddenly shy.

"Can Papa come with us?"

I stare at my son, happy he wants to be with his grandfather, but a little chagrined our outing should be pluralized with my father. D. T. senior has only been in my house twenty-four hours and already wormed himself into the heart of my son while I stumble around clumsily outside.

"Well, sure he can," I nod. "If he's in town."

Dale junior looks at me with real alarm.

"He'll still be living with us, right?"

I look at my only son and put my arm around him. I can only marvel at the unconditional love children bestow on adults who are so fucked up. Dale junior leans against me, and I realize then it's been a long time since I've hugged my son.

"I hope not," I say, winking at the boy of my dreams.

The two flat we bought when the credit line was young and we were foolish reminds me of Oakland. It is a mustard-colored frame structure with spires and the faded inspiration of the 1890s. The paint is peeling with long shards of baked, lead-based paint hanging off like curled wallpaper, boards missing on the porch, and gutters sagging. We bought on a street of other similar houses with steam heat, creaky floors, bulls-eye molding, sloped, leaning garages, and a city lot. If location is the key to real estate, then maybe we did all right. We are two blocks off downtown Charleston and there have been rumors of an urban renewal project on the boards for several years.

"I don't think anybody's home, son."

I had momentarily forgotten about D. T. senior, who had been finishing up a phone call in the car. I ring the doorbell again to my upstairs tenant .

"Looks to me like someone kicked in this boy's door," he murmurs, fingering a splintered hasp I had just noticed.

I don't come over to our rental property often. I am not the man to own a dwelling where others reside, because I am not handy and that seems to be a prerequisite for having rental properties. Whenever I do come over, I am greeted by the glares of the neighbors who regularly inform me they are calling the city because of numerous violations. I usually just cut the grass and leave.

I tentatively open the door and peer up into the gloom of the staircase.

"Chad!"

There is no sound. I breathe in my upstairs tenant's Marlboro 100s lingering in the worn-through carpet of the foyer. My father is still examining the carnage from the last time Chad couldn't find his keys. The jam of the door is splintered white and the deadbolt is hanging on by a thin sliver of pine. It is cold inside and I remember Chad's complaint of the heat and my promise a week ago to fix it. I peer up the stairs again, trying to gauge the effects of alcohol and possibly heroin on the body of a two-hundred-and-fifty-pound male. I don't relish the prospect of barging in on my tenant with his shirt off and tattoos on. Chad is very stout, hairy, and has the burly strength of a man who eats primarily beef and drinks primarily beer.

I switch on the light in the foyer and nothing happens. I flip the switch and remember the city of Charleston had let me know my tenant had not paid his bill. The letter went on to say that I would be fined fifty dollars a day until service was restored.

"Is he there?"

"I don't know," I admit, staring up into the darkened cavern of Chad's stairs. "I guess there's only one way to find out."

I look at my father in his immaculate blue suit and power tie. He looks like an undercover FBI or an IRS agent. I start up the stairs with him close behind. We are a couple of agents of the law or at least of the landlord police. I reach the top of the stairs, confronted once again with probably the stupidest thing I have done in the last twelve months—buying a rental property. Dirty clothes are piled in the hallway and in small mountains in the bedroom and living room. A television is covered with Styrofoam food containers and beer bottles. Cartons of Marlboro 100s are stacked in careful order against one wall. The kitchen is a sculpture of piled trash and putrefying food. I note the same waffle on the counter I had seen three months before—a testament to modern preservatives.

"Good God!" D. T. senior's mouth is open. "This man is one P-I-G," he intones in Elmer Fudd parlance.

I ignore my father's exclamation. My tenant has pulled me to my senses once again with the unflinching reality of a fossilized waffle, and I try to recall the demonic presence that persuaded me to buy this property. I blame it squarely on the media. Inured to the demise of the stock market, popular media proclaimed wealth to be found in the purchase of investment properties. Donald Trump slipped in with the morning news and I took twenty-five thousand dollars from the credit line and a month later closed on the yellow 1892 frame two flat in downtown Charleston. Then the bottom dropped out of the housing market, leaving me with the legacy of my folly.

"Well, now, this boy has some interesting artwork."

I turn and see a framed collection of soaps from the twenties designed for people of color—*Nigger Soap, Coon Soap, Uncle Remus Soap, Black Face.*

"For yo' black face," D. T. senior reads out loud.

"That should make you feel right at home, Dad."

D. T. senior frowns and looks at me.

"Now I don't go in for that kind of racism, son."

What kind of racism my father does go in for, I'm not sure. Right now I am trying to understand what to do with this cold, dark apartment. It is then I see the open window with the brown extension cord snaking over the sill. I pull the window up farther, following the weaving brown cord down into a basement window.

"That sonofabitch!"

"What's that, son?"

"He's running his lights and appliances off the downstairs tenant's electricity!"

D. T. senior sticks his head out the window. I see a neighbor shake her head at the two slumlords. She puts down her blind, and I return to the apartment.

"Well, he is a resourceful man."

"He's a drunk," I mutter.

D. T. senior steps back from the window, eyeing the bags of piled trash and beer bottles and various forms of organic decomposition. He fingers the waffle and examines a hardened piece of toast shellacked with month old jelly.

"You have to throw this man out, son."

"Thanks for the newsflash, Dad."

D. T. senior plants his feet and stares at the contagion.

"You can't have a man like this defiling your abode."

I look at him appraisingly.

"You going to pay the mortgage, Dad?"

D. T. senior frowns.

"That's not the point, son. You can't have someone like this living in your building."

I feel the frustration that is my father—the unreality that keeps him on the merry-go-round of jobs and broken marriages. It is the ascribing of values where there are none and practicality takes a back seat.

"What do I care how he lives?" I grumble, kicking a beer bottle away. "As long as I get the rent."

"Then you are nothing but a slum lord, boy."

I shrug. "I'm a slum lord."

"Boy, you have to have morals—"

"Oh, give me a break—"

It is then we both hear the reptilian gurgle of a man. The snore comes low and guttural, then smoothes out to heavy, labored breathing. My father and I stare at each other. I am suddenly cognizant of the fact I have violated the rights of my tenant by entering his apartment.

"I think yo' boy is here," D. T. senior whispers, looking toward the living room.

I wonder then if Chad "packs" and decide it is probable. A man who feels no need to fix his kicked in door or empty his trash and who posts *Nigger Soap* on his wall has a good chance of owning a loaded gun. I glance toward the stairs as D. T. senior nods toward the living room.

"Son, I think your tenant is on the premises somewhere."

"I think you're right," I murmur, walking into the family room of Chad's life.

The couch is empty, yet there is the definite low buzz of a man breathing. This is the belly of the beast. The only accommodations are the television and the couch and the low-slung table peppered with cigarettes, bottles, and dust-covered remotes. DVDs shine in the morning sun like flying saucers next to ashtrays and wine bottles. A bong pokes toward the ceiling like an obelisk. It is the college room of yesteryear.

"You might not find him in all this mess—"

I hear a low snort, not unlike pigs I have heard on farms. D. T. senior and I look at the couch again, then I notice a space behind it.

"Give me a hand, Dad," I say, grabbing one end.

D. T. senior leans toward the couch the color of camouflage, and we pull and get nowhere. It is a sleeper and very heavy.

"Hold on now …one, two, three!"

My father leans down and I yank the end of the couch from the wall.

"I'll be *damned!*" D. T. senior is breathing hard. "*How* do you think this boy got back there?"

The back hair is a mat of curly brown. There is the image of a corpse seen in so many horror movies. Chad is wedged into a face-down fetal position and I am dubious about disturbing his slumber. One never knows how a man waking from behind a couch will react. Chad suddenly stirs, then rises up slowly like a man from the dead. He turns around and yawns, moving his mouth experimentally.

"Morning," he says, nodding to D. T. senior.

My father nods back.

"Morning."

Chad scratches himself. He is a hairy man in his BVDs. He stares at me and nods, scratching again the plethora of inked figures crossing his chest, coughing, and clearing his throat as any man would after a solid eight hours.

"Hello, Dale."

"Hey, Chad. Getting a few winks behind the couch?"

Chad frowns, scratching his beard. He yawns again, looking around.

"Yeah … I must have dropped the remote behind the couch and fallen asleep when I went to get it."

This is a logical explanation for a man sleeping behind his own couch. He stands up, his belly clearing his briefs by a good three inches. He extends his hand to my father.

"Chad Hampton."

"Dale Hammer Senior."

Chad chews on this and then looks at me.

"Your father?"

"Right."

He yawns and stretches to the ceiling.

"You guys use your key to get in?"

"No, the door's been kicked in," I reply, nodding to the stairs.

Chad frowns.

"Yeah, I've been a little worried about security lately. I don't want anybody to steal my possessions."

I look around at the *possessions* and imagine the chagrin of any would-be burglar. He faces me, and I avert the Chad manhood pushing toward me.

"You here for the rent?"

"Yes."

"Okay, I've got a check for you."

Like a man moving through an organized office, Chad moves some clothes, pushes aside some Styrofoam containers, then picks up a check.

"Sorry it's late. I've been a little slow."

I take the check, emboldened from the accomplishment of my mission.

"Listen, Chad, I got a call from the power company—"

He nods, pulling on some jeans from the mountain of clothes in his living room.

"Yeah, I gotta get by and pay that."

"They're going to fine me fifty a day if you don't."

Chad shakes his head at the chicanery of corporate America.

"All right … You going to get the heat fixed?"

"I'll get someone over today."

"The toilet's leaking too, and I think the shower is leaking down into Rose's apartment—that's what she told me anyway," he says and shrugs. "By the way, tell the bitch to quit calling the police when I have a few friends over. It's very embarrassing to have police come to your door when one is entertaining colleagues."

I stare at the man that is Chad. I envision a tea party among the trash and moldering waffles, a collection of *colleagues* seated around the empty beer cans and last month's fast food.

"She wrote me a letter." I pause. "She says you were pretty loud … something about needles and drugs …"

Chad snorts in disdain.

"She's fucking nuts. She better talk to her son. *He's* smoking pot in the basement and has a band that he practices with down there. I can't get any sleep, and if it continues, Dale, I will have to consider other accommodations."

The Hilton, the Palmer House, surely other accommodations are beckoning the man who sleeps behind couches.

"I'll talk to her about her son," I murmur.

D. T. senior gestures to the rack of soap on the wall.

"That is some interesting types of soap you have here, sir. I am from the South, and I have not seen these type of … hygiene products before."

"I bought that at an estate sale," Chad says, nodding slowly. "I see it as emblematic of the Jim Crow South that still exists in a much more muted form today. While the civil rights movement addressed the most egregious aspects of segregation, my contention is that the mores and social habits of Southerners remain unchanged, and the Jim Crow South is still as prevalent today as it was fifty years ago."

He turns and looks at D. T. senior, tapping the soap. "While this soap seems outlandish to our present-day sensibilities, I contend it is merely the same racism today packaged differently." He pauses. "I did my Thesis on the philosophical origins of Southern Society."

D. T. senior and I exchange glances of mutual shock while Chad *the scholar* pulls on a T-shirt from another pile of clothes, walking into some army boots and slipping on a trench coat. The image of the crazed, drug-induced fiend is replaced by the Renaissance man who snoozes behind couches.

"It's amazing, isn't it?" Chad flips up his collar, pausing by the framed soaps of bigotry. "The complete *ignorance* of certain regions of this country."

I have a fantasy about reentering academia. In my fantasy, I become a professor at a college that is in New England and teach literature at a boy's school in a creaky old plantation house. I am revered by the boys and enjoy a pipe in front of my fire in the evenings and read drowsy literature and grade papers. This fantasy has nothing to do with the city college where I was a sweaty adjunct teacher working for pennies. In my fantasy, I will be nestled in New England, surrounded by like-minded people who discuss literature and the arts as we wilt our lives away in literary nirvana.

Whenever my life becomes intolerable, I revert to this fantasy—a sort of "Break glass and pull in case of high distress." I was thinking about this because at various times, I have considered the life of Chad. I envision a life of sleeping behind my couch, clothes at the ready, food for sustenance on the counter, mindless hours of television in an alcoholic haze that ends when I retrieve my remote. The thought that an educated man could not fall so low always saved me from this scenario. Now, another thought crashes in right behind this one—maybe Chad knows something I don't.

The scholar has gone off to find breakfast at some friendly diner that will serve a waffle not less than a few minutes old. D. T. senior and I wait outside the door of Rosa Casino, watching Chad become a small figure on the street. He is a man who walks with a jaunty step, his unlaced combat boots still audible to us, his long trench coat swinging in the wind. He personifies that famous Janis Joplin line, "Freedom's just another word for nothing left to lose ..."

The front door swings back as a woman with short black hair and a New York mouth sticks her head out. Her eyes are dark and predatory; she glances around and then hits me with the landlord glare.

"Yeah, Dale," she asks with the irritation that is Rosa Casino.

"Hello, Rosa. I was in the neighborhood and just picked up the rent from Chad ... I thought I would do the same with you."

The small, dark eyes narrow, the nose tweaks, and the neck extends.

"Didn't you get my note?"

"The one about Chad? Yes, I received your—"

"No, I sent you another one, but I also want to know what you're going to do about that *creep* upstairs!"

I nod, knowing what Rosa is referring to. I had received the note before on pink stationary with "Rosa Casino" in bold script across the top. A short, to the point, minimalist epistle.

Dear Dale,

Because of a loss of clients from my massage business, I will be unable to pay this month's rent.

Rosa Casino.

I have received notes from Rosa before like this. The woman has balls the size of canastas. She doesn't even bother to dodge me like other self-respecting tenants.

"Rosa ... did you get my messages giving you until the fifteenth to pay the rent?"

She frowns.

"I have a client right now, Dale, can we discuss this later?"

"Rosa, my mortgage payment is going to be late," I say more forcefully. "I need the rent!"

The two dark butterflies meet over her brow. The screen opens just wide enough for her mouth.

"Well that's too fucking bad, Dale. You should have thought of that before you decided not to fix any of the things I requested!"

This is true. I have been delinquent on many of Rosa's complaints, but the Rosa Casino litany of problems overwhelms the landlord mind. Many times I receive voicemails reciting violations of codes, clogged drains, washer malfunctions, dryer problems, leaks, windows broken, stoves not working, refrigerators that need defrosting, and grass that needs cutting. I ignore these complaints because to fix one would validate the rest and I had found Rosa usually forgot 90 percent of her complaints. I see now my dalliance is being used against me.

Rosa whips the space just below my nose.

"You *yuppies* think you can push working people around—well, you can't! I'll get you the rent when I get some more clients and you fix the problems I have told you about *numerous* times!"

I put my foot in the door she is already closing. The Rosa nose is an inch from mine, and there is a strong waft of black coffee on the Casino breath.

"Don't try using strong-arm tactics with me, Dale! That drunk upstairs is stealing electricity from me and every time he showers, it rains on my computer. I could call the city and have you cited for *many violations*, so just be glad I'm *cool.*"

"What—"

"If I may interject, madam."

I had forgotten about my father standing behind me, quietly observing his son the landlord. I turn around and hold up my hand.

"Dad, let me handle this!"

Rosa glances at D. T. senior. She frowns.

"Who's this? The fucking FBI?"

"Dale Hammer at your service, madam."

"He looks like the man," Rosa sniffs, using a term going back to a generation that thought it would die before it got old.

"If I may make a suggestion," D. T. senior continues, generating the languidness of tongue that bewitched three wives and a not a few corporations. "Might we have a minute of your time so we can work out our differences amicably?"

Rosa stares at D. T. senior, pauses, then miraculously steps back and gives up the screen door.

"I can give you a couple of minutes and then I have to get back to my *client.*"

We enter the Rosa Casino domicile. It is cleaner than Chad's, but of course the city dump is cleaner than Chad's apartment. The *client* is a large fat man lying prone in the middle of the room with a single towel draped over his ass. Rosa's clients lay on an ironing board table with a folding Oriental shade cradling their heads. Incense is burning and new age music floats out from a boom box in the corner. The man has a scruffy beard, one jowl pressed against the massage table.

"How ya doing," he says to D. T. senior.

"Dale Hammer."

"Nice suit," the man says and nods. "Brooks Brothers?"

D. T. senior hooks his thumbs in his vest.

"I wear no other."

"I'll be with you in a minute Al," Rose hollers over.

"No problem, take your time," he says, raising his hand. "It's just so relaxing to lay here and not hear kids screaming at me."

I notice an electric guitar and an amplifier in one corner next to stacks of CDs. A sepia-toned picture of a Spanish woman is on the wall. There is the faint undertone of a computer game coming from the back bedroom. The rock-and-roll son is in the vicinity.

I turn to my tormentor.

"That's another thing, Rosa. Who told you you could use the downstairs for your kid to be a rock star?"

Her eyes narrow and I realize then what a small woman Rosa is. Five two in heels and not much over a hundred pounds, she is wearing a black leotard shirt and looks every bit like a Puerto Rican mother from the Bronx. Rosa rolls her eyes, hacking the air.

"You told me he could practice down there, or are you going to lie about that like you lie about everything else?"

"I never—"

"Son." My father has stepped between us. "If I may ..."

I throw up my hands, secretly glad to have someone else duel with this woman.

"It seems to me Rose—"

"Rosa," she snaps.

D. T. senior smiles like the weatherman and begins a slow inventory of the apartment. He pauses in front of the picture of the Spanish woman.

"Your mother?"

"Yes!"

My father nods slowly and turns.

"Very beautiful."

Rosa shrugs, but murmurs, "Thank you."

Al watches from the table as D. T. senior takes a leisurely stroll around the living room. He is touching various items, picking up a picture of her son.

"How old?"

"Thirteen."

"I remember that age ... they are just beginning to act like they are twenty."

D. T. senior continues his tour, slowly draining the room, riveting his audience of three. He comes back to the center of the room and gestures to the room at large.

"It seems to me, *Rosa,* that you have some grievances you feel have not been addressed."

"Yeah, look at my computer ... *look at it!*"

Al, D. T. senior, and I turn as one. Sure enough, there is a pool of water next to her monitor with salty water stains on the desk. Black plastic garbage bags are taped over the monitor and the computer itself. Even now, a solitary drip falls from the ceiling.

"Every time that *fat fuck* upstairs takes a shower, I gotta put out a pot to keep him from drowning my computer!"

D. T. senior turns to me accusingly.

"Dale, are you aware of this problem?"

"I told him," Rosa nearly screams. "The same way I told him the motion light is out by the garage and the dryer doesn't get hot."

D. T. senior frowns at the slumlord and shakes his head.

"Have you been made aware of these problems?"

"Dad, let me handle this—"

"No, your dad is doing a better job," Rosa proclaims, nodding to D. T. senior like he's her attorney.

I feel a thud to back of my head, the arrow in my back.

"Well, son, have you addressed Ms. Casino's concerns?"

Rosa perks up at the use of her surname. Al is looking at me like I'm something that crawled up on the beach.

"I haven't fixed some of these problems," I sputter. "But that has nothing to do—"

D. T. senior holds up his hand for silence and turns back to his client.

"Then, Rosa, the reason you are holding back the rent check is because your grievances have not been addressed."

"Right … *right*," she nods righteously. "That's why I'm mot paying the rent."

"Hey, Mr. Hammer, are you an attorney?" Al yells from his table.

D. T. senior pivots, smiling faintly.

"No, I'm in sales," he answers, handing him a card.

"You really should be an attorney," Al says and nods.

"Thank you, Al. My father was a renowned attorney in Mississippi. Managed Senator Herrin's campaign in '46. He was the lead attorney for the B&E railroad for twenty years and carried Mississippi for the Senator."

"Is that right?" Al turns to his side, giving us all a shot of a very large scrotum. "That was a hotly contested race pitting the labor unions against the steel industry, if I recall."

D. T. Hammer turns back to the man whose dick now lies outside his towel.

"That's amazing."

Al shrugs nonchalantly, crossing his legs over his penis.

"I'm a bit of a political historian ... my father ran the twenty-second ward in Chicago for years, and my grandfather before him."

"We need to talk further," D. T. senior nods as Rosa pulls the towel over Al's privates.

"So ..." D. T. senior turns back to me, and then to Rosa. "Here is what I propose; you give my son three days to fix the said grievances."

"All right," Rosa nods tentatively, glaring at me, smiling at my father.

"You will give my son a check for the rent postdated by three days ... this will give you the assurance that the problems will be remedied by the three days. If the problems are not fixed by then, then you will stop payment on your check." D. T. senior pauses. "I know it is not your *intention*, Rosa, to not pay your rent, as this is a basic obligation, but you also have rights as a tenant, and your complaints must be addressed."

There is a moment of silence, and the axiom of my father comes back to me ... *don't talk!* Many deals are lost when the salesman speaks too soon. *Don't talk.* Rosa stands in the room, glancing at D. T. senior, then myself. A car goes by outside. My tenant walks over to her purse and pulls out her checkbook. She writes the check and hands it to D. T. senior.

"Tell him he has three days."

"Smooth," Al says, his dick falling free again.

D. T. senior turns to me.

"You have three days, Dale, to remedy Ms. Casino's grievances."

I mutter and grumble, pocketing the check.

"Smooth," Al nods again.

"Very good ... well, we will keep you no longer from your client, madam," D. T. senior says, shaking the smiling Rosa's hand.

"Thank you for coming," she says brightly and for a moment, Rosa Casino looks almost attractive.

D. T. senior does a quick victory tour of the room.

"It was nice to meet you, Al."

"It's been a real pleasure, sir," he says, shaking my father's hand, towel falling. "You might consider the law."

D. T. senior hooks his thumbs again in his vest and nods somberly.

"I have always thought the courtroom would be a fascinating venue."

"You should think about it, sir," he says and nods seriously.

We go to the door, and Rosa looks at me.

"Feel free to bring your father next time you come over. I'll give him a free massage."

My mouth drops as I realize Rosa Casino is coming on to my father. He then bows, rolling out his hand.

"I look forward to our next meeting with relish, madam."

"Smooth," comes from the naked Al behind her.

The Riverside Diner dates back to when mills and generators shoaled the riverbank and the diner enjoyed the status of the only diner overlooking the mighty Fox. There is a faint smell of the musty sediment in the tired carpet; the waitresses look like women who have had to man buckets and mops on not a few occasions. The river provides a vista of trickling brown water while one inhales eggs, protoplasmic omelets, or the *Riverside* burger—a half pound of glistening beef pooling in its own juices.

We have just slid into a booth for breakfast. I watch the muddy sludge while D. T. senior strikes up a conversation with the waitress.

"Have you been doing this long, Betty?"

Betty, devoid of teeth and short of temperament, is not up for University of Mississippi charm at this hour of the day. She tortures her gum and raises one drawn on eyebrow, the bloody mouth curling up on one side.

"Too long ... what you having?"

My father leans back and taps the plasticized menu.

"I don't really know. Now, tell me, what would *you* recommend, Betty?"

This is not a question Betty gets often. I am sure she is married to a man named Hank who works in the local body shop and is probably the best fender man in town and the biggest question Hank poses to her is where are his goddaamn cigarettes—after that, Betty is not called upon to answer anything. But here is Mr. Suave from the South looking at her like he could bed her or order eggs. I am amazed at how a prescient salesman like D. T. senior can miss the clues. Betty is not a good prospect; in fact, she's not a buyer at all. She doesn't respond to the refined banter of D. T. senior's generation where each encounter is laced with possibilities. Betty has been brought up on stupefying reality shows and my father has already been parked in the "some old coot" category.

"I don't know ... eggs are good," Betty says and shrugs.

"What *kind* of eggs, Betty?"

Betty shifts her weight and her eyes narrow. The party is over, but D. T. senior is just warming up, probing the prospect, fattening the goose. She clamps down on her gum.

"Look, I'll bring you your food, but I ain't going to order it for you."

"Dad—"

"You're right Betty, I am sorry ... but a woman of your *experience* must know the menu ... now how long did you say you've worked here?"

D. T. senior has brought out the heavy artillery—twinkling blue eyes, ingratiating smile. Betty shakes her head, deciding for the hundredth time to get another job.

"I didn't. Listen, old man, I gotta get to my other customers ... when you click on from your Alzheimer's, let me know, will you?"

Betty is now moving, and I yell after her.

"Two coffees!"

She glances back and shakes her head. I stare at my father.

"*Dad,* why didn't you just order the fricking food?"

D. T. senior already has his cell phone out, opening his day timer. He puts on his glasses, beginning to inscribe the day with a gold Cross pen.

"Just having a little fun, my boy," he murmurs.

"But she didn't think it was fun."

"That's her problem," he says, dialing, and then holding the phone to his ear.

I look at D. T. senior's shaking hand. I wonder about this genetic inheritance, bringing about the images of my grandmother, who had Parkinson's. What is amazing is how the fountain of energy has not dimmed over the years. I know D. T. senior will not fade out like some rural circuit getting weaker, but more like a circuit breaker that suddenly trips as he runs for a plane.

"Hello, Doris. I just wanted to let you know that I love you and whatever you decide, I am supporting you one hundred percent. Please call me at your earliest convenience ... I love you."

He closes his phone and looks up, following the figure of a waitress much younger than the recalcitrant Betty.

"Dad, how many messages have you left your wife?"

"Oh I don't know ... a few."

I stare at him.

"Dad, I've heard eight myself … you must have left her others I didn't hear."

D. T. senior finds another young waitress, following her with the blues eyes capable of undressing a woman in seconds.

"I've left her a few messages," he murmurs.

I know now that he has bombarded the hapless Doris with missals of undying love. *Repetition.* I learned this as a boy. A request to take out the trash was followed up by five more requests. *Repeat thyself until you wear them down.* D. T. senior isn't anything if not the persistent salesman. He overwhelms with thudding repetition, wearing down the prospect with repeated salvos of low-level insistence. I was sure Doris had disconnected her phone and barricaded her door at the unrelenting barrage that is my father.

Out of nowhere Betty returns and takes pity on us.

"Here's your coffee," she says, setting down two mugs and some creamers. "Do you guys know what you want yet?"

The gum is back in motion and the weight parked on one hip. Betty is not unattractive in a fleshy, used up way. D. T. senior lights up like the weatherman; twinkling blue eyes at the ready, the engaging smile, the distinguished gray goatee—who wouldn't be this man's friend and confidant?

"Ah, Betty, I knew you would come back to me, and I was just considering one of your omelets, but I don't know which one and—"

"Two eggs over easy with a side of bacon and a Denver omelet for my father," I interrupt, seeing the narrowing eyes and the flattening mouth.

"All right then," she says glancing at D. T. senior with the same regard someone would give a street person.

I lower my voice.

"Dad … you almost did it again!"

166

He looks up innocently.

"Did what, son?"

"You almost drove her off again! She doesn't want to have a conversation; she just wants us to order the food!"

D. T. senior now has out a blue Waterman pen, circling a number, jotting himself a note.

"As I said before, that's her problem, boy."

This is what drove my mother crazy up to the day they divorced—D. T. senior is fundamentally oblivious to the needs of other people. Someone could be bleeding in the street and he would ask them directions. The strength of any good salesman is not to hear objections and my father is incapable of considering the wants and desires of any other human.

I take a deep breath and try again.

"Dad, it was going to be *our* problem … not everyone wants to be sold. "

He frowns.

"Don't know what you mean, boy," he murmurs.

"I mean, the world doesn't care about a lot of salesman schmoozing anymore. People are too busy for that shit."

D. T. senior shakes his head as if I have just blasphemed in church.

"People are never too busy to converse, my boy."

"Yes they are, Dad," I say tiredly. "Most of them are just trying to get through their day."

"Well then," he says, closing his day timer. "That is their loss."

I watch D. T. senior check his tie and flick a crumb off his suit. He does one more survey of the restaurant. He is the consummate morning man, at his peak before nine AM. I wonder where he will funnel such energy now that he is not employed, and then I know the answer. He will funnel it into whatever he is doing—driving waitresses, mailmen, and the unfortunate street person crazy. He leans back against the faded green vinyl.

"So, how is the writing going, boy?"

This is out of left field and I give the question the inflection it deserves—I shrug, grunt, look away, and shrug again.

"It's going."

D. T. senior looks at me for a long moment, then shakes his head.

"Well, now there's your ticket, boy! You get one book that hits and you have it made and I can live on your back forty. "

"I'll get right on that," I murmur.

My father was my biggest booster in the lottery of mid-list authors hitting the bestseller list. He understood success in the blanket assumptions most middle-class people carry—*the one in a million hit is just a hop, skip, and a jump away for the rock star, movie star, and novelist. One hit out of the park, and you are set for life, you lucky sonofabitch.*

Never mind that the odds against hitting this proverbial homer make a lottery ticket a surer way to the warm milk of the American dream. Never mind I did everything short of climbing into Oprah Winfrey's limousine to get my book into her book club. D. T. senior can really only understand literary endeavor in its proclivity to hit the bell, cash in the chips, and get the winner out of the middle-class grind. After that, I am wasting my time.

"I always said that when you make it, then I am going to retire and enjoy the good life, boy," he nodded, dialing his phone.

I feel strange pangs of guilt. I too nursed this fantasy. Just a little luck, a little help from Oprah or a smitten *New York Times* reviewer and *wham*, I'm on the *NY Times* bestseller list and game over. Not such a hard climb after all. But I am no longer pursuing the burning story, and this all seems like a thirteen-year-old boy dreaming about becoming a professional baseball player or president.

"Jim … Dale Hammer here. I want to know if you heard back

on my contract and what the company is going to offer me in terms of a buyout ... my number is 708-565-5432 ... talk to you soon."

He puts his phone away again.

"Is that guy with your old company?"

"Who?"

"The guy you just called."

"Yes," he says darkly. "The cocsuckah."

D. T. senior says this loud enough for a woman in a booth to turn around.

"Dad ... are they going to give you some kind of buyout?"

"You bet your ass," he says and nods. "I have told them in no uncertain terms that if they do not give me acceptable terms, then they'll have a *whopper* of an age-discrimination suit on their hands ... *the cocksuckahs.*"

The woman from the other booth looks up again. I lean in closer, lowering my voice.

"Dad, was there anything in your contract with this company concerning *severance* pay?"

D. T. senior clasps his hands, doing another round of gawking at young asses and firm breasts. He strokes his goatee, putting on his reading glasses, picking up the menu Betty had declined to pick up.

"Well ... not specifically, my boy. But it was always implied as part of my arrangement."

I feel a cold sweat break out. Heat pours out of the front of my shirt. I now see the true landscape D. T. senior and I had been hacking our way through. I always assumed my father had the core survival instincts of a fox and that this latest twist in the D. T. senior roller coaster would prove to be another rube, another hidden canary in the coalmine. Now I see my dad might really be out on his ass.

"You mean ..." I breathe deeply. "You had no *severance clause,*

Dad?"

He sits back in the booth, his power tie bowing out over the starched white shirt. D. T. senior looks very donnish, holding his menu, looking over his glasses—a man in control of his destiny. Perception is reality. Remember that, boy.

"I don't work that way, son. I'm more concerned with my situation at the company, not what's going to happen when I leave. But they know what *will happen* if they don't do the honorable thing."

I feel a great hammer swinging down from the heavens, hitting the gong of my life. The man who produced a son who believed he could beat incredible odds and conquer New York publishing had just laid the fattest of eggs. This kind of talk always drove Wendy crazy. She could never understand how D. T. senior could ascribe the values of an English major to billion-dollar corporations. I could never explain to her that for D. T. senior's generation, companies were still accountable. I could never explain my father would personalize a company until he expected that entity to act with the moral certitude of an individual.

I shake my head, staring down at the worn Formica.

"Dad, they aren't going to give you *anything* unless it's in your contract."

D. T. senior drops his menu as if I have just missed some concept in the Riverside Diner seminar on corporate shenanigans.

"That's not necessarily true, boy."

"Yes it is, Dad," I say dully. "Do you have anything saved?"

"Of course I do."

I rub my eyes and see my own plight again. I know this is a lie. I know Doris has been taking lots of vacations. I know D. T. senior has been living paycheck to paycheck for years. I know this because this is how I live. My suspicion D. T. senior has reached the end of the working phase of his life has been confirmed. I stare at the man writing again in the day timer, glancing at his cellular phone for a call from his wife or his former employer— the man in a Brooks Brothers suit and a power tie without a pot to piss in.

He suddenly looks up and smiles at the woman who would gladly stick a salad fork through his heart.

"Ah, Betty, you have returned to me," he says as our food arrives.

11

"Get Gordon in!"

–Mission Control after Astronaut Dick Gordon blinded himself with sweat.

I see a sleek new hybrid in our drive with antique Christmas ornaments in the rear window, and I begin thinking about Christmas letters—the missives that land at our door informing the helpless about wonderful vacations, kids destined for the Olympics, and stock portfolios abounding. Wendy finds these seasonal epistles enlightening, enjoying the tidbits given now in two–sided, computer-generated flyers complete with color photos. I find it the next step in Andy Warhol's fifteen minutes of fame taken to its logical democratic denominator. The owner of the hybrid had sent us such a bulletin on the life of academics, a rambling Kerouac monologue written in the revelatory style of the cultural elite—informing us of trips to Africa with his African American wife and spectacular hikes with photos of Elliott Hammer in shorts and a safari hat—the Renaissance man complete.

The truth is I like my brother, but our ancient sibling rivalry had its roots in the twin pillars of older brother and fascist achiever—Elliott inherited the mantle of family artist, and I became his foil.

We have tried to forge a new relationship, but unreturned calls, slights, and outright rudeness over the years has slowly built up as barnacles on the good ship of brotherly love until it slowed to its present speed, wavering in empty lassitude—two forty-something men who have little use for each other.

I pull up behind the hybrid that is a sleek lime green. The antique ornaments glisten in the new light of day.

"Elliott's here."

D. T. senior looks up from his day timer and nods slowly.

"He must have got the word."

"Did you call him?"

My father frowns.

"No. I wonder if Doris told him."

I pull up behind the electric car and examine the ornaments again in the rear-view window. There are bloated antique bulbs, papier-mâché birds, a headless Santa, and the sharp edge of a Christmas star. Even though Christmas is a good two months away, Elliott is ever on the lookout for plastic Santas, old sleighs, and reindeers no one would claim. I imagine he stopped at some garage sale or garbage heap and picked up the ornaments on the way. He used to have parties where people would guess how many ornaments were on the Hammer tree and the number was in the thousands.

We go in through the garage and I am surprised to hear Elliott's wife. Apollonian is an angry black woman who switched gender preference for my brother; a no-nonsense English professor who takes trips to Africa frequently to dig up her ancestral roots. I look at my watch, confirming this is Tuesday and there are classes today.

We enter the living room and I see a man in Johnny Cash black, standing by the fireplace with one brogan up on the hearth. His hair is cut short in a blond Truman Capote delicate wave. Elliott is a multi-media professor with an emphasis on film and with his Buddy Holly glasses, he does look like a director. He holds his arms wide to D. T. senior.

"Father!"

They embrace in a sixties hug. Wendy is sitting on the couch next to Elliott's wife. Apollonian has Rastafarian braids and a tenting salmon -colored dress of some African design. She is a woman who eschews makeup, deodorant, and lets the hair under her arms flower. She plainly states her opinions in the tone of the dry English teacher. I am the one who introduced my brother to his wife. I had met her when I was teaching and she had just self-published a novel. She often speaks in the third person, announcing at family dinners that Apollonian Opokus will be signing copies of her new book at Barnes and Noble. She shamelessly promotes her own work, self-publishing her three novels with Xlibris, giving out cards at every occasion with a pen moniker, "Apollonian Opokus—NOVELIST." She has often included me in her Xilbris book-just out-yesterday fanfare, sending me chapters and invitations to book signings and parties.

"How are you doing, Father," Elliott asks, searching D. T. senior's face as if he has been beaten.

"Fine, son. Just fine, my boy."

Apollonian stands up and walks across the room and we are treated to another sixties embrace.

"Dale, I am so sorry."

I walk over and shake my brother's hand.

"How's it going, Elliott?"

He extends a limp fish.

"How are you, Dale?"

"Good ... no class today?"

Elliott prissily flattens his hair and gestures to Apollonian.

"We cancelled our classes when we heard what happened. We wanted to get out here right away."

I register the "we" that has become the subject in any Elliott

Hammer sentence. Between wives I see my brother and we go to the bars and the declarative "I" begins his sentences. Once Elliott is married, the singular is replaced with the plural, and my brother goes into the isolation mode that marks all his marriages.

"How did you find out?"

Elliott frowns, his eyes binding behind his horn rims.

"I called the house and Doris answered."

D. T. senior has sat down in a very old rocker.

"What did she say, Elliott?"

My brother starts moving the bracelets on his wrist—a dead giveaway that he is agitated.

"She said you lost your job and that you had separated."

Elliott has real pain in his voice. Apollonian stands suddenly and kneels by D. T. senior, taking his hand. She is in the yoga position with her long locks trailing to the floor. I can't help thinking she looks like she's offering her body up as sacrifice to the disquietudes of D. T. senior's life.

"I'm sorry, Father, but she was never worthy of you," my brother declares.

I see Wendy mouth these words and then meet my eyes. Elliott and Wendy go way back to when he was married to his first wife. They were Scott and Zelda while Wendy and I became June and Ward. She hated the box my brother put me in.

"Now, now … Doris is all right," D. T. senior says magnanimously.

Apollonian stares at him with tragic eyes.

"Dale, that is so good of you to say that after what she did to you."

"After you supported her all these years so she can fly back to New Jersey to drink and smoke with her Gloria Steinham cronies," brother Elliott grouses.

Doris had been vilified long before by my brother. Doris never worked in the classical sense and this was a proletarian sin as far as Elliott Hammer was concerned. He had conveniently ignored the fact that D. T. senior didn't require his woman to work. But to my brother, *Doris* had become the reason D. T. senior had no money, no pension, nothing short than the reason he had suddenly become old.

"The bitch," he mutters.

"Well now ... Doris just needs to work out her problems," my father eulogizes.

Brother Elliott nods and moves some more bracelets.

"Apollonian and I have been doing a lot of talking."

He suddenly stands up and walks over to my father. He takes his other hand and kneels by him. The couple at the altar with our Lord. Even D. T. senior looks uncomfortable with these open displays of filial devotion.

"We have it all worked out, and this is why we came over right away," Elliott continues.

Wendy has a strange look on her face now. It is the sight of my brother and his wife kneeling next to D. T. senior like he is the Pope.

"Father ..." Elliott pauses. "We want you to come live with us."

"He has a place to live," I blurt out.

My brother frowns at the obtuse student in the back row.

"Over a garage, Dale? I think our father deserves something better."

"I think your father be happier in a *real* bedroom," Apollonian nods.

There is a strange silence in the room. The assumption that my father doesn't want to be living over my garage is implicit in my brother's offer. I see now why class has been cancelled and the two academics have come rushing out to save the father from the bourgeois barbarian.

It is my wife who stands up and bails us all out.

"I think that's a great offer!"

I had put several two-by-three posters on the wall of my office announcing signings at Barnes and Noble, along with a blown-up picture from my dust jacket and an even larger picture of the cover of the third novel. When I was a boy, I knew a man who was a famous actor in Chicago and had then fallen into obscurity. Whenever I went over to my friend's house, he would take me upstairs to his father's office and we would stare at a wall covered with yellowed newspaper clippings, letters, awards, posters, and photographs of his father shaking hands with past presidents. I know now what that old actor gleaned as he thumbed up yellowed articles of past glory—that we do not disappear if we can become keepers of our own glory.

Elliott stares at the cardboard announcements and I feel self-conscious, like a boy who tacked ribbons to his walls even though everyone on the team received ribbons. He suddenly sits down on the futon, sinking farther than any normal man should into a bed. Elliott stares at his bracelets and then shakes his head.

"Father always liked you better."

It is a plain statement laced with the past. I know what my brother is saying; it is the reason my garage was the first port of call. My brother turns back to the posters. I thought he might comment, but I can think of not one instance where Elliott referenced any of my novels. Long ago I had become co-conspirator in the accepted way we would handle the publishing of D. T. Hammer novels—it didn't happen. It didn't matter how many novels I published, they would all be categorized with the trophies I received in high school for running track or wrestling. My novels were nothing more than nomenclature of D. T. Hammer—the fascist achiever. They did not admit the bearer entrance into the hallowed halls of art and literature. For Elliott and me to have any kind of relationship, my novels would have to become, in the old Soviet Union vernacular, *nonpersons.*

Elliott shrugs, still turning his bracelets.

"You were always his favorite. You did the sports and all that shit he loved."

I take this in, modulating my reply. To my brother, the fact I played sports in high school was a sellout to the powers that be. He saw this as nothing more than a maneuver by a master con artist to gain favor—never considering I might have *wanted* to play sports.

"But you could do anything and it was all right," I pointed out. "I had to stay to the set course."

Elliott looks down, and I can see myself behind him in a vest, staring into the distance in a very Hemingway pose. The book covers dance around his bowed head, shimming back and forth, *na na, hey hey, goodbye*—a taunting reminder that the years those books were written in were gone. In the early years, discovery quivers on the horizon and ideas come fresh, unadorned, and unintentionally original. Writing now is like writing in the fog of war.

Elliott frowns from his low-rider position on the futon.

"But Dad came to stay with you," he says and shrugs again. "He could have come to stay with us ... but he came to stay with you."

I know what my brother is saying. D. T. senior did not veer off the highway and park in front of the organic garden of my brother and his wife. The stated reasons D. T. senior stammered out in our living room were irrelevant. "Well, I really appreciate that, son, I really do, but I think I'm just going to stay here until I go back with Doris ... but I do appreciate ya'll's invitation, I really do." I knew this was smoke. Elliott knew this was smoke. The reason D. T. Hammer preferred to sleep over a garage would never see the light of day, but in lay terms it is something like this—I hold the secret prejudices and the same fucked up neurosis as the man.

D. T. senior had checked out to a large degree by the time his second son came along. He barely knew Elliott between his work, his golf, his disintegrating marriage, and the numerous affairs he had left all over the continental United States. I had gotten his name, the best years, and the unflinching loyalty any first-born son has with his father. In the South, there is nothing bigger than being the first.

"It was just geography, Elliott," I say, feeling bad for my brother. "My house is bigger and you know Dad, he needs his space."

He shakes his head slowly.

"We had the guest room all set up for him. He could have had his own bathroom. He could come and go by the back door. We are better set up for him than having him live over a fucking garage," he mutters, real anger spiking the corners of his eyes. "It's just the same old shit. He'd rather fucking sleep on a shitty bed in your *garage* than accept the hospitality I have always offered him and you never have."

This is true. Elliott was always calling my father, inviting him to dinner, taking him to Cubs games in Chicago. He would drive out to D. T. senior's house at the drop of a hat. He made things for D. T. senior, gave him golf bags he rescued from garage sales, and wrote poetry to dedicate the birthdays of my father. He *is* the better son, I readily admit. But D. T. senior can call me up and tell me a racist joke and I'll laugh. He can tell me a dirty joke and I'll laugh. I'll smoke a cigar with my father and not say a word, both of us enjoying the fine, burly tobacco after drinking bourbon on his porch. We are meat eaters and have little regard for our digestive tracks when it comes to inhaling ice cream, donuts, and gallons of coffee. We both complain of flatulence, getting fat, leer after women, and are capable of the inane conversation of Southern morons. These are things my brother the vegetarian, consumer of all things organic, attuned to the wants and needs of his liberated African American wife, master professor, drinking only with *colleagues,* wearing horn-rimmed glasses, lover of all things vintage, and careful counter of all things budgetary cannot claim.

"That's true," I offer. "But, who can figure Dad out?"

Elliott stares down at his black brogans.

"Well, we have to help him. This could really be a disaster."

"Right," I nod.

He looks up at me. "So, you ready?"

I raise my eyebrows and feel I missed some essential part of the conversation.

"Ready for what?"

"To go see that bitch, Doris!"

I stare at Elliott and feel another light go off on the control panel as the 737 D. T. Hammer takes a left turn and begins to lose altitude. The turbulence that is my father had sent me looking for smoother air, but I see now this has been in vain—D. T. senior has a way of bringing the storm with him.

"What do you mean?"

Elliott stands up, gesturing to the author on the wall.

"I mean, she's kicking him out of his house after he busted his ass supporting her! She can't do that!"

I pause, scratching my brow. I am still missing the germane point. I have never harbored any resentment for Doris. My respect for her only went up when I heard she had sent the Don Juan in Flosheims packing. But to my brother she is the devil incarnate.

"You're going to tell her that?"

"That's right."

"You're going to tell her she can't kick dad out?"

Elliott frowns at the slow student. Obviously, I was not listening to the lecture.

"She can't sponge off of Dad for five years and then fuck him over when he loses his job!"

I see the passion in my brother's eyes and consider he sees this as nothing short of saving D. T. senior from certain doom. Elliott gives no weight to Doris's side of the teeter-totter that kept D. T. senior from loneliness. He gives no points off for graduation from the D. T. senior Course in Marital Desertion. Elliott only sees my father like some hapless schoolboy ensnared by a scheming vixen. This actually goes back to the divorce between my mother and D. T. senior where party lines were drawn and D. T. senior was cast as victim and villain—it all came down to the view from your seat in the stadium.

Elliott is now standing up, gathering momentum as he crashes past the novelist D. T. Hammer gazing into the distance.

"I mean, what the fuck, Dale, what's Dad going to do? People die from loneliness, you know, and she's been whooping it up while he's been killing himself, and she can't just kick him out and move on!"

"I think Dad might have something to do with it too," I say gently.

He shakes his head at my reasoning.

"It doesn't matter. What's right is right, and she can't just *use him* until it's convenient and then throw him out the front door. I knew this was going to happen when she didn't get a job ... *I told Dad,* but now she's done it, and we can't fucking stand for it."

The injection of the "we" in the sentence has all the import of, "You are either for me or against me. I suddenly remember the look on Wendy's face when D. T. senior declined my brother's invitation. If D. T. senior remains in my garage, then there is probably a good chance Wendy and I will falter under the combined weight of money, filial pressures, and good old bourgeois living. This might be a way to inject my father back into his old life.

"All right," I say and nod slowly. "But I need your help on something else."

Elliott's eyes grow suspicious.

"Dad asked me to talk to Al about giving up the plot next to mom … so he can move in."

The professor evaluates the data. He sinks down into the futon, frowning, then nodding his conclusion.

"Yes. Dad should be there."

"I don't know about that," I say and shrug. "But I said I would talk to Al. I'm thinking of meeting him for lunch."

"Fine. I'll help you get the plot back, you help me with Doris."

"Deal," I say, not feeling good about either task.

Elliott stands up.

"Al should give it up anyway after he married that woman."

I lean back in my chair and pause.

"I'm not sure what Mom would think about all of this."

"She'd want Dad," brother Elliott states with absolute confidence.

I stare at the man who may not feel the favor of D. T. senior, but psychologically, they are dead ringers. Elliott has the same delusional quality my father shares and that leaves me as the unwitting devil's advocate to the *Abbot and Costello* of blind acceptance.

"We can get to Langford in three hours, and we'll come back tonight."

I pucker my lips, feeling this is a mistake again. Never mind that the logic of Brother Elliott is seriously flawed—the logic of the son who sees no wrong in the poster boy for matrimonial discord. If there ever was a man guilty of the cardinal sins against marriage, then it is my father—desertion, adultery, negligence, deception—the jury is just warming up.

"All right," I nod, hoping for a miracle. "Let's go."

Langford on first glance would not seem to be the perfect

D. T. senior habitat—a legacy of the rust belt with rampant unemployment, virulent crime, a healthy black population, and more riverboat casinos than any one town should have. But on the outer edge of this dismal town is Triton Shores, a white, upscale, thriving beach home community of pure white sand and million-dollar cottages. The incongruity of these two cities is accentuated by the fact there is no way to reach Triton Shores without driving through the heart of Langford. Like Oakland, Triton Shores is the white oasis reached after a river of squalor and despair.

The drive around Lake Michigan to Indiana is a drive of little visual interest. Steel mills, defunct and active, dot the shore and are smelled more than seen. Sulferous emissions betray the migration of Chicago industry and on sunny days, tiny, shimmering shards float in the air and blanket the Indiana landscape. The rust and chemical belt combine in one long, curving arc on the horseshoe of Lake Michigan, with Triton Shores on the farthest end of the shoe, just out of reach of the polluting effluvium.

My father's house is a brick ranch built into a hill of sand. Five blocks off the lake, the houses nestled in the foothills of Triton Shores are deceptively suburban with real lawns, trees, Malibu lights, and deck furniture, but beneath all of this is a sand dune that leaks out from under the tarred drives and brick patios. D. T. senior's house is built into one of these dunes with a sub-basement garage that is open. Two ELECT HILLARY signs dominate the front lawn. That my father married a woman who fronted protests in the sixties is really not surprising. D.T. senior always has prided himself on marrying progressive woman–a stepped up modern version of the Southern Belle who has an appreciation for our higher nature.

Elliott and I get out of the car to the screech of a miter saw.

"Doris is definitely home," I murmur.

"Good." Elliott says and nods, eyes focused, a man on a mission.

We climb up the hill of many cement stairs. Elliott and I huff up to the top and pause, taking in the vista of the neighborhood of Triton Shores, Indiana. The houses and cottages are all built on hills where vines obliterate chimneys and trees dwarf roof lines: a serendipitous mess of frame, ranch, and colonial homes.

"All right," Elliott says, getting his breath, reminding me of one of the great incongruities of Mr. and Mrs. Organic—they smoke.

"Let's go."

"What are we going to say?"

Elliott looks at me with professorial disdain.

"We are going to confront her on what she is doing to Dad and tell her that she has to leave the house and Dad stays."

"Oh," I say and nod. "I'm sure she'll be fine with that."

"She'll understand when I get done with her," he murmurs grimly.

I feel for the unsuspecting Doris. God hath no fury than that of a righteous organic professor on a soapbox. Elliott rings the bell as the miter saw whirls to a slow whine and stops. We listen to footsteps approaching the door, then a woman with long, flowing dark hair and safety goggles appears. Doris, even covered in sawdust with farmer jeans and safety goggles, is still imposing. She has large Semetic eyes that break us down in seconds. Her dark curly hair looks like it is still leading the protest marches she fronted in New Jersey in old blue pictures of a woman in calf high boots in front of a VW microbus. Now pushing sixty, Doris still looks like the type of woman who would tell you to eat the crusts to your bread because people are starving in India.

"Elliott and Dale, this is a surprise," she says with some reserve.

"Yes it is," I say.

"Doris, we have to talk," Elliott declares.

She pauses and something in my brother's diminutive,

dressed-in-black persona, warns her this is not a social visit. I consider the time it would take me to return to the car and just drive away. Elliott gestures into the house.

"Can we come in?"

Doris glances at me and I shrug slightly.

"All right, but the place is a mess," she says, giving us passage. "I'm working on my second orders of peckers."

Elliott and I exchange glances, then I remember Doris has started a business selling wooden letter openers that look like woodpeckers. My father has sung her praises many times as a woman who not only plays the organ and sings, but one who has already formed a women's group to front the second wave to "GET HILLARY ELECTED." There is a miter saw, saber saw, compressor, nail gun, saw horses, levels, and boards of every length. Doris has approached carpentry the way she raised her children after her husband joined a commune—she did it a step at a time and read from every manual printed under the sun.

"We can sit on the couch," she says, moving a stack of *Better Homes and Garden* and *Carpenter's Weekly*.

The couch is an L-shaped pit with lots of pillows. Elliott and I sit on one corner of the L, and Doris is on the other. My brother clasps his hands and pauses. His tone switches to that of a counselor, a professor of good will.

"Doris, Dale and I," he begins, glancing at me. "Drove out here to talk to you about the situation with our father."

Doris nods, but I can see her stiffen. She taught inner city kids in New Jersey before moving to Chicago as a trainer for IBM, where one Southern gentleman swooped her off her feet.

"Obviously, Dad has left, and you and he have some issues," Professor Hammer continues, stretching out his brogans. "That's *your* business … but our father just lost his job, and he now has nowhere to stay." The good professor pauses again, glances at me, then lets his missile fly. "The fact is, Doris, my father has supported you in a very lavish lifestyle for the last seven years, and I find it unacceptable that you have turned him out of his house! Frankly, I think you have to reconsider the situation."

Doris has grown stone cold during my brother's dissertation. She speaks like a man with a gun.

"You think I have to reconsider the situation?"

It is a rhetorical question dripping with knives and icicles. She is confirming the condemned's guilt, but the professor sees this as nothing more than a student reiterating the proctor's charge. Elliott nods, and I see him falter and I remember suddenly the Achilles' heel of one Elliott Hammer—*he is no good at confrontation.*

"The situation is, Doris, my father has no real retirement, and yet you let him go out day after day and *kill himself* while you work on your, your...peckers."

Doris has large lips and they are protruding now. They are not lipo lips, but real lips of righteous indignation. I imagine those lips cowered white helmeted cops long ago and smoked many a joint in their day. They curl like an octopus toward the offending new age man in the small spectacles and slicked hair. Her eyes narrow slightly, then she laughs at my brother.

"You don't think my peckers are work you arrogant little shit?"

I mentally put on my helmet. Doris has just pulled off her goggles and is eyeing the visiting professor like someone about to swat an errant fly. I look at Elliott and see his face blanch red.

"I don't think you have to call names, Doris," he sniffs. "We are all adults here, and I think we can work this out amicably."

She looks down for a long moment then reaches for a pack of Virginia Slims. Doris lights the cigarette like a man and eyes my brother again. She blows a long, slow cloud of smoke across the professor's face. Elliott waves the smoke away testily.

"The simple fact is, Doris, my father has treated you decently, and now you have to treat *him* decently." Elliott gestures to the domicile under construction. "Maybe you can live in different parts of the house, but you have to understand he is unemployed now. He needs your support, and I think making him leave the house is very cold and cruel. Frankly, the best remedy probably is for you to find another place."

Mr. Frankly just walked in the room and I wait for the counter-offensive. Doris is smoking quickly now, ashing her cigarette in a Big Gulp cup. Elliott is growing emboldened and leans back on the couch and opens a hand to reason.

"Maybe the thing for you to do now is to start supporting my father while he tries to get back on his feet. I think it is only fair in view of his support of you and your ..." Elliott glances around with the intellectual's distain for the trades. "*Hobby.*"

Doris ashes her cigarette, grinding the butt to a stub. She slowly raises her head and stares at my brother like a strange new life form. The fact is, I always liked Doris. She understands the shortcomings of one D. T. senior and often is able to laugh at his most irritable qualities. I see now what a colossal mistake it was for me to assent to my brother's mission of mercy.

The benevolent soothsayer gestures to the portable phone on the table.

"So, why don't you pick up the phone and give Dad a call, and maybe you two can go to therapy or even speak with Apollonian."

Doris stares at Elliott like he just shit on the floor.

"*Apollonian?*"

"Yes," Professor Hammer nods. "She had a double major in psychology and has done some therapy work with couples. I think she would be more than willing to let you and Dad work out your differences and charge you a minimal fee."

A slight smile crosses Doris's lips, her eyes laughing.

"Just who I want to get in the middle of my marriage," she

murmurs. "A bisexual black woman married to a man who talks like Tweety bird."

Elliott preens to a new shade of red and wrings his hands. I grin. It is true; my brother does have a small voice.

"I resent—"

"Are you finished?"

Elliott stares at her, then glances at me.

"Dale, do you have anything you want to add?"

"No, no," I say and shrug. "I think you … covered it," I mutter, eyeing the door.

"Yes … I think that sums it up, then," Elliott says and nods, turning to the woman watching him like a mark.

"Okay," Doris says, standing up. "I'll show you to the door."

Elliott glances at me as I stand. My brother remains seated.

"Doris, I think we still have some unresolved issues here—"

"No, we don't."

I start to move toward the door. It is time to go and I have a fantasy we can escape before Doris strangles my brother.

"Doris, I'm not leaving like this," Elliott declares, still sitting.

"Yes, you are," Doris says like a man.

Elliott looks at me. I mouth, "Let's go." He turns back to Doris. Class is being adjourned, but the professor is not finished with his lecture. He wants to make his point again; he wants to be sure his student understands his basic thesis.

"But what about what I said?"

Doris then speaks in an amazingly level tone.

"You sanctimonious little shit … your father deserves everything he gets and probably worse."

Elliott stands finally and shakes his head, crying out.

"How can you say that after everything he's done for you?"

I watch Doris's tongue move against the inside of her mouth, deciding which way to garrote my brother. Her mouth moves so quickly I am not sure she spoke.

"Amber."

The word is defecation on the floor—a grenade Doris has rolled to our feet. Professor Hammer stares at her, not comprehending the meaning of her one-word missive that I know very well contains the rhyme and the reason why D. T. senior is now over my garage.

"*What?*"

"Amber," Doris says again.

I grab Elliott by the arm.

"Let's go," I say, staring him in the eye.

"No, *wait a minute!* She can't just throw him out like this ..." He shakes me off and turns to the woman who is a good head taller. "Who the fuck is *Amber?*"

Doris is by the door, a stone mannequin. I manage to move Elliott toward the door, wanting to clear the entrance before the other shoe falls. My brother pauses in the door, staring at the woman who would gladly kill him with her hammer.

"I want to know who the fuck Amber is!"

Her mouth moves around gritted teeth.

"The secretary he *fucked,* you condescending prick!"

My brother's mouth drops open as the door pushes us onto the porch. The miter saw starts back up, and we descend the twenty cement steps like two chastised boys. Professor Hammer has the dazed expression of a man hit with a two by four.

I back out of the drive.

"Well," I say putting the truck in gear. "I think that went well, don't you?"

189

12

"I ain't got the fuel, sorry."
—Astronaut Pete Conrad Gemini 5

The bright yellow of Dale junior's soccer ball scores a goal high and to the right into the net of parental guilt. I tried to block the shot, but as I pulled into my drive, I realized the price for being thrown out of the carpenter's lair is I had missed my son's soccer game. How many times could I promise one nine-year-old I would be at his game and then not show up? In the beginning I was true and held fast to my *uber* parent maxim and missed nothing. Then, slowly, life pushed in. The seamy truth is I am committing the sin of the father and becoming fundamentally oblivious to the needs of my son.

"Who's car?"

I turn from the lone soccer ball on my lawn and stare at the silver Cadillac and register the second comet to land on the D. T. Hammer planet. I had already clipped the famed Cadillac once before and offered to pay the five-hundred-dollar deductible. My in-laws declined my offer, opting to hang me out in effigy instead; a good Dale Hammer transgression is worth much more than the five hundred dollars.

"My in-laws," I say and nod.

I breathe heavily, seeing my father-in-law emerge into the garage. Dick is a tall, lanky man in his eighties with Ronald Regan hair who spends his time trying to find anything mechanical to putter around with. He is a retired science teacher who made a million dollars on a patent for correctible ink he mixed in his garage. I know he has found something to fix in my house and is trying to run down the appropriate tool. This could take him all day, as my tool bench has become a catchall of paint cans, insecticides, painting tarps, and hardened brushes. I watch Dick navigate between my new tractor and the car, moving the spurious items of my life into precise order. To say that Wendy didn't marry her father would be an understatement. We are two men who wouldn't recognize the same apple in the road—to Dick it would be a red sphere slightly off balance—to me, it would just be the apple I ignore.

I watch Dick stack several cans of oil neatly on the hood of my tractor and then turn to Elliott.

"I better get in there and see what Dick is looking for in my garage," I mutter, opening the door.

"You mean that guy in your garage?"

"Yeah."

We enter the garage where Dick has already cleared my workbench and is now in the process of replacing the tools, paint cans, brushes, an old compressor, tarps, insecticide, cans of WD-40, a backyard fogger, a power sprayer, masking tape rolls still in sealed plastic, a container of Lime-Away for the water stain on the side of our house, small cans of two-cycle oil for a chainsaw I no longer own, instruction manuals for the garage opener, and a mélange of parts and papers no man could readily identify—all these things he was putting back in precise order.

"I found the adjustable wrench under these paint cans. Your toilet upstairs won't stop running. The float just needs to be adjusted," Dick informs me.

My father-in-law always completes the question not asked. Many times I find myself on the short end of a conversation already in progress. "These condensers always go out first," he would say, holding up some small part, already on his way to the garage before I can reply. He finds the concrete fascinating the same way I find the abstract absorbing. Consequently, we are two men with little of interest to say to each other. We can talk war and nostalgia, but after the History Channel, we are two ships in the night, not remotely interested in stopping.

"Take whatever you need," I say magnanimously. "Dick, I don't think you've met my brother, Elliott."

"How are ya, Elliot?" he says, flashing a rare smile. "Yeah, you just need to tighten up that float and she'll stop."

"I'll have to get on that," I mutter, moving toward the house.

"I got it covered," he says, moving tools aside, brushing dust from the counter. I am amazed. In minutes, Dick has brought order to my garage the same way he marched off to make the world safe for democracy and then returned to raise a family, start a business, and retire as the man complete. My generation can't even keep their fucking garages clean.

"Someone cut it down last Saturday night."

My mother-in-law stares at her daughter and then at me. I had just walked into our family room. Wendy is sitting on the couch while Apollonian is holed up in the other Queen Anne with a book, making notes, glancing occasionally at the earthlings in her midst. Betty commands from the other Queen Anne.

"What do you mean *someone* cut it down last Saturday night?"

"Someone cut it down with a saw," Wendy replies to her mother.

Betty stares in disbelief. She is a thin, rail hardened woman, rich beyond belief, fierce, and determined, the last of a certain matriarch that vanished when the frontier was settled. Dick long ago gave up the field to the superior force and has found refuge for years in garages. I foolishly tweaked the whiskers of the tiger years ago. That I was not worthy of her daughter is a given—that I talk back is salt in the wound.

"Well *Jesus Christ*, did someone call the police?"

"Yes," I say and nod, giving her a quick, dry kiss. "You've met my brother, Elliott, before, Betty?"

Betty's eyes dull behind her wing tipped glasses. She never gave up the beehive from 1965 and with age it has given her the import of a queen with a nest of hornets overhead. Her mouth is permanently turned down in dissatisfaction over the world at large, her bony hand wearily acknowledging the man with too many bracelets and a suspect vocation.

"Hey, Elliott, how ya doing?"

"I'm fine." My brother gestures to the woman in the chair. "Have you met my wife, Apollonian?"

Betty breathes tiredly, regarding the type of woman that didn't exist until the latter part or her life—liberated, black, bisexual, and a career woman. Apollonian is the type of woman she could clearly do without. Leave it to her son-in-law to bring all these freekoids into her domain.

"We met," she says dully.

"Yes, what did happen to your sign?" Elliott murmurs, frowning.

Betty gestures to the ceiling.

"What kind of *nut* would cut down a sign in the middle of the night?"

I shrug to my mother-in-law.

"I guess someone didn't like the sign."

Betty inflates, her mouth filling, her eyes growing wide.

"Didn't like the sign! Jesus, that was a *beautiful* sign! What kind of a person wouldn't like a pretty turquoise sign like that with pictures of ducks and children playing and grass?"

I gesture out the window.

"Well, you can probably take the two pieces. I'm sure nobody would object."

Betty looks through me and shakes her head for the millionth time. She is a woman with the rude knowledge of the farm wife combined with the thrift of the Depression. After fifteen years, we give each other a wide berth. Dick is the one and only exception to her unsaid edict: *men are good for only one thing, and they aren't even very good at that.*

"Well, I think that's ridiculous! I hope the police catch whoever it is and put him in jail a long time ... imagine, cutting a sign down in the middle of the night! As if you didn't have something better to do with your time."

Wendy is daring me with her eyes, and so I beg off. Betty suddenly looks up from the tragedy of the sign and nods to me.

"So I heard your father moved in with you."

"That's right ... just temporarily."

I know this is the real reason for the unscheduled Betty visit. My mother-in-law does not sanction independent thought or action. The simple act of reading a book in her presence is suspect. D. T. senior moving in with us hit all the buttons, the biggest one being that if anyone should be moving in, it should be *Betty.* My mother-in-law has lobbed long-range disapproval for years at my father over his jobs, his young wives, and the fact he's still roaming the planet at seventy-three while she glides in motorized chairs. If D. T. senior had any respect at all, he would be whiling his days away in front of *Jeopardy* like decent people his age—not traveling hell to leather in pursuit of the almighty American buck.

"Well, that's what they all say," she says airily.

I frown, taking the bait anyway.

"What's that?"

Betty holds up her hand.

"*Temporary*. They always say it's *temporary* when they come to stay with you and before you know it, five years have passed!"

I smile.

"I don't think my father is going to live over my garage for five years."

She holds up the hand of logic.

"Don't say I didn't tell you so." Betty looks over her glasses. "So his wife threw him out?"

"She didn't throw him out," Elliott declares hotly, looking like he just swallowed an onion. "My father is giving her *some space* while she sorts out a few things."

"Sorts out a few things?" Betty snorts. "Sounds like she sorted out a few things and *he* was one of the things that got sorted out!"

Elliott's face darkens.

"I think they are going to work it out," I intone, trying to head off the impending cultural morass.

"I take offense to that," the professor states, his pallor now a dark chartreuse, adjusting his spectacles. "In fact, I take *umbrage* to your tone."

Umbrage to your tone, I mouth. Now I know we are in deep shit. Betty gives him a look not unlike Dick's expression in the garage. The ten-dollar words have the same affect on this Greatest Generation—more bullshit from the generation that specializes in bullshit. "Umbrage" was not a word used when people were busy fighting to make the world safe for democracy.

"*To what?*" Betty says and frowns. "What are you talking about?"

Truly, the eloquence of one multi-media professor is lost upon this child of the Depression. My brother stands up from the arm of the Queen Anne, adjusting his glasses. The professor never lectures sitting down.

"I take *umbrage* to what you just said about my father."

My mother-in-law stares at the Martian in horn-rimmed glasses.

"*Umwhat?*"

Elliott's eyes dull for the child.

"Umbrage ... I take *umbrage!*"

"*Umbrage* ..." Betty scowls. "What the hell is that?"

My mother-in-law looks to me for interpretation.

"It means—"

"It means I take *offense* to what you said about my father!" Elliott roars, turning another shade of red.

He is standing, his cheeks scarlet, fine beads on his brow.

"Then why don't you just say *offense*," the student wants to know.

Elliott raises his eyebrows; surely in his fifteen years of teaching he has not had a student so obtuse.

"Because *umbrage* describes more precisely my feelings—a more accurate adjective," he informs the freshman.

Betty stares at Elliott as if he just stepped out a spaceship.

"I didn't say anything about your father. I just said his wife sorted him out—"

"*And I told you that he left on is own volition,*" Elliott roars again, screaming at the old woman in the chair.

"His own *volition*," Betty cries out in protest to my brother's ten-dollar words, violating the clear tenant of the minimalist writer. "*Volition* ... why don't you just say what you mean, for Christ's sake?"

Elliott stares at her and smiles suddenly. He has written off the student—nothing left to do but flunk her.

"What I said is that my father left on his own *volition*, which means he left because he *wanted* to leave!

Betty shrugs, meting out the simple logic of the last century.

"I heard he lost his job and his wife threw him out the door and now he's living here because he doesn't have anywhere else to go."

Elliott stares at Betty, the perspicuity of the Multi Media professor overruled by the clarity of the working class. Clearly, this student does not belong in his class.

"I don't think disparaging someone's parents is very constructive," Apollonian ventures, her jaw set in disapproval.

Betty shrugs.

"You reap what you sow, I always say," she hums out.

Elliott turns and stares at me, his eyes blazing.

"I can't believe you are letting her say these things about our father in your house!"

I look at my brother and cannot decide whose side I am on. Elliott is actually breathing hard, while Betty looks cool as a day in January. I could have told my brother not to cross swords with a woman who has bested a certain novelist for years.

"Elliott … *chill*. Betty doesn't mean anything—"

"What, you're taking her side now against our father?"

"I can't believe he'd want to stay here," Apollonian mutters.

"Oh come on," my wife says, standing up. "You were rude to my mother before and deserve whatever you get."

Apollonian's mouth drops open.

"What? I was rude? *I was rude?*"

Wendy is now standing, the lawyer punctuating her position.

"All your bullshit about climate studies, when all my mother said was she liked the fact it was warmer now … but you have to go on *a rant* about global warming, criticizing everyone who hasn't read the obscure texts you cite."

Apollonian holds up her hands, shaking her head. I can see now that I should not have left these three women together—a lawyer, a humorless English professor, and the unsinkable Molly Brown. Apollonian throws one of her braids over her shoulder, moving her jaw in black woman indignance.

"*Sorry* if I interject with something other than the price of

197

mayonnaise at Kmart."

"What's wrong with the price of mayonnaise at Kmart?" Betty wants to know.

"Nothing," Apollonian shrugs. "It's just I get tired of a consumerist culture where the only thing people find worthy of talking about *is* the price of mayonnaise."

"I think we better leave now," Elliott says.

"This place is a fucking racist nut house," Apollonian declares, shaking her head and getting up.

"And the two nuts are leaving," Betty murmurs.

Apollonian pauses in front of her chair.

"You are a terrorist old woman."

Betty looks up, a small grim smile on her lips.

"I heard you were a lesbian before."

The professor roars, veins swelling in his neck, his finger slapping the air.

"How can you talk to my wife that way?"

Betty shrugs innocently and looks at me.

"That's what Dale said."

Elliott glares at me, and I open my mouth. Apollonian suddenly leans down toward my mother-in-law, speaking in a low voice.

"You should try eating some pussy sometime."

Betty's mouth drops open, and her eyes tear up.

"What!"

Betty looks at me, then turns crimson—the first time I have ever seen my mother-in-law truly embarrassed.

"Dick!"

"Get out of here!" Wendy shouts, pointing to the door.

"Dick!"

"I can't believe you let people talk this way in your house," Elliott shouts from the door, leaving it open.

In times of real crisis, I become weirdly practical. No need to leave a front door open, even if people are trying to kill each other. I walk into the hallway and see Elliott and Apollonian have already pulled their car down the drive. Their hybrid actually squeals rubber and then goes down the access road and wheels around in front. Elliott puts his arm out the window and flips me the bird, a disembodied "Fuck you," coming across the country air.

13

"Find out what happened ... and fix it so it never happens again!"
–Mission Control

When I return to the living room, I attend to the wounded. Dick has now entered the fray and like the hapless General coming to the scene of a battle already fought, he is trying to find out what happened from the dead and the wounded. The toilet float he holds in one hand is a possible weapon to avenge the honor of his wife. He is the true member of the Greatest Generation—improvising to use whatever is at hand to fight the Japs, the Krauts, the organic academics.

"Dick, I have been insulted in my own daughter's house," Betty declares, still residing in her Queen Anne throne.

Dick stands in the middle of the room with his old-man pants pulled high and the bulbous float from my toilet. He wears a blue nautical sweater with some sort of yachting emblem on the right side. Soft-soled boating shoes complete the ensemble his wife laid out for him on his bed. Dick now stands in my family room, a yachting captain trying to decipher how his ship ran aground.

"Who insulted you, Betty?"

She gestures widely toward the front door.

"That ... that black *lesy, that's* who!"

Dick touches his hearing aid and looks to the front door.

"Black Lesy ... what's a lesy?"

Betty rolls her eyes, slapping the arm of the chair.

"Oh God, Dick, a lesbian...*lesbian!*"

The yachting captain spreads his arms wide in frustration—Mr. Rotor Rooter with his toilet float.

"What black lesbian, Betty?"

"Elliott's wife, Dad," Wendy says dully, flopping down on our couch.

Dick frowns and brings down his float. I know in his mind, he craves the sanity of a world where the buoyancy of a plastic bulb will stop a toilet from overflowing. The world at large does not respect the laws of physics or any other laws. He has become the old male capable of focusing on one problem at a time—win the war, lose the peace—the modern world is one of bits and bytes—a multitasking hell he cannot keep up with anymore. He zeros in on the central issue.

"Elliott's wife is black?"

"Oh Dick!" Betty shakes her head. "That lesy said something to me I can't even repeat!"

"Don't repeat it, Mother," Wendy warns sternly.

Dick shrugs, gaining confidence.

"Well, if you can't repeat it, then I don't see what I can do ... it can't be *that* bad."

"It was that bad, Dick," Betty says, staring at him.

The captain walks over and puts his hand on my mantle. He looks at me. We are men, after all.

"What, did she call you a name, Betty?"

Betty looks up at Mr. Nautical and shakes her head. Missionary position with the lights off has ruled the roost for a long time, and the carnal acts of whores and prostitutes are restricted to the upper cable channels. The Greatest Generation is all about tradition.

"She told me I should do something."

Dick glances at me and grins. *Women.* It's a good thing men are around to protect them.

"C'mon. What was it? It couldn't be *that* bad."

Betty stares at her husband then shakes her head. The lights will remain off for the duration and oral sex will not be spoken of.

"I can't do it. I don't think you have ever *heard* words like these, Dick."

He rolls his eyes, waving the toilet float through the air.

"Betty! I fought in *World War II* for God's sake ... I've heard the words—*trust me.*"

Betty stares at the yachting captain, then turns to my wife. "You tell him."

The cycle is now complete, the children are parenting the parents.

"Dad." My wife lowers her voice. "It was something *sexual.*"

Dick's eyebrows go up. A shell has just landed on his foxhole. Pull up the anchor and head to sea. The Gatling gun of their marital life has been brought out—*something sexual.*

"*Sexual* ... she said something *sexual?*"

Betty rolls her eyes and stares at the captain of the good ship lollipop.

"Dick, for God's sake, it concerns female *private parts.*"

This is enough for the captain, who now gives the abandon ship order. The lines were clearly drawn years ago when training bras and periods were handled while he was safely in the garage. It is now every man for himself.

"Oh ... okay ..." he mutters, abdicating in light of female private parts. "Fine ... fine ..."

Betty stares at me suddenly.

"I don't know what's wrong with your brother, but he sure hit the bottom of the barrel with that black broad."

I offer no defense, holding up my hands as a beaten man.

"But you see what happens when family comes to live with you?"

I look up, truly baffled.

"No, what?"

Betty stares at me as if I am the dumbest rock on the planet. *"This … this* happens!"

"Oh …" I nod slowly, now waiting to know what "this" is.

The doorbell chimes in staged timeliness, and I wonder if my brother has forgotten something.

"Who is that?" Betty demands, incredulous someone should be ringing the doorbell when the donnybrook of female private parts has been breached.

"I don't know," I murmur, walking into the hallway.

I pull the door open to a crew-cut man in tennis shoes. The detective is at my door with his boy standing next to him. He smiles.

"I hope this isn't a bad time, Mr. Hammer."

"No, no … How's the investigation going?"

Detective Clancy is almost sheepish as he hands me an official-looking document.

"I have a search warrant here for your garage."

"For my garage," I say, trying to think of at least one cop show where the accused has to field a search warrant for a garage.

"Yeah," Detective Clancy says and nods. "I wanted your whole house, but the judge was pretty conservative and in light of the crime, thought your garage would be adequate."

I look at the search warrant and sure enough, it instructs me to turn over my garage to unknown persons.

"Well, I'm certainly glad I got the kilo of coke out of there yesterday."

Detective Clancy glances at his son, who frowns. *Coke? Coca*

Cola?

"This is serous, Mr. Hammer," the detective informs me.

I shrug.

"Sure, go ahead. My father is probably sleeping above the garage, so try and keep it down."

Detective Clancy's antenna goes up. He squints suspiciously.

"Your father is sleeping over the garage?"

"In my office. He came to stay with us a few days ... he's a known operative in covert operations for Al Qaeda."

Detective Clancy nods slowly.

"You're kidding, right?"

I shut the front door and lead the way to the garage.

"You met my boy, Brian?"

I nod to the crew-cut, lanky boy I recognize from boy scouts.

"How are you doing there, Brian?"

"Fine," he mutters, following his father.

We reach the wreck that is my garage.

"Well, here we are, scene of the crime. Help yourself."

"We'll be brief and discreet," Detective Clancy says in a confidential whisper.

"Fine, fine, I'll go see if my father is up there. He hates to be wakened. Last time he woke in a murderous rage and killed three people before I could stop him."

Detective Clancy touches his belt where his gun should be.

"I'm joking."

I go up to my office and immediately see D. T. senior is not there. The lights are off and the bed is made. My office seems very peaceful at this moment, and I contemplate lying down on the bed. I walk to the window and see his car in the drive. I wonder where D. T. senior has found to hide during the battle of female parts. I look down toward Georgia Barnes's house as two people emerge on the porch. The woman puts her hand on the arm of the man. I stare, feeling sweat break out all over my body. The man is wearing a yellow Brooks' sweater, smoking a cigar, and possesses the unmistakable air of someone who just completed a successful date.

If a man can take more than he is given, then it is probably a good thing. I readily admit the rolling dervish on the log knows more than I do. He has kept open his range of possibilities and that is what drives people and not the thudding toil with the promised nirvana at the end. Humans are fundamentally present minded. Lest I forget this, all I have to do is watch the man walking toward me with his hands in his pockets, the shibboleth of good fortune riding herd on all he possesses.

I reach him out of breath, having run the last twenty yards. He stares at the sweating, quivering man and removes the toothpick from his mouth.

"Are you all right, boy?"

"No," I gasp, breathing heavy, leaning on my knees. "What … what are you … " I gulp for air. "*What are you doing?*"

"Just finishing a very pleasant evening, my boy."

"Dad … what were you doing there?"

"Having a mighty fine meal," he replies, rubbing his belly. "She's a very nice woman."

"You mean, Georgia?"

"Yessssss sir," Don Juan drawls slowly, crossing his arms. "And between you and me, I think she is a very *lonely* woman."

"*Oh shit!*"

D. T. senior frowns and removes his toothpick again.

"Keep your voice down, boy. You don't want to be swearing like that."

I begin to pace back and forth in the drive. Clearly I am too late. The master salesman has identified the prospect, zeroed in on the decision maker, and identified the problem to be solved. All that is left is the close.

"Don't even *think* about it, Dad. *No way, no how!*"

He frowns at his highly agitated son.

"Son, what are you talking about?"

"I'm talking about *Amber*, Dad! We saw Doris and she told us the real reason she threw you out. I'm talking about keeping your dick in your pants for once! This is not your next port of call. This is not your next safe haven. Georgia is not going to be your sugar momma, *all right?*"

D. T. senior removes the toothpick again and squints. His blue eyes are clear, his goatee well trimmed, and his sweater has a small alligator on the right tit. It is amazing that God gave such an exterior to the most unctuous con man this side of the Mississippi.

"Now, boy, are you feeling all right?"

I back away.

"Don't ... " I back farther away, shaking my head. "Don't play me, Dad. I know your method, and I know your madness ... what did you there besides have dinner?"

"Not a thing," he replies sincerely. "But I must say, Mrs. Georgia can cook one mean crab cake, and her mint juleps are out of this world ... she's from Atlanta, you know."

"Oh shit." I rub my forehead, pushing back the throbber moving into the frontal lobe. "You had crab cakes and mint juleps?"

D. T. senior nods widely.

"Tha's right. And big, fat shrimp cocktail. The woman does know how to cook."

"Dad, you are not to go near her again."

"Well, now, it's a little late for that, son."

"What do you mean?"

"Well," DT drawls. "We are going on a picnic on Thursday. I think it would do her good to get out. You know, she hasn't had any beaus since her man left."

"Any *beaus!*" I shout, stopping in the drive. "Dad, you can't do this!"

D. T. senior looks back at me, blinking innocently.

"Do what, son?"

"You can't screw Georgia Barnes!"

D. T. senior frowns. The prig returneth. He may be a libertine, but to vocalize the act of sex always gave my father the fidgets. He is strangely prudish even as he is persistently promiscuous— staying in the tradition of genteel Southern intercourse done in the dark, missionary style.

"Now, boy, what kind of talk is that?"

"What …" I sputter. "What about this thing with Amber?"

D. T. senior draws in a deep breath.

"A tragic situation I now regret. Doris was a good woman and deserves better."

The slip to past tense regarding Doris is unmistakable. She *was* a good woman. She deserves better. The woodpecker activist has already been parked in the back lot.

"What do you mean she deserves better? *She deserves you!*"

"No." D. T. senior shakes his head. "I think it is better for both of us to move on now."

"Oh fuck!"

"And I hope she finds what she is looking for," he says magnanimously.

"*Dad!*"

I feel like I'm about to implode. The man moves with lightning speed. That's what the corporations in America love about this man. He could drive out and come back with a whopper of a sale. He has the touch, *the gift.*

"Yes, son?" he asks innocently.

I stare at him, trying to coax reason back into the man with tunnel vision who rarely looks behind at the piled up bodies.

"*You* are what Doris is looking for," I sputter. "Don't you want to reconcile … don't you want to get back with her?"

D. T. senior examines his toothpick one last time before flicking it away.

"Now I have been givin' this a lot of thought, boy, and I think it is properly best for all concerned to realize we made a mistake. Doris and I are in the past now. I think it is healthy for us both to move on and find our true *soul mates.*"

I scream out in agony. The seventies just landed with a disco ball and a therapist. Burt Bacharach is playing on the radio and everyone has facial hair.

"*Soul mates! Soul mates!* Dad you are not a fucking *soul mate!* You are a *salesman!*"

"Now, now, I know it may seem sudden to you," D. T. senior nods tragically. "But sometimes love just happens that way."

"*Love!*" I shriek. "Dad, you don't love anybody! You are incapable of love! You are a traveling salesman! You love hotel rooms and expense accounts—*not people!*"

D. T. senior frowns again.

"Now, boy, that is not true. I love you and my grandchildren and whole lot of people."

"That's because you have to, Dad! But you don't love other people—you are elusive, you can't commit, and you are confusing love with being *lonely!*"

D. T. senior starts walking again, speaking like a man holding a traveling seminar.

"Now, I didn't go looking for anybody. I saw this fine woman walking up her drive when I went out to get your newspaper, and we spontaneously began to converse. I won't say it was love at first sight, but I think our mutual attraction was in evidence."

"Love, love, love," I mutter, thinking this goofy dream will end and I will wake up in my bed.

D. T. senior stares at the painted horizon and nods slowly.

"Sometimes it just happens like that, son. You never know

when it's going to grab you, and sometimes you have to throw caution to the wind."

I stare at the man who threw caution to the wind so long ago he has nothing left to throw. I try one last time.

"And I guess the fact she's loaded has nothing to do with it?"

D. T. senior raises his eyebrow.

"Now, son, I am not a man driven by material goods, but a dowry is always a helping hand in any new relationship."

"*A dowry!*"

I have died and woken in 1865. Rhett Butler is standing in my drive in a Brooks Brothers sweater. The darkies are in the fields, and the suitor is contemplating all that will be his with his marriage. I shake my head.

"A dowry, Dad, is for a young daughter not yet wed, given by the parents to the suitor …" I sputter. "Who the fuck is giving you the dowry, *her ex- husband?*"

He tilts his head and shrugs.

"Means are not important to me, son. I am beyond that at my age." D. T. senior looks at me as the man transformed. Gandhi has just landed over my garage. "Do you know she has a Negro who makes her dinners?"

I hold my forehead. The movie has begun and it is really bad—black and white, old costumes, hackneyed phrases, and a tired recycled plot. *"Negro?"*

"African American, Dad," I shout.

He shrugs away the last fifty years.

"Where I come from boy, they are Negroes … but like I say, money is not important to me anymore."

I stare at my father, wondering how he can say such things with a straight face. Then I realize, like all great salesmen, *he really believes his own bullshit.*

"Oh, like hell, Dad! How can you say shit like that?"

He shakes his head tragically.

209

"I think you better reexamine your values, son. Living out here might not be such a good thing. There are things more important than money, son."

This is my line and it has been hijacked by Errol Flynn. I shake my head; a pounder of a headache has descended. The blanket assumptions of my father are impossible to shake because he truly *believes* them. I rub my brow.

"Son …"

"What?" I mutter.

"There is a man coming out of your garage."

I look up and Detective Clancy has emerged from his search. D. T. senior frowns and gestures toward my garage.

"Now, why is that boy taking your saw?"

After Detective Clancy sped away, clutching my saw like a man who had just found the Holy Grail, Dale junior walked out of the garage in bright blue shorts and a teal jersey with "HAMMER" on the back. I inhale another full quotient of father guilt in one gulp. Three games of not standing on the sideline talking to Dan Rodgers from Wayne, a wealthy suburb to the east of Charleston, while yelling at our sons to kick the shit out of the other team and score, *score!*

"You missed my game," he says, looking at me with real hurt.

I nod and grovel.

"I'm sorry about that, Dale. I had to go somewhere with Uncle Elliott."

He frowns, a puzzled expression on his face. He looks up at me, the gapped teeth whistling slightly when he speaks.

"I saw Uncle Elliott flip you the bird."

I glance at D. T. senior, who has now picked up the basketball. I didn't know Dale junior even knew about "the bird." He could even be flipping people "the bird," and I wouldn't know it. I have reached the point with my son where lies and half truths are preferable to reality.

"He was waving ... Uncle Elliott waves with his middle finger," I explain.

"He's been doing that since he was a little boy," D. T. senior nods. "I mean, waving with his middle finger," he continues, giving me the bird behind Dale's back. "How about a game of pig there, boy?"

"Sure," my son screams, forgetting about the transgressions of the father for good clean fun with the grandfather. No expectations, no guilt, and you leave when the baths and the homework begins—being a grandfather is not a bad gig.

"I'll make the next game ... I promise," I say, but Dale junior is already laughing at D. T. senior's antics.

"That's P," D. T. senior calls out, and then turns to me. "So who was that man in the white car?"

"Nobody," I mutter.

D. T. senior takes a free throw and tilts his head.

"Looked like the law to me."

"He was nobody, Dad."

The garage door slams. Angela comes out trailing her blanket and munching on a cookie.

"Grandma brought cookies," she proclaims.

D. T. senior pauses with the basketball.

"Betty and Dick are here?"

"Yes," I say and nod. "And if I were you, I would stay clear."

"You're preaching to the choir, boy."

"P," my son shouts.

"I want to play!"

Dale junior stares at his nemesis, his little sister.

"Papa and I are playing a game."

"I want to play!"

"Can she play with you guys?" I ask, seeing the large tears forming up.

"No … she always ruins the games," Dale junior grumbles.

"That's not true, Dale—"

"You always take her side."

"No I don't—"

"*Yes, you do.*" Tears well up in the son. "You don't come to my games and you always take her side *and I hate you!*"

I watch my nine-year-old accuser stomp through the garage.

"Dale!"

The garage door slams in exclamation. D. T. senior stares at me.

"Don't say a word."

He shrugs and swishes from the half court.

"Hey, little lady, how about a game?"

Angela lights up and jumps up and down.

"*Yes!*"

I know I should go up to my son's room, but I really don't want the accusing eyes of Wendy's family. They are the Midwestern brigade of thudding ritual with the implicit: *Look how fucked up your family is compared to ours. Your brother is married to a black lesbian, and your father is sleeping over your garage. And your nine-year-old son hates you and with good reason. You never make his soccer games!* I know that Betty and Dick went to his soccer game. It is a mission in the missionless life of the retired: cruises and shopping and grandchildren.

"I'm going up to my office for a moment," I announce.

"Sure thing, big boy," D. T. senior nods, throwing the ball to Angela.

I head up the stairs, thinking about Wendy suddenly. I wonder about the last time we went out. We used to make a point of getting a sitter every other weekend. Before we moved, we put our social life at the top of the heap. But after our second child and the move, we found out money did matter. Besides, our kitschy restaurants and old-time movie theatres and comfortable coffee shops are now fifty miles to the east. Now we are at the mercy of fast food chains, bad local restaurants, and bloated fifteen-screen movie theaters overrun with bored teenagers.

I open the door to my office and shut the outside world down. It is quiet. D. T. senior is a neat man and the futon is folded and his suitcase and briefcase are lined up. My small pine writing table sits by one window. I cross the room and sit down. There is a fine sheen of dust on the computer. No sebaceous glands have anointed the keyboard for many a day. I consider flipping on the computer, watching the flat screen come to life, but then I think, *to what end?* I am the mid-list writer extant—living on past glory and cached web pages—checking the library for titles never checked out. Worst of all, there is no burning desire to tell the world of my life now—just some faint coals from a fire that is slowly, but surely burning out.

14

"I've got a bunch of computer alarms. Abort the landing ... ABORT!"
–Apollo Simulator

I can see out of my pumpkin. There is a small eyehole and I see small, white projectiles raining through the air. The papier-mâché still smells like paste and crinkles from each marshmallow. I can hear the soft thook of over a hundred boys aiming over a hundred PVC pipes at my person. The pumpkin sways from side to side. The marshmallows are sticking to my shoes and collecting in my socks. I am walking on a gum of soft white confectionaries. Sweat is blinding me. Whoever designed my round edifice didn't consider the ambient heat of a grown man. A porthole at the top would do wonders, but all I have is a stem. I am a bowl of body-heated air collecting the mass of a thousand mini marshmallows spittoon at twenty miles an hour from a thousand slender PVC pipes. I am a forty-six-year-old man wearing a large, orange papier-mâché pumpkin who has become the moving target for budding adolescents of the far west suburbs.

I am the Great Pumpkin.

There was a time when the world was right. We were in our small house in Oakland and I was home with my son. Wendy and I split the time of watching him like a pie divided into thirds. The nanny was there for Monday through Wednesday, I picked up

Thursday, and Wendy had him Friday. My Thursdays were a joy and a burden. I would write while my son slept and then we would play in the backyard or I would make some lunch. One day we had a picnic in the backyard. We sat outside and crunched on chips and floated away on Orange Crush. Spring had come with those amazing, warm gusts of humus rich air where the world seems to breathe again after a long winter. My son was four, maybe five then, but suddenly I was gripped with a knowledge I didn't want. It is the ache in the heart that the small time with our children will come to an end. He was our only child, and I was my son's best buddy, *his dad*. We had the closeness that comes when children are young and so are the parents. I desperately want to get back to that closeness, to find some glimmer of the two buddies, but it is lost under the juggernaut of parental responsibility while trying to make a buck.

I think on this as I drive Dale junior to Pack Night—a scouting jamboree where the scoutmasters get to hold a microphone and blare announcements in a gymnasium while two hundred glandular cases run wild. The lights of the elementary school are burning as I pull into the lot. Prairie Creek is a cinder block palace able to withstand tornados, floods, and any other natural disaster the planners could foresee. A long, flat obelisk with short windows and a flat, green roof, the school conjures up a time when the blue ink of mimeographed copies smudged fingers, and men with fat ties and sideburns lurked in the halls.

We clear the windswept parking lot bulging with cars. I had actually parked on the lawn next to Brad Jones's command vehicle with BSA stickers in the rear corners of his windshield. Dale junior emerges from the car in full regalia with pins and badges and his Cub Scout cap. D. T. senior extricates himself from my Yukon, glancing toward the blazing lights of the school.

"Looks like big happenings in there, boy."

"Oh yeah," I nod.

We cross the lot and pass through the glass doors into the indescribable smell of warm caramels that is any public school. The cinder-blocked walls have been painted tan and are covered with paintings of native Americans, a few presidents, and the famous scowling farmer and his wife from American Gothic. A desultory janitor with the standard jingling keys and rag blossoming out of his back pocket passes us. We pass a large poster announcing the Great Pumpkin contest. Dale junior turns suddenly.

"You want to see my pumpkin, Dad?"

"Sure."

"I'm going to use the facilities," D. T. senior calls, ducking into the boys room.

We peel off to a side hallway and pass through two doors as the roar of Pack Night is silenced. We walk past doors marked *"Nurse," "Lounge,"* and *"Counselor."* The art of some Thomas Kincaid ne'er-do-well asserts itself and we pass sunsets over lakes, loons breaking the horizon, and a campsite of day-glow orange on the edge of another lake. Hanging gliders proclaim, "Respect" "Quiet," and "Be Courteous." I see the hand of caring women all around me and I know this is a good thing. Let the men stay outside where they can bash around and screw up the world—here is where we incubate the future.

"Here it is!"

Behind a glass case in the hallway are a long row of decorated pumpkins. Dale junior's pumpkin is painted black and white for the Chicago White Sox and has a ribbon on it. The paint runs together and the letters are slightly crooked. Compared to the store-bought quality of his classmate's pumpkins, I know the Hammer pumpkin is destined to command no prize

"I got third place," my son announces suddenly.

Dale junior then smiles with the same gapped two front teeth I had growing up. There are moments when my son reminds me so much of myself. I know his insecurities, his fears. He has this vast uncertainty at the core of his being and I blame myself for this. For the hundredth time, I vow to be a better role model, a better parent, a better father. I stare at the red ribbon on the Hammer pumpkin and see no less than fifty other pumpkins with red ribbons. It is the jamboree of third-place pumpkins. I see again the egalitarian hand of the mother in the background. No child will lose, they will all be winners—at least in this world they will be.

"Hey, that's great, Dale! It is a beautiful pumpkin and very worthy of third place."

He smiles again, beaming at the crooked smile on the Soxs' pumpkin.

"I think they gave out a lot of third places," he whispers, glancing at me, a small cloud passing through his eyes.

"Nah," I say shaking my head. "Yours is the only third-place ribbon I see," I say, placing my body between my son and the other fifty pumpkins.

Dale junior turns back to his small orange globe of confidence.

"Yeah, you're right," he nods.

"What do you say we get to the meeting? I have a lot of things I have to do."

"I'm so lucky you're going to be Rocket Man, Dad," he says as we head down the concrete corridor.

I put my hand on his shoulder and my son leans against me. Our shoes fall on the tiles of time, and we shuffle down the cinder-block walls of our common fortune. It is spring again and we are having a picnic, munching on chips, and drinking cold soda, and for a moment, I feel the warm rush of two old buddies.

I have attended these pack meetings before like the reluctant storm trooper at the Fuehrer's ball. The sight of so many button-down people in one room with middle-age men in uniform makes me wonder what planet my spaceship crashed on. The men bulge out of their green khaki, standing at rapt attention, while desultory scouts bring in the flag and another scout blares, "Taps" on his horn. Some men salute as the flag passes and women press their hearts. "Taps" has run out of gas, and the pledge of allegiance has been sacrificed as we all wait for the boys to get the flag into place. The Scouts salute the Scoutmasters and everyone drops their hands in relief. The Scout jamboree can now begin.

I am suddenly in a sea of blue-uniformed midgets, a Lilliputian army of short brimmed hats and yellow neckerchiefs. The gym already has the sweaty warmth of children in motion. I see fathers in trench coats, Blackberries in hand, leading their sons, some with cell phones pressed to ears. The mothers guide their sons with a tonal efficiency that is lost on the men, who set their sons loose into the chaos of an open kennel—the gymnasium of Prairie Creek.

"Can I go and play, Dad?"

"Sure ... I have to go take care of rocket business," I nod, looking toward the cluster of uniformed men standing behind amplifiers and microphone stands.

D. T. senior has already struck up a conversation with a man in a Burberry trench coat. I turn back to the men milling around the front of the room. I see Brad Jones and Jim Mesh, then spot the Scoutmaster and his wife, Mike and Barb Smithy. Mike bears an absurd resemblance to Fred Flintstone and Barb is a pinched mouth brunette Wilma. There are other men in uniform, stringing more microphones. One of the scout leaders taps a microphone with his index finger, bringing a dull thump from the rafters, nodding that all is well with *Scout Rock USA*.

Brad Jones turns around when I walk up. I notice Brad is in full regalia with a matching Scouting hat, army-green Scouting socks, badges sewn in rows across his shirt with a canteen, key chain, scouting knife, compass, and flashlight, all hanging from his utility belt. Dark brown BSA shoes are shined to an impeccable luster. He greets me with a frown reserved for the private who cannot get his bed made right.

"Dale," he says wearily.

"Brad."

We shake weakly.

"Big turnout."

"Oh yeah ..." Brad wipes his brow. "Have you talked to Mike?"

There is something in his tone that sends off my alarms.

"No ... should I?"

He nods darkly.

"You should talk to Mike. I think there has been a change."

"A change?"

Brad Jones retreats into protocol.

"You should talk to Mike."

The Scoutmaster rivals a general in badges and metals. Barb Smithy is behind him in a brown shirt, testing the sound equipment behind us. Jim Mesh looks fairly rugged in his khaki ensemble. I am the man who the Scout military despises; a longhaired man with stubble in a long coat wearing Tony Lama cowboy boots. *Civilians! Jesus, if only they knew the sacrifices we make so they can dress like down-on-their-luck writers.*

"Hello, Dale."

I shake hands with the Scoutmaster.

"Mike ... Brad says I should talk to you."

Mike snorts, his nose twitching. He reminds me of a man who has eaten too many donuts and sat through way too many meetings. His eyes are dull and his bowl haircut does nothing to dispel the cartoon quality of his square jaw. I remember someone told me he was a fertilizer salesman and I wonder if the twitching nose and bad sinuses has come about from too much nitrogen.

"Dale, I think we are going to have to make a change in

regards to Rocket Man."

I am still feeling a glow from my son's one sentence: "I'm glad you're going to be Rocket Man, Dad." Now I feel that old bowling ball bearing down on my few pins of good fortune.

"A change?"

"Yes," Mike says and nods. "Jim Mesh is going to take over. Brad is very busy with his job and other commitments, but frankly, Dale, we're not sure you're up to the job."

Now I am falling back into my old self. *Fine. Fuck Rocket Man. Take the job and shove it.* But while Rocket Man is nothing I aspired to, it has become the one thing that will make my son happy. And so I begin to fight for something I never really wanted in the first place. I pull back my hair and stare this doughboy in the eyes.

"Give me another chance, Mike. I've had a rotten couple of weeks."

And even as I say this, I see Detective Clancy giving me the ultimatum to pay up or face the risk of incarceration. I think of the lone middle finger of my brother. I think of Doris throwing us out of her house. I think of Chad rising from the dead behind his couch, and then the strange look in Georgia Barnes's eyes when she stops her Maserati to tell me she thinks my father is charming. I think of the elusive Jed and Ellie Mae who could well torpedo my job on Friday.

I dig in for Rocket Man to make my world right.

"What do you say? I'll shape up and fly right. Brad doesn't have to do it. I'll handle it, *I promise.*"

"If you returned some of our calls, then you might find people more willing to believe you," Barb weighs in, standing slightly behind her husband.

"You're right," I grovel. "I should have been more ... attentive."

This does nothing to back Barb down. She smells blood.

"You know we work hard for the boys, and people like you who give scouting a bad name. We do this for you, Dale, so *you* can have a good time with *your* son, and I wonder if you understand this. I don't think half of you parents understand that we do this for *nothing*. We are volunteers, and we have busy lives just like you."

I meet the two cold blue eyes behind coral-colored wings. Her glasses would be in style if Barb had not purchased them thirty years ago.

"I know, Barb, you are right," I say, groveling in earnest. "I am not appreciative."

She flips a finger into our small space.

"And now you want us to believe you are going to straighten up and fly right because now you think you can't be Rocket Man? Well maybe this is something you should have thought about before, Dale," she snaps, anger welling into a crimson rage burning in her cheeks and pulsing in her temples.

I consider throwing myself at her mercy, clawing her bodice, weeping in contrition. Mike suddenly clears his throat.

"Well, maybe we can work something out here if Dale feels he can fly right."

Barb makes a sound in her throat, huffing off in tired disgust. *Men.*

I raise my three fingers in the Scout Oath. Mike glances at his lieutenants and then at Jim Mesh. I look at Jim and something passes between us. I remember Jim's basement office and the turning clothes of his dryer. I remember the kids' rooms all newly purchased from Sears.

"Well, I tell you, Mike," Jim says suddenly. "I can see giving up Rocket Man, but we don't have anyone to be the Great Pumpkin tonight, and …"

Mike looks at me, raising his eyebrows, nose twitching.

"What do you say, Dale? Be the Great Pumpkin, and Rocket Man is yours!"

I hold my arms wide and acquiesce to what I know not.

"I'll be whatever you guys want me to be."

It is hot inside my sealed space. I am not unlike those early deep-sea explorers descending to the depths in my sealed orb. I move in the same murky darkness, not sure where to place my feet. I imagine that being on the bottom of an ocean would not be so different. I only have one small port hole to see out of and it keeps moving with every step. Essentially I am blind, a man who can only guess where he is going by sound and feel. I know the cement walls will eventually stop my forward motion. I stumble across the gymnasium inside my papier-mâché fort—a man inside a pumpkin looking for salvation.

Outside my small peaceful enclave is a roar, a wall of sugar-jazzed boys screaming at the top of their lungs. The sound comes near and then suddenly retreats. Hot breath pours into my porthole as boys inject their voices.

"Hey! Anybody in there? What are you doing ... Heeeeeey!"

It is not unlike being inside a trash can with people yelling in the top. The sound waves have nowhere to go and ricochet around my circular dungeon. The cloth straps that rest across my shoulders have become suddenly heavy as I am propelled forward. Someone has just shoved the Great Pumpkin and I run like a man in a fast movie. Another shove sends me off sideways, and now the blind man is doing a two step fast walk to keep from falling.

"Anybody in there!"

The hot breath of marshmallows fills my pumpkin. Another shove sends me reeling. I am breathing hard to keep up with my legs. I remember Jim Mesh's admonishment suddenly. "Look, all you have to do is walk from one side of the gym to the other and let the boys pelt you with marshmallows. It's easy."

Another shove sends me running like a man about to fall

forward. I glance out my porthole and veer from the cement wall. I am the center of a moving colossus of boys chasing the strange, orange-colored orb across the shined basketball court. I hear men laughing, then D. T. senior's voice rushes up and comes in the eyehole I can no longer locate.

"Son, I always knew you would amount to something sooner or later."

Then he is gone and a boy's mouth appears.

"*Heeeeey, anybody in there!*"

I am now walking on some sort of gum. The ritual of the Great Pumpkin is one of hunting. The boys are all armed with five-inch sections of PVC pipe and pockets of mini-marshmallows. An enfilade of marshmallows pelt the curved walls of my fort as I hear the soft thuds of baked sugar puffs. The problem is that the floor has become covered and I am now walking like a man in a marsh. A small white pipe appears in front of my nose as a marshmallow hits me between the eyes.

"*Hey!*"

The short snouts of PVC pipes fill my eyehole with marshmallows fired at point-blank range. The air suddenly fills with white projectiles.

"*Ow, you little shit,*" the Great Pumpkin shouts.

Another slender tube is inserted and the assailant catches me in the eye. I reel and stumble backwards. I can only see out my left eye as three more marshmallows pepper my cheek. The Great Pumpkin has lost his balance and stumbles backward drunkenly, then falls forward. Another well-aimed pellet finds my other eye.

"*You little shit,*" I scream, crashing on blindly.

Another white gun comes into my domicile and I put my mouth to the tube this time. I open my mouth as a marshmallow is fired down into the pit of my stomach. I gag and cough and nearly throw up. Tubes are now crashing though soft spots of my papier-mâché. The chicken wire is poor reinforcement. I have become a turkey in a shoot with a thousand guns. The air inside my tank fills with projectiles as I am pelted in the face, the head, and the arms. Marshmallows torture me from every angle.

"Stop it," screams the muffled Great Pumpkin.

Another tube comes in and I grab the tube and shove it out. I hear the wail of a fallen Scout and take solace in taking one with me. But I can't stop the onslaught. Tubes perforate my papier-mâché skin like attacking piranha. I am hit with no less than fifty mini-marshmallows at once. The air is white, smelling of a confectionary. The moist, warm air causes the soft gelatinous blobs to stick to my skin. I hear little pops as they find their targets. The air is fouled with nine-year-old breath pumped in by way of a hundred PVC tubes. I can take no more and the Great Pumpkin starts to run in a long paean of adult agony.

"Fuuuuuuuuuuuuuuuckkkkkkkk!"

I run across the gymnasium and the roar becomes distant as the marshmallows cease. I have cleared the teeming hordes, but I don't know where I'm going. I smash into something very hard as chicken wire and papier-mâché give up against the impermeable wall of cinder blocks. All goes black.

It is the memory of Brad Jones's mouth over mine that makes me cringe. I would have been fine even if Brad hadn't breathed day-old garlic into my mouth, which produced a gagging fit. Brad stood and nodded to the crowd that I would be fine, that he has brought back many Great Pumpkins this way. My one thought when I emerged into this world with fifty pubescent boys staring down at me was this—*at least I am still Rocket Man.* Such are the small victories we settle for.

By the time D. T. senior and I reach home, Dale junior is snoring in the back seat and I feel the peace of a day well spent. My head has settled to a dull throb and I sit in the drive with

D. T. senior, who has lapsed into a moody silence. The moon is low over the trees and coyotes are hissing about in the wetlands. Occasionally a howl does break the night as we are treated to moments before men with subdivision grids moved into fertile soil and put mammon over God's land. Betty's car is still in the drive, mirroring the lunar night in a thousand suns of lacquered beauty. I wonder then if she and Dick are staying over. The life of the retired is one of being at sea until a port opens up, then the good ship *Jeopardy* moors until they are gently nudged out again.

"A Cadillac," D. T. senior says, staring at the low-slung car.

"They have three of them," I murmur.

My father stares at the car as if he is seeing all three. To say Dick is the inverse of my father would not violate the rule of understatement. He is retired. He goes to Florida for six months of the year. He travels at will. They have no financial worries other than the performance of their mutual funds. My father-in-law lived a life of prudence and is now reaping the reward, while D. T. senior's life of controlled chaos has come for its due. The only thing my father has over Dick is that he stayed in this world as the cynosure of all that is American—the active man.

"That old broad is loaded." I hear my father shift in the seat. "How did Dick get so much fucking money?"

"He worked for it, Dad."

DT Senior raises an eyebrow.

"I work for my money too, son, but I don't make that kind of money."

I slouch down in the car. Dale junior's snoring rises behind us.

"You have to live a boring life, Dad. You can't get divorces and go after rich divorcees."

D. T. senior stares out the window and shrugs.

"Sounds like a high price to me."

"I rest my case."

We are staring at the garage and I see D. T. senior look up toward the two dormered windows. Does he register that he is now a man over a garage? I don't know. I envision what the room over Dale junior's garage will be like. I hope he uses a good carpenter and insulates the floor as well as the walls. I hope he will add some dormers and utilize baseboard heaters. I see myself as an old man over the garage while Dale junior's wife threatens to leave unless I do. Dale junior will then toss and turn in his sleep, wondering if another garage waits for him too.

"You never think your life will end up the way it does, that's for sure."

I look over at D. T. senior. His white beard makes him look absurdly like Ernest Hemingway for a moment. This is not the first time this has happened. I have a picture of the last great dead white male in my office and Angela has more than once said, "There's Granddad." Ernest always made sure he married up, one wife richer than the former. I suppose in that way he is smarter than D. T. senior and myself—a man thinking of the future at an early age.

"I tell you, boy, you always think that you have more time to fix things," D. T. senior murmurs. "You think you'll have one more chance to beat the odds and get another job, turn things around before it's too late ..." He moves his head slowly. "Then you're out of time and there's not a thing you can do about it, and all that's left to you is to play out your hand."

I would like to offer some sage advice, but the truth is out there under the heartless sky, and not the moon or the stars can deny a life lived and its consequences. D. T. senior turns to me.

"Don't end up like me, boy."

"I don't know, Dad," I mutter. "I think I'm on a rocket headed for your planet."

D. T. senior laughs suddenly.

"You'll be all right ... I guess I will too."

I look at my father and realize the salesman code has just descended. *Never feel sorry for yourself. Never talk down. Never be anything less than positive.* You don't wallow. D. T. senior has just turned on the high beams of undaunted optimism. I look back at the garage.

"Elliott was pretty broken up you didn't want to stay with him."

My father shrugs.

"He has himself a good woman and a good life; that boy doesn't need someone like me fucking it up."

"No. I need someone like you fucking up my life."

D. T. senior turns and says in perfect deadpan.

"Son, your life was already fucked up."

"You got me there."

We sit for a few moments listening to the early crickets. The wind hisses appreciatively.

"You really not going back with Doris?"

"I don't know, boy ... I don't think she'll take me back."

"So you're after Georgia Barnes."

D. T. senior frowns.

"Let me tell you something, boy. A lot of people in this world live every day of their life in pain, and if I can bring a little light into that woman's life, then what the hell."

My father says this with a straight face, and I know that he has convinced himself he is one with the man ringing a bell outside of department stores—*the Salvation Army of spurned lovers.*

"So it's a mission of mercy, not a mission of a million dollars."

"I am not a shallow man, but if a woman comes with a sizable dowry, then so be it."

"Dad, you should have never left Mississippi."

"I have thought that many times, son," he nods slowly.

"Speaking of that, did you speak to that cocksuckah about your mother's plot?"

I look over at the hurricane that is my father.

"How can you say that when you are trying to get into another woman's pants?"

"Don't worry, boy. I'll just have a little fun and move on."

"That's exactly what *I do* worry about dad. You'll move on, and I'll be stuck."

"Seems to me like you're going to moving on too," D. T. senior murmurs.

"What the hell does that mean?"

D. T. senior rolls his shoulders, gesturing to my house.

"Just that in my humble estimation, you and your wife have become *radically* different people."

"Dad, you have never liked Wendy," I say tiredly.

"Not true, boy, but the difference between you two is that she *likes* this life out here while you could just walk away."

"I like my house, Dad."

"It's a goddamn baron, cultureless land."

I stare at the dervish of social commentary.

"C'mon, Dad. I don't what's so great about living outside of Langford in a golf club community."

"You know what I'm saying, boy," he shrugs.

"At least I live *somewhere.* You have lived the last forty years out of a suitcase."

"And I like it that way."

"That doesn't mean it wasn't a fucked way to live, Dad."

D. T. senior rolls his shoulders again.

"Maybe so, but I'm not going to apologize to anybody for it."

"No one's asking you to."

My father punctuates the darkness with his finger.

"And you are going to be right with me, boy. You going to be right outside of this house soon enough."

"Yeah, well, misery loves company," I mutter, staring at the house in question.

I think on this scenario. *Would I look back?* Would I mourn the loss of our three fireplaces, our two and half baths, our three-car garage, my office, our acre and a half? How much do these things weigh in the scale of home and hearth?

"That fellow across the street is a nice guy," D. T. senior says suddenly.

I turn, frowning.

"What fellow?"

"That man there ... what's his name ... George—"

"George Campbell?"

"That's right."

"When did you talk to him?"

"He was over talking to your wife in the yard yesterday. You were gone somewhere."

I admit to a strange stirring down in my soul. George Campbell had gone from the Boo Radley of my life to this strange presence. A man whom I had not spoken a word to for over two years has been defended by my wife and now my father is saying he was a decent guy.

"You better be careful, boy. I watched them talk from the upstairs window for about thirty minutes. I think that boy likes your wife."

I give D. T. senior a look, hoping my expression will convey that he his bordering insanity. Like most married men, I can't imagine my wife being attracted to anyone but myself.

"I don't think a geek like Campbell is going to give me much competition, Dad," I mutter.

"It's those geeks who have all the money, boy."

I roll my eyes at the tired aphorisms of my father.

"He's not Wendy's type, Dad."

The salesman slices the air with his hand.

"Women like men with money."

"Not this woman."

D. T. senior laughs softly.

"What ..."

"I used to think money didn't mean shit too and then I spent my whole life trying to *get it* when I realized it meant everything."

"That's where we're different, Dad," I say and nod. "I *know* it doesn't mean shit."

D. T. senior looks at me.

"You in a world of shit, son."

We sit in silence.

"So ... you going to talk to that sonofabitch about giving up that plot?"

"I thought I'd give him a call tomorrow, if you can wait until then to move in."

"I can wait, boy, but you never know when the grim reaper comes for you. They say they saw something on my last stress test."

I turn to my father slumps down in his seat.

"And?"

"And they wanted me to do another test, but I told the cocksuckahs I wouldn't do it!"

"So, that's it?"

"Tha's right. I'm seventy-three years old, boy. They can take their tests and shove it where the son don't shine for all I care. I smoke cigars and drink bourbon and eat shitty food ... fuck 'em."

"Brilliant, Dad."

D. T. senior leans back, his beard white in the half light.

"Sometimes, boy, you have to say enough is enough. I've been prodded and poked all my life, and I'm tired of all that shit. If I'm going to fall over and die, then so be it."

I stare sinto the moonlit night and sigh.

"I'll talk to Al tomorrow."

I take a bike ride. It is night. These are the rides I like best. The balminess of late October is mixed with something more mysterious, a hint of winter to come, the rustling leaves, the clouds over the moon. I feel suddenly young and it is this feeling that gets me hunched over my bike, pedaling like a madman down the drive and into the wide-open night.

My wife will wonder what has happened to her wayward husband. There are issues to be discussed, fights to be fought, and problems to be solved. All more fodder for a forty-six-year-old man to mount the same two-wheeler he did as a boy of twelve and head off into the countryside. I start up the hill that is Belleview and pass the homes of the upper middle class. Big-screen televisions flicker out into the night and I imagine families gathered around movies with a dog by the heel, a cat snuggled on a couch, an early fire burning in a brick hearth. Yet, here I am, a man alone, pounding up the hill like a laboring diesel locomotive. I turn at the top of the hill and head off into the country, passing the jagged edges of the blue sign.

The moon is now over the cornfields and I don't need my light. The road rolls out before me as a long, dark strip with the center line pacing out the rationality of man, the belief that two cars may pass each other at sixty miles an hour and not veer across. I compare this landscape to the one I just left. I see how Belleview is the anomaly; a manufactured community of homes on the edge of an agrarian land. No wonder the farmers hate the suburbanites. Here in the country breeze among the fanning stalks are real lives, real loves, and real histories. Behind me are a processed group of people who have no allegiance to anything except a vague worship of the almighty buck.

And I am one of them.

I pedal faster, enjoying the true anonymity that comes with the night ride. I have taken other nocturnal cruises before and I love the invisibility that comes with it, the passing of homes where people know nothing of the man who is silently speeding by just outside their four walls. My head clears and for the first time in days I am at peace. I experience the same emotions I did when I was a boy. I feel power rushing into my legs and I am invincible again. Youth surges into my tired body like a drug and I wonder if age is nothing more than too many problems and responsibilities, with no sure way of solving anything.

I see a far sign blinking. It is a stop sign in the middle of nowhere with a flashing red light letting all know they will have to pause to consider. I approach the intersection and then brake and stop. My breathing fills the air. I am at the intersection of four cornfields. I am literally in the middle of nowhere and it is here my life comes back to me. I consider that in a mere twenty years I will be my father. Sixty-six or seventy-three, there is the law of diminishing returns. The office over the garage is the room waiting for me. I have no magic bullet to change my course. Detective Clancy is one of the signposts along my road. I will either be booked or confess. Wendy and I must have our reckoning sooner or later. D. T. senior will stay or go. Rocket Man must either rise or fall. The trajectory of my life is approaching the curving arc where the booster engine sputters and all that is left is the parachute and the hope of a safe landing. I consider for the first time the possibility my wife might be having an affair.

Where this comes from I'm not sure, but incredibly, I suspect George Campbell. His strange, wavering eye and the mention of him by D. T. senior and then the surprise that Wendy has spoken to him on several occasions hardly adds up to an indictment. But the flashing stop sign, the slight tick of the light, the breeze coming across the field, all hold some sort of presentiment of the future. Like the friends I never see anymore, the parties I never attend, I feel the surprise of a man who occupies a life he is not familiar with. Yet, it is of my own doing, and I understand finally—we are our own worst enemy.

15

T-3

…and counting

Wednesday

"So it's Wednesday … what happens on Wednesday?"

"Nothing."

So it went in my bus of one. On Wednesday I was in a particular hurry because of a promise to meet Ellie Mae and Jed at Starbucks. He had called and moved our meeting up a day. I push down the accelerator, trying to coax the line of minivans with young charges into moving faster. I shiver against the morning cold, wishing I had time for a cup of coffee. The preternatural quiet in the car is something different. Usually there is some question pertaining to baseball, chess, or basic physics concerning the planet, which could cover global warming or where do birds go in winter. But today Dale junior is quiet, and I wonder if there is something more than just the natural depression of a child going to school.

"Wednesday is a good day, then?"

"It's all right," he says and shrugs, staring out the window.

"Gym class?"

"Yeah."

"Music?"

"I hate the music teacher."

I glance in the mirror again at my school soldier ready for his drop with backpack, lunch, and zippered flight gear. His expression has become morose, and I wonder if this could all be put on Mrs. Beamer, the hapless music teacher.

"Why do you hate the music teacher?"

"Because she always yells at me."

I take this in, turning down Crane Road to the school. This is a straight shot between McMansions, a few recalcitrant cornfields, and a cemetery from 1906. The stream of school-bound SUVs, minivans, and Hummers has swollen to a line not unlike morning traffic on the expressway. I ride the bumper of a minivan with a vanity plate: "PROCHOICE."

"Why does she always yell at you?"

The shrug again.

"She says I always sing out of tune."

A Hammer trait. No Hammer I know of is musically inclined. I don't hold this against my son and I think it is actually a good thing. A man who has but a few talents is better off than the man of many—it is really a matter of focus. I hit the brakes suddenly and nearly shove "PROCHOICE" into the backseat of the minivan in front. The snaking caravan is a dominoes game of starting and stopping as children are dropped, makeup is applied, and morning cell phone conversations are pursued. I am but one of the few male drivers in our omnibus of grade-school charges.

"Well, I wouldn't let it get to you ..." I slam on the brakes again, swearing silently. "What else happens on Thursday?"

"Writing."

I look in the mirror and nod.

"Now that's something to cheer about, huh?"

My son shrugs again, keeping his lonely vigil of the passing countryside.

"Yeah, I guess. I do like writing the best."

"Of course you do," I say, hitting the steering wheel. "English and writing were always my favorite. Are you guys working on stories or anything?"

Dale draws an imaginary figure on his window.

"Yeah. But Mrs. Measly says I wander too much in my story, and I have to stick to the plot."

I consider this migration of minimalism down to the fourth grade. *No. No. Don't meander, stick to the plot!* A child at least should be able to explore and play in the realms of creative writing. Later, they can be beaten down into submission, writing the one-dimensional stories and novels the public demands. Conformity comes earlier with each passing generation.

"Well," I say gingerly. "It's all right to meander, Dale. That is where the meat is. I think what she is saying is that eventually you want to make it back to your central theme."

"Nope." Dale junior looks in the mirror. "She cut six pages out of my eight-page story."

"Six pages!"

The feeling of evisceration is something I hoped to spare my son at least until he was old enough to drink. I press down the accelerator, finally getting a clear lane to make up for lost time.

"Yeah, there was practically nothing left."

"That's ridiculous—"

"Dad!"

I look up and just miss the yellow "School Zone, 15 MPH" barriers, jamming on the brakes, trying in vain to stop several tons of man and machinery, seeing the wide mouth of a woman with a bowl haircut—the antichrist of all that is wrong with suburban America. It is my nemesis in the orange neon smock, brandishing a red stop sign. I hear nothing, but I watch her mouth move in a steady motion as I recognize my proctor from just days before.

"It's Mrs. Thomas," Dale shouts in real agony. "*You did it again, Dad!*"

A common theme as of late; the Dad who is now on the back of the cereal box of Dad Buffoonery. Take a wrong turn, lose a sock, piss on the toilet seat, or just have a bad day, and it all winds back to *dad the clod.* I am the cog with the broken tooth in the smooth machine of women and children, and I certainly have just brought the whole machine to a screeching halt.

"Dad!"

"I know, I know," I mutter, looking in the mirror at Mrs. Thomas and her two barricades. She is the commando stealthily approaching the enemy tank. Determination is her righteous emotion as she marches toward my window. Her face is red, her mouth still open. It seems to me that she is yelling, "Stop!" over and over.

"Oh man, is she mad," Dale junior cries out fearfully.

The truth is, I feel my son's fear as well. This is the woman I have avoided all my life. The woman who was never asked to prom, always returned her library book on time, and ended up giving blow jobs because that's all the boys wanted from her. This woman has now reached the back of my vehicle. I know I am guilty, but I take my foot off the brake and begin moving at a guilty ten miles an hour. I assumed Mrs. Thomas might flip me the bird, note me in her report, or cuss me behind my back. Never did I countenance the steely determination of the enraged crossing guard.

"Dad!" Dale screams out. "She's *chasing us!*"

It is true. Mrs. Thomas has broken into a determined jog, her large, muscled thighs breaking the pleat of her khaki shorts, great breaths expounded from her red cheeks, the stop sign held aloft not unlike the Olympic carrier of the torch. I watch in the mirror this billboard for the modern American matriarch, the equiangular red stop sign seeming to float in space behind me.

"No she's not," I mutter, keeping my eyes on the mirror, accelerating to twenty miles an hour. This will surely do in Mrs. Thomas. She is not a marathoner and while ten miles an hour may be doable for the *in-shape* crossing guard, certainly twenty miles an hour will convince her the effort is not worthy of the cause. But to my chagrin, the neon besmocked Mrs. Thomas with her red octagonal warning sign is now running full steam down the centerline of the highway. She has ramped up her speed and I know then she has trained for this moment and I'm much more than just the scofflaw who blasted past her barriers for the tenth time. Nothing less than the clarion of the trumpet charge of middle-class morality is chasing my truck. Minivans pull to the side as the mothers watch Mrs. Thomas execute her duty to God and country—not unlike the reactions citizens have when a cop pulls his gun.

"Dad!"

"I see her, I see her," I mutter, losing my faith that an internal combustion engine can outdistance a pissed-off crossing guard. Dale junior is hovering just below the seat, watching the huffing Mrs. Thomas. She is now beet red, her fists pounding the air, the stop sign tucked in under her armpit. She is not unlike the jet pilot locked and loaded for combat with wings swept back and guns locked on the target.

"Aren't you going to stop, Dad?"

It is the question, but like the robber in the commission of a crime, I realize I have gone too far. If I pull over now, I will have to endure the sweaty wrath of the middle-aged woman who wants my ass. But if I continue, there is still a chance Mrs. Thomas might run out of gas and just say fuck it.

"Eventually," I murmur, watching my son, who is peering over the seat like a man under fire. I look in the mirror again, slowing to ten miles an hour as traffic has slowed to watch the drama unfold. Mrs. Thomas neatly closes the gap, and like the hound, she knows she will soon have her prey. Traffic is following behind the heavyset, bright orange marathoner not unlike a caravan of the long distance marathoner, urging on the runner, lending their support for the final mile. They are clearly on her side, this mélange of minivans moms who want to see me defrocked as much as Mrs. Thomas. All I can do is continue toward the school with a fifty-year-old woman jogging behind me. I envision the life of one Mrs. Thomas and know then she must have her vindication. She is probably ill used by her husband, sexually deprived, the workhorse of the middle-class grind. As the years have passed, she has come to hate the errant male. She has been used and abused while her husband travels and bangs the latest stripper before returning to the *man-woman* snoring on the far side of the bed. Mrs. Thomas now demands recompense. The target of her sublimated wrath is one white SUV trolling toward the school parking lot.

"Dad, she's still coming," Dale junior breathlessly reports

"I know, I know," I murmur, watching Mrs. Thomas settle down to a respectable jog.

I wonder then if she has been working out on the treadmill, envisioning exactly this type of emergency where she is required to go beyond the usual duties of the crossing guard. A steady thirty minutes, working off sexual steam, then maybe a good-night session with a vibrator finishes off the monastic life of the suburban house mom/crossing guard.

"She's still coming, Dad," Dale junior informs dully, peering low over the backseat like a man who might be shot any minute.

I now see the entire Prairie Creek School has stopped their migratory morning to watch this drama unfold. I keep hoping Mrs. Thomas might give up the ghost, tire of sucking in my exhaust, her lungs giving no more, and having made her point, she retires to the side of the road to flip me the bird. But Mrs.

Thomas comes on like the possessed warrior she is.

"Dad, she's still *there!*"

"I see her," I mutter.

Mrs. Thomas is huffing now. Her sign is carried loosely, like a football player who knows he will cross the goal line and all he has to do is not fall or fumble. I turn into the circular drive with Mrs. Thomas trailing like the dog that chases the car to a standstill. The drive is where the principal greets the returning students— it is where Mrs. Thomas will have her day. She is huffing greatly now, breath blown from red cheeks, sweat smoothing the bowl haircut, the sign hitting the concrete.

"We are going to die," my son moans from the back, slumping down in his seat as we wheel around the circle.

I come to a slow stop and see Mrs. Thomas lean on her knees briefly. Mr. Boner the gym teacher and Mr. Young the principal have come to her aid. She is holding the stop sign aloft as I leave the safety of my warship. It is time to face my nemesis.

"*You …*"

Mrs. Thomas is still trying to catch her breath. She is spitting nails, glaring, spitting phlegm, sweating, and coughing out exhaust and road dust.

"*You … You … are … a …*" She swallows again. "*A … criminal!*"

I feign surprise and hold my arms wide. I think pleading ignorance is my only chance. Maybe I am a man who never looks in his rearview mirror.

"I'm sorry," I say sincerely. "Were you behind me?"

The bald and suited principal, Mr. Young, eyes me as if I'm a child predator. He is a man combining the vagaries of middle age with a suit ten years out of date and the comb-over hair of a man defying male pattern baldness. The hated Mr. Boner, gel haired, blue *Target* sweat suited, with monstrous gym shoes, snorts and shakes his head.

"I might have *known* it would be *you* and your son."

Mrs. Thomas suddenly breaks from the principal's grasp and swings her fiberglass sign. The hard fiberglass catches me in the shoulder like a large paddle.

"*You always speed … You are going to kill somebody, you selfish asshole!*"

The sign then swings again and I deflect it with my hand, jerking the sign from Mrs. Thomas. She falls to the pavement, losing the balancing stick of her journey.

"*Ahhhhh!*" She screams. "*He hit me!*"

The mothers of Charleston come to the aid of Mrs. Thomas. I am confronted with the large jaw and dull eyes of the physical education instructor. "Mom, I'm going to major in physical education," said long ago with the tacit nod from parents who realized junior was no rocket scientist. The breath is laced with Colgate, the teeth perfectly flossed.

"Pretty easy to pick on a woman, huh, guy? Why don't you pick on a *man?*'

"I would if I saw any," I say, inhaling the toothpaste of one Don Boner, PE.

"*He speeds every day … every day … I hate him … I hate him!*" Mrs. Thomas wails, surrounded by teachers, nurses, social workers, and mothers.

"I didn't hit her," I explain to the red-faced principal. "She chased my car and then hit me with her sign."

Mr. Boner places a fat index finger in my face.

"Because you speeded, *asshole,*" he yells, spraying me with saliva. "No wonder your son is such a fricking *knucklehead.*"

I stare at the narrow eyes taunting me from above. Enough is enough.

"Fuck you, Mr. Pituitary."

Mr. Boner's mouth drops open. No on has said these words to this man for a very long time. He is *the gym teacher,* after all.

241

"You want to say that again?" he says, stepping closer.

"Sure ..."

"Dad?"

I turn and there is Dale junior standing in front of my car. He looks scared; his eyes are full of tears. I have caused a mini-riot at the school, and his gym teacher is about to take a shot at his father. I turn back to the principal, fuming, audibly growling at me. He is a much smaller man than Mr. Boner, but he does not need physical force. *He is the principal.*

"I'm sorry," I mutter, looking down. "I didn't mean to speed. Tell Mrs. Thomas I'm sorry."

"You tell her, asshole ... " Mr. Boner shouts.

The principal in the polyester blend suit turns to Dale junior

"Young man, I want to see you in my office, *now."*

Dale junior starts crying.

"Hey, don't take it out on him," I shout.

Mr. Boner smirks as the principal puts his hands on my son's shoulder.

"You should have thought of that before, Mr. Hammer."

I meet Ellie Mae and Jed at the Starbucks on the corner of Main Street. I have frequented this coffee watering hole many times before, snagging one of the overstuffed chairs in the corner, slipping into caffeine and sugar nirvana, ignoring the cell phone calls that come the minute I pull out a book. This Starbucks occupies a converted furniture factory from the last century. It is cavernous, with hardwood floors that steel dollies rolled over at one time. The artists are missing, replaced by bluetoothed men on laptops and children inhaling whipped-cream monsters. I don't have to wait long; a mountain man and his stockcar moll blast through the door, garnering glances from businessmen and moms alike. Clearly they are in the wrong Starbucks.

"Hi guys," I say, shaking hands with Jed first and then Ellie Mae, who immediately vacates to order up.

"You need anything, Dale?" She calls across the room, a sexpot in shorts pulled halfway up her ass and a low-riding shirt. The mothers eye her dubiously. The businessmen catalog an image to be used when they squeeze their dicks with all that Republican rage. After that she is a cartoon character straight out of the *Dukes of Hazard*.

"No, no, I'm fine."

Ellie Mae turns and gives the entire coffee shop a very defined ass crack. Jed flips a chair around and sits down on it backwards, spinning his Dale Earnhardt cap around, the truck driver gang banger of our culture. His knees are like tabletops and his hands engulf mine. The image of Ellie Mae spinning around on top is faintly hilarious. I know they met through the Internet, and I imagine old Jed sat down one night after long, weary days on the road and punched in, *woman, trailer, double wide, NASCAR, nice ass, big tits, no education required, smoker preferred, Alabama.* Google matched them up in lightning speed, blacking out the screen, throwing up the single name that would change his life: *Ellie Mae.*

I actually like old Jed. He knows Ellie Mae is certifiable and that most things in life aren't for free and lonely hours in a truck are the only real way he will make money. His Internet bride still believes there is gold over the next rainbow, and if she watches *Oprah, Jerry Springer,* and *Who Wants to Be a Millionaire* enough times, then she will turn over the rock of fame and fortune.

I spread out a good faith estimate in front of Jed.

"These are the numbers, then," he says and nods, stroking his beard.

"Yes. These are the closest I can come right now. The only thing I don't know is how much your mortgage insurance will be."

He looks up, his eyes darkening.

"I don't know what all this shit mean, but is this my payment?"

"Yes."

He pushes out his lip, sounding out the number like a first grader.

"Sixteen hundred and one."

I nod slowly. "Like I said, the bank has not gotten back to me with their number for the mortgage insurance, so I took an estimate."

"Hmmm.'"

It is an amazing deal, really. Jed is not putting down one cent of his own money, the sellers are kicking back six thousand in closing costs, and with the tax credits, my client stands to buy a house and get money back in hand. To say nothing of the eighteen thousand in back child support payments the bank chose to overlook and the judgment that was being paid at closing—only in America could a man with no money buy a house and walk away from the closing table with cash. But there would be mortgage insurance and this was the one number I could not nail down.

"I'm going to let Ellie Mae look at these fucking numbers, I can't make head or tail of 'em, but if we go above this sixteen hundred and one, then I'm fucking walking out the door."

"You are getting a house for no money down and cash back. Let's not be too hasty in walking out the door," I say gingerly.

Jed leans back and crosses his arms.

"I'm telling you, Dale—"

"Here you go, honey."

Ellie Mae has returned and I mentally gird myself for battle. I need this closing for a lot of reasons, but any source of income, no matter how pathetic, still beats zero. This all floats through my head as I watch Ellie Mae and Jed eat a caramelized whipped cream creation that would give a regular man a heart attack. Jed motions to the good faith estimate with whipped cream flecking his beard.

"You look at those numbers; I can't make shit out of 'em."

Ellie Mae picks up the paper, frowning, moving a finger of spangled silver down the line. She is not a dumb woman, just misinformed, which actually makes her worse—she really believes everyone *can be* a millionaire and that if she could just get on *American Idol,* she would show those girls how to really sing! Ellie Mae puts the paper down and stares up, her blue eyes not unattractive if they weren't placed against some sort of spray-on tan that has turned her skin permanent orange.

"What the fuck is that number?"

She speaks through her nose as many southern girls do, turning *fuck* into *fug.*

"That is the underwriting fee," I nod, territory we have been over many times.

"I never saw that there before," she says, looking at Jed, who has just finished his coffee and whipped cream creation the size of a Big Gulp. He still looks sleepy, the sugar and caffeine doing nothing but coating the whiskers around his mouth white. Ellie Mae turns back to me. "Did you add that in?"

"As I said before, I am paid by the bank; I just turn over the fees they charge me."

"But that weren't there before."

"Yes," I say and nod. "Yes it was … we even discussed it."

She looks back at the paper, moving on to find better fish.

"What in the fuck is that?"

The mothers look over and the businessmen yawn. I look where her silvery nail is tapping.

"Those are your title fees."

"Nine hundred fucking dollars!"

Now all of Starbucks has tuned into the trio from the last

remake of the *Beverly Hills*. I guess I am Mr. Drysdale, forever trying to swindle Jed out of his millions. I pause and see that Jed has come out of his sugar buzz to see if crazy Ellie Mae has actually found something.

"Ellie Mae, I am not the title company, and those are pretty standard fees."

"You're fucking ripping us off! How much are you making, huh?"

I nod down to the paper. "You can see what I am making right there on the paper."

Ellie Mae looks down and then cries out for all to hear.

"Three thousand fucking dollars!"

Jed is now brooding over the paper. He determines maybe Ellie Mae is on to something and scooches his chair up closer.

"Dale, my sister recommended you, but she said you got to keep an eye on you." He points a huge finger at me. "Listen, Dale, you probably *are* a swindler, and I don't really care. Hell, we all gotta make our money, but you better keep me at sixteen hundred dollars, or I'm walking."

There are moments where it all comes crashing down. There are moments when what you are doing meets you right in the road, and then you have a choice. You can either say, "You can't call me a swindler," or you sit there and say nothing. I make no move; only my skin has changed color. Ellie Mae and Jed are now standing. They have done their work and are looking down at the man with his page of numbers. Jed nods down to me.

"I don't give a shit how much you make, Dale, but you better get me that fucking payment."

I mutter something, smile, and try and shake hands, but they are gone. I sit back down and feel the eyes of the businessmen and mothers who know something untoward occurred in the Starbucks. I hear them leaving, going back to where fine upstanding people always do the right thing.

Billy Goat's Tavern is on lower Wacker drive and has the darkness of a diner from the forties. The black-and-white pictures circa 1940 accent this feeling of being lost in time. It is the place made famous by John Belushi in his skit, "Cheezeburger cheezeburger cheezebuger." It is the place where newspapermen came to drink and smoke after long days at the Chicago Tribune or the Sun Times. So it makes sense this is the place Al suggested we meet on his lunch break from the Tribune.

"Is he here yet?"

Elliott is standing in the smoky haze of the bar with an expression of a school marm in a boys' bathroom. The academic does not approve of men in suits eating God's chosen animal in a subterranean bar. He glances back at the door, ready to vacate the moment things become intolerable. A man dressed in black with more jewelry than Norma Desmond does not frequent watering holes catering to iron workers and office dregs. A sushi bar is more my brother's speed, or a sanctioned university bar with coeds and alternative music.

"I'm only doing this for Dad, you know," he informs me while pulling out a stool.

I smile wryly, thinking that for two men who had just parted ways under the hail of black lesbian anger and matriarch rage—we were doing all right.

"Really? I thought you were doing this for me, Elliott."

The professor ignores this and straddles the bar stool, dropping a pair of black leather driving gloves on bar.

"Apollonian didn't want me to come at all, but I figure Dad needs the support," he says darkly, ordering a cosmopolitan.

That was another reason I knew Elliott would be present and accounted for—any campaign to further the cause of one D. T. senior has Elliott as a shoe in. I can see my brother has already framed this mission in the same light of Doris the embezzler. So now we are the Brothers Karmazov once again. I have already downed one bottle of beer and have started on a second. Elliott inhales a martini and orders another. Several construction workers have turned to look at Truman Capote and the disheveled man sitting at the bar. We are an unlikely pair—no one would guess we were brothers.

"You think he's going to be an asshole about it?"

I shrug.

"I don't know."

Elliott frowns, shaking his head.

"It's not fucking his! It's Dad's right to be there."

"He's not Southern," I point out wryly.

"Exactly," Elliott nods, himself having been born north of Mason-Dixon line in New York.

I swig my beer and feel suddenly tired. I stare at a photo of a gas station from fifty years before and feel suddenly the presence of all those people who have passed. It isn't good to go tampering with the dead.

"I wonder what Mom would say," I muse out loud.

"She'd want Dad there," the professor states emphatically.

"They grew up together and they raised children together. Al was only there at the end."

"Some would say that counts for more," I point out.

"No way. She'd want Dad there."

A shadow blocks the pale light dribbling in from lower Wacker. I turn to a man with close-cropped hair and a skeletal jaw. A faint resemblance to athletes of old clings to Al Milner, maybe Johnny Unitas or a thin Dick Butkus. Since my mother's death, Al has become a workout freak.

"Hey, guys, sorry I'm late," he says with an easy handshake and a grin that is Al.

I remember then I always liked Al. His demeanor hearkened back to a time before men with Blackberries and digital cameras.

He has the air of the gumshoe reporter on a beat with his craggy, lined jaw and flinty blue eyes. The old newspaper man still lurked in his loose-fitting sport coat with patches on the sleeve. My mother's attraction to this hard-bitten guy with the soul of a poet was understandable.

"You guys eat?"

"I've had two beers," I say, holding up my bottle.

"I'm not hungry," Elliott replies tersely.

"Well, I am. I'll take a cheeseburger and Miller."

The bartender leaves and we make small talk.

"She's great, great," he says, pulling on his Bud. "She's taking an art class now … there are easels all over the place."

I smile, thinking how everything to Al must seem like a cycle. Married to an artist before who filled his loft with easels, paints, and canvases—he now shares his life with another woman who prefers the scent of paint thinner and stained palates to the conventional living room and couch set. His new wife had moved into the loft with a lot of my mother's paintings still on the walls. I imagine it would be intimidating to have the former wife of her husband lording down from on high without trying to add her own statement.

Al's cheeseburger and fries arrive and he picks up a bottle of ketchup.

"How the kids?"

"Great," I say and nod, feeling Elliott's stare. "How's the newspaper world?"

Al stares ahead, upending his beer.

"Busy."

Elliott and I exchange glances. Whenever we asked Al how his work was, he always gave only one reply—*busy*. It became a running joke and we began calling Al "Busy." Of course, this was all before my mother got sick and Al became a saint for his heroic nursing.

"You sure you guys don't want something to eat?"

I shake my head, ignoring the imploring expression of my brother.

"Al … listen. I have a question for you."

"Shoot," he says, wiping his mouth.

I pause.

"I visited Mom's grave last summer."

He turns, chewing his burger, his light blue eyes circling the bar.

"Did you see the bench?"

"Yeah … that was nice."

"Glad they finally put it there," he nods.

Al wipes his mouth and swigs his beer.

"And I noticed there was a plot next to my mother … empty, of course."

"Yep," Al says, taking another large bite. "It's mine."

He grins suddenly and I feel a little better.

"Not looking to move in too soon either," he continues, winking.

"Well, I guess what I was wondering Al is … well, now that you are married, do you think you would actually, you know … want to be there?"

Al continues chewing, then sets down his cheeseburger. He takes another swig of beer and turns. The dispassionate observer of the human condition is there, the journalist gathering the facts.

"Why?"

It is the question. I look at Elliott, who looks like a spurned housewife dying to give her two cents.

"Because that plot should go to our father," the professor announces to the auditorium.

This is not the way I wanted things to go. I wanted to ease into the question, flank it with several probes, and test the temperature

250

of the water. Elliott just dove in and didn't even see if the water was deep enough. Al's eyes cloud over. His expression is that of a man who just walked into his living room, only to find some aluminum siding salesmen.

"Really?"

I begin damage control.

"Al, what we are saying is that if you aren't going to use it then … well, we don't know who will end up there—"

"Not that sonofabitch."

The professor blanches. Even I lose my breath over the sucker punch. Al has clearly finished his lunch. He turns on his stool and appraises the two brothers coolly. All good will has vanished, and I know then Al has considered this question before. Like all good journalists, he has considered every angle and maybe even saw the day when two brothers would come down to a subterranean bar, sniffing around for the last dregs of a marriage that ended years ago.

"I don't think that kind of talk is constructive, Al," the professor informs the old newspaper man.

Al shakes his head, stabbing a fry into the sea of blood.

"You guys have a lot of balls."

"Al, it is a family plot," I say tentatively. "Forget about my dad. We just wondered if you wanted to sell it to us."

"What, you're going to move in?"

A slight gleam is in his eyes now. I shrug.

"No, but maybe down the line."

"Nope. That place is not for your father."

There it is—the simple declarative sentence that Hemingway built a career on. Amazing how much can be packed into a few words. Al rolls his tongue around the side of his mouth. He fixes me with a stare and then stands up. His eyes are flat. My brother has not given up the fight yet. He always felt in some way it was Al's fault our mother didn't go to Mayo or some alternative clinic where her life would be saved with alfalfa sprouts and ginseng.

"I think you are being ridiculous, Al."

"You do, huh."

His expression is not that different from Doris's. The academic is milk toast to this man who has dueled in the real world for forty years.

"Yes, everybody has their price … we just need to know yours," the professor says coolly.

Al grins suddenly and I know then he is laughing at Elliott.

"All right. Ten grand and it's yours."

Elliott frowns, looking closer at this man who looks like he is chiseled from stone.

"How much did you pay for it?"

"Two thousand."

Elliott looks at me, then at Al. The epiphany spreads through his face, a scarlet rage of the disenfranchised.

"You are trying to rip us off!"

Al smiles coldly.

"That's the cost, boys." He looks at me. "Tell your dad I won't take a check. It has to be cash."

Al then finishes his beer and throws a twenty on the bar.

"Thanks for lunch, guys."

After lunch I drive over to the far south suburbs in search of Carl Sanchez High School. The drive is long and sulfur-filled, with the reek of water treatment plants letting everyone know where Chicago pumps its waste. I find the largest high school in the state and park among BMWs, Hummers, and bright convertible Volkswagens. The scent of the high school hallway is one of chewing gum, the gun-metal scent of lockers, a tang of erasers, paper, and a lingering whiff of towels in a locker room. I inhale bad cologne and too much perfume as I navigate the hallways, asking more than one suffering teenager where the main office is. Finally, I spy the large, glass-enclosed aquarium complete with the rotund secretary.

"Can you tell me where the English office is?"

It is the same question I ask every year and the flat mouth and dull eyes catalog our little dance as another ritual endured for the sake of a pension. It is the same question I ask every year I come to Carl Sanchez High School and stand in front of twenty students and field questions about the origins of my first novel.

"Room C15, down your hall and to the right," she tells me, already gearing up for her next performance in 365 days.

I sail back into the streaming tide of young America. They ignore the man in cowboy boots and leather jacket, slouching along in the sea of students, teachers, advisors, coaches, and administrators. It is a ritual, after all. Ten years of appearing in front of children who have read my first novel and fielding the questions prompted by one Tom Hector—my one-man cheerleader who claims my coming-of-age novel supplants *Catcher in the Rye* in relevancy, nudges out *A Separate Peace* in pathos, and clearly knocks *To Kill a Mockingbird* on it's ass with pace. The one caveat to these heroics is that I would come to the school and spend a day talking to his students.

I find room C15 and open the door to a cinder-blocked office of desks facing each other. There is the roasted coffee burned under the dripomatic in the corner and an open carton of moldy coffee cake complete with a white plastic knife. A man in a sweater with a sash (circa 1975) is reading student papers while inhaling coffee cake, raining crumbs down upon the steel grey desktop. He doesn't look up, but reaches for another slice of rubberized pastry without taking his eyes from the paper now fairly covered with dehydrogenated dough. It is the English office.

"Dale!"

I turn to a tubby, short man with glasses and grey hair, standing up from a far desk by the window. Tom Hector weaves his way past rows of To *Kill a Mockingbird* and S. E. Hinton's, *The Outsiders*, greeting the man who has now given up on the student paper, reaching me with his hand outstretched.

"Dale. Good to see you."

"Hi, Tom. Thanks for having me."

Tom Hector is a round, cherubic man with ocular glasses giving him the air of a middle-aged boy. His quiet enthusiasm has steeled him through years of administrative politics and an English department under siege for validity if not relevance in the digital age.

"Well, this is it," Tom says, glancing around the cement-walled office. "I retire after this year."

I realize then Tom Hector is not much older than me. I envy this man who is now able to cash in on a promised retirement to proudly wear the headset of McDonald's or the smock of Home Depot. A quick examination of the road not taken in my own life leaves me to the same conclusion—I will work until the day I die.

"You're a lucky man, Tom," I say sincerely.

He shakes his head wistfully.

"I don't know … I'm not sure what I'm going to do without my kids …"

"The school will certainly be less for your absence."

Tom Hector smiles and like all of us who have pinned our lives to something than the almighty buck—he has the moment of recognition that the halcyon glory of altruism might be nothing more than walking out and driving home.

"I'd like to think so," he says in a low voice.

I look at Tom Hector and want to give him some reassurance that what he has done will mean more than all the Donald Trumps in the world.

"Well, you always pushed my book because you believed in it, and I think you probably were the same way with your students."

"Thanks, Dale. I'm going to miss this place." He smiles suddenly. "Even this shitty office."

I look around the English office and feel something inside me relax, some sort of guard coming down. I had forgotten the warm congeniality of educated people with a common belief in something other than the dollar.

"Well, we better get to the classroom. The kids are waiting," Tom says, opening the door.

"Showtime," I say and nod.

Tom Hector is an artist in hiding. His classroom has a Dionysian gloom. It is so dark I can barely see the students as I ramble on about my career, the ups, the downs, the anecdotes, the pithy phrases about writing and reading. The shaded lamp in the corner throws shadows against the wall, obscuring Tom Hector's posters of popular culture—a movie poster of Marilyn Monroe and James Dean, *The Boulevard of Broken Dreams*. There is pleasure here. I can see people holding my first novel. It is dead center on the one-armed bandits and I realize then how long it has been since I saw anyone holding one of my books. The questions are coming fast now and I am like any talk-show host, picking people out of the crowd, orchestrating, cracking jokes and witticisms.

"I write in the morning and leave the rest of the day for reading," I say, painting the picture of the successful artist. "I treat it like a job and take the weekends off like everyone else," I inform my wide- eyed ninth graders. "You have to do what you believe in. I knew when I started my first novel, that *this,* this is what I wanted to do for the rest of my life, and I dedicated myself to that task. I told myself that even if I wasn't successful, I would continue writing, even if I never got published."

I stand in front of the podium and look out at my young brethren, winding up for my summation. I have reached the nirvana of any self-help guru who suddenly believes his own bullshit and I am flushed with emotion as I give away pearls of wisdom.

"One day you will come to a crossroad, and you will know that there is something out there—something you want to do more than anything else in the world—and you will have a choice then, either to pursue it or join the rest of the people who say I will take the easier road, the road everyone takes, and throw in your lot with the mass and take the easy money."

I pause for dramatic effect and walk out from behind my podium. This is the pinnacle of my small rock concert, the encore, the song they have all been waiting for. I play it like the old hand, the impresario at the top of his form—the successful artist of mass culture.

"But if you decide to take that road less traveled, if you decide to become the actor, the musician, the painter, the writer, then you will find a hard road, no doubt, but you will be very lucky because you will know who you are, and no one can take that from you. Thank you for having me."

There is polite applause in Tom's classroom. I smile in the darkness, nodding to the students I have wowed. They must be enraptured with the man who easily charted off interviews in the *New York Times, USA Today, People Magazine,* radio, television, and the anecdotal conversations with Hollywood producers. It has been a very good class with wide-ranging discussion, and now it is time to wrap up by signing books. A lone hand in the back goes up. I see the lounging young man who has peppered me with questions as to how I get paid. I have handled him easily, giving him the specifics of percentages and advances and the economics of trade book publishing. He is good-looking, athletic, a popular student already. He lounges in the back of Tom's darkened classroom, grabbing twenty winks between doodling on his paper—drawing pictures of tanks next to naked women. He has the natural instincts so key to an athlete, and his instincts are telling him there is a strut missing in the D. T. Hammer concert—a weak link in the chain mayo of my story.

"Yes," I say, nodding.

"Yeah," he sits up and kicks back his hair, lounging over the small desk. Blond, blue-eyed, well muscled—the *uber* man of young adulthood. "I went online, Mr. Hammer, to find your books, and I couldn't even *order them* because they said they are all out of print ..."

"Todd," Mr. Hector warns ominously.

I can see Todd has been the thorn in the Hector realm. The dubious naysayer to the teacher's last year, robbing epiphanies, destroying moments with a muttered, "Yo bro," flashing wannabe gang signs while peeling off a rap lyric from a city far away from suburban Orland Park.

"No, no, let him go," I say, nodding. "Let him ask his question."

"Yo ..." The ghetto hand extends in rapper style. "So I went to all these different sites, and none of them even *had* your books. I even tried to special order them and it said the only thing I could do was get *used* copies. I went to Amzon.com, and it said you're like two million down in ranking, so I called my main homeboy Jack who works at Barnes and Noble and I told him, like, to get me one of your books."

Todd kicks back into a prime slouch and holds up his hands, a thin smile as he stabs one more phony.

"But, like, he called me back and said, 'dude, this guy's books are *dead, man.* They aren't any anywhere. We don't even carry them in our database. He's DOA, man.'" Todd pauses, letting go his final torpedo. "He said there is *no way* you can make any money from your books because he says people *can't get them.*" Todd frowns, holding up a hand in gangster fashion. "So, like, I don't understand how you can stay at home and write and stuff, when you don't have any books to sell."

Tom Hector is throwing daggers toward Todd. He has violated the basic covenant of the guest speaker—*thou shall not show up the guest speaker for the fraud he is.* But Todd has laid out his case and the class is waiting for me to rebut. The arrow is easily knocked down. It is really a lob over the wall and I could throw it back with the realities of book publishing followed up with a few veiled references to foreign royalties. But I pause.

I look down at the podium. Even in this sanctuary of non-reality, the truth has followed me. The hapless, non-book reading Todd has plunged to the truth I have been glossing over for the last hour. It is the question I get: *do you do anything else to support yourself?* I know, too, that Todd is the realist of our times and I am the fake—painting a picture that doesn't exist. The students deserve better, because one of them might believe a man writing literary fiction no one reads could *actually* make money.

I look up at the lounging man of the future in the back row.

"You're right, Todd," I say slowly. "You can't get my books anywhere. They have been out of print for the last five years." It is quiet now in the classroom, and the students still clutch the novel of their hope. I hear a pencil roll off a desk. "The truth is, I can't make a living at what I do ... " I look up. "I've done a disservice here by painting a picture that I am successful author."

Todd has a faint smile on his face. He has scored mightily and taken down the bullshit speaker.

"I broker loans for a living." I shake my head. "I need to make a certain amount so I can live in my house and have a big car and support my two children."

I pause and look around the room at the stricken faces.

"So ... stay in school and get yourself a good job. You don't want to be in my position ... it's a bad feeling to not be able to be who you really are."

I can hear Tom Hector moving. He did not bargain for this in his final year. He wanted an uplifting speaker, not a man who decides his students are to be his confessors. I should have quelled the rebellious Todd. I should have sloughed him off with humor or with vague references to Hollywood deals. I had done it before under the banner of the mysterious income of the author. But he deserved better; *they* deserved better.

Tom tries to rescue his class. The silence speaks volumes. His students are not sure what the man just did in front of them, but it is not something they have experience with. "All right, it's time for Mr. Hammer to sign your books!"

I wait at the podium, examining the fine laminate.

"C'mon, I know you want to get your books signed," Tom Hector urges.

I stare at the podium. Every other year I am flooded with students wanting their books signed, but I see now the spell is broken. I am not a celebrity. I am not even an author. Busted by the sleepy leviathan of Todd, I have been taken down by one of their own and have fallen below the status of a teacher.

The bell rings and I hear the fast shuffle for the door. I pick up my annotated copy of my book and sling on my jacket.

"Yo, Mr. Hammer."

A book lands on the podium. I look up, and it is the Lord himself.

"I liked your book, man," Todd says and shrugs. "Could you sign it for me?"

Wendy is standing in the driveway with her arms crossed, watching a tow truck loading up D. T. senior's Jaguar. It is one of those trucks that pulls the car onto a flatbed and then drives away. A fat man with a mustache is moving a lever on the side of the truck, watching the reluctant car slide up onto the back. Of course he has a cigar and seems relaxed, humming to himself as another car levitates onto the back of his truck. Wendy's expression carries the accusation of a woman confronted with yet another billboard for the modern dysfunctional family.

I jump out of my car, approaching the man who is now whistling.

"Pardon me."

He turns, sending out a fine puff from his wet stub.

"You own this car?"

"No," I say, shaking my head. "But my father does. Who are you?"

The Jaguar has now come to the end of two red tracks and the man presses the lever forward. I watch as the car levitates to a level position and then slides forward to the cab of the truck. It is a rather impressive if not a civilized way to repossess a car. There are none of the movie histrionics of a tow truck sneaking up in the night.

"Auto repossession," he says, breaking his humming again to reach into his pocket. He hands me the pink slip from a multilayered form. The paper is a work order to pick up a silver Jaguar.

"Your dad just lose his job?"

I look up at the man who has friendly brown eyes.

"Why?"

He shrugs.

"Most of the cars I repo for this company are guys who lost their jobs."

He lets go of the lever and begins threading chains through the axles of the car. He is the dispassionate laborer and I envy him for this. His life will go on regardless of the fate of D. T. senior's black Jaguar. I don't know where my father is, but I know once his car is taken, we have lost all bargaining power.

"I think there's been a mistake."

The man looks up, then removes his wet pacifier.

"Call the company. I just do what I'm told."

"Stay right here while I make a call," I instruct, walking up to

Wendy, who is now standing inside the garage. "They are repoing Dad's car."

"I can see that," she nods coolly.

"Do you know where he is?"

My wife shakes her head and I know this has put D. T. senior securely in the dog house—*the man can't even be present at his own repossession.*

"Well … I'm going to call—"

Just then I hear the tow truck fire up. The placid man of many tunes is already driving down our drive.

"*Hey! Hey!*" I take off at a sprint. "*Come back here!*"

Even now I am cognizant how this looks to the neighbors. There is a man in a leather coat and cowboy boots running down the access road after a black Jaguar on a tow truck. *Writers! Jesus! Why doesn't he go back to where he came from?* I inhale exhaust and road dust down to the cul-de-sac, but the impresario of the whistled tune hits the gas and gives me a final black cloud of exhaust. I come to a stop, grabbing my knees and breathing like an asthmatic. I watch the Jaguar float down the road and then take a right turn and disappear.

I turn and see George Campbell watching me from his zero-turn mower. He has on his golf shirt, accountant glasses, gripping the turning levers like a fighter pilot. He grins, pivoting on a dime to go cut his grass down to the proper three-eights of an inch.

"Why'd they take Granddads car?" Dale junior asks, frowning.

"It was broken…they're going to fix it."

I turn and walk back toward my house. Wendy is staring at me, waiting for the official press release.

"Why'd they take his car, Daddy," Angela screams, tooling around on her training wheels.

"His car was broken," I repeat.

"It didn't look broken to me," Dale junior mutters, staring at where the Jaguar had rested.

"Well it was."

Dale junior shrugs and then goes into the backyard with his football. I turn to find my wife staring at me.

"What?"

"You want to tell me what happened to my mother's car?"

I go over my list of transgressions and remember the bumper of the cream Cadillac. In my haste to get milk the night before, I had nicked the in-laws' chariot. It was a very close call, our cars chafing as I slid down the side like the Titanic. I had jumped out and inspected the Cadillac and seen no visible damage.

"You want to tell me about it?"

"What?"

Wendy drops her arms and gives me her best, "Oh, come on" expression.

"My mother came out and started screaming that someone vandalized her car and then your son says, oh no, Grandma, no one vandalized your car, *Dad hit it* with his car."

I close my eyes momentarily. The effigy of one D. T. Hammer would be burning in Betty's yard tonight.

"All right," I say, holding up my hands. "I nicked your mother's car, but I didn't see any real damage."

"Save your bullshit for the loans, Dale."

"It's not really working there either."

Wendy pauses, her tired eyes a testament to the fact we have been on a dead run for a long time.

"It's not working anywhere, Dale. The fact you would tell your own son to lie for you is repulsive."

"I didn't tell Dale to lie."

The two butterflies arc into her brow.

"Really? What do you call telling him to not say anything about *vandalism*?"

"Vandalism ... I don't think a scratch is *vandalism,* Wendy. And as far as telling Dale not to say anything, I just figured since there was no real damage, why get the old girl into a tizzy? You know how she reacts to her almighty possessions."

Wendy looks down her long, slender nose.

"Well, if you worked for anything, then you would understand the pride they take in what they own."

"I'm the one working," I point out.

Wendy comes nearer and even in battle, she is an attractive woman. It is hard to fight with a woman you would like to take to bed.

"What you do is not *work.* You go sit up there and write God knows what! You go to coffee houses and read old novels no one cares about. You moon around and talk about how you are surrounded by morons while your loser brother insults my mother, your father insults everyone, and you are *oblivious!*" The lawyer steps in close for the summation. "All you care about, Dale Hammer, is what is happening *to you,* to your sensitive artistic nature, while the rest of us go down the shitter."

I nod slowly, wiping sweat from my brow.

"Anything else?"

"Yes," Wendy nods. "You cut down that stupid sign and now we will have to move because we have been *ostracized* by the entire neighborhood! But I'm sure that was your plan anyway."

"I don't think anyone convicted me," I say quietly.

Wendy stares at me dully.

"That Detective Clancy came by. He told me about the saw. He told me that all you have to do is pay for the sign and there will be no trouble. He said you had been very rude to him and that you were making more trouble for everyone."

I shake my head slowly, feeling I have become the whipping boy for everything that is wrong with our lives. Even while I argue, I know Wendy is right, but that doesn't make it any easier to admit culpability.

"You have them all lined up."

Her eyes narrow.

"You lined them up yourself, Dale. You have always had to rebel, but you are *forty-six* now, Dale. You are not the truculent artist anymore; you are just the middle-aged fuckup!"

I pause.

"And what are you, Wendy?"

She stares at me dead on and nods.

"I'm a fool."

My son catches my lobbing spiral with his fingertips. He turns and runs back with the ball. I watch his long, gangly legs and realize he has grown another few inches in just the last week. I know this is not true, but when did he become taller than Wendy? It is still a sure signal on the railroad of fleeting childhood. I have had to fight the urge to tell my son to slow down several times, that he will grow up fast enough and I need to catch up with him. But I know he is on a train that will only chug faster and faster until I see only the caboose lights rounding the grade.

"Hey, Dad, throw me another long bomb," he says, face flushed, breathing hard after running the length of the field.

I take the ball.

"All right ... Hut hut, hike!"

Dale takes off and I watch him run, long-legged, nine years old, gangly, a carbon-copy of myself at his age, all enthusiasm, all drive, little coordination, and all heart. I let fly a long, sailing bomb. He dives and scoops the ball and then begins a long run back to me. He has the natural ability of the boy athlete who makes plays a half-dozen adults would never attempt.

"You can throw the ball back, you know. You don't have to run it back."

"I know," he says and shrugs. "I just want to get some ball-carrying experience. I'm going out for football next year."

"*Football!* Then we better start practicing."

"Okay, what's my next play, Dad?"

"You're going to return a kickoff."

"All right," he says, tearing down the length of the yard again. "*I'm ready!*"

I let one fly. Not a bad kick for a man who hasn't kicked a football in many years. The ball lands near Dale junior and does a couple end-over flip. I take off, playing a zone defense, gauging the boy scampering toward the house. I cut him off and grab his shirt and we both go down in a long slide. I grab the ball from his hands and roll over.

"*Fumble!*"

He jumps on me and we end up on our backs. The cold scent of early dew is on the grass; there are a few clouds drifting through the twilight, fluffy golden pillows of shortening days. I lay there with my son against my arm, smelling the earth.

"Dad?"

"Yeah."

"I'm sorry about letting Mom and Grandma know about the car."

I look over at this boy of my heart and rub his hair.

"Hey, I should have never asked you to do that. You did the right thing. You told the truth, and that's what you should always do."

Dale junior frowns, tossing the football up and catching it.

"Yeah, but Grandma was pretty mad, and I thought maybe I shouldn't have said anything."

I envision Betty staring at the hairline crack in her bumper, a deep scarlet spreading over her baby cheeks. She must have felt the satisfaction of a general who has tried to root out the guerillas in the forest for years—only to find they have come into the open suddenly and she was there to cut them down.

"Listen," I say, staring at my son. "What you did was the right thing; what I did was the wrong thing. No matter how mad someone gets, you have to tell the truth. I was wrong. So, you see, you know more than your old man."

Dale junior smiles suddenly.

"I've always known that, Dad."

"Don't rub it in," I say, lying back down.

"Hey, Dad?"

"Yeah."

"Who's Marty?"

I turn.

"Why do you ask?"

He shrugs.

"I don't know … Mom's been on the phone all day with some guy named Marty. He keeps calling back and asking for her."

I sit up and stare at the house and can see Wendy in the kitchen. *Marty*. The name has all the import of receiving a summons from the IRS. Suddenly the house is not mine and this yard is not mine.

"Did you ever wonder, Dale," I murmur. "That there's something everybody else knows and you don't?"

"I feel like that every day at school, Dad."

I stand up and brush the grass off my pants.

"Hey, Dad, you still didn't tell me who Marty is."

"He's our attorney," I call back, walking toward the house.

I open the door to the kitchen and all is quiet. Wendy is dicing an onion with a glass of merlot on the counter. She has on a light blue workout suit with tennis shoes. She is the picture of the wife who has all things under control, winding down at the end of the day with a glass of wine. Angela is on the couch dissecting *Blues Clues* for the hundredth time.

"Hey."

Wendy looks up, cleaving the hapless green onion into small pieces

"Hey."

Our customary greeting—so far so good. I watch the salad being prepared, considering how to open such a Pandora's Box and then just blurt it out.

"Dale says you have been talking to Marty."

"He told you," she murmurs.

She asks this without meeting my eyes. I lean down on the breakfast bar and nod.

"Yes, the summons was delivered by my son."

Wendy looks up and smiles wryly.

"You should be used to summons by now, Dale."

I digest this and let it pass. *Stay focused.* There is a nugget of truth in all of this.

"So …" I paused. "Why did you call our attorney?"

The onion is now being diced into small squares. Wendy doesn't pause and I wonder if she even heard the question. She speaks quietly.

"Why do you think?"

"I don't know. Are we having legal problems?"

"Don't play coy, Dale." She looks up, her eyes a dark cerulean blue. "You know why I called him."

The feeling of spinning out of control is there. I am back on the ride when I was ten and that car is beginning to turn. I can feel the G force building and suddenly I don't feel good. I might vomit, I might die. I nod slowly, letting the word roll off my tongue slowly, hearing it as someone else might say it.

"A divorce?"

Wendy is now dissecting the hapless onion into pieces no human could spear with a fork. We are long past the salad, her preparation has now become a pagan ritual and our marriage is certainly on the chopping block. She stops her knife, her finger holding the blade against the old wooden cutting board.

"It's not working anymore."

"What's not?"

She looks up, exasperation moving out tragedy.

"*This* … this thing we have been dancing around with for the last fifteen years."

"This," I repeat slowly. "You mean our marriage."

"Bingo."

Bingo, I mouth. Where is the tape for this one? One always tries to reference some moment before, something you can refer to as how a scene should proceed, but I have nothing in my repository. We are in the category of marriage, death, childbirth—life-changing events that have no equal.

"Wendy," I begin quietly. "Our marriage has never worked, but show me one that does. Besides, that's no reason to get divorced."

The knife finally stops; the fine wine has turned her lips purple. The lawyer has returned and will steer my wife through the shoals of marriage dissolution while I flap back and forth—a sailboat in the doldrums.

"What is *the reason,* Dale? We have sex like automatons, we barely touch, you are in trouble with the law, my parents, your job, and your father has now come to live over our garage … how *the fuck* are we ever going to surmount all of that?"

Wendy's curse is like a spark in a rainstorm. She *does* mean business.

"Sounds like normal middle-class life to me," I say weakly.

"It is not *normal,* Dale."

I lean back against the counter and stare at Angela glued to the television. Steve is demonstrating the concept of sharing, and I feel an urge to sit down with my five-year-old and relearn the basics of being human. I wonder if the producers of *Blues Clues* have covered the basics of Mommy and Daddy splitting up. Maybe Blue will find several clues. The first one will be a redial on the phone to a lawyer, the second would be a divorce settlement under a table. Steve will exclaim to the television and bring out his handy-dandy *notebook* ... lawyer ... settlement ... I know, I know ... *divorce!*

I look away from the scampering blue dog and face Wendy.

"Did it ever occur to you, Wendy, that all our trouble started when we moved out here?"

Her eyes dull.

"Don't put it on the house again, Dale. You put *everything* on this house. This has not caused the problems in our marriage."

Even as I postulate my theory, I know it is full of holes. But I need time; I need time to maneuver, to think.

"I think this move has been a death knell for us. "

Wendy puts the knife down and I can see a sort of onion mash on the cutting board.

"Dale, I *like* our house. I like this life out here. I even like the people out here. You are in love with some idea of how we should live—some idea of living in a crappy house in a crappy neighborhood with crappy schools so you can feel edgy and have no guilt that you are living a bourgeois life." The knife is now airborne, slicing air in front of me. "The life of the down-and-out artist is *over,* Dale! It ended when you had kids, though you didn't know it. You have to face the fact *you are* a bourgeois, you do *live* in a conservative area, and that *you have* become someone you have always hated."

Wendy shakes her head firmly, the knife at sternum level.

"But you cannot drag your family down with you! I'm sorry you aren't successful, but you have to move on because I can't stay with that man looking for salvation in a beat-up house and an old car. *I can't do that anymore.* So if you want to stay in this marriage, then you have to change."

I see daylight, and yet I am cautious. There could be life here, but I do have to sample the air first.

"Change?"

Wendy nods.

"That's right, Dale. You have to finally grow up."

I pause and then squint.

"Is that a threat?"

Wendy smiles faintly.

"Still the little boy, Dale. It is not a threat. I talked to Marty to get information, but if you do not change, then I will file."

"Oh," I say and nod. "*You'll file.* The lawyer *will file*," I shout.

Angela turns from the land of the animated.

"Will you guys keep it down?"

"Don't worry, sweetheart," Wendy says, sounding like she is discussing the salad with her husband. She turns to me like a cop. "Keep your voice down."

I turn and see Dale junior making his way to the house. This is one thing I have never gotten used too. I don't mind the fact we have to hide having sex, that a good movie has been reduced to watching the Disney channel for the hundredth time, that I trip over toys every day, that my son listens in on our conversations like a hawk now—but I have never gotten used to not being able to fight like two married people.

I am suddenly pissed. Like the man threatened with bodily harm, behind the terror comes real anger. I'm pissed I am being pushed against the wall; I'm pissed because I am on the defensive. I'm pissed because I have lost control of every part of my life.

"Let me ask you a question," I say, my voice trembling.

Wendy looks at me, ready for anything.

"Since when did a house mean so much to you?"

My wife shrugs lightly and holds up her merlot.

"Since you showed me the good life, Dale."

The son will inherit the sins of the father. I can't help but think this as I watch the man strolling up from Georgia Barnes's driveway. He exudes confidence and wealth—a contented man. There is no sign that he lives over a garage, his wife has thrown him out, he's lost his job, or that his car has been repossessed. I examine him from my office window and look for some sign of such obvious catastrophe, but he is walking in the same slow, meandering way—a man who has not a care in the world.

When I catch up with him, he is still making his slow pilgrimage; a mislaid Southern gentleman wooing the last authentic Yankee damsel in distress. He takes the cigar from his mouth. The last slants of autumn slash the lawn.

"How come your life keeps getting better while mine is going in the shitter?"

D. T. senior shrugs, puffing his cigar again.

"Bottom rail on top now, Massa. You just have to roll with the punches, boy."

I turn over this basic maxim.

"They took your car, you know."

My father nods slowly, examining the wet stub of his cigar. His eyes darken as if there is some flaw in his cigar troubling him.

"I saw that, boy. I figured it was a matter of time."

He keeps his eyes on the cigar and then slowly places it back in his mouth.

"Next time let me know, and I won't go chasing the tow truck."

"I am sorry about that."

I watch some Canadian Geese land in Campbells' yard. They squawk and honk, jumping around in the wet grass. I wonder if they are gathering to leave for the migration south, but they seem disorganized, flying around in circles ceaselessly. I turn and look at my father.

"Well, I might as well give you all the news. I spoke with Al. He wants ten grand for the plot next to mom."

D. T. senior takes the cigar from his mouth again.

"Why that Yankee sonofabitch!"

"Funny, he said the same thing about you, except he didn't call you a Yankee."

"Why, he is trying to extort money for my rightful resting place!"

I take this in, feeling like a man in an *Elvis and Costello* act. The line is so hackneyed and out of place, I have to laugh.

"Cash, Dad," I say and nod. "He said he wouldn't take a check either. He wants cash."

D. T. senior grits his teeth.

"That *sonofabitch!*"

"That does seem to be the word of the day," I murmur.

He frowns and then eyes me suspiciously.

"What'd he pay for it?"

"Two grand."

D. T. senior smokes angrily.

"I wouldn't give him a goddamn nickel," he grumbles.

"Well, he wants more than a nickel."

I can see the D. T. Senior combine kicking in. He is walking in circles on Georgia Barnes's driveway, his southern dinner churning over because of the disturbance of a placid evening. He stops then.

"*Cocksuckah!*" He bellows, and the geese in Campbell's lawn take sudden flight. "A bunch of *whoreshit* is what it is!"

Now the geese are flying erratically over our heads in convoluted circles. Man or fowl—it seems no one knows what the fuck they are doing.

"You just have dinner again?"

D. T. senior takes another long pull on his cigar and his anger is drained off in the memory of a good meal.

"She just made the best batch of Southern fried chicken I have ever had. She even attempted some yams." He lowers his voice. "I must say that her chicken rivals your mother's, although she did make a better mint julep than your mother."

I shake my head, thinking of the meal I didn't eat. I had left the scene of my impending divorce for the brooding darkness of my office. Now I realize I am very hungry.

"She made you fired chicken?"

"That's right, boy," D. T. senior nods, puffing away like a locomotive. "Don't you know the way to a man's heart is through a man's stomach? She made me some pecan pie, too, for desert, and a most *delicious* cup of coffee. I must say for a Yankee woman, she is a very good cook."

I am reduced to cold pasta while my father dines like the great Kingfisher.

"A fucking mint julep ... great," I mutter, shaking my head.

"That's right, boy. And a delectable aperitif. We ate on the veranda by candlelight while I regaled her with stories of the old South, which she now wants to visit in my company. I think she would even consider moving down there if we so desired."

D. T. senior starts singing in a low voice.

"*Wish I were in the land of cotton, all old cares now forgotten, look away, look away Dixie land, wish I were in*

Dixie ... "

I look up suddenly, thinking the absurdity of my life is commingling with my father's—a very scary thought.

"Dad, what are you doing?"

"I beg your pardon?"

"You're fucking with me, right?"

D. T. senior pulls the cigar from his mouth. I stare at him in front of the white-columned house and realize it *actually* fits. All D. T. senior was ever missing was the backdrop of money—insert backdrop complete with mint julep and Cuban cigar, and he is now the picture of landed gentry, dropped straight from the late nineteenth-century, prejudices intact.

"Dad, you are not going to marry Georgia," I say flatly.

He takes a deep breath, gesturing toward me with his Cuban.

"Now listen to me, son. Not any of us knows our destiny. Why, you might leave your wife tomorrow and end up with some prostitute in Chicago." My father touches his chest. "That would not be for me to pass judgment on *your* actions. Consequently, you cannot pass judgment on mine. None of us know which way the sands of time will blow us. We all have to do our own thing, boy."

"Dad, that's such *bullshit!*"

He raises his eyebrows, clearly tolerating the student who cannot grasp these fine pearls of wisdom.

"I tell you, son, I have been doing a lot of thinking. *A lot of thinking*. I had a conversation with that cocksuckah Bill Jersey, and I realized then that these people will never rehire me, and they don't care if I sue them either. So I sat there up in your garage and I said to myself, well, you cannot determine what is going to happen to any of us. You have to just go with the flow." D. T. senior holds up his hands to the sky. "I could sit up there and curse Doris for throwing me out, or I could lament that I have lost my job, or I could go on with my life. And so that's what I decided to do, and I must say my life looks better to me now than before."

I feel like a man who has just had buckets of mud thrown all over him. Whenever D. T. senior has an epiphany, it is faintly hilarious and always self serving.

"Dad," I say sternly. "Going on with your life is not screwing Georgia Barnes."

He stares at me, clearly disappointed.

"Now there you go again, boy. You are not listening to what I said one iota! Now, I did some more thinking over your garage and another thing came to me. I was thinking about Doris, and then I thought about my former wife, and then I realized something ..." D. T. senior holds the cigar in front of him. "I should never have split up with your mother."

"I think she left you, Dad," I say dully.

My father holds his hands wide.

"But I let her! See, you are getting lost in the details boy. See, that doesn't matter. What I am saying is that I should have never *let her leave* because we were really at our best together."

I roll my eyes, not letting this one pass.

"Is that why you traveled all the time and screwed around?"

He shakes his head and stares at me in exasperation.

"Now there you go, boy! You keep going down to the *lowest* common denominator. What I am trying to say here is that your mother was good for me. She brought out my *higher nature,* you see. These other women, Doris, for instance, bring out my *lower* nature. I don't think it is their fault; I think it is a difference between a true Southern woman and these Yankee women. You see, a Southern woman appreciates the *finer things,* although I will say this Georgia woman seems to appreciate them too."

"You mean because she's a millionaire?"

D. T. senior grins slowly.

"That doesn't hurt, boy, but what I'm saying is your mother, God rest her soul, was probably the love of my life, and that only comes once."

"It takes Mom being dead for six years for you to realize this, Dad?"

D. T. senior looks up from his cigar.

"I have suspected it from time to time, boy, but sometimes you need bad things to happen to you so you can see the light," he finishes somberly." I know now she was the woman I should have always stayed with for all time."

I stand in the twilight and know I should just nod and agree, but old grievances rise up out of the dusk. The frustration that is D. T. senior has me by the lapels. I stare at the driveway for a long moment.

"Then why did you always put work first, Dad?"

He frowns, holding the cigar low.

"I didn't put *work first*, boy. I had a family to support!"

I step up close. I am surprised by the emotions I feel, old wounds surfacing from twenty years before. But I am in the past and present as I watch my own life unravel in not much different fashion than my father.

"Dad, tell me you didn't think work was the most important thing in your life. More important than Mom ... more important than us."

He snorts, waving his wet stub through the air.

"Don't be ridiculous, boy! I never put work first over your mother or my chillun'."

"Okay, then why did you work all the time?"

He stares at me as if I am the last idiot on the planet.

"Because, boy, I had to support your mother in *the style* she was accustomed to!"

"Oh," I say, nodding. "You just wanted to keep Mom up in that Southern belle tower of lace and verbena."

D. T. senior eyes me and puffs meditatively.

"That's right. Your mother was not equipped to work! She was brought up to be waited on hand and foot, boy. For a writer, I would think you would have figured that out by now."

I shake my head and know there is some truth here; it's just hidden in the musty cotton patches of D. T. senior's map of the world. I laugh shortly.

"Too bad all the darkies are gone, huh, Dad?"

D. T. senior jabs his cigar toward me.

"I was your *mother's darky*, boy! Your generation may not understand this, but your mother was a Southern belle, and you have to make considerations and the truth is, boy, I did not make enough money for her."

I suddenly remember the many fights between my parents. They were epic affairs, with my mother's verbal virtuosity doing a tap dance on D. T. senior's bowed head. My mother had a mountain of psychic energy built up from a day with children and an intellect fired on voluminous reading. When D. T. senior gaffed, she unleashed a torrent of rage and verbal abuse on the man in the fedora and Florshiems.

I breathe deeply, looking at my own house.

"Ah, what the fuck," I mutter. "My wife just threatened to divorce me. I'm going to lose my job, and the cops are going to book me on Monday for destroying public property, and my son probably thinks I'm a lousy father." I stare at D. T. senior and shrug. "So who am I to pass judgment on you?"

He stops, pointing with his cigar.

"I didn't think you were working much … does your wife know?"

I shake my head.

"I didn't tell her. I thought I might get something else before I did." I pause. "I'm a lousy broker."

"I knew that, boy."

"Thanks for the encouragement, Dad."

D. T. senior chuckles and puts his arm around my shoulders.

"Now don't you worry."

I frown, afraid to ask the question.

"Now why shouldn't I worry?"

"Because, boy," he says grandly. "There are *lots* of garages in this world."

16

T-2

....and Counting

Thursday

Dixie is floating out from my office window.

"I wish I were in Dixie, hurrah! Hurrah! In Dixie Land, I'll make my stand, way down in Dixie. Look away, look away, way down South in Dixie!"

I continue up the stairs and open the door to a haze of Old Spice and cigar smoke. D. T. senior is ready for the day with suspenders, a bowtie, a striped pinpoint Brooks Brothers shirt, and tennis shoes. I stare at the man of Florsheim descent. *Tennis shoes?*

He is tweaking his bowtie in front of a cracked mirror.

"... In Dixie Land, I'll make my stand, oh way down in Dixie. Look away, look away, how way down in ... Dixie!"

"Al Jolson, move over," I mutter, flopping into my chair.

"Hallo, boy. Another beautiful day in paradise!"

The salesman mantra; the sun rises and there is a chance to overcome all adversity. I stare at D. T. senior.

278

"Are we going on a picnic?"

My father is busily placing potato chips, grapes, a Diet Coke, and one beer into one of my blue coolers.

"Well, why not, boy? It's a *beautiful* fall day, and those pricks I work for are having second thoughts now that I told them I will sue for age discrimination ... so Miz Georgia and I are going for a picnic in the country."

I put my feet up on my desk and yawn.

"A picnic?"

"Tha's right. Miz Georgia and I are going to find a nice, shady tree and have chicken salad sandwiches and wine. I might even bring my banjo along to strum her a few tunes."

I raise my eyebrows. Life starts out strange some days and then just gets weird.

"Dad, I didn't know you owned a banjo."

"I don't, boy," he says, adjusting his tie again in the mirror. "But I can always buy one. Miz. Georgia says she loves a man who plays an instrument."

D. T. senior's picnic lunch is now finished. He actually has a mahogany-colored basket with a red-checkered hanky sticking out of the top. He slips on a straw-colored fedora with a cigar in his top pocket.

My cell phone rings.

"Mr. Hammer, Detective Clancy here."

I can hear a police radio hissing in the background.

"Yes, Detective Clancy?"

"I'm wondering if you have given any more thought to our situation."

"Our situation?"

"C'mon, Mr. Hammer. Why don't we stop fucking around here?"

"All right. Let's."

"I've talked to Dr. Petty again. He really wants to solve this situation quietly. He doesn't want any bad publicity for the neighborhood, and if I have to arrest you, then it's going to be in the paper, and it's going to make Belleview look bad."

I nod slowly.

"You mean property values could drop?"

I hear the police radio again.

"Look, I know you are not a stupid man, Mr. Hammer."

"Thank you."

"You got a lot of people in your neighborhood who came out there and built their dream home. You got a lot of people who are selling their houses for over a million bucks. They are trying to establish a market out there. Dr. Petty is a very savvy man and understands what's going on. All you guys are in this *together*. Your own house could suffer if people think something *weird* is going on in Belleview."

"Hmmm … like a crazed sign-hacker on the loose?"

"Exactly." Detective Clancy sounds a friendly note. "Now, I know you did this. I got the saw. Your prints are on it. It matches the teeth marks in the wood. I know and *you know* you cut the sign down. You are on record saying you hated the sign. Fine. Now, all I'm saying is give Dr. Petty a call and tell him you will replace the sign, and I'll bury this thing." A long pause. "Otherwise, come Monday, I'm going to book you for damage to public property, and it ain't going to pretty, Mr. Hammer. You don't want your kids to see your name in the paper for hacking down a sign, now do you?"

"Certainly not."

"Good. Then we have an agreement of sorts?"

I pause.

"We just have one problem."

"What's that?"

"I didn't do it."

I hear the police radio again.

"You're a hard case, Mr. Hammer. Expect a squad at your door at nine AM on Monday with a warrant for your arrest."

"Good talking to you, Detective Clancy."

I close the phone. "The Battle Hymn of the Republic," suddenly stops, and I turn to my father. D. T. senior is examining me from my writing table with the unlit cigar in his mouth.

"Boy, it seems to me you are in a world of trouble."

"Well don't worry about it, Dad. It never bothered you before."

He raises his eyebrows.

"That supposed to make me feel guilty?"

"Dad, guilt is the last thing I expect in you."

D. T. senior pulls the cigar from his mouth and examines the label.

"Well, you're right. I am not a man who feels guilt. It is a worthless fucking emotion in my estimation."

"Really?" I stare at the man in the straw fedora. "Some would call it a conscience."

D. T. senior eyes me.

"Some would call it a boy pissing in his milk."

"You do have the metaphors."

D. T. senior leans back and I can see he is trying for something beyond the official emotional repertoire of one D. T. senior.

"Listen, boy. There is something you should know."

I lean back in my chair. Truly I am played out, but like a good soldier, I brace myself for the next barrage. D. T. senior glances toward our house and lowers his voice.

"I think your wife is having an affair." The word *affair* is said like "a fair." Having this proclamation delivered in Southern patois is more sauce for the goose. I stare at my father dully.

"Really?"

D. T. senior nods sagely.

"While you were out gallivanting last night, your wife had a visitor. *A gentleman caller.*"

I see magnolias, I see lace, and I see a wide-columned porch with Clark Gable slinking from the shadows. *A gentleman caller?*

"Really," I say again, not liking the strange tickling down in my groin.

My father begins a slow pace.

"See boy, I have often thought young people have no concept of marriage. People nowadays just go out all the time or they go out separately. You cannot leave your wife home *alone* but so much before they start *to wander* boy. Even when I was traveling, I made a point of calling your mother and making sure I was in touch."

I nod slowly.

"Oh, I see. So it's okay to travel all week, but call in just to make sure Wendy doesn't have an affair? Is that why your marriage lasted so long?"

D. T. senior pulls the cigar from his mouth.

"Boy, we are not talking about *me*! I have fucked up my marriages, and I admit that. I am trying to give you the wisdom of my *experience* and keep you from going down the same path. I will tell you this—when your mother and I were married, I did not go out to the bars and leave her home!"

"No," I say and nod. "You went to other states and left her home."

"That was *work*, boy."

"How convenient, Dad."

D. T. senior sits down at my writing desk and leans back.

"You can say what you want about me. It doesn't bother me. But I am telling you." He points the cigar. "I have seen this man around several times, and now he came over last night and let me say he stayed *mighty* late."

I pick up a stapler from my desk and eject a staple onto the wood. It is true I went out for a beer with an old friend, but I do not believe my wife would take the opportunity to carry on a clandestine affair.

"And who is the Dangerous Dan Grew of the old South?"

D. T. senior glances mysteriously out the window.

"That Yankee boy across the street. The one with the mower."

I stare at my father and break out in laugher.

"George Campbell! You think Wendy and *Campbell* are fucking around?"

D. T. senior shrugs, holding his arms wide.

"I don't know his name, but yes, I would say from my observations you had better stick close to the castle or you might just lose it."

"Dad, I have probably already *lost* the castle, but not to George Campbell."

My father stands up and regards me tragically. The unlit cigar takes its place.

"Okay. I have told you my suspicions. That is all I can do, but let me tell you, it always the person *you least expect,* boy."

"Dad," I say dully, "Campbell and Wendy are two *very* different people."

"Opposites attract, boy," he shrugs.

"No way."

He picks up his picnic basket.

"I have more experience in this area than you do, son."

"What experience is that, Dad?"

"Why the experience of *amore. Love, boy!* I have been around the block a few times, and I've seen it all. You better keep an eye on that girl."

"Sure, Dad." I wave him on. "Enjoy your picnic."

"I will … oh, I almost forgot. Tell that sonofabitch I will give him what he paid for the plot and not a penny more." DT takes the cigar from his mouth. "Tell him he is trying to *poach* on a family plot, and if he thinks he is going to end up there, then he has another thing coming! Tell him I will personally come dig him up and remove him if I have to."

"That presupposes you will be the last man standing," I point out.

D. T. senior nods confidently.

"I will be, don't you worry about that, boy."

I listen to his footsteps go down the stairs. I sit for a long moment and then go to the window. A Maserati slows down at my drive. D. T. senior gets in and disappears into the bright sunshine.

17

"I can make out very, very small farmland … pastureland below. I see individual fields, rivers, lakes, roads, I think. I'll get back to reentry attitude now."

–Astronaut, Mercury Atlas 7

Like Dorothy in the *Wizard of Oz*, I have decided I really would like to get back to Kansas. All I have to do is give back the ruby slippers to the Wicked Witch of the West and tell Glenda the Good Witch that I have had enough and I don't care if they want to keep the house, just blink me home so I can wake up in my old life with students and teachers looking over my bed, shaking their heads, *We thought we lost you there for a minute!* I foolishly believe that like Dorothy I can go to Oz and enjoy the fruits of that life and then after all is said and done, just go back to who I was, conveniently ignoring the fact that the wizard is a charlatan just like me.

It is late when I return to my office and D. T. senior hasn't come back from his picnic yet. I wonder if a man can elope who is still married, but I know D. T. senior would talk his way around that, postdate the check, and negotiate with the judge to do a mock ceremony valid once his divorce went through. *"Listen, judge, I'm good for it. Just do the ceremony and we will fix this up later."* I admire that shibboleth on the log able to make ham hocks out of lard, but I am a linear man, believing a straight line is better than a circuitous maze.

I sit at my writing desk and look out into Campbell's yard. It is not unpleasant, this pastoral country evening—geese flying, a slight breeze of humus, and good old earth—a distant child screaming in the lassitude of another beautiful fall day. So why do I feel like the dark cloud of the last universe is over me? I could point to many reasons, but of course the underlying one is that I cannot tap my shoes together and go back to that man of three years before. But I can try.

"Bill Contraire."

I clear my throat, thinking best how to proceed.

"Mr. Contraire, this is Dale Hammer. Chris Keystone referred me to you regarding teaching. He said you might need someone for our intro classes."

A pause.

"Chris Keystone … right, right … I did say that … but I said that *last spring.*"

I finger the slip of paper given to me at a block party almost a year ago.

"Right … well, I had some other obligations I had to attend too, but now my schedule is clear and I'm raring to go!"

I sound like someone from the musical *Oklahoma. Clickety clack, clickety clack.* Bill Contraire is taken aback, but not taken aback enough to stop typing on his keyboard. Another crazy desperate adjunct teacher has just weighed in, and it's time to get that memo to the department. *To All Interested Parties—Thou shall not give out referrals to desperate adjunct novelists! Repeat. Thou shall not refer writers of mid-list fiction into the sanctuary of tenure and a pension because they will not perform to the exacting standards of faculty meetings, curriculum necessities, and they will always be late to class!*

"Ah ... I'm glad to hear that, but unfortunately, Mr. Hammer, we filled that opening last summer, though, if I recall, Chris said you have had several novels published, and frankly, I wish you had contacted me. That would have been a nice addition to the faculty."

"Instead you filled it with some just out of college adjunct happy to receive the shitty salary and hours you have to offer," I mentally finish for him.

"I understand," I say, hearing the speed of his typing increase.

"But send me your Vitae; you never know what can change."

"I certainly will ... thank you for your time."

"Thank you, Mr. Hammer," he finishes, clickity-clacking away.

I hang up my last resort.

"Al here."

"Al ... Dale Hammer."

A pause.

"Yes, Dale."

"I told my father of your ... offer, and he ... well, he has a counter."

"I'm listening."

I lean back in my chair.

"He will pay you what you paid for the plot."

Another pause.

"Tell the sonofabitch the price just went up to twenty grand for insult and injury."

I laugh shortly.

"You're kidding."

"I'm not. And frankly, Dale, I'm surprised you would do his dirty work."

The phone goes dead. I rise from my desk and walk over to the window. George Campbell is walking away from our house. He has on his tie and the rolled-up sleeves of a man of business. I watch him cross to his house, then see a white Maserati speed up the drive and drop off a man with a picnic basket. The sun is slanting as this man in tennis shoes whistles, strolling up through the twilight that belongs to him. The tune is perfect, executing the high notes with precision, rivaling Bing Crosby. Dixie never sounded so good.

"I left you sitting at that desk, and you are *still there,* boy."

I have degenerated to looking for any new sites referring to my books. One is never so low as to surf the electronic void looking for references to one's books. This latest site is in German, and I can't read a thing. Somebody in Germany might be raving about my novels, informing the reading public of Germany that this is an American author they should read. I hit the translate button and wait. The site reads, *"A View to Mississippi ... powerful man overtakes lawyer in good drama of courtroom ... good condition ..."* I find another site. A teacher in Taiwan teaching English as a second language has listed my second novel as one of his favorite books. It is a cached posting from four years ago, but what the hell, it's new to me. Another German site promotes my first novel. I convert the currency, a whopping two bucks for a slightly used copy. Not exactly setting the Prussians on fire.

I turn from the screen and look at the man who is slightly sunburned, a basket next to him on the bed, lounging like a college student.

"How was your picnic?"

"Magnificent, boy, just magnificent! She is quite a woman."

"I want your life," I mutter.

D. T. senior shrugs.

"You can have it any time you want, boy." My father pulls out a cigar from his top pocket and nods in my direction. "What did you do today? You look tired."

"I told Al about your offer."

He cleans the cellophane from the probe.

"Uh huh, what did the sonofabitch say?"

"He said, 'Tell the sonofabitch the price went up to twenty thousand for insult and injury,'" I murmur.

"The sonofabitch!"

I nod, doing a new search.

"You guys really should get together. You speak the same language."

"Cocksuchah! That's a bunch of whoreshit!"

"Hmmm … now those are invectives Al doesn't use."

"Sonofabitch!"

"Now, you're speaking the same language."

D. T. senior shakes his head and stares out my window.

"I will have to rethink this," he says distantly.

"Or pay him twenty grand," I say and shrug, finding another site selling my books in Japan. "I don't know if I would do another counteroffer."

"Cocksuckah … So what else did you do, boy?"

"I went to hear an author I know speak," I say, reading the Japanese site referencing one of my books. I convert a review, *"Much good, but author wanders in conventional tale of aging … three dollar American."*

D. T. senior nods slowly, popping off one of his tennis shoes. "Where was that?"

"The library in Chicago," I answer, reading another Japanese translation: *Road That Shines—Out of Print.*

D. T. senior parks his cigar.

"You drove all the way down to Chicago to hear another

writer?"

"That's right," I answer, thinking of the article that got me into the car on my knight's mission.

"You knew this fellah?"

I have just found a girl from Budapest on *Myspace* who lists one of my novels as a book she has read. I surf through lots of photos of bald men who are her friends; a photo of a fat girl implores me to join her site. This is my reader and I study her face for any signs of intelligence. She seems devoid of any mental pabulum.

"We gave a speech together once," I murmur, moving on to an African American bibliography that lists my second novel. "I saw that he was giving a reading and thought I might say hello ... not a big deal."

"Uh huh." D. T. senior leans back on the bed, crossing his one tennis shoe over his knee. "So, did you get what you want?"

"What do you mean?" I ask, noticing on the Barnes and Noble site that people who have bought my book also bought *The Minute Manager.* I try to think of a connection between my novel and *The Minute Manager* and consider my novel could be read between appointments, fitting into *The Minute Manager* paradigm of no time wasted.

"You didn't drive all the way down to Chicago just to hear some boy talk about his *writing.* So, I ask you again, did you get what you want?"

"Dad, not everyone is on the take," I murmur, moving on to a nine-year-old interview in the *New York Times.*

"Don't bullshit a bullshitter, boy! You went down there to get *something,* and I'm asking you a flat out question ... did you get it?"

I read the interview again with the next "hot" novelist. The author talks about the divine inspiration of his writing. The author sounds like he is full of shit, but it is the *New York Times,* and I am in awe for a moment at this man who managed to bungle his way into such an illustrious newspaper.

"Dad. I hadn't seen this guy for a long time, so I thought I'd go down and support him," I continue, reading a sixth-grade rating of my first novel as "Highly readable—good for problems readers. Average intelligence."

D. T. senior rolls his tongue around the inside of his mouth.

"Seems to me, boy, that if *he* is the one giving the speech, then *he* is not the one who needs support."

I turn from the computer. I have stumbled into the references to Civil War soldiers of the same name. D. T. Hammer the novelist is being supplanted by another D. T. Hammer who enjoyed his fame in a size seven shoe on a diet of hard tack and cold black coffee. I wonder that Google should place a veteran higher than a defunct novelist. The truth is, one should never be allowed to read one's own press. It is like digging up a corpse. D. T. senior is waiting for my answer now. I know better than to give any information to this bulldog under the bridge.

"No, I didn't get what I wanted," I mutter, turning back to cemetery references to other people with the last name of Hammer.

D. T. senior for once in his life is silent. Of course it is the one time I want him to open that gigantic trap of his.

"I'm sorry, boy."

I turn and look at him.

"*That's it?*"

My father looks at me.

"What?"

"You smoke me out to say, 'I'm sorry, boy'?"

D. T. senior pulls the cigar from his shirt pocket again.

"I can't very well cry for you when you haven't told me what you were trying to do in the first goddamn place."

I shake my head, thinking a retreat could be in order about

now.

"Now go on and tell me what you were trying to accomplish," he says, flaring the early darkness.

I breathe heavily. What the hell. I am on the ninety-fifth reference to D. T. Hammer—a man who came up with his own Clam Chowder. I pivot in my chair and shrug.

"I hoped he might give me the name of his agent."

"Uh huh, but he didn't."

"No, he didn't."

D. T. senior pokes his cigar in my direction.

"And you feel like a big piece of cow dung now. Is that right, boy?"

I look up at the man smoking a cigar.

"That's right, Dad," I reply dully. "I feel like a big piece of cow dung. *Jesus.*"

"Well. What do you expect, boy?"

I frown, squinting at the man leisurely smoking his cigar.

"I'm sorry?"

D. T. senior gestures with his cigar.

"You got *more* problems than that, boy! I don't see you working on anything here. I don't see you doing your job or doing your writing."

"And you're going on fucking picnics," I retort, holding my arms wide. "So what's that prove?"

"Boy, you and I are at *different stages* of our lives. I have *raised* my family."

"You could call it that."

"Doesn't matter how you think *I did* it, the point is that phase for me is *over,* but you are in *the family-raising* years, boy, and you are fucking it all up."

"The patriarch speaks," I mutter, picking up a dog-eared copy of my second novel.

D. T. senior holds his cigar in front of him.

"That's right. But we aren't talking about *me* right now. We are talking about *you,* and I'll tell you straight out what your problem is."

"What a surprise."

D. T. senior points with his cigar.

"Your problem, Dale, is that you are living *a lie.*"

I stare at him flatly.

"Thank you. I didn't know that."

D. T. senior smokes for a moment, tearing away his smoky phallus suddenly.

"Uh huh. You may think you *know it,* but you don't! You think you can have it *both ways,* boy. You think you can do your writing and live your life of integrity while dipping into the well of the goodies. *But that ain't the way it is.*" He thumps himself on the chest. *"I know.* I lived the life of shit that you can't imagine! I wake up in hotels. I sit through boring-ass meetings that you could not tolerate for a second. I take assholes golfing and sit though fucking dinners that would stunt a bull and compliment morons on their bratty, spoiled-ass children. I have bosses that are your age and are as wet behind the ears as you are."

D. T. senior pauses, exhaling a blue cloud.

"But you see, I *made* that deal, I took the money, and I can deal with the shit! You *think* you can take the money and not deal with the shit, but I'm here to tell you, boy." D. T. senior points his smoky cigar. "It ain't that way. You have taken the money, and now you got to pay the price.'

"Thank you, Sigmund Freud," I say, clapping.

"Uh huh." D. T. senior regards me though a white haze. "You are a smart man. You are smarter than me. You read more books. You and your mother used to laugh at me and how dumb I was, I know that," he nods, examining his cigar. "But I had to go make a living and bring up my family and as smart as you are, Dale, you haven't figured out how to do *that.* You sitting here in your big house, with your neighbors you can't stand, in your fucked-up financial situation, and your wife is about to kick your ass right out the door. So who's the smart one, Kingfisher?"

"You know nothing about Wendy and I, Dad."

"I know you never talk to her, boy!" He exclaims, holding his arms wide. "You think because you don't travel that you are some kind of fucking saint! You might as well be traveling, boy, because you are so wrapped up in your own shit you don't know what your kids or your wife is thinking half the time! I hear you on the phone. I know this house is breaking you and you are headed for the poorhouse. And there ain't no shame in that either!"

D. T. senior waves his arm toward the ceiling. He is warming up into one hell of a sermon.

"Your mother and I went through same times and we survived. The only shame is that you won't *own up* to your responsibilities to your kids, your wife, or yourself, for that matter."

My father pops his cigar, shaking his head slowly.

"You won't own up, boy, to who *you are*, and until you do that, you are going to drift and continue to fuck up your life."

I stare at the floor.

"Are you finished?"

D. T. senior puffs on his cigar and shrugs.

"Reckon I am."

I pause, thinking of several different roads. One would take me back to the world of ancient references to a man who doesn't exist—the other would address this sonofabitch who is really pissing me off.

"The man living with his son over his garage speaks," I say, feeling a strange trembling in my chest. "The man who goes through marriages like rain, never saw his kids because he traveled so much, then gets thrown out by his wife because he fucks around with his secretary, then loses another job because he's so fucking confrontational—this man, this man is now moralizing to his son about his relationship and his life!" I lean forward. "Don't you see the hypocrisy in what you are saying, Dad?"

D. T. senior shrugs and answers in cold-water honesty.

"No," he says in perfect deadpan. "I guess I don't, boy. I'm seventy-three years old; I can say whatever the fuck I want."

"Dad ..." I say dully, realizing I have already been trumped.

"Yeah, boy."

"You have *always* said whatever the fuck you wanted."

18

"The SOB is damned lucky to be alive."
–Mission Control, Mercury Atlas 7

We must at all times be the patriarch or matriarch of moral certainty, even if we have the authority of a whore in a brothel. I have gone from berating my father to berating my son. This is generational of course and is only a matter of age. I am amazed at several things. One, is my son's foot is rapidly approaching the size of my own. I see this in the two long, skinny skis that are cadaverously pale. I have already mixed up our tennis shoes several times and I realize that in six short years my son will be eyeing the car to buzz around in with his learner's permit. All right, maybe seven, but it is coming.

But right now there is a crisis at hand. Dale junior is solemn, staring down at his hands on the couch. His warm-up sweats move slightly. I can see his leg jiggling. I try for the patriarch, the man who speaks from a platform of order in an increasingly chaotic world.

"Dale, your mother informs me you are no longer doing your homework."

My son continues staring down at his hands. I look at Wendy, who is waiting for me to move beyond the obvious. She has been wrestling with Dale junior for the last year over his inability to get his homework finished. My own years in elementary and high school were marked by the same kind of failure. *"He's a very smart boy, but he just seems lazy."* Lazy is a word teachers were still allowed to use in the sixties and seventies. Now a child is ADD, hyperactive, retarded, a Ritalin candidate—I would have certainly been the drug-crazed zombie of Ritalin descent if they only had the medical science.

"Dale," I say sternly. "If you can't do your homework, then we are going to have to look at pulling you out of some of these sports programs."

Dale junior looks up in terror. I have just thought of this, thinking it might squelch the fire of indignance in my wife's eyes. The cried lament of, "Just do something" is right under the table with those two brand-new size seven and half feet.

"You can't do that," he cries out.

I stare at this blond-haired boy of my youth. Of course I can't. What will it prove to banish him from sports under the guise of academic purgatory—a Dickens character at a lone desk while his classmates whoop it up?

"Yes I can and I will, unless you tell me what's been going on," I say with false authority.

"Nothing," said down to his hands once again.

I am not good at this role. I am much better at a pickup game of basketball or football or playing some chess in front of the fireplace. Usually I leave Wendy to be the heavy. It is hereditary, some sort of dodging of basic responsibilities. D. T. senior never sat on a couch between his parents. He was raised by a black mammy and a mother lit on too many highballs. So I see now this is about much more than homework; this is about a life over a garage.

"Dale, I'm going to give you one more chance," I say judiciously. "I want you to tell your mother and me why you have not been doing your homework."

It is an idiotic question—do I know why I can't keep a job or get my literary career out of park? No, it is some mysterious confluence of circumstance and heredity, but this doesn't mean I can give a nine-year-old a bye.

His knee bobs faster. Wendy piles it on.

"Dale can't even remember his books. His teacher tells me he never brings his books home. She also told me he never showed us his report card." Wendy is glaring at me and I feel like maybe I should be sitting next to Dale. "He doesn't remember his coat, his gloves, and he has lost his violin."

I stare at my son. *Wow.* He can't remember a fucking thing. Neither can I.

"You lost your violin?"

A shrug.

"Yes."

"Do you know where it is?"

"No."

I stare at my hands. Somewhere I had lost contact. Somewhere I had lost knowing the basic nomenclature of my son's life. I didn't even know he *played* the violin. Maybe he is playing the piano, the oboe, and the harp in some dusty classroom with the last rays of three PM blanching the floor. Maybe he is a chess master, a savant, a magician of unbelievable duplicity while his old man laments over a garage.

"Well, let's start with your backpack," I suggest.

"He left it at school," my wife fills in. "He has left it at school all month!"

I nod. I am trying to give my son some wiggle room. I am trying to give him an exit from the box he has created. I know the feeling—with all options exhausted, one gives into the obvious truth. Failure is an integral part of my being.

"Where's your report card, Dale?"

Shrug.

"Don't know."

"You *don't know* where your report card is?"

"No."

All this information is conveyed in perfect head-down posture. Angela picks this moment to skip in.

"Hi, Daddy!"

"Hello, sweetie." I breathe in the five-year -old on autopilot. She at least is staying the course so far. But girls are like that. You could be on a sinking ship and Angela would inform you that you don't have your life vest on correctly. Boys can't hold a candle to that kind of concentration under fire. "Can you give us a little room, sweetie? We are having a conversation with Dale here—"

"Why don't you talk to her like you talk to me?" Dale junior asks and scowls.

I turn to two hot eyes full of injured pride.

"Because she didn't *lose* everything and not do her homework and not show us her report card," I tell the prisoner.

My son goes back down to his hands.

"Wait," he mutters.

Wendy intercedes.

"Angela, why don't you go watch some television?"

"All right, Mommy."

She skips out of the room and we turn back to the convict. His knee is doing a fast bounce and I feel his pain. There is a reason behind all of this, and I suspect it has nothing to do with my son. Something is knocking him off the path of nine-year-old competence; something is messing with his ability to order the basic parts of his life. I suspect it is one forty-six-year-old interloper who leaves dissension in his wake like a fast-moving boat.

"Dale, it seems to me like we have an organizational problem here," I begin again.

He looks up. The adult has switched to problem solving. I am only too happy to give him this bone now.

"What I do is write down the things I want to get done," I explain. "It helps me organize my day. Maybe we could get you an organizer of some kind."

The *One Minute Manager* has arrived. No wonder the man who read my book also ordered this pamphlet of common sense—he gleaned the *One Minute Manager* waiting in the wings behind the purple prose. Wendy gets up and pulls a small notebook off the coffee table.

"He has his assignment book. It's where he is *supposed* to write down what he has to do each day."

I take the notebook. "Dale Hammer" is written in block letters next to pictures of machines guns and zombies. A good psychologist could have a field day. I used to doodle pictures of machine guns and bombs and men with their heads cut off. I know now this was not normal, but what is normal in the juggernaut of mass culture?

"Good. Then we already have the tool," I say to the hopeful eyes. "Let's see."

I start thumbing through the organizer that has each day of the week. I pass swastikas and bombs and more machine guns. The normal doodling of any nine-year-old?

"There's nothing in it. He has never written down one thing," Wendy says, busting my son once again.

I had hoped for something to work with. I had hoped for some glimmer of effort I could build on, but all I am left with is the detritus of WWIII.

"Mrs. Measly says that if she doesn't see some effort from Dale to catch up, she is going to have to request a *team visit.*"

I look at my wife.

"A team visit—"

"Social worker. Ritalin police," she mouths.

Now I am sweating. Dale junior has suddenly gone into the

"might really be fucked up" category. I throw the assignment book on the coffee table and shake my head. I have lost the good-guy role, the father who can still vouch for the son and give him some room to maneuver. *Team visit? No fucking way.*

"Dale. I don't see any alternative. I think we have to stop the sports until we can get a handle on this."

He breaks the hand meditation. The adults have thrown a curve ball, not to be endured but to fight back. They have gone right past the thudding platitudes to violating the central kid tenant—*thou shall not fuck with my sports.*

"No way," he shouts.

"Yes way. You are in trouble, and we need something to wake you up."

Dale junior is off the couch now, holding his head, gushing tears.

"What about soccer. *I have a fucking game tomorrow!*"

The two parents' mouths drop open. *Fucking? Fucking?* A word that Wendy and I employ more than we would like to admit, but I never thought it would jump the bridge so early to the son.

"Watch that language, young man!"

Wendy looks at me. Clearly my response to front line swearing is inadequate, but it is tinged with the guilt of the giver of the arrow. A long wail comes from the boy who falls to the floor. I look at Wendy, who nods back.

Dale suddenly springs up and points an accusing finger.

"*It's your fault. You tired to run down Mrs. Thomas and now they're taking it out on me!*"

"I don't think so—"

Dale junior is crying profusely now, his mouth in agony. His missile has hit home and Wendy gives me a look that could fry a private. My son is not finished.

"*And all you guys do is fight! You shout at each other all the time. I can't do my homework. I can't do anything in this house ... all I want to*

301

do is leave because you hate each other … I know it … I know it … "

Wendy and l look at each other.

"What's wrong with Dale," Angela wants to know, appearing from television land.

"Nothing," he shrieks. *"Just leave me the fuck alone!"*

Then he is gone up the stairs and the door to his room slams. I bow my head and stare at my hands. It is not the swearing, not the total inability of the father to reach his son that has me breathing like a man at the bottom of a pool. It is the simple aphorism that no man should throw a stone that lives in a glass house.

Like witnesses to a crime, we hang around the scene and wait for the next van of detectives, evidence technicians, and gawkers to arrive and tidy up the guilt splattered all over the living room. Wendy and I sit across from each other listening to our children cry. Angela has decided her allegiance lies with her brother and not her parents. After running into the room and pointing an accusing finger at me, *"You can't take Dale's sports away. You're mean and I'm never going to play with you again,"* she ran upstairs and joined her brother in a crying chorus. The parents sit on the couch. I am waiting for some sort of righteous piety to guide me through the channels of my arbitrary decree, but all I feel is hypocritical, guilty, and cruel. I fight the urge to run upstairs and give Dale some ice cream, promise a trip to the toy store or a sports event—anything that will put his world right and restore mine.

"Don't do it."

I look at Wendy. Her reading glasses are low, eyes firm.

"Don't go upstairs and try and smooth it over. The kids have to understand that we are *parents* and not playmates."

"I think Dale gets that one," I murmur, rubbing my hands together.

Wendy picks up a magazine from the coffee table and folds her legs up under her. She has the seeming ability to make the quick emotional shifts while I loiter looking for sustenance for self inflicted wounds.

"It's all right for his father to put down the law," she says, paging through *The New Yorker.*

"The law feels pretty shitty about now."

Wendy turns another page.

"His principal called today."

A fresh second wave of seasoned guilt descends. I look at the woman who seems the picture of a suburban urbanite—legs tucked under, reading glasses low, reading the *New Yorker* while the world churns on.

"What did he want?"

The eyebrows dance high.

"He wanted to let me know that you are not allowed to drive Dale to school anymore."

A quick glance from the rarefied polysyllabic world of *New Yorker* fiction and then another page. I stare at my wife, showing as much indignance as a man can muster who has been chased by a crossing guard.

"That's ridiculous!"

Wendy throws the magazine on the coffee table. She purses her lips.

"You've also been banned from school property."

"On what grounds?"

My wife slips into lawyer mode and instructs her client on the particulars of the case. The glasses are used as a prop, angling in the corner of her mouth.

"The principal (the accuser) claims you endangered the lives of the students and the crossing guard by wantonly speeding and failing to obey the command of Mrs. Thomas to stop."

I'm pacing now, injured pride in my red face.

"That old bitch has had a hard on for me ever since we moved here."

"I would think that would be anatomically impossible," the lawyer sniffs.

I stop, pleading my case.

"I sped *once,* one time I went a little too fast, and she has been on me every time I drive past her. So this morning, I was going a little fast, I admit it, but then the crazy woman starts chasing me down the fricking road!" I stop, throwing myself on the mercy of the court. "I mean, what was I supposed to do? I'm in traffic, I have this crazy woman chasing me, I can't really pull over, so I pull into the drive of the school and then the crazy woman *attacks me* with her sign! What I really should do *is sue her* for physical abuse," I say, nodding. "Maybe that's what I'll do. I'll sue her for attacking me!"

The lawyer squints, frowns.

"Not much of a case … any witnesses?"

"Only the whole school."

Wendy tilts her head.

"They would be on her side and no one would say she attacked you."

"Dale, they could ask Dale," I point out.

"He's your son—biased. They don't like to put children on the stand."

I jam my hands down in my pocket.

"This is bullshit, Wendy."

There is a slight smile on her face.

"You know when I married you, Dale, I said one thing to my mother who asked me about marrying a man who was unemployed, unpublished, and looked like he would never settle down."

I wait for the verdict.

"I said, 'Mom, I know all that, but I will never be bored with

304

Dale.'"

"And that's been true," I point out, breathing some relief.

"Hmmm …" Wendy stares down at the *New Yorker on* the cocktail table. "But I wonder if I should be bored at a point. Maybe too much chaos is too much chaos and relationships need some boredom to stabilize."

I sit down on the couch and stare at my hands.

"I know things have been crazy," I say in a low voice." But things will get better … I will change."

She taps her reading glasses, tilting her head down.

"Now I know you're lying."

I look at the two crystal blue eyes that arrested me so long ago.

"At forty-six, you're who you are and I'm who I am." Wendy pauses. "I guess the question for both of us, is can we be who we are together?"

I look at her and think of Campbell again. If she is having an affair with my neighbor, then she wasn't being very secretive about it. But one theory I had heard lately is that some spouses *want* to be caught. They want to do something on the lines of a Pearl Harbor to start the war.

"What do you think?" I ask in a low voice.

Wendy looks away and shakes her head. "I don't know, Dale. We've been together for fifteen years, and it has been crazy, but I'm not sure I can take any more crazy. I'm not sure I can take another fifteen years of crazy."

"You want boring, then?"

Wendy tilts her head, twirling her hair.

"Boring is not necessarily boring. Sometimes it's just stable. I mean, no one out here strives to be cutting edge. No one wants to break the mold and find out what happens when everything blows up." She shrugs. "They just want to raise their kids."

I frown, feeling a great gong coming down from the

heavens.

"And you think that's a good thing?"

Wendy stares me dead in the eye.

"Is it so bad, Dale? Is it so bad to be normal and middle class and just raise your kids? Shouldn't that be enough?"

I jump up, staring out the window at our four dead trees. I turn around from the ten-thousand-dollar mistake and look at Wendy.

"You want me to be like fucking George Campbell?"

Wendy stares at me and then I know. I have scored a direct hit and the lawyer is bleeding. She reconnoiters.

"I don't know where that came from, but a little George Campbell would help you. He is a nice man who can listen, Dale. Do you know you cannot listen *to anybody* but yourself? Its all about what *Dale* wants, what Dale *feels*. Do you know I can't even tell you what I feel *about my life*, because I'm so busy making *you* feel good about *your* feelings. I have to play the stooge to all your antics … I have to be the rah-rah, because you are so busy tearing everything down."

"I never asked for that," I point out weakly.

Wendy chews on the end of her glasses, shaking her head slowly.

"It's what you demand of *everybody*—of me, the kids. It's all who can make *the great* Dale Hammer feel better." My wife shrugs. "Maybe I do appreciate a man who can listen instead of spewing all the time … a man who can put someone else first."

Now I know I'm fucked. Campbell has moved in on my life. My father was right. It's amazing the speed at which the man with the zero turn mower has supplanted me. I never should have talked to the sonofabitch. I stare at the fireplace, the floor to ceiling windows; this is the great room of our lives. I never felt it was our cozy room of family life, because I was always floating in a vast space, unable to adhere to anything, unable to pull in my family into the tight circle of closeness, of home and hearth, of secure people in secure surroundings.

I look at Wendy and gesture to the man in waiting across the street.

"Maybe I should get a fucking zero-turn mower and become a lawyer."

Wendy ignores this.

"You can attack these people for anything you want, Dale, but at least they are leading their lives. At least *they know* who they are."

"You mean George, don't you, Wendy? *George* knows who he is?"

She stares at me and frowns.

"Whoever, Dale. The problem is not these people, it's *you. You* don't know who you are!"

Strange I should hear the same words out of my father and my wife's mouth in the space of an hour. A theme does seem to be emerging, but I don't really want to recognize any validity right now. It is time to dig in. Besides, I'm pissed. I nod slowly, glaring at my wife.

"You want me to roll over and fucking die. Is that it, Wen? You want me to become some brain-dead robot so you can live in a big house and give our kids the kind of life you think they should have?"

The lawyer rolls her eyes.

"Please, Dale. We aren't talking about a lobotomy. I just don't understand why you have to push everything, why do you have to test *everybody?* Even the crossing guard woman … you have to *even* fuck with her!"

"She deserved it," I grumble.

Wendy looks down, tapping her knee with her glasses.

"That's what you say about everyone, Dale. You probably even say that about me."

"Sometimes," I respond, feeling real anger welling up in me. "I didn't create this mess, Wendy. I'm just the stooge everyone can blame it on."

My wife stands up and this is my signal. The lawyer is about to give her summation.

"What I want to know, Dale, is who told you that you were the divine arbiter of culture and that you had the moral upper hand while all the rest of us have to worry about making a living and raising the children?" Wendy suddenly is in front of me. "Why do you have that prerogative to decide *who* is worthy and who isn't?"

I look up, shaking my head.

"Because these people," I say dully, "are too dumb to even know they're alive. They are cattle, waiting for the next call to eat, to work, to sleep, to fuck. I know I'm alive," I say and nod. "I may be fucked up, Wendy, I may not have a clue what the next day will bring, but at least I'm out there swinging! These people never had the balls to take the first fucking pitch."

Wendy pauses, crossing her arms.

"Is that why you cut down the sign, Dale? To show you were *still swinging*? Is that why you drive an SUV over someone else's land? Is that why the police are coming to our house? Is that why your father is living over our garage after his wife kicked him out and his car is repossessed and he is now trying to get into the pants of a woman half his age? Is he still *swinging* too, Dale?"

"Georgia is not that young," I correct her.

"Whatever."

I sit down, suddenly tired of our dueling banjos. I remember the way D. T. senior used to bow his head when he fought with my mother. I remember the weariness in his posture, the surrender of will to the forces allayed against him. My wife is a worthy opponent and I am tired of fighting. Wendy sits down too, holding her brow. I can hear the water softener downstairs, the

308

pump of our well pumping in more water for the D. T. Hammer household—the mechanics of my life continuing unabated even as the iceberg lies ahead. She turns and looks at me from under her hand.

"Don't you think that's all pretty pathetic, Dale?"

Wendy continues holding her brow as if she has a terrific headache.

"Hacking down a sign to show everyone how different you are?"

I stare at my hands. Dale junior is on to something. When the shit rains down, stare at your hands. I shake my head slowly.

"I can't do it that way, Wendy ... I just can't."

She looks at the floor, then at me, her eyes filling suddenly.

"That's too bad, Dale, because I can't do it this way anymore."

It is a beautiful night out on my front porch. The bullfrogs are enjoying the last balmy night of autumn in the wetlands and the occasional coyote is howling in ecstasy over his latest kill. The moon is low over the trees. I smell cigar smoke and hear the creak of the rocker down on the far end of the porch. The glowing orange stub announces D. T. senior is also sampling the night air before retiring.

"Another happy night in the land of Ozzie and Harriet," he says, referencing a show I never even saw.

"Were we loud?" I ask, settling in the other Adirondack rocker.

He shrugs, blowing out a long ghostly stream.

"Don't worry, son, I have heard far worse. *You* have heard far worse."

This is true. Many were the nights I went to sleep with a pillow over my head. I became a pro at humming, keeping the voices out of my head, the anguished adults lacerating each other. I have more empathy now for those two people dealing with financial pressure, too many kids, too many expectations, the slow leaking away of physical vitality.

"I always swore I'd never fight around the kids after you and mom," I murmur, watching the mist rising over the wetlands. "But I guess I couldn't keep that promise either."

D. T. senior eyeballs me in the dark.

"You want me to get you a violin, boy?"

"I could go for some sympathy about now," I nod.

He shrugs, staring off into the wetlands.

"Everybody fights, boy. If you don't fight, then you are dead. Part of the human condition."

I tilt my head, considering this latest D. T. senior aphorism.

"That may be true, but fighting feels like a failure right now."

My father goes back to smoking.

"You be all right, boy."

The cigar smoke smells very good, and I relieve D. T. senior of his second, inhaling the sweet, burly tobacco. Cancer, emphysema, heart disease, bring it on. I want to settle down into the tranquil haze of nicotine. I stare off into the wetlands and think maybe it was a better age when men worked and smoked and drank themselves to death without self knowledge. At least there wasn't all this goddamn worrying or all this *whoreshit* to use D. T. senior's word.

"Believe it or not, your mother and I swore we would never fight in front of you kids either," D. T. senior says in a low voice, rocking slowly. "Your mother came from a broken home, and she wanted to give you all the things she didn't have. That's one reason we were always in debt, because she couldn't stand for you not to have things she thought you should." He pauses. "I guess I did too."

I pull the cigar away. The tobacco is doing the trick. A soft veil has fallen over the world. A little bourbon and I would be set. I look at D. T. senior sitting in the rocker, his leg crossed over his knee.

"You were right."

"What's that, boy?"

"You were right what you said up there. I am fucking up."

D. T. senior tilts his head, tapping his ash over the side of the porch.

"You just doing what I did. You trying for something you just can't get, and that will drive a good man to drink. We all want the right things, want your kids to have a good life, your wife not to work, nice house like you have, but the world doesn't give a shit about that. The world wants your balls and usually gets it."

My father nods, pulling the cigar away.

"Look at me, boy. I am sitting out here at *seventy-three* without a pot to piss in. I was just sitting out here figuring how much longer I have to live. You know, dying doesn't seem so bad sometimes." D. T. senior picks me out of the darkness. "I don't mean suicide or anything, but just to be able *to rest,* just to be able to put it all down once and for all."

I stare at the man pulling on his cigar, one luminous white tennis shoe on his knee. I should be feeling some concern that my father just said dying doesn't seem like such a bad thing, but I can't work up the moral indignation that God's greatest gift should be tossed aside like the ash of a cigar.

"You know, boy, you just get tired of the struggle. Tired of the struggle." D. T. senior holds his cigar low and shakes his head. "But then you go on, because there is nothing else to do *but* go on." He gestures to me, his cigar flaring. "Everybody has their day in the pickle barrel, and this is yours, but you'll get out. You may even have to sell this house and pay off your debts and start over, but you'll survive. Many a good man has gone through exactly what you have and survived. Hell, I did, and your mother did too."

I stare off into the uneven darkness where the moonlight is christening the fields. Right now the world seems very beautiful. I wonder then how long the world has gone on without me. But it does. The world goes on with or without you.

"I think Wendy and I might split up," I say in a low voice. "I think she has had enough."

D. T. senior spats over the side of the porch.

"No, you wrong there, boy. She is just waiting for a signal from you."

I tip my cigar in the garden and shake my head.

"I don't think so, Dad. I think she has had enough signals."

"*Whoreshit.*"

"I think we are in alignment on that," I say wryly.

"No sir." D. T. senior shakes his head. "You are confusing your failure as a father, as a provider, with being a husband." He glances behind him. "You may have to sell this house to pay your debt. You may have to walk the streets to get another job. But many a good man has gone down the same way and gotten back up on the horse to do it again. Just look at me, boy."

"I'd rather not," I say wryly.

D. T. senior holds the cigar below his mouth.

"I don't blame you there, boy, but that woman in there doesn't give a tinkers *damn* about a house or how much money you make …" D. T. senior suddenly pokes me in the chest. "What she cares about is what's in your heart."

I frown.

"I thought you said Wendy cared about the house and I didn't."

"I was just trying to use reverse psychology, boy."

"Freud speaks," I murmur, feeling even mellower from the tobacco.

"What's that?

312

"Nothing."

D. T. senior rocks slowly and gestures to the night.

"You'll see I'm right, provided you are not too dumb to tell her how you feel about her."

I look over at the man in the checkered shirt with the tennis shoe over his knee, this soothsayer living over a garage.

"You are a crazy old fuck, Dad."

D. T. senior pulls on his cigar and nods slowly.

"Takes one to know one, boy."

19

T-1

....and Counting

Friday

Riding like the wind, I take my morning ride down the Great Western Trail that began as a wagon road leading to Chicago, then became the path for the Milwaukee and Ohio Railroad before turning into the limestone-covered bike trail I now pedal down through the six AM frost. It is exhilarating, these early-morning bike rides, where for a moment the troubles of the previous day are left at the jagged edge of the Belleview sign. I pass farms and sleepy old cows and a light on some barn, finally reaching the field where the old wagon trail tunnels down through the trees and head out into the country. I begin a slow, steady pump that turns into the breathtaking ride, zooming over old plank bridges and gullies, passing the old telephone poles with their glass conductors, plunging back through the history of the plains that men and women crossed looking for their dreams.

I am one with those people as I push myself to my limit of endurance, fueled by a couple of bottled waters and last night's carbo load. The body settles down and does what it does best without stress or equivocation,

314

cleanly burning fuel and propelling me down the path at twenty miles an hour. The morning sun is dappling through the turning branches and the mist is rising over the fields as I go even faster. I pedal out the stress of my disintegrating marriage, my moribund literary career, and my failure as a provider for my family. The world is behind me while D. T. senior sleeps over the garage and Dale junior and Angela sleep in their beds clutching stuffed animals and Wendy wraps herself deeper into her comforter while the man of the house passes abandoned silos pink with the dawn, then an old bank that probably died in the Great Depression, never seeing the man in the green Gore-Tex shirt slipping past as a phantom of the future. Detective Clancy is having his morning coffee while his perpetrator throttles across an old railroad trestle, still pumping harder, trying to outdistance himself from himself in the age-old contest of man and his environment, while Jed and Ellie Mae are shaking off too many beers and cigarettes as they groan to life.

I pedal on while the world grows older.

Usually closings take place at title companies, but occasionally they take place at the office of the attorney of the seller. I follow the directions from Mapquest into Roselle, driving past the address again. Mapquest has sold me down the river several times before and I figure it must have gotten the address wrong because Jack's Auto Repair occupies 500 W. Wayne Road which should be *Ravioli and Associates*. Roselle is a Chicago suburb that had its glory days before they built the expressway that now roars overhead through the center of town.

I turn around one more time, staring at my directions, starting at Jack's Auto Repair. I turn into the parking lot of small storefronts with empty glass boxes. I see a small door next to Jack's Auto Repair and make out, "Ravioli and Associates, Attorneys-at-Law." I am actually fifteen minutes early and roll into Frank Ravioli's office that smells of motor oil. A woman with hair piled up on her head looks up from a desk. Her breasts bulge out in the current breast culture style that fits in with the cheap paneling, the dropped ceiling, and the fine coating of smoke that breathes from the used-up carpet.

She gets off the phone. Her nails are amazing, blood-red claws. Lill Ravioli engraves a gold-painted plate.

"Can I help yous?"

"Yes, I'm here for the Haller closing."

A shrug and a look to the open door where a pneumatic lug wrench is whirring off tires.

"Yeah, Frank's not going to be here today ... he had to get a car."

I stare at the woman who is so skinny she looks like she might crack in half.

"You mean, he owns Jack's Auto Repair as well?"

"Oh yeah ... but his name is Frank. He just calls it that for marketing."

One can see old Frank Ravioli sitting up with a napkin stuffed into his chin, a bottle of Lambrusco open, ravioli spinning around in his plate, sounding out the consumer appeal of Frank's Auto Repair versus Jack's Auto Repair.

"But it ain't no big deal. We already got the docs from the lender."

I feel a great sense of relief. The loan documents are the final hurdle. All that is left is to sign. I thank Lill Ravioli profusely, going into a small paneled conference room. I sit at the end of the long table and put my briefcase by my leg. There really isn't anything in my briefcase except for a calculator, but carrying a briefcase gives one an air of commerce, deals completed, and deals in the works. I pick up several magazines from a small table, *NASCAR, Napa Auto Parts, The Law Review* from 1985. Clearly, Frank Ravioli is a Renaissance man who walks both sides of the street.

I toss the magazines back on the table when a bald man peeks in.

"Haller closing?"

I stand up.

"Yes, Dale Hammer."

"Tom White ... I'm the sellers' realtor. They aren't coming today, but we have power of attorney."

"Great," I say and nod.

Things were looking better every minute. No sellers, no lawyer shenanigans trying to get last-minute concessions, no drama. Just a sign, sign, and we're done. Tom White takes the far end of the table and sits down. He opens his briefcase of files and calculators and pens and note pads and stickers and his phone neatly clipped to the one of the pockets. I admire a man who is really what he purports to be. So many of us live dual lives, one foot in and one foot out, I guess we don't want to be too committed to any one thing lest we miss the next boom, gold rush, or IPO.

I hear the bell on the front door, and Ellie Mae and Jed skulk in. Jed shakes my hand and groans down into a seat, tossing his oil-stained Chicago Bears cap on the table. Ellie Mae doesn't even look at me, but turns up the corners of her mouth, baring breasts for all to see in a low-rider halter top. I act as master of ceremony, introducing Tom White.

"Good to meet you," he says, and Ellie Mae smiles at Tom White's resplendent baldness. He is the type of man she has little contact with except in custody battles for "her babies" (ages seventeen and eighteen respectively) who still reside in Alabama. Not able to garner respect from the lambasted mortgage broker, she turns on the low beams for the smooth-headed Tom White, who wears a light blue polo and khaki pants. To Ellie Mae, he looks good enough to eat.

"So you represent the sellers, then?"

Tom White nods, paging through documents, dialing yet another call.

"Yes, and I must say, you are getting quite a deal."

This perks up Jed a bit, who is sitting in his beard, chin to chest, staring at the dirty linoleum floor. He looks over at Ellie Mae, and I can see now the tug-of-war that has been in play.

"See, honey, I told you we were getting a good deal."

Ellie Mae smiles back at Tom White, who cannot keep his eyes off her breasts, though his effort is mighty. I am sure in the sales seminars the guru chants to the lambs—*and never ever look at a woman's breast. You could lose the deal.* But Ellie Mae has leaned even lower, and we can all see the beginning of her pink nipples.

"Well, we'll see," she says in a saccharine tone. I know then that Ellie Mae has made a life out of driving men to distraction. Her body may be used, but like an old hotrod, it can still be pulled out of the garage. I think that is one reason Ellie Mae and I never hit it off. I simply didn't find her Ellie Mae persona attractive, and without the leering eye as her compass, she is unsure of her position.

"Is there an attorney present?"

"Ravioli isn't coming," I nod.

Jed sits up. "My attorney said he had a conflict, but if there were any problems, I could call him on the cell phone."

Lill has just crashed into the room in her spikes, putting the closing papers on the table and then turning back around. It was all like a dream come true. At most closings the documents are delayed, the attorneys are late, and the clients are lost. I spin around the loan documents and page through, going to the first page. The HUD is long and legal and has all the numbers—it is the Bible of the closing.

Jed and Ellie Mae are huddled together as I explain what the numbers mean. Jed cuts to the chase.

"Where's my payment?"

I look down the long list of numbers.

"It should be ..." I trail my finger down and see the payment total. "Well, it looks like it is a little higher than we thought ... 1610.00. Not bad; we were only nine bucks off."

Jed stares at the number and then looks up sleepily, his eyes dark and his tattoos swelling outside of his cutoff sweatshirt.

"Nope. I told you sixteen hundred and one was my top."

"I know, Jed, but we are only nine bucks off and—"

"You fucking liar!"

Ellie Mae has brought forth all of her trailer charm, her prescient ability to be the boldest in the park, giving Dwayne the first blow job while the other girls gagged. She always had lots of sass and found that between her ass and her mouth, she could go pretty far.

"Ellie Mae ... I don't think—"

"*You're a fucking liar.* You told us it would be sixteen hundred and one, and now it's nine fucking dollars higher!"

I am sitting back on my emotions. The cool play is what is needed. I can take anything, as long as they sign. I have never had anyone walk out of a purchase, but this is a new era. Banks are losing billions on these type of loans, and the correspondent lender who is offering these terms is no more—we are all a footnote to something that has already passed.

Jed shakes his head dubiously.

"Dale, I told you I wouldn't sign if it was anything above sixteen hundred and one."

Jed is more rational and I take heart that he is actually holding the pen.

"That's true, but I also told you, Jed, I didn't know what the mortgage insurance would be exactly. I came pretty close, but yes, I was nine dollars off."

Jed is picking at his beard while Ellie Mae scrutinizes the numbers. Tom White rescues us all and I am thankful for the smooth, dulcet tone of the counselor.

"Listen, guys, this is a *great* deal. You are getting a *great* house, and I understand you put no money down. My feeling is this is a once-in-a-lifetime opportunity, and I wouldn't let nine dollars stand in *my* way."

Ellie Mae looks up and smiles warmly.

"But Tom, he lied to us," she says in a low Tammy Faye voice. "He's lied to us about *everything*. So tell me why we should we trust him now?"

Tom White and I lock eyes. His expression is one that conveys he gets paid on commission too, and I didn't really fuck this thing up, did I? I can feel the blood rising up my neck and I think briefly about just walking out. Tom White smiles, gesturing to the sinner at the far end of the table.

"Well I can't speak to that, Ellie Mae, but he seems to be *very* close to his estimate."

"He's a fucking bald-faced liar, Tom! He's lied about the interest rate, how long it would take, and now the payment is fucking higher." She looks around the room as if just now discovering it is full of men. "I mean, Jed can do what he wants, but *I* wouldn't sign it … I wouldn't step foot in that house!"

Jed is picking at his beard while Ellie Mae flips her hair, dropping her top even lower, as she sticks her ass in the air. The sun has heated up the cheap paneling and years of necrotized resins are being released into the air with old motor oil and car exhaust. We are in a bad movie, and even then we are the scene that will get cut for being too over-the-top, too unbelievable. Lill looks in at the bent-over Ellie Mae, her thong clearly visible through her white, skin-tight shorts and then withdraws, thinking her father should really concentrate more on the automotive side of the business.

And there we are. Sitting in the stifling room, heated sunlight coming in through sooty windows, exhaust wafting over from the auto bays, everyone in the room staring at me like I just stole the family jewels. I look at this woman of sallow complexion, her breasts pushed high by the latest fashion of *American Idol,* and I know I have finally met the charlatan who has been me.

I breathe heavily and look up at this woman of the twenty-first century, educated by reality television and slick advertising.

"You can't talk to me that way, Ellie Mae."

Her mouth drops open, amazed I would stand up for myself at this late hour.

"I can talk to you any fucking way I want, and if you're going to sass me, then I'm getting the fuck out of here!!"

Then Ellie Mae bolts out of the room. Jed breathes heavily and looks at me and Tom White.

"Sorry, boys," he says, shaking his head and dropping the pen. "But booty is booty."

And then he walks out the door, crossing the parking lot to his pickup and screeching away. It's as if we were all playing blind man's bluff and suddenly someone broke the rules. Borrowers threaten not to sign, they negotiate concessions, but they don't leave and jump in trucks and squeal away. I stare at Tom White, who has his mouth slightly open, two men who just lost thousands of dollars in commission.

"Booty is booty!" he cries out in disbelief.

Even the ever-industrious Tom White knows something has happened that never occurred before. I listen to the torque gun in the auto bay next door and pick up my briefcase. Tom White stares at me, looking for an explanation, reason, sanity. Men in polo shirts and khakis are rarely exposed to the true heart of the American psyche.

"Booty is booty," he cries out again.

"Dale, open the door."

I had returned from my closing and found myself once again outside my son's door. I stare at Thomas the Chipmunk and SpongeBob. They taunt me from their secure position on Dale junior's door. They at least have a role in my son's life, a reason for adhering to the outside of his door. SpongeBob has his hand up, walking with his buddy Patrick along the Bikini Bottom. I wish I had the pull of SpongeBob right now. Maybe I could get the door to swing open. I knock again, modulating my voice between an order and a plea, the patriarchal supplicant trying to get into a room of his own house.

"Dale ... open the door."

"*No!*"

The voice is muffled, a heaving voice between sobs. I stare at SpongeBob and notice for the first time how his middle finger is extended. *Why hadn't I noticed that before?* No doubt about it, SpongeBob is flipping off the world. I am sure Wendy didn't notice this either when she carefully taped the poster next to Thomas the Chipmunk, who has no fingers. Bird or no bird, I must gain entrance into the nine-year-old sanctum.

I knock again.

"Dale ... *please* open the door."

"No, go away! You *hate me* anyway."

I breathe heavy.

"I don't hate you. Open the door."

"No ... forget it, you *doofus.*"

I take this in stride, although it is a first. My son has never called me a doofus before. Soon *fuckhead, dickhead,* and *shithead* would follow. It is only a matter of time. But for now I stay focused on the subject at hand, gaining entrance to my son's room. I stand as the doofus outside the gate.

"Dale," I say rapping on the white enamel, "open the door, *now.*"

More forceful, with a hint of implied consequences. I wait. A door clicks and I realize it is the other door to my son's room. Our upstairs is one big circle with a landing between the second and third bedroom. Dale junior appears on the far landing with blotchy, red eyes. He is essentially in the castle while I stare across the moat.

"There, the door's open. What do you want, *doofus?*"

The *doofus* wants to be let in. This is a new sensation—being insulted by my nine-year-old. I don't know what a doofus really is, but the inflection tells me it is not something anyone wants to be. I breathe heavy, seeing the blotchy skin, the red eyes. I am a doofus.

"Dale, open the door."

"I just did."

I point to my door, briefly considering a sprint through my daughter's room to the landing. I try for parental control, yelling across the moat of contained space.

"No, open *this* door."

Dale wipes his eyes again.

"Why? So you can *yell* at me some more?"

"I didn't yell at you, Dale," I say in a calm voice.

"Yes, you did," he shouts, fresh tears appearing on both cheeks.

I feel the absurdity of the situation—we are arguing across the wide-open space of the stairwell. Dale junior is standing essentially on a balcony and I am beggar outside the castle.

"Dale, walk around and unlock this door, and we will discuss what just happened."

He grudgingly gives up his balcony with a muttered, *"Doofus."* The door clicks and SpongeBob and Thomas the Chipmunk swing wide. I glance at SpongeBob again and his middle finger and then turn to Dale junior, who is sitting on his lower bunk, crying again.

"Now, tell me what is wrong."

"What do you care?" he cries out. "You're just a *doofus!*"

I nod slowly, sitting down on the far side of his bed.

"That may be, Dale, but I still would like to know what is really bothering you. Is it because I told you you couldn't play soccer in the house?"

Fresh tears, accusing eyes. The man of the hour has just blown it again.

"Yes ... you never ... let me do ... *anything* ... if ... I ... do *anything,* you tell me to stop it ... I can't play basketball or hit a balloon ... or play soccer ... *you let Angela do whatever she wants!*"

I stare at my hands, a habit I have picked up from my son. It is true. I do give my daughter far more latitude. I don't have the expectations of the father for the son. It is easier. We are separated by gender and that makes all the difference. Angela's world is largely sealed—dolls, princesses, and magical horses. We can come to a neutral place, a sort of wonderment. But it is no excuse.

"Dale ... I have told you," I say in a level voice. "You can have the entire basement to play whatever sports you want—"

The blotchy red face turns on me.

"*You're lying.* You said that before and then you told me to stop playing basketball down there!"

"Now that's not true—"

"*I hate it out here* ... there's nothing to do ... all I do is play football by myself ... why did we ever have to fucking move out here!"

The linkage my son employs is not surprising. I ignore the word "*fucking*" as a moment of passion. Soon I will be treated to every obscenity I have murmured in his presence.

"You have lots of friends, Dale—"

"No I don't," he shouts, wiping his face, showing the gap in his teeth I had when I was a boy. "Why did you make us move out here? *I hate it.* It's not my fault you're losing your job, and now you and mom are getting divorced!"

The last hatchet catches me between the shoulder blades. I had never told my son I was fired or that my wife and I were going through difficult times. Yet these children know with the prescience of a shaman. They know far more than we can ever tell. Still, I am reeling. Dale junior has achieved the equivalent of a body blow. I regain myself, trying to pull *the man in control of his life* out of the garbage.

"Where did you hear that?"

"I heard mom on the telephone … she talks about it all the time."

Now I am winded. Now I am pissed. My son knows more than I do. This is not good.

"Dale, your mother and I are not getting divorced."

He shakes his head.

"That's not what she said…she has the papers and everything!"

I stare at my son, trying not to show that he is kicking my ass. *Papers and everything…*My mouth is open and I am looking around for the prowler who is about to steal my life. I could well be on my way to the small divorcee apartment, headed for Sears to create the rooms used on the weekends for the part-time daddy. I feel ill, but I pull it together, trying to save what is left of my authority.

"Dale, listen to me … look at me. " He turns and my heart breaks, because there is real fear in his eyes. "Your mother and I are going through some rough times, but we aren't going to get divorced … here, wipe your nose," I say offering my sleeve.

Dale takes a deep breath.

"I know you aren't getting divorced, Dad … but *she is,* and it's all because we moved out to this shitty place."

Another first. My son is now using the word *shitty. Doofus, fuck, shitty.* The world has changed.

"I hate it here … *I hate it* … and you're the one who made us move out here!"

The crying resumes and like a duck hit on the head, I don't

quite know what to do.

"And you don't come to any of my games ... "

I rub my forehead. Parental solace is predicated on the fact child logic is in error, but my son is hitting the issues dead on.

"And you don't let me do anything ..." Fresh tears. "You're a ... a *doofus.*"

What my nine-year-old has said is not wrong. His lists of transgressions are a machine gun of my peccadilloes. I try and regroup, looking for the logic of the adult against the passion of the child. My marriage is going down the toilet. The move out to the land of million-dollar homes has not been a good thing. Should I compound my sins and add lying to it?

I look at Dale junior and rub his neck, sitting on the bottom bunk, giving in to the boy who only speaks the truth.

"You're right," I say, rightfully convicted. "I am a doofus."

In our old life the jack-o-lanterns were real pumpkins and the turn-of-the -century homes looked haunted. The good people of Belleview have improved on the traditional pumpkin by inflating the equivalent of the Hindenburg on their front lawns. These giant pumpkins loll in the wind, anchored by long steel cables. Pneumatic pumps whirr day and night, keeping these orange dirigibles at just the right PSI. The pumpkins are bathed in orange spots and their giant smiles can be seen a mile away. Georgia Barnes has the largest pumpkin and it sits on her lawn like some sort of rotund lord, tugging gently at the anchor cables, the smiley face of suburban plasticity.

Dale junior is a vending machine for Halloween, and already his M&Ms and Milky Way have fallen off the large box he wears over his shoulders. D. T. senior and I enjoy our chocolate windfall while following my son to various houses. We have gotten a late start and forgot a flashlight, so now we stumble along in total darkness. Other trick-or-treaters go by in a hail of flashlights and glowing necklaces. We have to stop several times while D. T. senior catches his breath.

"Good lord, boy, we going to cover the whole neighborhood?"

I thought we might, judging by the vending machine moving rapidly ahead.

"Maybe you should cut down on the cigars," I observe, watching him gasp for air.

"It's not *the cigars* that are the problem; it's this *walking* that's the problem, boy."

I wait by the curb while Dale junior goes up to another porch. D. T. senior is breathing heavy, bent over at the knees. It's like this sometimes. My father usually produces such a whirlwind you never even see his age, but suddenly he will become mortal and I realize again he is seventy-three.

He stands up.

"All right ... I'm okay ... where'd that boy go?"

I can see a faint box moving toward another house.

"He's a good two acres ahead of us."

"Let's walk slowly and catch the boy on the return, then."

We start down the street. The moon is low over the trees and the air is balmy. D. T. senior pulls out a cigar and licks the end.

"Those aren't helping your wind."

"I'm just going to suck on it, boy."

We pass some other trick-or-treaters in the darkness.

"So ... why is your boy so mad at you?"

I turn and look at D. T. senior, who has lit his cigar.

"Who said he was?" I ask and shrug, thinking of the sullen vending machine with no smile, a strange condition for a nine-year-old on Halloween night.

"Don't bullshit a bullshitter. The boy won't even *look* at you."

I breathe tiredly.

"He's mad because I cut off his sports until he gets his

homework under control and I wouldn't let him play soccer in the house. There, that's what he's mad about."

D. T. senior takes the cigar and holds it down by his side. His blue eyes look strangely luminous in the evening light.

"Boy, you are just batting a thousand! Got your wife pissed off at you and now your boy. You better be nice to me, because I'm the only friend you have left."

"Don't worry about it, Dad."

"I *do* worry about it. He's my grandson!"

I glance at D. T. senior. This sudden assignation as master grandfather is comical. If his job called tomorrow, we would all be breathing D. T. senior exhaust. The grandfather suit would be traded for the latest Brooks attire and phone calls would rain down from airports and motels. It is only because he is a captive over my garage that he has discovered his role as grandfather.

"No offense, Dad, but you haven't exactly been that much of a grandfather until now."

The scuff of D. T. senior's loafers slow, his cigar brimming with oxygen.

"I don't know why you say that, boy."

I turn and face the man in Ol' Miss garb: sport jacket, sockless loafers, and cigar.

"Because even when you have an appointment in the area, you would rather stay in a hotel than stay with us. You could see your grandkids, but you would rather sit in some hotel room and fall asleep watching HBO movies. You don't remember their birthdays, not that I really care, but when I tell them their grandfather is staying in a hotel right downtown but not coming out to the house, then they have to wonder why their grandfather doesn't really give a shit about seeing them."

I know I am being rough, but I don't care. My life is fast becoming a mirror of my father's, and I blame him fully.

"I have to work, boy. I am not retired."

"I understand that," I say and nod. "Just don't play the grandfather card now; it's not yours to play. I'm glad you're here now. I'm glad you're getting to know my kids better, but when Doris takes you back or you get a job, then you'll beat it the hell out of here and never look back. You'll travel, you'll call, you'll have dinner downtown, and you'll never come out to the house, and I'm not even sure *you* know why." I shrug. "Maybe you didn't grow up in some basic way, maybe you just have to be the bad boy. Who the fuck knows! Just do me a favor. Don't tell me how to raise my kids."

We stare at each other. D. T. senior nods, probing his cigar toward me.

"Good fucking speech."

"Thank you."

We begin walking again and reach the end of the cul-de-sac. Dale junior has appeared two houses up, and I can see he has hooked up with some other kids. D. T. senior is staring off at one of the small mansions. I feel bad about my outburst, but my nerves are shot and anything is possible now. The one positive of massive failure is that it gives one the clarity of vision of the doomed. D. T. senior turns and puffs his cigar quickly, glancing at me several times. I have hit a nerve and this is puzzling. My father had shrugged off marriage counselors, therapists, clergymen, lawyers, and doctors for years with the indifference of a school boy in a study hall. Why I should be able to land an arrow now made no sense. He stops in the street, tearing the cigar from his mouth.

"Well, that sounds like a bunch of fucking happy *whoreshit* to me!"

I stop and we are two men in the middle of a road.

"That doesn't surprise me, Dad."

"I'm sorry I can't be like Dick and come over for every fucking birthday party."

"I don't expect that," I answer, seeing real anger in his eyes, maybe even hurt.

D. T. senior stops, holding the cigar high for divine retribution.

"Let me finish here. It's true, I *do* stay in motels when I'm in town and I can't be the doting grandfather when I'm doing business. It's just the way I am. You want a different kind of grandfather, boy, then you better call Dick. I'm not a good father the way you are, never was, *never* will be, but I can still give you advice. That is my prerogative. You don't want to listen to me, boy, then that is your prerogative."

Now I feel bad. I am taking things out on the wrong person. He has not changed. D. T. senior has been consistent all his life. It is me who has changed. It is my own inadequacy as a father that I using as a club.

"I'm sorry, Dad." I hold up my hands in surrender. "I'm just fucked up."

He suddenly shrugs, turning back into the rolling shibboleth. The passion has gone like a wave and we are walking again.

"We all fucked up, boy. Just don't try and solve *all* your problems at once. You are just going through what we all did. You just like every other man who has had a family and had to support them in this crazy, fucked-up world."

There is bitterness in D. T. senior's voice and I remind myself that life has not done him any favors lately. I have not been cognizant of his three AM terrors, dying a lonely man without a penny or a wife to look after him. I am foolish to think he doesn't wake and feel the dull terror of an uncertain future. We walk in silence, hearing the distant screams of children in the evening air. I am drifting back now. It is one of those nights where one can see all the way back.

"Dad, do you remember that rocket ride I went on when I was a kid?"

D. T. senior is holding his cigar low again. He puffs, tilting his head.

"The one I took you off of?"

"Yes." I pause, feeling the terror of that moment again. "I thought I was going to die on that ride …" I look at him. "How … how did you know to get me off of that thing?"

My father squints down the road.

"Well, your mother thought you were going to be okay, but I knew you wouldn't say anything. I knew you'd rather die than say what the hell you really think, but I could tell from your face you were in trouble, and I had to do something. "

I slow my pace until we stop again. It has grown dark and I can barely see his face. But there is a question out there. It is central to my life now and I realize it is one that I should have asked a long time ago.

"But how did you get that man to stop that ride? I mean, the man was in that booth, and you had to get him to stop the whole ride for one kid … how did you do it?"

D. T. senior shrugs, puffing lightly.

"Well, I told him to stop the ride."

"And …"

He shrugs. "Man said he couldn't stop the ride for one boy. I said, that is *my boy*, and you better stop this fucking ride right now."

We are still standing in the street, a raw October moon over the trees.

"But he didn't stop the ride, right?"

"No." D. T. senior shakes his head. "Nope. He didn't."

"So…what'd you do?"

D. T. senior puckers his lips, nodding slowly.

"I pushed the sonofabitch out of the way! Then I pulled back this long red handle and stopped the ride myself."

I suddenly feel young again, the years out there in the misted fields. I had assumed D. T. senior had *asked* the man to stop the ride and he had done it. Now I see that bit of rationality did not exist. Even when a boy is in trouble, the world doesn't care. Not content to follow the rules, D. T. senior bodily threw a man out of the way and throws levers, turns switches, does what he has to do to save his son. *Would I do the same for Dale junior? Would I come to his rescue and battle his demons?*

"Then you got me," I finish for him, suddenly exhausted.

D. T. senior nods slowly.

"That's right, boy. They said they were going to call the police and every other thing ... but sometimes ... sometimes, boy, you got to take things into your own hands and make things right."

We start walking again. I listen to the sound of our shoes, D. T. senior's breathing, and the sounds of the deepening night. It is such a simple thing, but unknown to a man of my generation. The authority to destroy systems for moral order does not exist for me. But I am grateful for what a man did for me thirty some years ago. I didn't yell then; I didn't scream to get off. I felt I didn't have that right.

I put my hand on my father's shoulder, saying the words so hard for the boy then.

"Can you take me off this ride now, Dad?"

D. T. senior frowns, smoking his cigar and then shakes his head with true regret.

"I wish I could, boy."

20

T-0

Saturday

Blastoff

The Ford is loaded with enough explosives to launch the Space Shuttle: five hundred rockets, engines, parachutes, launchers, igniters, batteries, wadding, barricades, police tape, remote controls, and hundreds of feet of red twelve-gauge wire. The end of the yellow barricades stick out the back window with the yellow police tape flapping in the breeze. The wind whistles around the interior of my ten-year-old SUV, ruffling Dale junior's hair in the back seat, tweaking D. T. senior's beard in the front, shooting errant trash on the floor of my car.

It is a beautiful autumn morning with blue sky and brilliant sun painting the old barns. There is not a cloud in the sky and the sun is beating on the high corn as we head farther out into the country. We are following the directions of one tired Brad Jones who I managed to get hold of at six AM. Rocket Day is to be held in the middle of a Park District field lodged in the middle of numerous cornfields. I am sure the farmers had a good laugh when the Charleston Park District purchased the ten acres for families to enjoy the great outdoors. I can hear the farmers laughing still as I become hopelessly lost.

Brad's directions didn't take into account that each road looks the same and many are unmarked except for cryptic numbers. Even though I have lived out in the country for almost three years, I still have no idea how to navigate roads marked by signs: RR21. I am a man of gas stations. I could circumnavigate the globe as long as there is a lone Pakistani behind bulletproof glass telling me where to go in an unintelligible tongue. The world may have GPS, but I will always be the man running into the scent of gasoline, tracing an oil-stained map on a wall next to the men's room.

I look down the road and see no gas stations. What does come down the road is an unmarked police car that roars up behind me like an ill wind. I start to pull over when the lights flash on in the headlights and the siren burps.

D. T. senior stares at me.

"Were you speeding, boy?"

"Dad, it's the cops!"

"Thank you, son" I say, dryly, rolling to a stop on the shoulder.

I watch the door open and a man with cop glasses and a crew cut emerges. I feel a strange blend of relief and apprehension as the cop in tennis shoes approaches my window.

"Could I see your license please, Mr. Hammer?"

"Detective Clancy," I murmur, squinting into the sun. "Slow day in Charleston?"

He says nothing as I fish out my wallet and pass over the laminate. The good Detective holds my license, and it is then I see his shoulder harness and a small cannon. I squint into the sun again.

"Was I speeding, Detective?"

He shakes his head and hands me back my license.

"No. Would you please step out of the car, Mr. Hammer?"

I take a deep breath. Not an auspicious start to Rocket Day.

"Is he going to arrest you, Dad?" Dale junior questions.

"I hope not," I mutter.

We reach the end of my Explorer and Detective Clancy removes his wire-rim sunglasses. His eyes are cold, his manner efficient. *Just the facts, ma'am.* I smile, looking for levity with the law.

"Are we having a rendezvous, Detective? We really should stop meeting like this."

Detective Clancy gives me a tight smile. He crosses his arms and runs his hands over the eighth of an inch crew.

"Hair number ninety-nine is out of place."

The tight smile again.

"So did you give any thought to our little situation?"

Our little situation. I can only think Dr. Petty must give a lot of money to the Charleston police department. What I really am staring at is an errand boy for the good doctor. Dr. Petty is before me in jeans and tennis shoes with a .45 on his shoulder. That sign had really racked him off.

"I take it you are referring to me confessing to a crime I didn't commit?"

Detective Clancy puts back on the sunglasses. He is wearing a Members Only jacket and Target gym shoes. The Dirty Harry persona is wilting under the suburban dad who has to run his son to soccer practice in an hour after playing cop.

"Why don't you get wise to yourself, Mr. Hammer?"

I look out at the wide open space, the agrarian sun beating down on two men in synthetic tennis shoes and polyester blend jackets. We really don't belong to this planet anymore. I look at the detective.

"Get wise to myself? Now we are in a bad movie from the forties."

Detective Clancy ignores my reference to film noir and thumps the air with his forefinger.

"You are the only one buying off on your own bullshit. I hope you know that. I know you did it, and *you know* you did it. All you have to do is pay for the sign to be replaced."

I look out into the wide fields and nod slowly. *Confess thy sins and be cleansed.* If only it were that easy.

"So all I have to do is pay for the sign and everything will be forgotten?"

Detective Clancy smiles. He is seeing daylight. A little Saturday-morning police work and a confirming call to the good doctor. The bird dog doing his duty.

"That's right. This will go no further than right here … otherwise I'm going to have to arrest you on Monday. You will be booked, fingerprinted … might even spend a little time in a holding cell."

I chew on this, watching a farmer harvesting his corn.

"There's only one problem."

The smile retreats.

"What's that?"

"I didn't do it."

Detective Clancy stares at me through his polarized shields. I know he would like to draw his cannon and report back to Dr. Petty that the "sign issue" has been taken care of. The good doctor would slowly nod by his pool. That will teach people to fuck with the Belleview banner.

"I'll see you on Monday, then, Mr. Hammer, and it won't be pretty, I assure you … not pretty."

Even though I am weak in the knees, I give no quarter.

"Is that a promise, Detective Clancy?"

The good detective turns by his door. He has had enough of this. There is real crime to be pursued—kids to be hassled, scofflaws to confront.

"Bet on it!

I am then treated to a hail of Chevy Caprice exhaust and spattering gravel. I walk back to the car and get in, ignoring D. T.

senior's imploring eyes.

"What in the hell did that boy want?"

I shrug, putting the truck in gear.

"Big drive on for donations … I gave him a couple of bucks."

"Did he arrest you, Dad?"

I glance into the rearview mirror.

"No …not yet."

"Dad, we're lost."

We have just stopped at one of these intersections with two green signs informing us that RR 25 and RR28 have just met. These two roads are not part of Brad Jones's directions. I sigh and consider the intersections that are my life—nondescript, no direction and each turn leading into certain oblivion.

"You're lost, aren't you, boy?"

I glance at my father.

"Of course I'm lost; there are no fricking road signs out here."

"You better call Mom," Dale junior groans.

This is a common lament of my son. Dad is habitually lost, so call Mom. I don't think Wendy can give me the directions on this one. I don't know if the woman who sat at the kitchen table last night with the legal documents would answer the phone. Of course this was after the strangest encounter of the night with my neighbor. The doorbell rang at ten PM. I opened the door to a stout man, curiously naked without his mower.

"George Campbell coming to my house. What a surprise. You usually come over when I'm not here," I say, keeping a firm hand on my leaping emotions.

Campbell hands me a long envelope.

"Consider yourself served. Tell Wendy to call me with any questions."

I watch him waddle away, holding the envelope that clearly has a return address, "Campbell and Associates, Attorneys-at-Law."

"Well, you better do something, boy. We can't sit at this intersection all day!"

I look over at my father. D. T. senior chooses action, even the wrong action, over no action at all. It is the reason he will fly across the country to have a business lunch with a plant manager who will not buy anything from him. It is the reason he will drive five hundred miles to meet a man who has a complaint about a single box. The *action* is important, not the result. I am the next generation of this philosophy—I think about the action taken and then generally take no action at all.

"Call Mom," my son urges.

D. T. senior slashes the air in front of us.

"Just pick a goddamn road, son, and we'll follow it to where it goes!"

I look at the Zen Master who expressed the desire to accompany Dale junior and I by appearing in a checkered shirt and tennis shoes. He is now the executive in charge. (*Just do it, boy*) But I have always let men like my father rule. If there is an area of lesser concentration, then something will move into it. In science class this was osmosis, in real life social Darwinism. *Just fucking do it, boy!*

I nod slowly and stare at my father in the sudden quiet of rural America.

"That's sort of the way you've led your life, Dad."

"That's right!" He nods indignantly. "And you would be better off to adopt some of my habits! Don't *overthink* everything, boy. Your whole goddamn generation thinks it can't take a shit without an *e-mail* or a *Web site* to tell you where to squat—just take a chance and *pick* a road and go down it and keep going until you hit another road and maybe you might find your destination at the end of that road!"

I breathe heavily and look in the rearview mirror.

"You hear that, Dale? There's a philosophy for your life. Write that down. "

Dale junior looks out the window and shrugs.

"Granddad's right, Dad. You probably should just pick a road."

Now my nine-year-old has thrown in with the man over the garage. The simple logic of the child has combined with the neurotic to bushwhack me. I should be the one giving sage advice, but Dale Junior has picked up long ago that Dad is riddled with angst and indecision. At least Granddad *does* something.

I glance at the directions once more and shrug.

"Fine. Fine. We'll take this road," I mutter, turning right onto *RR 27.*

D. T. senior claps.

"There you go, boy! *Congratulations.* You just made a decision," he says and nods, extracting a long cigar from his top pocket.

"Don't smoke in the car, Dad," I say quickly.

The man from the South rolls his eyes and puts the cigar back in his pocket. I take this small victory, but even cheap revenge doesn't feel the same anymore.

Metaphors do justice when applied with a deft hand. That I am now hopelessly lost does seem like justice. We barrel down the road for another ten minutes, passing two more intersections that look just like the one I had sat pondering. Now I am sure we are hopelessly lost in the great bread basket of America. We pass horses and cows and sheep and chickens. We pass men on tractors and women on porches. I am getting more lost by the second, and I have the same feeling when I sat with George Campbell's envelope. It is the sucker punch, the errant fission of catastrophe.

Wendy is motionless, a lawyer with a legal document in front of her.

"I didn't know George was an attorney," I mutter, wishing now he had been my wife's paramour. I find this thought much more preferable than being my wife's attorney. I want to ask whatever happened to Marty, the family attorney. But of course I know what happened to Marty. He was passed over for a divorce attorney. George Campbell had broadsided me. The man in the button down shirt and zero-turn mower had just kicked my ass in the worst way.

"I thought he was a salesman," I complain again, feeling like Campbell had violated our secret covenant of mutual loathing.

"Wrong again, Dale," is all my wife says.

"Boy, we are *lost!*"

I look over at the pale blue eyes of the original soothsayer. The man of action has now become the disgruntled executive who can't believe the perspicacity of moronic underlings. I look over at D. T. senior and raise my eyebrows.

"Whatever happened to just choose a road and follow it?"

"Well, you chose the *wrong road,* boy."

"And you know this, how?"

"Granddad's right, Dad," comes from my number one son. "You are on the wrong road."

I consider now the role of the American dad. It is one of being the constant whipping boy of the blockhead. Since I have become married and had kids, I have become the doddering fool forever making the wrong turn, picking up the wrong dish, turning on the wrong program, not servicing the car on time, taking out the trash, or cutting the lawn. I have been parked in the back lot of wife and children to fulfill my role as the hapless has-been of the progenitor. Even D. T. senior gets more respect than the man who is the supposed master of his home.

"I'm going to ask for some directions," I mutter, seeing a restaurant at the intersection.

"Why don't you call Mom?" comes from the back

I turn and look at my son who presses back against the seat.

"Mom doesn't know where the hell she's going either, Dale!"

I turn around, feeling D. T. senior's eyes.

"My, my," he murmurs.

"What?"

He shakes his head slowly.

"Talk about double entendre, boy."

I glance at my father and am truly surprised.

"I didn't know you knew what a double entendre was, Dad."

He shrugs, the diffident air of the scholar descending like a glove.

"I know more than you think, boy," he says mysteriously, implying libraries he has frequented, tombs read, and theories discussed.

"I hope so, Dad," I say, getting out of the car.

I walk up to this shack of a restaurant that has a sign boasting 1921 as its original date of inception. I toy with the idea of just walking past the restaurant and continuing down the road like those men from the 1930s who walked out a back kitchen door and hitched a ride on a passing freight. That ride must have been one of sorrow, but also one of immense freedom. D. T. senior and Dale junior would tell years later how I walked off to a restaurant and never returned. There would be rumors of alien adduction, foul play, and spontaneous combustion. Finally, the consensus would be that D. T. Hammer just couldn't take it.

I open the door to the restaurant and walk into 1925.

The diner is all farmers. They are in coveralls with low-brimmed hats, weathered skin, and sunburned necks. Thick fingers gnarl white porcelain cups, swiveling their necks to stare at the man in sunglasses with cowboy boots. The sound of the diner has been drawn down to a radio playing somewhere. Blue smoke from another era floats in the morning sun. A woman with her back to me speaks without turning.

"Just keep going down the road."

The woman sits and continues smoking on the shiny diner stool. She has both elbows on the counter and her cigarette zips smoke into the light.

"I'm sorry—"

"You heard me, just keep on going down the road."

I look for a mirror. Surely she has seen me in the reflection of something. I clear my throat.

"I'm looking for—"

"I know what you're *looking for.* They all come in here. Just keep going down the road and turn right, and you'll see what you're looking for."

The farmers are staring at me. The woman doesn't turn around.

"You mean—"

"You *know* what I mean."

I stare at the woman's back. She tips her cigarette again. I pause, torn between a dream and a moment.

"Thank you."

The farmers return to their coffee. The woman presses the cigarette to her lips.

I walk back to the car and get in. D. T. senior has the victory gloat all over him.

"So boy ... how lost are we?"

I pull onto the road, squinting down the deserted two-lane highway. I look at my father with a confidence that gives him pause.

"For once, Dad, we are exactly where we should be."

21

"Houston, Tranquility Base here. The Eagle has landed."
—Neil Armstrong, Apollo 11

Brad Jones and his entourage are standing in the middle of the field like the Joint Chiefs of Staff. Brad is in full regalia with shined medals, BSA camouflage green hat, neckerchief, badges running up and down his shirt, BSA camouflage green pants, combat boots, and dark glasses. I stop my SUV on the edge of the field while General Jones surveys my vehicle, approaching cautiously.

I roll down the window to cop glasses.

"I wasn't speeding, officer."

Brad Jones smiles faintly.

"Good morning, Dale."

"Good morning, Brad." I salute, turning to my copilot. "This is my father, Dale senior."

"Good to meet you, sir," Brad Jones nods, then turns back to me.

"Dale, I think you should set up your launching site at approximately center field, that way you can maximize your protection against the possibility of drift into the far trees." He checks his watch. "Scouts should be arriving at o-nine hundred,

343

so that gives you an hour to erect your barricades for launching your vehicles. We will be preparing the rockets at this station with the engines and wadding while you will arm the rockets and of course, launch the vehicles."

I salute. Brad doesn't smile.

"I have to caution you, Dale," he says, his face darkening. "No more than one rocket may be launched at any one time, so you will be pretty busy arming and launching the rockets in succession."

"Affirmative."

Brad pauses and then knocks on the top of my car twice.

"Good luck, Dale."

I salute once more and Commander Jones salutes back.

"That boy has watched too many *Rambo* movies," D. T. senior murmurs.

"More like John Wayne."

I follow Brad Jones's directions and stop in the middle of the field. It is a beautiful day, and the morning sun brasses the straw-colored grass. We tumble out of the car, staring dumbly at a wide blue sky. It is the prairie, after all.

"Well, I guess this is where we will set up base camp. Dad, why don't you and Dale start unloading the barricades?"

"All right, boy."

D. T. senior and Dale junior begin pulling out the yellow barricades as I take out the boxes of rocket engines. I set these by the back of the truck and begin unraveling wire and connectors and igniters. I try and remember Dean Heinrich's instructions, but they are back in the haze of a week filled with change. I take out a large battery and put this in the middle of the field. All things will revolve around the battery. My barricades will be at a uniform distance and I will string the yellow police tape around in a large octagon. I turn to the job of figuring out which wires go where. *Red to positive and black to negative.* I start with the battery and begin to unravel the Dean Heinrich design. Suddenly the launch site coalesces; the barricades are up and the tape is strung. The two sawhorses with launchers every three feet are in the middle. I string the launch wires back to another saw horse and have D. T. senior and Dale junior attach the launch controls. When Brad Jones arrives, our base camp is complete.

He walks slowly around the perimeter of our operation.

"It looks good, Dale, I'm impressed," he says and nods, standing in combat regalia and mirror sunglasses, hands on his hips.

"Thank you, Brad."

He nods to my truck.

"Dale, I came to get those rocket engines."

I instruct D. T. senior and my son to assist Brad in carrying the rocket engines back to the base tent. There are three boxes of engines and wadding and extra rockets. They leave and I am left in the middle of the field with my twenty-five launchers, twenty-five launch rods to the sky, yellow tape, and barricades. I sit down and unzip my jacket, then lay back on the warm grass. I close my eyes and see George Campbell's documents on our kitchen table again.

Really, I consider it a bill of sale. A bill of sale for the purchase of a house, a life, two kids, a single wage earner, a tax bill, middle-class debt, angst, stress, middle-class maladies, polarization, loneliness, a bill for no blacks, no Indians, no Chinese, no Mexicans, no Japanese or Jews, a bill for Western European people of blue eyes and blond hair (I lost count of the number of blond-haired children in our neighborhood) no crime, no dissent, no poverty, no bums, no old cars in the drive, no boats, no solicitors, no sheds, no unkempt lawns or leaning garages, no beggars or thieves, no protestors of solicitors, no holy rollers, no Krishnas, Muslims, pollution or city lights, no people with bad teeth or bad breath, no people who say *ain't* or *got no*, no RVs in the drive, no accents, few beards, no telephone polls or electric wires, no planes overhead, no traffic around, perfect lawns, patios, marble bars, no trees, and no bugs.

"I thought he was a salesman," I mutter again.

"Lawyers *are* salesmen, Dale, you should know that," Wendy says.

I still wished Campbell had been having an affair with my wife. I preferred that scenario much more than the designer behind the dissolution of my marriage. The documents were impressive, with "Divorce Decree" across the top. The work that had gone into this legal document was obvious. There was a clear blue folder that enfolded the crisp white documents with "Campbell and Associates, Attorneys-at–Law" in gold letters. I imagined George Campbell sitting in his den, laughing manically, glancing across the street. Or the other scenario where it is just another divorce case to pad the Campbell wallet.

I open my eyes and hear a strange hum. I sit up and stare at my steel launch wires leading up to the sky like so many antennas. They gleam in the sun, moving slightly in the wind. The rockets slide up the launch wire, blasting off toward the heavens until the ejection charge fires and the chute opens. It all depends on wind and the physics of rocket propulsion.

"Why did you go to Campbell?"

Wendy looks down at the table.

"I couldn't use Marty, you know that." My wife looks up, her eyes pained but firm. "He is solid, Dale. He is fair. He's not like you; he doesn't care what other people think of him. He just does his job and raises his family and I know he's a good lawyer. I think you should find a good lawyer too."

I stare at the document I haven't touched. If I touch it, then my marriage is over.

"I told George to be fair, and I think I came up with some equitable proposals concerning the children … the money …

the debt."

"That should be the easy part," I mutter.

"Not necessarily," the lawyer says.

Still, I make no move. I cannot believe that this fire we have been dancing around for the last year is really spreading now. I can see how a divorce starts. It is much like buying a house. Once you start looking, then it really just a matter of time before lawyers and counselors and mediators move in to seal the deal.

"I'm not going to open that."

"Dale—"

"No. I'm not going to."

Wendy looks down and shakes her head.

"You're going to make me do the shit work right up to the end, aren't you?"

I stand up from the table and feel the back of my legs shaking. The knowledge that my life is spinning out of control in a far more rapid speed than even I could have predicted is scaring the hell out of me.

"I need to regroup. I need time to think."

Wendy looks up from the table, her eyes hard. I can see she has made her decision and there is no going back now. Wendy is like that. Once she makes up her mind, then that is it.

"How much time?"

Her question is emotionless, hard.

"Give me until tomorrow. Let me get through Rocket Day."

"All right," she says, putting the blue folder back in the envelope. "We will settle this tomorrow."

I look across the field and watch D. T. senior and my son walking toward me. My father has his hand on Dale's shoulder, and I realize he has become more stable than me. Regardless of what happens, he will still be Dale junior's grandfather. He will still see his grandson with the regularity he chooses, while I will be subject to the dictates of an impersonal court.

I hear the hum again, a low, sonic hum really. I stare at the steel launch rods as the wind blows again, vibrating and singing in the sun.

Rocketry is really all about pushing boundaries. The rocket blasts off for the heavens and depending on the type of engine, it can go a mile up into the sky. Many times the rocket becomes invisible and only the smoke trail can be seen. The rocket engine gives up its thrust and then it glides for a few second up above the clouds. The rocket acknowledges gravity and begins to arc over, and it is then a flaming charge of gunpowder ignites and blows off the top of the rocket, propelling the parachute into the slipstream. If all goes to plan, the parachutes fills with air, and the rocket floats back to earth.

But many rockets never return. Some go up into the sky and are lost from sight. Some rockets blow up on the launch pad. Some rockets blow up in the air. Some rockets seem to continue going until they disappear altogether. Some rockets go up and their chute doesn't open and the rocket slams back into the hard earth. Some rockets shoot off in a crazy arc and smash into a tree or a telephone poll. Some rockets never fire and just sit on the launch pad. Some rockets catch fire when the parachute charge goes off. Some rockets float back to earth and hang up in a tree. Some rockets simply don't go high enough and fall back to earth. And then some rockets arc over, their chutes open perfectly, but they just float away.

It is within this concept of pushing boundaries that I rediscover Dean Heinrich's one flaw. I imagine it was something he could not have foreseen, or I like to think Dean Heinrich had something more to him than granny glasses and a numbering system for his tools. The *master control* is a large steel button that I hold while the Scouts take their position behind the yellow barricade. In front of the scout is a small yellow plastic launcher with a single red button. Upon my command, the scout steps forward and presses the button. The rocket sitting with an igniter shoved up the bottom end is connected to the scout's launcher, but it is also connected to mine.

Dean Heinrich's words float back to me as if from a vision. "I put the master control in because I didn't want to end up with a rocket in my eye socket. So I came up with this little gizmo," he said that night, holding up the gleaming metal button with the thick yellow wire trailing back to the battery and the phalanx of launchers. "The scouts can't launch shit unless I press this baby. In this way, I stay in total control."

I wonder now about Dean Heinrich's assertion. *Total control—* an illusion taught to us in school that if we follow the rules, if we do what we are told, then we too will be in *total control*. But of course, the adults are in cahoots to keep from children the central secret of their expiring lives—*one loses control as one ages and not the reverse*. It is in childhood that one has control over a bike ride or a walk to the park, or reading a book on the couch. The child mind is present minded and seals out the dark forces that tell one we are clearly *out of control*, for what could be more emasculating than the knowledge that as we age we move closer to uncontrollable oblivion?

I imagine when Dean Heinrich came up with this button on some rainy night, he convinced himself that he had wrestled back some of that childhood control the way he had wrestled his tools from obscurity with the knowledge he could reach for any tool at any time. But then came Dean's moment of truth as he tested the launcher. The first position, the first click, the scout's rocket becomes activated and the scout's launcher is now live. The scout can then actually control the launching of his rocket. I'm sure Dean Heinrich went through many tests, hearing the small *phssit* of the igniter, watching the smoke waft in his garage, a small point scored against his corporate job, his corporate life.

Maybe it wasn't that first night, but some other moment when he had two rockets on the launch pad, when Brad Jones's edict of *one rocket at a time* was ringing in his ears that he pushed the metal button to a second position that shouldn't have existed. This unknown flaw then lit up the second rocket and Dean Heinrich watched in horror as two rockets blasted off together.

I'm sure he then conducted many tests with the door of his garage open to a drizzly spring wind, errant gusts from storm clouds fluffing his baby fine hair while he tested and retested the master launcher, only to conclude that the flaw in his system was real. If one pressed the button all the way down, then *all* the rockets were live and potentially a juggernaut of rockets could blast off to the heavens. This must have disappointed Dean as he contemplated another variable in the universe he had not accounted for.

He probably tried to redesign the button. Maybe the exigencies of time defeated him, along with the sneaking suspicion that if he fixed this hole in the Heinrich universe, another one would surely pop up. The best way to handle the flaw was to be scrupulous and instruct all Rocket Men to never *ever* push the master launcher to the *second* position. It was with the utmost urgency Dean Heinrich instructed me that night that *under no circumstances* was I to ever contemplate a dual launch. That technically it should not be possible, but because of a flaw in design, multiple rockets *could* be launched, endangering the lives of the scouts and all present on the launch field.

Therefore, one must never tempt fate, one must be circumspect, and press lightly on the launch button to the first click, and *never* continue beyond that safe position.

Rocket Day progresses like most organized events—fitfully. From my position in the field, I can see Brad Jones and his entourage under their green army tarpaulin. The Scout leaders stand behind a long table, congratulating each other on finding a reason to wear paramilitary attire as middle-aged adults and not be arrested. Nowhere but the Scouts can a grown man wear knee socks with tassels and a neckerchief and not be accused of being a sex offender.

I lie in the grass and watch Dale junior carry a rocket to the first launch pad and carefully thread it down the steel rod and then scamper to the launcher. He turns and faces me expectantly. I hold the master launcher lightly in my hand, looking over at D. T. senior, who has retreated a good twenty yards to the middle of the field. "I don't want to be around when you blow yourself up, boy," were his final parting words, showing no faith in my ability to organize an event that will not end up in destruction and mayhem.

"Go ahead, boy," he calls, his voice carried away by the wind.

I sit up and face my son, who is all smiles.

"Ready, Dale?"

"Yeah," he shouts.

I finger the large silver button and then slowly depress it to the first position. The launch pad is now live.

"Launch when ready, Commander," I shout.

Dale presses his red button and the twelve-volt battery delivers its charge to the sulfur pod of the igniter. The rocket seems determined not to move when *whoosh!* A long curl of white exhaust blasts out as the rocket shoots for the heavens in a sonic whine, becoming a small dot in the blue sky.

"Wow," Dale shouts.

I put my hand to my brow and see a puff of smoke as a red chute billows out. The first launch has been a success. Even D. T. senior has to admit that for once I have succeeded in what I set out to do.

"That thing really moves," he says, watching Dale junior run after the gliding, drifting rocket heading back to earth on the far side of the field. "I didn't think it would be like that."

"You remember these, don't you," I say, looking at D. T. senior. "We used to launch these same rockets."

He frowns and shakes his head. I stare at my father and realize he doesn't remember the autumn nights when a boy and his father stared up at the sky and had a moment together, a moment before the dusk, before the sweeping away of the short time between men and boys. I feel sad that D. T. senior's life has progressed to the point where old memories are fading and he has lost recollections of his years as a father. These years with Dale and Angela are the best years—I even know this.

"Uh oh. Looks like the Lieutenant General is coming to pay us a visit."

I turn and sure enough, Brad Jones is crossing the field in full regalia. His combat boots crunch the stiff grass underfoot, his badges cutting the dark khaki of his uniform. He now has on a BSA beret that is cocked on his head in Green Beret fashion. Brad's field glasses are around his neck, and he stops once to follow Dale junior's rocket to the earth. He then strides into the launch area.

"Dale, could I have a word with you, please."

"Sure, Brad."

I follow Brad to the far side of the launch site. He carefully takes off his mirror sunglasses and hangs them on his top right pocket. His cell phone, keys, compass, pager, flashlight, Swiss army knife, canteen, and first aid kit all dangle from a black utility belt on his waist. He is efficient, organized, and ready to face any exigency. I tuck in my shirt to show I am also ready.

"Dale, why was that rocket launched?"

I stare at him, feeling the smile fading from my face.

"Just checking things out."

Brad frowns, and I see the man so aghast that I drove across a vacant field a week before. I know that Brad probably lost some battle to get me stripped of my duties as Rocket Man—thwarted only by the fact no one else would do it.

"That was an unauthorized launch, Dale."

I stare at the poster child for anal retentiveness

"You're kidding, Brad ... right?"

The glasses come back on.

"No, Dale. I will not have any more unauthorized launches on my site. I am responsible for the safety of everyone here. You are only to launch when I send a Scout down with a loaded rocket, and then you are only to launch *one* rocket at a time. If I see anymore unauthorized launches, then I will relieve you of your duties." Brad then takes his glasses from his eyes. "Do I make myself clear?"

I stare at this man who I could easily kick in the balls.

"Taking this a little far, aren't you, Brad?"

"I beg your pardon?"

I shrug.

"Sure ... whatever, Brad."

"Good! I'm glad we understand each other."

Then he strides out of the area like MacArthur returning to the Philippines. I feel sick to my stomach. If there is one fear I am loathe to admit it is this: *That I will become what I abhor.* I can feel the creeping tentacles of acceptance weaving their way through chinks in my armor. There are times when I take pride in my large home and my wide lawn, and there are times when I am glad we are all white and my children don't have to deal with the messy issues of multiculturalism. There are times when I watch the news and see the world as sweaty hordes trying for a piece of the pie. It is like the slow infection of a drug, and not kicking Brad Jones in the balls is surely another hit of valium.

I turn and see D. T. senior has been listening. I know he wanted to let Brad Jones have it in the worst way, but he saw that this would break a boy's heart. D. T. senior walks over and puts his hand on my shoulder and says in a clear Southern drawl, "That sonofabitch should get that stiff poker removed from his ass."

I look at my father, knowing then; I am not the man to perform such an act.

22

"Failure is not an option."
–Mission Control

Now the scouts are drifting from Brad's command post to my hapless octagonal in the middle of the field. The boys are shy, rude, aggressive, and polite. I take the rockets and insert an igniter into the engine before handing it to D. T. senior and Dale junior. They put the rocket on the steel rod and connect the wire clips to the igniter. The Scout takes his position at the launch barricade. I push the button to the first position and tell the Scout to fire when ready. *Whoosh!* Another rocket rushes skyward, blasting through the short thrust stage to the ejection charge. The Scout takes off at a dead run, running for his rocket drifting downfield.

Now the scouts begin coming like an assembly line and we are busy. D. T. senior is connecting the igniters while Dale junior continues putting rockets on the launch pads. We steadily fall behind as the air fills with burned rocket fuel. My small island in the middle of the field has become crowded. I see fathers walking over with sons. They are men my age, some younger, some older. They walk across the field with their hands on their sons' shoulders, looking for a moment. Rocket Day is in full swing.

The day gets hot and I have good sunburn going on the back of my neck. My hands are black from rocket exhaust and the ground is littered with igniters and spent rocket engines. D. T. senior and Dale junior have gone to get something to eat while I enjoy the lull of noontime before the afternoon rush.

"I know you from somewhere."

I look up to an old man in a baseball cap and glasses. He is with a Scout who is the last one before lunch. I put the Scout's rocket on the steel rod of the launcher and look at the old man again.

"I never forget a face … what do you do for a living?"

"I'm a writer."

"Is that so?"

I go down on my knees and connect the igniter to his son's rocket.

"Maybe you read one of my books?"

I get up as the old man shakes his head doubtfully.

"I don't read. I used to, but since I got older, I can't stay in one place anymore, can't sit long enough to read. So I don't think that is it."

"All right," I say picking up the master control. "Ready to launch"

The boy nods eagerly.

"Let's do a countdown. Ready, ten, nine, eight, seven, six, five, four, three, two, one …"

I press my button and the Scout presses his as the rocket flashes skyward. The old man cranes his neck.

"Well, I'll be!"

We all watch as the red parachute flashes against the clear blue.

"Better go run and get it, Toby," the old man says and nods as the Scout takes off.

He turns to me.

"My grandson ... he's got some problems."

"Don't we all," I say, putting down the launch control.

The old man takes his hat off and smoothes his hair.

"His mother is my youngest. Her husband ran off on her a few years ago and that's affected the boy." He shakes his head slowly. "He was making good money as an insurance executive, had a big house out here, three kids, seemed like everything was fine. Then one day, he just comes home and says he doesn't want to deal with the pressure anymore and quits his job. Then, another week later, he gets a job at some not for profit setup for peanuts." The old man pauses. "Well, one day he doesn't come home from work. My daughter called me worried and all, and I tell her I'm sure he'll be home soon, but the sonofabitch never does come back."

I begin scooping up dead engines from the field.

"What happened?

He shrugs.

"Nobody knows! Seems he just disappeared. Resurfaced a year later in Las Vegas after he gambled away everything he owned. The police brought him back and now he lives with some woman and never sees his kids. It's been hard on the boy."

We both turn and look at *the boy* who is far down the field, still chasing his rocket floating back to earth. The old man shakes his head doubtfully.

"I don't understand this generation. My son-in-law had no business buying that big house. He didn't have the money. *Hell,* I work in a lot of these houses and most of them don't have any goddamn furniture. What the hell is that?" The old man stares at me accusingly. "I'll tell you what it is; it's a buy now, pay later generation, except they *can't* pay because they don't want to do the work. My father worked three goddamn jobs during the Depression to keep food on the table and he never complained!

He always supported me, even when he knew I was wrong, and I was wrong *plenty* of times. He'd just say to me, 'I hope you learned your lesson,' and that would be the end of it. But he never thought about abandoning us," he continued, his eyes suddenly filling with tears.

"Even when his back was hurting him so bad he'd cry at night. But in the morning, he'd go to his job as an electrician with the railroad and right up to the day he died, he never complained." The old man wipes his eyes. "At the end he told me he's had a good life and a man shouldn't complain who has had the kind of life he had." The old man touched his chest. "Same with me. I've had a good life. Six kids, saw the world in the war, had my own business, bought and sold more real estate than any man should and now I'm retired officially, but I still get up at five AM and drive to the office. My son runs it now, but I can't help myself. I have to do *something*; I can't just sit around and do nothing."

His grandson comes huffing up.

"That rocket went pretty far, Toby."

"Sure did, Granddad," the curly haired boy says and nods.

"Wow, look at all those launchers!"

He leans against his grandfather, then suddenly runs to the other side of the field, holding his rocket high. The old man stares after him.

"Like I said, something is not quite right about the boy ... they have all these fancy names for it, ADD, DDD, who the hell knows, just a lot of bull for not having his old man around."

I stare at his grandson and can see Toby's problem. He is running with the rocket over his head, but every few minutes, he looks back to his grandfather. The old man shakes his head and looks at me.

"I spend a lot of time with him, but I don't know what will happen to him when I'm gone. I'm eighty-one; I'm not going to be around forever."

We both watch Toby hold his rocket aloft, running through the field.

"That goddamn sonofabitch should be shot," the old man says.

I sometimes have dreams of other women. They say the sure sign of a mid-life crisis is to dream about one's youth in the form of a younger woman. Sometimes the women in my dreams are women I would never consider sexually attractive. They invade my dreams, the fat, the moronic, a strict old teacher from my first grade. It is bizarre, and I spend a moment contemplating what these alien invaders could mean to my life and I have no answer. But one dream that occurs with some consistency is this one: I am looking for Wendy and she is not to be found. I am looking all over the house and then outside. In my dream, I come to the conclusion she has left and then I wake in great relief, finding her sleeping next to me. It is a dream I have never told her about.

I used to pick her up after work on my motorcycle. She worked at a law firm on Michigan Avenue and sometimes I picked her up at one AM and we went to the three AM bars on Rush Street. Many times we ended up walking along Lake Michigan, watching the sun rise, with Wendy carrying her high heels, the surf lapping her ankles. I was working various jobs then, trying to get started as a writer. It was the eighties, with all that unbridled ambition pumping through the country. I was working part-time jobs and living with my parents, playing rugby and ratting around on a motorcycle. Wendy had a serious relationship with a man she had dated in college.

"He wants me to be a housewife. He wants me to settle down," she said one night after we had stopped at a bar. "I don't think I can do that."

I assured her I would never expect her to be a housewife.

"You don't worry about anything," she replied. "You're free.

But I don't know if I can trust you."

I explained that just because I was working in a bar, living with my parents, and riding a motorcycle with no real plans except to be a writer—it didn't mean I wasn't trustworthy.

"I just get the feeling you'll leave one day," she said, peering into my soul.

"What do you mean?"

"Just that one day you will decide things are too hard and you will leave."

I pointed out that you could not predicate a decision today on something that might happen in the future. Still, Wendy could not make up her mind between the man who would be stable and the Svengali on the motorcycle. She consulted therapists, palm readers, her mother. Everyone told her to follow her heart and to be careful, because decisions have consequences.

"I want you to know that whatever decision you make, I will be okay with," I lied one night when it seemed fate was going against me.

"I just don't know if I can trust you," she replied tearfully.

"Follow your heart," I counseled.

"He bought an engagement ring. He's going to give it to me Friday night."

I mooned around and lost weight. I took midnight motorcycle rides that turned into morning vigils outside her apartment.

"He is stable, but he will limit you," I pointed out weakly.

"I know that."

"You will have to put part of yourself away for that security," I continued. "You will have a barrier against the world, and he may be a good father and a provider, but you will not be able to be yourself and you will never know what you might have evolved into because he can't go there."

"I know that," she whispered.

"You could be someone else with me. You could become a

totally different person. Who you are with limits you."

"I know," she whispered and went out on Friday night and left me in the dark.

She called on Saturday, and we went on my motorcycle and then walked in Lincoln Park. She had told me nothing on the phone. I was dying.

"Well …"

"Well, I told him I wasn't going to marry him."

She said it just like that and I felt reborn. Wendy had her hands in her leather coat and stopped and turned.

"I told him I wanted to bet on something else. I told him we were different."

"That's great," I nearly shouted.

Wendy shrugged.

"I don't know if it's the right decision. But I know one thing …" She paused then, looking me dead in the eye. "I will never bored if I am with you."

I kissed her and we married two years later, and then suddenly fifteen years later, I am launching rockets in the middle of a field. I sit next to my launchers, listening to the wind in the far trees. I wonder if I have kept her entertained. I wonder if the edict of never becoming bored is enough. I wonder if she did make the right decision on that Friday night—or have I become that man on the motorcycle again, speeding down the midnight highways of my dubious design?

The afternoon juggernaut of Scouts has begun and I immediately fall behind. We have picked up every straggler Scout and father who made a side trip for one last father-son activity before the day's end. They are coming in waves now. Ten or twenty Scouts in a bunch and they are building up outside my perimeter. I am launching as fast as I can, but I am falling steadily behind. The igniters begin to malfunction from the carbon build- up on the wire clips. The exhaust gases have turned our hands black and I see creases on Dale junior's face. Every time an igniter fails, I have to climb under the rocket and pull out the old igniter. The wind has ceased as Indian summer swoops in for one last hurrah.

It is getting hot.

Brad Jones stops in to see what the problem is.

"What's going on, Dale?" he asks, surveying the mob gathered outside my police tape.

"Too many people, Brad. We need to launch more than one rocket at a time," I reply, wiping carbon all over my shirt.

Brad adjusts his BSA sunglasses and tips his beret.

"Scout protocol calls for one launch at time."

I am on the ground under a rocket, rubbing the wire clips together.

"Brad, the igniters aren't firing because of the carbon build-up on the clips. I can't get through all these people just firing one rocket at a time! You have twenty-five launchers here; why not fire more than one at a time?"

Brad sets his jaw, his finger becomes a piston.

"I went through this with Dean Heinrich. I told him we did not need multiple launchers, because we can only fire *one rocket* at a time. He insisted on the multiple launchers, and I think it works out so we can prepare the rockets in advance, but *no*, you may only launch *one* rocket at a time. That's final!"

Brad Jones strides off, leaving the private to face angry parents and frustrated Scouts. These are men with short haircuts who wear suits during the week and do not have time to lose. I stare at this horde of frustrated men and know I have finally experienced my version of hell: surrounded by men in golf shirts and polyester blend shorts who are yelling at me, "*This is why we can't stand Democrats; they can't get the fucking job done!*"

"C'mon use some of these other launchers!"

"Another screwed-up Boy Scout operation."

"This is why I don't go to these things."

For the first time, I am with these people. I am usually in the audience voicing the same complaints at the interminable pack meetings or the camping trips that seem to degenerate into endurance tests for the parents. But now I am on the other side, the man who is the target for the venom of overworked, stressed, white, middle class parents who find themselves in the middle of a field on a Saturday.

I stumble on through the smoke and carnage.

I have often suspected that exhaustion plays a key role in life. The man with energy, with the verve in his step, is much more likely to be successful than the man who is slowly losing his zap. I could attribute key decisions to exhaustion—the purchase of our home, for example. We had tired of looking and settled on the house that was more expensive than we could afford. I had stopped writing because I had become exhausted, played out by the ceaseless rejection of bad novels. Even fatherhood was a direct answer to exhaustion—the good father finding time and energy to be that good father—the bad father waving off to the couch, seeking rest.

Rocket Day became no exception. We worked tirelessly under the blazing sun, firing off rocket after rocket. We became carbon-coated minstrels slogging through the flattened grass, kicking aside burnt engines, threading yet another rocket on the steel launch wires in the mind-numbing procession of one-rocket-at-a-time. I had developed a deep hatred for Brad Jones after inhaling sulfurous smoke for the better part of seven hours. Still, the Scouts continued to stream across the field. It seemed every boy in Charleston had come bearing a rocket to blast off. I could not keep up and by the time the sun is slanting behind the trees—I have an angry mob on my hands.

Still, I am not allowed to break the log jam. I am the victim of procedure, of the rule enforced even though it makes no sense. *One rocket at a time.* The Brad Jones edict is a rock in my shoe as I lie on the ground, shoving faulty engines into rockets, hearing the grumbling from parents who don't understand why. It is the proverbial grocery store clerk who will not speed up. It is the line at the Division of Motor Vehicles where one lone woman holds up fifty people. It is the modern condition of a world moving faster while humans labor under the effort of their own folly.

It occurs to me that failure on a spectacular scale is a bit like being a professional athlete. Only a few people know of the true isolation that thudding, redundant rejection on a colossal scale can bring. The athlete is immersed in his privileged cocoon of wealth and specialty, but few know what it's like to stare down a one-hundred-mile-an-hour fastball. There is insight in the extreme edge of failure or success. The privilege is the view afforded to those who can endure the pressure, the vagaries, and the threat of oblivion.

Rocket Day has merged into my volcano of errant motives. We are having a complete technical malfunction. Strangely, I think back to when I was a child and the television screen would suddenly go blank. The national anthem would play and then a test pattern appeared with a low-frequency hum. Even as a boy I realized this meant the day was over, that the world had gone to sleep and even television had turned in for the night. How I yearn for that type of world now, a world that rested, a world that ends. Now we face the madness of a world crashing on forever.

I go down on my knees and peer up under one of the rockets. My son has been connecting the igniters backward, putting the red clip where the black clip should be, and causing the igniter to short-circuit.

"Dale," I shout. "*You are connecting the igniters backward!*"

He looks up from another rocket he has just finished.

"Goddamit, Dale."

His face turns pale as I cuss a blue streak.

"Dad ... I didn't know."

"I explained it to you. Can't you get it right? "

The tears well up, and one crisis breaks for another.

"Don't take it out on your kid when you're the one screwing up," one man closest to me shouts from the crowd.

I glare at the man and he shrinks back. I consider then walking out of the octagon of hell. In truth, I am surrounded. There are disgruntled parents and Scouts on every side. I want to run; I want to hide, because I can no longer participate in what has become my life. I can't even perform the duties of Rocket Man. I wonder what central cog is missing in my psychic makeup. What is it that allowed these people on the other side of the yellow tape to perform so flawlessly? I realize then that if actions are predicated on thought, and thought comes from basic beliefs in what one is doing, then I must not believe in anything I am doing.

I turn to my son, who has taken refuge with his grandfather. I turn and stare at the mass of angry people. They are the mob I have avoided all my life. They are my secret horror, the majority, the conservative mainstream that I cannot come to terms with. And I had been foolish enough to think that I could hide out among them. We are separated by just a yellow tape, but it is all the difference in the world—*they believe in their lives*. It is in their frantic desire to get it all done. My brethren of khaki-clad men with five-hundred-dollar watches and cell phones and Blackberries and shaved necks and full bellies are taking a gamble on something as amorphous as a dream. I, on the other hand, believe in nothing, and that's why I do what will ensure my fate.

"Dad," I say tiredly, looking at D. T. senior with my son. "Reverse all the igniters on the rockets and take every rocket from the Scouts and stack them on top of each other on the launch wires."

D. T. senior stares at me as if I had lost my mind.

"You aren't—"

I meet his eyes.

"It's the only way, Dad."

D. T. senior shakes his head slowly.

"That boy is going to stop you."

"No, he won't. Get Dale junior to help you."

I turn to a box Dean Heinrich gave me and pull out forty extra igniter wires with clips. These are extras that Dean said we could swap in if the igniters become tainted with carbon. I then begin taking the rockets from the Scouts and their fathers. They hand the rockets over without comment. Someone is taking charge and this will get them to the next thing. I slide the rockets down the steel rods, one on top of another, and begin clipping the igniter wires. It is a great circuit all in series. Soon we have every single rocket ready for launch.

Dale junior is staring at me with a new expression. I had seen that expression when I went four-wheeling across the lot to Dairy Queen; I had seen it when the crossing guard chased us down the road and when I lit our Christmas tree in the burning pit. It is the expression of the boy seeing the parent as something other than a parent—maybe a compatriot, a co-conspirator—maybe a friend.

"You going to launch all those at once?" one man asks.

I just look at him and he nods slowly, mouthing, "Jesus Christ." These are family men, men whose lives had become a thudding daily grind, and someone is about to do something outside the purview of Middle America. Something that could go horribly wrong or horribly right. They watch as we hook up every single rocket, then step back. I count no less sixty rockets on twenty launch rods. Three to a kabob. Then I turn to my crowd.

"We are going to do a simultaneous launch," I announce

loudly. "You might step back a bit, as there will be quite a bit of exhaust."

All of middle America runs back ten steps. D. T. senior comes over to me, a strange look in his eyes.

"You sure this is going to work, boy?"

I shake my head, picking up the master launcher.

"I have no idea if it will work or not."

He bites the inside of his mouth, then nods slowly.

"Good luck, boy."

I turn to my son.

"Dale."

"Yeah," he says, his eyes still red, suspicious.

I hand him the launch pad with the large red button.

"I want you to have the honors."

He holds the master control and looks at me. I nod slowly.

"We will do a countdown, and then you will press this button as hard as you can until you can't press it any farther. Then I need you to hold it there, all right, Dale?"

His eyes light up and the smile of a nine-year-old boy gives me heart again. I put my hand on his shoulder and look at the rockets pointing into the dark sky. I turn and it is amazing how action, *any action*, can make one feel in control again—even if one is about to blast off sixty rockets with no idea of the outcome or the consequence. My father is right on this score—*just do something*.

I turn and see the people standing back, staring at the madmen in the circle.

"Let's do a countdown," I shout to the crowd. "*Ten, nine, eight, seven, six, five ...*"

The chant begins. Boys and men join in our great conspiracy. They all know this is a risk—but for once we are all on the same side. Republican and Democrat, liberal and conservative, we are all strapped in for the same flight. Maybe it is the secret desire of all middle-class people—to just to say *fuck it* once and for all.

"—*four, three, two*—"

"I command you to stop!"

I look up and see Brad Jones has just jumped into the launch area. His face is red, his sunglasses hooked on his shirt. He stands as the lone figure of authority among sixty missiles pointed to the sky. He whirls around seeing the wires, the stacked rockets. He runs to one rocket, then another, and then turns. Incredulity has pinched his brow, his eyes burning in indignation. He centers on my son.

"Dale, I command you to put that down! *This is illegal.* I order you to cease and desist!

I stare at him and feel this man of authority. He stands there in regalia, the creeping policeman of our times. *You will not do this, you will do that. You will follow our rules.* He is my shaman, my Buddha in the road. He is the man I have pledged to fight all my life and he is here in full Scout regalia, holding a cell phone in one hand and a flashlight in the other. *He will have order. He will have it his way. It is not who we vote for but it is who we vote against! You are either for us or against us and we will have our way. You are not like us and you will not be allowed to participate. You are the enemy. We have seen the enemy, and he is us, and he must be slain.*

I turn from the man with his finger extended like a baton. The son of my heart is staring at me.

"Press it, Dale," I say, nodding to his questioning eyes.

"*Dale! Put that down!*" Brad Jones orders.

Dale junior hesitates, and I can see the nine-year-old dilemma. Follow authority or follow the old man? *Is it ever any clearer than this moment?* We can give our children so little. They will have to meet the world on their own terms as much as we try to protect them. I know his little soul will never be the same after this moment. The world he will inherit will be even more conformist, more ruthless in the price of men's souls. I look at my boy and try and give him courage in his hour of need.

I put both my hands on his shoulders.

"Go ahead and launch the rockets, Dale," I say calmly.

Brad Jones is walking steadily toward us, passing our glittery missiles posed for the sky while the crowd remains silent. I know we have no time left. Brad will soon be close enough to take the launcher. Dale's eyes have filled with tears and mine too. I want to help him in the worst way, but I cannot take the launcher from him—he must make this decision on his own.

"Dad …."

"Dale!"

A clear voice calls out from the crowd, a woman standing in front with a little girl. My son turns to his mother. Wendy is there with Angela. She is standing in front of the crowd, her blond hair pulled back. Our eyes meet and she sees it all. She sees Brad Jones and her husband. It is fifteen years before again and it is Friday night and she has to bet on the man on the motorcycle or the man who wants a wife. Her son wavers in the balance.

"Tell him to put that launcher *down*, Mrs. Hammer," Brad instructs the lawyer, mother of two, wife of one. "This is illegal, and there will be *serious* repercussions," he says ominously. "Tell him to put the launcher down … *now!*"

I don't know, but maybe it was Brad Jones in the end who tipped the balance in that moment; maybe he unwittingly put the single piece of straw on the side of reckless abandonment. Maybe a full-grown man in a beret and a utility belt with tasseled socks finally illustrated my point better than any shenanigans. But for whatever reason, Wendy stared at Brad Jones the way someone might look at a palm reader, realizing before it was too late the shaman behind the cards, the charlatan behind the curtain, turning away from the supposed authority of our destiny.

"Dale junior!" She called out crisply. "Do as your father tells you."

Commander Jones has his mouth open, turning back to me just as I utter my final command as Rocket Man.

"*Launch!*"

Dale junior presses the button all the way down to Dean Heinrich's hidden flaw. I know now it was Dean Heinrich's secret wish and that is why he left the defect intact—some nascent, primeval wish of all men just to blow it all to hell and start over and who gives a fuck if your tools are numbered—blow the *whole fucking thing sky-high.* For a second, there is silence as that current flows through sixty igniters, sixty different wires, completing the circuit into sixty different engines and then sixty igniters fire and sixty engines fire and Commander Jones is obliterated into a hail of oxidizing orange fire and exhaust. I see him run for cover, vaulting over the yellow wire like the solider he always wanted to be, diving for the fox hole. The crowd is lit by the yellow exhaust and a mighty *whoosh* that turns into a mighty sonic whine breaking the air as sixty rockets streak skyward in a blazing hail of glory.

Sixty orange missiles zoom up into the coal sky as one and it is beautiful. There are a few early stars as the rockets go off at crazy angles, arcing across the simmering horizon as a thousand meteorites streaking through the sky simultaneously. The roar of throaty voices go up from men and boys who have had nothing for which to cheer for so long. They are cheering and clapping, and I know then my brethren yearn for freedom as I do, for they are rocket men also, strapped in, desperately waiting to see where they land.

Then the sky erupts into sixty brilliant white and orange fireballs as the ejection charges fire into stars all over the sky. The chutes open like blossoms of free will as men and their sons go tearing off to find where those rockets will land, where their individual trajectories will find them, knowing they are burning though the best years of their lives in the process.

"It's beautiful, Dale," my wife whispers, wiping her eyes.

I turn, and Wendy is standing next to me. She takes my hand as we stand side-by-side under our son's independence day. One may think it is of no consequence that a boy could defy the world and launch sixty rockets simultaneously, but it is these moments we remember, the small victories we take with us to the grave. I slowly put my arm around my wife as we watch the dangling parachutes float back to earth.

"You are bad at logistics, work, organization, and you whine and are like a child, and you can be the biggest jerk I have ever known." She pauses then and looks at me with the same amused expression I saw all those years before. "But I never married you for those things."

I frown, genuinely curious.

"Why *did* you marry me?"

Wendy looks then at the people tearing across the field in the darkness, Brad Jones standing like a man who has lost his command, and the smoking remains of sixty rockets in the field. She looks at the boys and men laughing, running through the near-darkness in a moment they will remember for the rest of their lives. She turns to me and brushes soot from my cheek.

"So I would never be bored."

We hug and we kiss, something we haven't done for a long, long time.

"Wow, Daddy, it's *fireworks,*" Angela screams.

D. T. senior is holding my daughter on his shoulders and it is a strange sight. He is a man who would put a little girl on his shoulders now to watch fireworks. He turns like a man with a neck brace.

"Boy, you done good."

"He has done good," Wendy says and nods, hugging me again.

I feel my son press against me. He is looking up at his father, and I see now I had made the right decision. Dale junior is a boy with confidence. I know he will have to fight more battles and he will lose some. We all have to reach the line where we say no more, enough is enough, and I know Dale will have to find those lines all through his life, but maybe, maybe this first one will be a reference point.

"Thanks, Dad," he says, hugging me.

Real tears fill my eyes as I look at my son, my father, my wife, and daughter. And for once, for once in my entire life, I know more than I can say.

Post-flight

There is a scene at the end of the movie *A Christmas Story* that has always stayed with me. It is after Ralph finally gets his BB gun and goes to bed. The camera then breaks for his father and mother by the Christmas tree watching the snow fall. The camera pulls back even farther, back outside onto the street, and now we see a small bungalow with an old Hudson parked next to it. The street is quiet and snow covered. That is what I always imagined my childhood should have been: a Hudson parked outside a modest home on a city street with everyone safe and warm, asleep in middle-class slumber. So it does not surprise me that we ended up in the small town of Riverside.

Riverside reminds me of Oakland before it became trendy. I even have a driveway on the side of our house for the old Ford. Our bungalow is strangely spacious with rooms hiding in the dormered attic and bathrooms crouched under the stairs. The yard is a city lot with a garage blocking the back where we have a small fence and a small garden. We do miss the big yard, but Dale junior and I soon became adept at throwing a ball down the drive. We have taken out a few windows during batting practice.

Wendy has taken some real estate closings and I am teaching ad hoc classes again for pennies, but we made some on the sale of our house and between it all, we scrape by like every other middle-class family. I guess you could say we are downwardly mobile, but I really don't look at it that way. We are where we are supposed to be.

D. T. senior has come to visit us a few times. After Doris let him back in the door, his short courtship of Georgia Barnes drew to a close. They never talk about the time he spent over my garage and I'm not sure what made Doris take him back. He never did get another job in the corporate world and has taken up real estate with the same fire that drove him for years to travel the world in search of customers. The word is he misses the traveling, but I have noticed a slowing down of the old bundle of energy, a softening of the old ruffled feathers. He also gave up on the plot next to my mother. I don't know if that was because Al wouldn't sell it to him or he decided he wasn't going to be moving in any time soon.

Elliott and I talk occasionally. I think my move back into the realm of normal houses has allowed him to stomach my lifestyle again. Who knows, maybe one day we will become friends. We have been able to talk about teaching now that I have a few intro to literature classes at the community college. It is nice to be around like-minded people once again. I have even used the word *colleague* a few times.

My lawyer marched down to the police station that Monday after Rocket Day and had a few words with Detective Clancy, and we never heard from him again. Of course my lawyer is very good and very sexy. I never see any of those people from my years as a Rocket Man. I suppose they are all on their trajectories and I do wish them well. The big news for me is that I am writing again. I have started something that I am excited about. It is good to have the old feeling of a secret once more. I suppose writers can't help themselves. They do stupid things like move out to the far west suburbs and then do all the wrong things, but the result is a new story, a new novel. My agent says I shouldn't tell anyone about this novel, but I'll just read you the beginning:

I guess in retrospect it was the slow culmination of events that led a man of forty-six, a fully grown man, to grab a snaggle-toothed saber saw and attack a hapless wooden sign in the dead of the night. Time of the crime? Oh, about three AM. Scene of the crime: the entrance to Bellview, bordered by two blue evergreens, five small, round, green bushes, and many fake-looking flowers that never seem to grow, lose their buds, or change color, be it rain or snow. The weapon? A crude saw. Motive? Destruction of the ugliest sign in the fair town of Charleston.

Clearly, there is a lunatic on the loose.

1516708

Made in the USA